The Price of Happiness

A Medieval Tale
Book 5

By Lina J. Potter
Translated by LitHunters

Copyright © 2018 LitHunters Ltd. (http://lithunters.com)
All rights reserved.
ISBN: 9781794084889
LitHunters, 2019.

Contents:

Prologue	5
Chapter 1	
The first knot	7
Chapter 2.	
Anagnorisis.	66
Chapter 3	
Black pawn, white pawn	102
Chapter 4	
A solemn arrival	124
Chapter 5	
Princess' fickle game	223
Chapter 6	
The Second node	259
Chapter 7	
Young fruit.	297
Chapter 8	
A glimpse into the future.	323
Epilogue	331
Post-epilogue.	
Two hundred years later.	339
Chronology	346
LitHunters:	347

Enjoyment adds strength to our desire.
Desire, old tree, for whom pleasure is the ground,
while your bark thickens, as you grow higher,
your branches long to touch the sky you sound!
Astounding travelers! What histories
we read in your eyes, deeper than the ocean there!
Show us the treasures of your rich memories,
marvelous jewels made of stars and air.
Charles Baudelaire, Le Voyage

Prologue

Pen in hand, the woman brooded over a blank piece of parchment. She paused for an instant and moved a golden lock of hair from her face. Suddenly, a fresh sense of resolution overcame her, and she began scribbling with speed and confidence.

This letter belongs to those who find it.

It took me a long time to gather the courage to write this letter. Besides, no one knows my own language here. I will write down the alphabet later. If not, let it become the Rosetta Stone of this world—the world of Ativerna.

It is impossible for me to open up to anyone, therefore consider this letter a confession. I hope that by the time someone finds this letter, I will be long dead. I also hope that the world of Ativerna will be purer and better than my own. Yes, my friend and reader, whoever you are, you shall be the one to hear my story. My name is Lilian Elizabeth Mariella Earton, the Countess of Earton, of maiden name Broklend.

My real name is Aliya Vladimirovna Skorolenok. I am a doctor, which is like a medicus here. Back in my world, I cured people and dreamed of doing it for the rest of my life. I suspect that I died back there, in my own world. My parents died as well; that I know for sure. It is hard for me to realize that I will never visit their graves. I am struck with grief at the knowledge that I will never again see my friends, my fiancé, or my native land, which I loved with all my heart in spite of everything.

I am writing to those who will be born after me. Upon coming to this world, I realized that it was purer than my own. Although it was filled with cruelty and bloodshed, I promised myself to introduce this world to only good things. I sincerely hope that I can leave this place in a better state than when I found it.

Should I describe my former life? It is better not to. It is enough to say that I used to live, love, and learn. As for the rest, my world had too much evil. Aldonai forbid (I even speak like a local now) anyone borrowing harmful ideas from my letter! No, it is better not to disclose anything.

When I first came here, I was in stasis. I was scared and hurt. Gradually, I realized that I owed this woman for letting my spirit occupy the frame of her body. She had departed so that I could live. It was a big sacrifice to make.

I don't know which things I will be remembered for. I know that history is written by politicians; those who paint their characters in whatever color they want. Let it remain so.

Who is Lilian Broklend? A bitch? A cow? Someone who loves power and breaks laws to bring strange and alien things to this world? I don't know. My only motivation is to survive.

No one liked the former Lilian. To speak plainly, they brought death upon her by sending the murderers to her house. I defended myself. Anyone who happened to suffer at my hand was chosen by fate. I will not justify myself for wanting to live. The most peaceful ones can choose to perish.

I have become harsh. I have turned cruel.

I have learned to make ugly decisions and bear their consequences. Do you think I am trying to justify myself? This could partly be the case.

I sincerely hope that everything good that I bring to this world and every soul I save from death will outweigh my acts of immorality, the acts which my mother would not approve of.

Whoever you are, I ask for your understanding.

The candle burned; the golden feather of artisan Helke Leitz scribbled on the parchment. The woman feverishly wrote her wandering thoughts. She signed it: *Lilian Elizabeth Mariella Earton.*

Chapter 1
The first knot

"My Lady?"

"Yes, Leir Tremain?"

"My boys have brought me some news."

"What is it?"

"Someone is preparing an attempt on the life of your glassblower."

"What?"

"What else did you expect, My Lady? You have negotiated with other guilds, but the glassblowers are very offended, therefore—"

"Therefore they are going to play dirty tricks on us. I see. Tell me everything."

"Our glassblower is a young lad; he gets infatuated very quickly. There is a pretty widow on the outskirts of Laveri, a forty minute brisk walk from here…"

"What's your idea, Hans?"

They had started calling each other by their first names long ago. It was more convenient. Besides, both Hans and Lilian held it true that all titles lost their significance in the presence of mutual respect.

"Look on the map; here lives a certain widow. The road that leads to her home is very solitary. It is the perfect place for an attack and kidnapping."

"Do they want to interrogate him?"

"I suppose so. They would make him talk and then get rid of him after he gives away all our secrets."

"Bastards."

"Lilian?"

"Tell me your plan, Hans."

The man and the woman exchanged malicious glances. Neither of them was going to stand on ceremony.

Whoever comes to us with a sword will perish, thought Lily, suddenly realizing the truth of these words in the world of Ativerna.

Having stayed alone, Lilian Earton looked out the window. The dark glass reflected a pleasing image of her face. She had done more than enough to achieve such a result.

It was "the hidden law of a probable outcome" that ruled over her life, just like in the song.

A year ago, Aliya Skorolenok could not have even imagined such a twist of fate. She was living, studying, working, and about to get married. Her life had been like anyone else's—before the car crash and subsequent reincarnation in someone else's body with all its unimaginable consequences.

Having found herself in the body of a medieval countess, Aliya had inherited all her responsibilities and her medieval husband with all his rights. Everyone around her had nothing but contempt for the donor.

She had had to put everyone in their place, and she had been rigorous. The outcome that had befallen the most disrespectful individuals had been deathly. The new Lily had had to appoint people in place of those she had removed. She had also needed to earn their respect.

One thing had led to another, and another… Lily had not even noticed that she had started working her fingers to the bone. She had wanted to live in a clean castle, take baths, and look at the world through clear glass—not pieces of parchment.

Aliya had not even noticed how she had attuned herself to the world of Lilian Earton and become burdened with the countess' duties and responsibilities. The king had soon taken notice of her inventions and called the woman to the capital. It was then that Aliya had realized her knowledge of the Middle Ages was utterly false. She had previously imagined beautiful ladies, noble knights, castles, and tournaments. *As if!*

The women were unwashed, the knights did not even know that they ought to fight in tournaments, and the castles were drafty all over. The only people that had taken an interest in the Countess of Earton had been hired assassins. They would have welcomed her in their arms any time of day or night.

So, Lily had gone to the capital to figure out who might be responsible for her attempted murder. All had been in vain. Upon realizing he could profit from the countess, His Majesty had placed a heavy load on her fragile shoulders. The king had asked her to adjust the whole production of manufactured goods. Perhaps she should have objected, but it was the custom to never refuse the will of the king.

The guilds did not like her interfering with trade, but that was their problem. Every individual who was unhappy with the present order could speak to the king.

Alas!

The guilds were unhappy to such an extent that Lily now felt like she was lodged on top of a sleeping volcano. Her fears were soon confirmed. It was one thing when they made attempts on her life; she had the Virmans to guard her safety. Trying to kill her artisans was another matter entirely. She could not ward off the danger facing every artisan, apprentice, and student. The only way was to repel the first attacks and establish strict boundaries. Her message to the villains was dead simple.

We don't interfere with you; you don't touch our people. If you, nevertheless, decide to meddle in our affairs, remember that strangling yourself to death would be less painful than our punishment.

Lily and Hans had discussed it before. But now was the right time to bring their plans to life. One way or another, it was a stressful task.

Should I start drinking valerian root? Maybe I should. Health is like honor; it needs preserving from a young age.

ಬ ಸಿ

The lover of young widows was Timo Richert. He was ambling around town whistling a tune. Life seemed to him a total blessing. *Who could have thought that only a year ago I was nothing?* Back then, he was an apprentice. *Pass this, bring that, get out of my sight, you idiot....* These words used to ring in his ears all day long.

Now, he was a respected artisan, and everyone called him Master Timo. Although the local guild was not entirely happy, they had given him the title.

It was all due to the Countess of Earton.

Once more, Timo blessed the moment that he decided to leave his native Altver and commit to the unknown. Indeed, he had left his dear ones in Altver, but he sent them money through the Virmans. The generosity of the countess was unsparing; working for her had been a sheer delight. He and Marko had found their own apprentices and become their own masters; they could live as they pleased. Taral was a fine, cozy place, and Timo had already found a room there. In addition, the countess had assured him that he soon would be able to buy himself a house in the capital, and a couple of horses too. She considered him a valuable artisan.

Lily made Timo realize the true price of his skill. He and Marko worked relentlessly. In five years' time, it would be fit for them to marry.

The countess surely would not mind them getting wives now, but they needed to accumulate some wealth first. Besides, both of them liked to frequent different women.

Timo's life was good, especially with a pretty, twenty-year-old widow waiting for his arrival. She was not an alley cat, but it was tough for a wench without a man. She had happened to run into Timo back in Laveri. He fixed her porch, gave her a little mirror, gave her a hand with a heavy basket…

They had met each other by accident. The girl had come to the city to sell milk just when Timo had gone looking for apprentices. He had suddenly craved some milk, and an affair had ensued. One thing had led to another…she named the place and the time. He came once, twice… Such an affair would never have happened in Altver; had he stayed back there, he would have remained an errand boy.

ಐ ಞ

Olivia had been somewhat sad. Nevertheless, she had greeted the young man with all honor. She had offered him milk and other pleasantries. The trouble had come in the morning, on Timo's way home. It hadn't quite been morning, just before sunrise. The young artisan had been walking and whistling, when suddenly…a bolt from the blue.

ಐ ಞ

Timo woke up in a strange place. He was lying on the floor, his hands and feet tied, surrounded by three bandits. One of them was picking his teeth with the end of a knife, the other two were playing dice. All three had instantly noticed their captive regaining consciousness.

"Give a holler to our master and tell him that the prisoner is awake," ordered one of the players.

The man with the knife stood up and left without a word. One of the players slowly rose, approached Timo and grabbed him by the scruff of the neck. The lad saw a flash of a knife blade.

"Huh," gasped Timo, trying to escape the sharp blade.

"Yes," confirmed the man who entered the room. "Do you understand, you scum, that we can do anything we want with you?"

Timo understood it well and nodded.

"Good. You will now tell us about the method you use for making glass."

"What h-happens after?"

Considering the man's smirk, there was no "after" for Timo.

"I will not tell you anything!"

Timo was suddenly surprised at his own bravery.

"What if we break a couple of your fingers? Or skin you alive?" The man was clearly serious. "You will tell us; there is no way out of it."

Never had Timo been so happy as when he saw Hans Tremain enter the room with his humble dark cape, expensive weapon on a sling, tall hat with a feather and thin lips curled into a sly smile.

"Leir Tremain!"

"That's right." Leir entered the room and looked around with a face of regret, saddened to be wasting his precious time.

"Everyone drop your weapons, or I will give the order to fire."

" Give it to whom?"

"The Virmans, of course. They are severe people. They don't understand jokes."

The main man swore filthily, and a short arrow hit the floor beside his foot.

"I am not kidding. Does it hurt you to know that you are missing out on so much money? Some amateurs from the middle of nowhere found the secret to making glass while your whole guild was idling about! Ha!"

The man grimaced but did not have the courage to answer back.

"Get dressed, Timo. From now on, all your visits to wenches will happen only with my consent. Do you understand?"

The young lad understood very well. His memory was as sharp as the dagger that had been held at his throat some minutes before.

"As for the rest of you, get ready as well. We will speak to you someplace else."

The villain's face switched from white to red, marking the change from surprise to anger.

Not like anybody gives a damn.

ಌ ☐ ಐ

Lily told off the glassblower— and the young man comprehensively embraced the criticism. Hans Tremain had defeated the whole band of criminals, a deed that was recognized by the king himself. His Majesty was quite content with the outcome of the affair.

As it turned out, the glassblowers were extremely angered. They bore heavy losses and lost dozens of apprentices. The guilds were never going to give recompense and simply left the tradesmen to their own devices.

The morals of the guild-members were like those of spiders. All the money that passed through their hands disappeared without a trace. In search of justice, the glassblowers decided on a hostile takeover.

The meeting with Olivia had been a set-up—and after one such meeting, they had kidnapped the youth in order to put him to questioning. They would have slit his throat with a knife and thrown his corpse into the sea to feed the hungry fish. They had even hired a couple of rogue men from the gutter for the job, who were meant to drag the captive to the designated basement.

Before the operation, they wondered: should they let the rogues question him? The glassblowers did not trust the men's honesty. There was no guarantee. Would Timo tell them the truth? Could they remember correctly?

No, they would try out the recipe that Timo gave them first. They resolved to keep the young man in their basement. He was an asset too valuable to trust anyone with.

As a result, the whole gang was caught red-handed.

His Majesty was indignant; Lily was outraged; Timo remained inside the castle, too frightened to poke his nose outside, and rightly so.

Lily wished to lock everyone up in Taral and prepare for a siege. And yet, she still needed to find the murderer. She had set up a trap, and all she had left to do was wait.

The first visitor turned out to be Baron Yerby with his wife and children. Praise be to God that Hans happened to be at home. He nodded to Lily asking her to buy some time and swiftly took off. Amir was also in the living room, on his way to leave for a walk with Miranda.

Grandfather Yerby turned out to be a lively man of about sixty. The man was short, bald like a knee-cap, with the countenance of an outright rascal. If he were an actor, he would be perfect for playing a crooked servant.

"My Lady, I am overwhelmed with joy to behold your presence!"

Before Lily could mutter a word, the baron cupped the countess' palm and touched her glove with his lips, covering it with kisses so profusely, that the thin lace instantly got soaked.

Lily somehow managed to withdraw her hand (a growling Nanook helped greatly) and raised her eyebrows.

"If seeing me brings you such joy, I will give you my portrait to behold. I hope you arrived safely."

"Yes, My Lady. Let me introduce you to my wife. Honey, come forward. Valiana, the Baroness of Yerby, it is my pleasure to introduce you to Lilian, the Countess of Earton."

The amber-headed lady with remarkable cleavage dropped in a half-curtsey. Lilian's breasts looked miserable in comparison, resembling two pimples.

"My Lady, it is a great honor to meet you."

Lily bowed her head slightly. "I am glad to welcome you in my house."

"Our children—Renard, Julie, Alina, Maria and Denise."

The bunch of ginger kids began nodding and kneeling. Lily unwillingly remembered the ginger Weasleys from the Harry Potter films.

"It is nice to meet you," said Lily in a singing voice.

"Can we leave now, Momma?"

It was Mirrie. She stormed into the living room like a whirlwind. The child looked charming. The blue of her riding suit enhanced her black hair and azure eyes; her white cheeks were ablush, and her lips were smiling.

"Of course, little lady. Who is with you?"

"I promise to be careful." Amir was smiling. Dressed in white, with black hair and tanned skin, he was an impersonation of a romantic dream, a hero of tales of the beautiful Orient.

Pity that the local children have not seen the films with Omar Sharif!

Lily nodded in approval. She knew that Amir would not let anyone offend either her little daughter or him; having been poisoned with quicksilver in the past, Amir had learned how to avoid danger.

"Miranda!" Valiana Yerby gave off a shriek, trying to grab the little miss in her arms. Miranda's training bore fruit. She swiftly escaped the disgusting embrace and hid behind Amir's back.

"Who are these people, Momma?"

"This is your grandmother," Lily responded loudly and saw the baroness' face drop. "Your grandfather, your uncles and aunties. Would you like to spend time with them?"

Mirrie shook her head.

"I better go for a walk with Amir."

"Of course!" Lily seemed to regain some lost knowledge. "Let me introduce Amir Gulim, a crown prince of the Khanganat."

The Yerbys were dumbfounded. Meanwhile, Amir grabbed Miranda by her hand and headed to the exit. Even though they were eager to leave, the prince did not forget to say his long-winded 'it pleases me to have become acquainted with you' behind the closing doors.

The doors reopened shortly to reveal Hans, who was as sweet and charming as an African viper.

"Ah, Yerby! I am so glad to see you…and all your family."

The baron got nervous. Perhaps it was because of Erik, who followed Hans into the room and blocked the heavy door.

"I am also glad to see my granddaughter well! What a teacher you have found her! He is a charming young man, and so talkative!"

"Yes," confirmed Erik, smirking like a hungry crocodile.

Lily suppressed a scornful laugh.

"I would also like to hear some explanation. Your protégé caused me some unpleasant moments."

Yerby was good at taking a punch—better than his wife.

The latter's face dramatically changed as she uttered, "Our p-protégé?"

"Damis Reis," Lily said with a smile.

"Who fully confessed to everything, repented and is waiting to be sent to penal servitude," grinned Hans.

"Yes," confirmed Erik in a deep voice. A dagger appeared in his hands out of nowhere.

"You have no right to…"

"That right was given to me by a royal representative. Should I show you the proof, or do you trust my word, Yerby?"

Hans looked so scary that Lily would definitely take his word for it. The baron flinched and wallowed in defeat and self-pity.

"I did not hire anyone. They deceived me…"

"You will have the chance to tell it to the king during questioning."

"Are you going to interrogate my husband based on the evidence received from some smug-looking scoundrel?" Valiana came forward with all the breadth and depth of her bosom. Lily grinned.

"How do you know what "that scoundrel" looks like? I never mentioned it."

"Y-you said he was charming—"

Hans smiled.

"Baron and Baroness, I suppose you will surrender willingly. I don't want to have to ask Erik to help you."

Like a cannibal, the Virman bared his teeth and stepped forward. Yerby's face turned the color of skimmed milk, white with a tint of blue, as he obediently followed Hans.

Valiana took a deep breath, but Erik took another step forward and took out an axe from behind his back. The woman immediately gave in and trotted slowly after her husband.

Lily knew what would happen next. They would be brought to the local bastille called Stonebug. Their fate would be decided by the results of an interrogation.

As for the children—

Lily looked at the young baron.

"Honorable Renard, I suppose your visit is now over. It might be a good time for you to leave."

It seemed that Renard had decided to swallow a nasty answer. Erik was still in the room, and the youth did not have the guts to be voluble. Renard flashed his eyes (never a crime) and proudly left, accompanied by his ginger sisters.

Lily sighed in relief.

One less problem? I hope so.

ಏ ⎵ ಊ

In three days' time, Leir Tremain told Lily about the Yerbys' confession. As it turned out, the money was his sole motive. In addition, he blamed Jerisson Earton for everything. All villains always blamed others for their own faults. *It wasn't me! The devil beguiled me,* they would say, although the devil wasn't even a thing in this world. *Poor devil,* thought Lily.

Yerby's first wife, Miressa, was rich. *But alas!* He had given his daughter Magdalena in marriage and exiled his son for sacrilege and disobedience. As the official version went, his son worshiped Maldonaya and had tried to ruin his father. After the executioner took out forceps for removing teeth, the non-official version came out. It turned out that the spouses argued almost every day, and the subject was the disrespectful behavior of Yerby's son toward Valiana.

The wife of Yerby, a "night cuckoo" was the main puppet-master. When Hans and his people questioned Valiana, they found out that Yerby's son had committed a disgusting act against her person. You see, the woman really liked her stepson. The feeling wasn't mutual; she interested him neither as a woman nor as a person. He did not want to make a cuckold of his father, especially not with an overripe matron. Valiana then began to tyrannize the young lad and drove him out of his own house. Valiana howled. It was an act she much regretted.

Yerby was as poor as a church mouse. All the money belonged to Miressa's children. As a father, Yerby was entitled to use his children's property until they were of age or married. The moment he drove his son away and gave his daughter into marriage was truly disastrous. The son's money returned to Miressa's parents. They, for some reason, did not approve of Yerby's second marriage and cut all contact. As for Magdalena…

In another bout of desperation, Yerby had suddenly remembered that he had a rich granddaughter. *If only I could get custody of the child!* It was impossible with a living father, Jerisson Earton, though that little obstacle did not change his plans. Yerby made inquiries and realized that he must get rid of Lilian Earton first, and then of Jerisson.

"Why?" Lily asked.

As soon as she had married Jerisson, Lily had officially become Miranda's mother. If something were to happen to Jess, she would get custody—either her or Earton's sister, and Miranda's dislike of her relatives was famous.

"How so?"

There was an easy answer. Miranda's nanny Calma had accumulated her dowry by selling information.

What a bitch! Lily thought. She was happy they had gotten rid of the nanny. She resumed listening. In short, Yerby hoped. His hope was minuscule, but a drowning man would hold onto anything, even to a poisonous viper swimming in the river.

Alicia would never take care of Miranda. She simply shrugged at Lily's indignation.

"Spare me, I am too old for minding children."

Lily refrained from comment and nodded.

"I see. You would have refused."

"Yes, I would have, lest His Majesty had asked me personally, and even so—"

Lily nodded. It was Yerby's last hope.

On the one hand, there was the sister of Lily's husband, whom the little girl hated with all her might. On the other hand, there were her grandparents. They could make the girl like them. They would throw themselves at the king's feet and bribe the little granddaughter with sweets. Their plan could have gone through.

Hans snickered gravely, implying that Yerby probably had a trusted person at court and had promised him interest from Miranda's inheritance. However, such bald claims required prior investigation.

Hans assumed that Yerby's first target was Lilian Earton.

Killing her would have been too costly. It was easier to find a random gigolo who would tempt the bored lady with a romance.

Yerby was convinced that Lilian wouldn't have resisted the charm of a handsome young man with good manners. It would have profited Yerby immensely for he would have gained a chance to blackmail Lilian into anything, even into giving him custody over the orphaned girl. Besides, had the court found out about her promiscuity, they would sooner have sent her to a monastery than given her custody. To find a lover was a sure way to make the "cow" disappear without a trace.

The "stupid cow" image that Jess had created of her saved Lily's life. If the killer had considered her to be clever, he would have prepared differently. The plan had been to seduce the "cow," to bribe Miranda, and to murder Jess.

They had begun taming the child in autumn. When Mirrie was suddenly sent to Earton, Yerby's protégé nearly failed to follow her. His task was to gain the girl's trust and make her side with her grandparents. Lily had destroyed that scheme.

The child received a lot of new information. The countess was present at her lessons, and there was no way the protégé could spread his ideas. Damis was not successful—he failed to even report back to his master.

Thank Aldonai spying is tricky without cell phones and landlines. They have not even invented Morse code yet, thought Lily, noting it down in her notebook. *I need to introduce them to all those things. The Virmans will certainly enjoy playing "Capture the Flag"!*

There was nothing left for the protégé to do but to act at his own risk, which turned out to be unsuccessful. *How was he going to kill Jerisson?* In a very primitive way. The earl frequented brothels. He would give the wench an "arousing potion" to offer Jerisson. It was not hard to find a whore; they charged very little. Most often, to the sorrow of her ladyship Lilian, Jerisson could be found at the brothel on the royal street. Yerby himself was a frequent guest. It was easy to make a deal with one of the girls without getting caught. Killing was certainly easier than curing; it required want, not brains.

Lily bit the end of a golden goose feather.

My husband ought to be grateful to me for saving his life so many times. Would he appreciate it if he were to find out? Something told Lily that he wouldn't.

She thanked Hans for the information and went back to her calculations. *It is good in theory—I want a store, a coffee place, a kitchen...but where will I find a suitable place for them?*

How hard it is to live in this strange, wide world!

ಹಿ ☐ ೧೪

If Lily were to have seen her husband at that moment, she would have been glad to find out he shared her hardship.

Jerisson's ex-lover had brazenly disappeared. Suspecting that the earl still harbored tender feelings toward his former mistress, the "Old Pike" scolded him in rich local jargon for helping her go into hiding.

Jerisson defended himself as hard as he could. *Why would I care about that whore? Ativerna is full of them.*

"Yes, there are a lot of prostitutes around, but not everyone tried to help you get rid of the annoying wife," countered the duke.

Jess protested. He managed to convince the duke of his innocence, but not entirely, for there was still a trace of suspicion in his eye.

ಹಿ ☐ ೧೪

Even Richard was of no consolation. The earl paced around the prince's chamber with wild eyes, getting in the servants' way as they packed his belongings.

"As if I would poison the cow!"

"A probable scenario; not gonna lie," Richard said, entertaining himself.

"Are you in your right mind?" retorted Jess.

Richard nostalgically thought that Jess viewed him not as the crown prince, but as the boy he used to prank Edmund with. He sighed.

"Think, Jess. You complained about your wife all around, right?"

"Right." Jess nodded unwillingly.

"While at the same time, you praised Adelaide Wells."

Jess nodded again. "I could not imagine that..."

"Yes, you only judged her by the size of her breasts." Richard ignored Jess' raging eyes and continued. "In short, she attempted to kill your wife, argued with you after failing to do so, and disappeared."

"So what?"

"One could suggest that you have done something with her."

"Something?"

"Anything! Murdered her or helped her escape; hid her in a village to visit twice a month. You better pray that no one else attempts to kill your wife, because this story got you in a lot of trouble."

Jess dropped into his chair.

"The question is whether I got into this trouble myself or if someone else wanted it. If my wife had not come to the capital, no one would have found out."

"Or if your wife had not been born, she wouldn't have been your wife?" snapped Richard. Sometimes Jess really got on his nerves. *While he is not a fool, he is completely in the wrong!*

"I understand everything," replied Jess. "The "cow" is not guilty of trying to save her life. She saved Miranda, too. I am grateful to her in some ways."

"But not in others."

"Would you have been?"

"I would have also been mad," Richard admitted honestly. "Think on this: you are going home now; are you going to throw a fit right upon seeing your wife?"

"I don't know…"

"Exactly. What does my father—I mean, the king—want from you?"

"He wants me to make amends, that's for certain. Otherwise, he wouldn't have treated me like a naughty schoolboy."

"Very well. Instead, will you go home and lose your temper as soon as you see her?"

"What do you suggest?"

"Practice keeping face. You are not guilty of what happened. It is not her fault, though, that you found such a mistress."

"Bugger!"

"The worst thing is that Adelaide's escape makes you more vulnerable."

"What do you mean?"

"If your wife wants to get a divorce, she can do it very easily. She has proof of your infidelity and of attempts on her life. Can you guess her next step?"

"She will divorce me on the grounds of the attempts. Even the Aldon will not be able to protest."

"Why do you think she is still not—"

"I don't know. The options are plenty."

"Even after all her letters?"

Jess rolled his eyes.

"Richard, I refuse to believe that she wrote them herself! Those were the letters of an experienced, clever, and cynical person—cruel if you will. There is no way that little brat could have written them. She is so much—wait, how much younger is she?"

"Jess, my friend, do you even know when her birthday is?"

"I don't remember…"

Richard wanted to help his friend. They were in their last days in that place, meaning that all their outings had to be with a view toward solving Jess' problem.

"Let's go for a tour around the city. You could get something for your daughter."

"But I have already…"

"It is not enough! Have you not learned yet that a woman's love is proportionate to the presents she receives?"

"Not always…"

"But often."

Jess sighed and rose from his chair. Anything was better than sitting and letting his blood get poisoned with stupid anger. He could go for a walk, think of something pleasant; it wasn't such a bad idea, after all.

"Fine, let's wander around. Who knows what we will find?"

Richard brightened up. *Much better!*

ಏ ಔ

Adelaide Wells was not exactly happy, but rather satisfied with herself and the world around her—the world enclosed inside a comfortable carriage that was taking her to the border with Ivernea and Wellster. To be more precise, the carriage was heading to Limayera, where accompanied by trusted people, she would take a ship northward. She was instructed to disguise herself, but that was only temporary. They would fix her looks and give her in marriage.

The messenger sent to Adele told the plain truth. "Because you are known to have a reputation, it would be best to not appear at court for some time. We have found a nice nobleman for you. He is a baron, but his title is not hereditary. He is not rich or young and has no children. Everything is in your hands. If you keep loyal to Count Lort, he will sort everything out. You will eventually have money and will be able to appear again at court. As for now, we are grateful to you for Lydia."

The man issued her new documents and a new name: Lydia Renard, a lower middle-class leyra, also a widow. Her only task was to seduce the candidate. Adelaide didn't mind it.

To marry an old man? I have done it before. I will have plenty of money and young lovers. This time, however, I will not liaise with either cousins or nephews of my husband. Aldonai save me! As for Count Lort, he is frightening, but at least he pays, which is the most important thing. Lady Wells was not going to stand idly by while someone else decided her fate. She had tried to settle in with the Earl of Earton but failed.

I will act more wisely next time. Something big is coming; I can feel it with all my heart.

ರಾ ೞ

Count Altres Lort was busy preparing for the departure of his brother and king. Therefore the orders regarding Lady Wells were given in passing. No, his demeanor did not suddenly become good-natured or graceful. He had a family in mind. The candidate was not a bad person. He was a loyal workman whose service earned him the barony. *Why not help him?* Women reacted somehow negatively to his scars and the burn across his whole face, which he got in a skirmish with pirates. Lady Wells would eat it heartily and thank them for such a husband, for her alternative was...

Altres thought exile to a monastery to be a fit punishment for her crime—if not hanging.

It all depends on how useful the Countess of Earton is. Besides, Adelaide Wells was an excellent pressure lever. She was ready to confirm and sign anything for a trinket. *I can make her admit that Jess offered her money to murder his wife!*

Altres had a boundless imagination. The count really hoped to drive a wedge between the Earton spouses to ensure their permanent separation. He wanted the countess to begin looking for a new home. Altres was prepared to do anything for his brother.

Why not in Wellster, if that would profit Gardwig? Why not give shelter to such a useful woman, or at least push her into divorcing her husband by sending over a cheap whore?

He would get rid of Lady Wells later. As for now, he was saving her for his service.

All my efforts are for the sake of Wellster.

☯ ☐ ☥

"Amir, when are you going to go home?"

His Majesty glared at Miranda. "Well, in a year perhaps."

"In a year? So soon?"

The girl was genuinely upset. Amir had become an older brother to her and a good friend.

"Do you want to visit us?" His Majesty squinted. "I will be glad to receive you. I will introduce you to my father and my horse."

Miranda reflected. The invitation was attractive.

I am curious to see where Lidarh and Shallah came from. I am eager to ride the Avarians, to gaze at the desert, to spot saxaul, which Lily told me about, to look for cactus, to see the sunrise amid the boundless sea of sand...

"Do you think Lily will let me go?"

"We will invite her as well."

"Do you think she will agree?"

"I don't know. We will implore her to come."

Miranda nodded, content.

"Deal. If not, I can come alone, when I am older."

"Great."

Amir looked at the girl with a smile on his face. He genuinely liked Miranda. As for now, she was like a little sister to him. It was too soon to think of anything else. Nevertheless, the prince didn't want this girl to disappear from his life. He needed to talk with Lilian Earton.

Everything will be fine. I will speak to Lilian and persuade her.

☯ ☐ ☥

How long does it take to build a store without having to bother with bureaucracy and formalities, provided the approval of the Crown and unlimited resources?

Lily figured out that it shouldn't take long at all.

She was right. The soil next to Laveri was rocky, and the quarries were not too far away. All the houses here were built of stone so she could use part of the old building materials for the construction.

As for the workforce—when it dawned upon the people that the landlady, though noble, was paying daily, crowds of workmen flooded in. The construction began so fast that Lily was even scared.

I hope it doesn't fall apart!

Her fears were unfounded. The workers were scared that bad work might cost them their lives. The most difficult thing was to make stained-glass windows. They had enough imperfect colored glass that they could easily make a pattern.

Lily considered such glass to be faulty. However, being a novelty here, the faulty glass fit the purpose just fine. One question remained: how they would prevent the street boys from throwing stones at the windows. The only thing that Lily could think of was to put a metal net over them. She instructed the blacksmith on how to make it, and the question was closed. It was not her bother anymore. She had to think about where to put the kitchen, toilets, demonstration rooms, and so on.

Lily got terribly offended by the Crown for how they dealt with the Yerbys. She discussed it with Hans over dinner.

"What will happen to them now?"

"Nothing, your highness. The king will order him to stay at home and not show up at the capital. His older son will become the official heir. That's it."

"Just like that?"

Lily was genuinely outraged.

That bastard! If his plan had succeeded, Miranda wouldn't be here right now! Poor orphans are cared about only as long as they are rich; once they become financially poor they are thrown away like garbage!

"My Lady, his plan failed."

"So what?"

"We have nothing on him—only the testimony of a commoner."

"And what if Reiss was a nobleman?"

"It would have made things easier. Otherwise, what do we have against him? His evil thoughts?"

"He tried to do evil and got caught," snapped Lily. "What about his confession?"

"He confessed under torture."

"He did confess all the same!"

"The nobles have already made a fuss over the Yerbys, to quote, 'being captured, held hostage and found guilty on the grounds of pathetic evidence from some pedagogue.'"

"So, the king had no other choice but to give in."

"Alas!"

Lily put down her fork. She had lost her appetite completely.

"This means that he will be able to cause my family more trouble."

"Not anymore. He doesn't have any profit incentive anymore—"

Hans realized that his argument sounded unconvincing.

"I will ask the king for a mandate on Yerby's lands and will send them our representative. Would it suffice, My Lady?"

Lily nodded. Either way, her mood had now been destroyed.

"Hans—"

"Yes?"

"Who supported Yerby?"

"They swear that it was the Duke of Falion."

"WHAT?"

"Duke Falion, My Lady. Not the marquess."

"Does it even matter? Like father, like son."

"You can talk to the son."

Is it worth speaking to him? Had it happened before, she would have rushed to get things straight. But now there was no guarantee that Falion was telling her the truth. *What if Yerby himself was lying?* They had not checked him with a lie detector. However, they had shown him the torture chamber and even made threats.

But would I have been able to maintain a lie under such circumstances? Depending on what was at stake. Sometimes telling a lie is the only way to stay alive.

What if—

"Hans, are you aware of the fact that any crime leaves a financial trail?"

"My Lady?"

"Look. They needed money to pay for my murder. They handled the transaction through Karl Treloney. Indeed, the money did not come out of nowhere. It was either withdrawn from somewhere else or received as a tax payment."

Hans nodded. "You want to see if there is a connection between the Yerbys and Falion, am I right?"

"Absolutely. If interpreted correctly, financial reports can tell a lot of things."

"Unfortunately, I have no hours in the day to—"

"I will find someone to handle it, someone from the Eveers, they will take to it like a duck to water. Besides, if they want to maintain a good relationship with me, they will say yes."

"I agree. They would do anything. Do you think it wise to—"

"And what alternatives do I have?"

"You could leave it as it is. You could simply stop trusting Falion."

Lily bit her lip. She could not believe that Falion could trick her so covertly. She refused to believe that she had been told lies. This upset Lily. She had trusted that man; he seemed so serious with her.

"The duke tried to help me make peace with my husband."

"Is that so? Did he tell you to create a family with him?"

"N-no, not exactly."

"In that case, do not delude yourself. Make no mistake, Lilian. I respect and love you dearly, so please hear me out. I advise you like your elder brother: never trust anyone from our high society, ever. The honey of their words has long been poisoned."

"I don't know. I don't want to offend him with mistrust, but I also don't want to be a fool. The best option is trust but verify."

Hans shook his head.

"My Lady, you cannot allow for even the tiniest spot to mar your reputation—"

"Do I have a reputation?"

The question was ironic.

"I promise to be careful, at all times, but I want to know, Hans! Do I not have a right to know?"

"As you say, My Lady."

"I implore you, Hans."

"I will do everything in my power. You might want to speak to Helke."

"I will. Whoever visits next will be quickly subjected to examination."

"We will do everything to make sure the criminals pay for their deeds."

Lily nodded contentedly and continued with her dinner. Boiled broccoli was not the most delicious of dishes, but very healthy. A sure way to looking fit was to settle business matters while dining—it guaranteed a loss of appetite.

Hans stabbed a piece of meat with a fork, finished chewing, and gathered the courage to speak on an unpleasant subject that he had been putting off for a while to not worsen his relationship with the countess.

"Lilian, are you aware of the fact that the embassy is coming back soon?"

"I am," sighed the countess. "I know, Leir."

"Your husband is coming, too."

Broccoli suddenly tasted like a boiled rag. Lily's appetite was totally destroyed. She pushed the plate away and sighed.

"I know."

"I—"

Hans's unconfident blundering reminded Lily of her former father, the Major Skorolenok. She stopped him with a wave of her hand.

"Say it. It is the king's order, am I right?"

Leir looked at her with gratitude.

"Yes, Lilian. The authorities issued an order."

"What does His Majesty want then?"

"He wants you to make peace with your husband."

Lily sighed, pushed aside her disgusting dinner and looked at Hans.

"How exactly do you envision it? Do you imagine him saying 'Darling, you survived despite all my efforts, and I am happy, so let us be happy together?"

Hans only shrugged.

"As far as I am aware, they plan to talk sense into him before letting him speak with you. Are you all right, Lilian?"

She remembered what talking sense into someone meant and chuckled. She waved her hand.

"Don't worry, Hans. Imagining it makes me laugh."

Hans imagined the king spanking the count, and it made him put his glass aside. It was not proper to laugh with a full mouth. Watching Hans struggle made Lily laugh even harder. This shared fit of laughter made them look at each other in a different light.

"His Majesty ordered me to have a conversation with you. Can I be honest with you, Lily?"

"Of course."

"Making peace with your husband is your only option."

"Is that so?"

"Your projects are too profitable for the treasury. His Majesty would sooner kill you than let you leave Ativerna."

Lily had no doubt about it. The story with the Venetian artisans had made a strong impression on her.

"I can stay."

"Stay and divorce? Believe me, that would make you an outcast in high society; it would be a scandal."

Lily sighed.

"What if I become a widow?"

"His Majesty will not let you remain a widow for long. He will find a person who is loyal to the Crown and make you marry."

"I suppose he won't take my preference into account."

Damned be the medieval mentality, to Maldonaya with it, thought Lily.

"So, I have to make up with my husband and live happily ever after?"

Leir Tremain shrugged.

"You have taken the first step, haven't you?"

"It was to save my own life and the life of Mirrie."

"Now, do the same to make your lives better."

Lily grimaced.

"To sell myself for money?"

"No. Just try to arrange your life in a more comfortable way. Is that so frightening?"

"To be forced to live with someone? Yes."

"Maybe you could try to fall in love with your husband? Maybe you will like him."

"I have no doubt that many find living with my husband quite satisfying," hissed Lily.

"So what if he could be yours?"

Lily resembled an angry cat.

If! I cannot be entirely open with Hans, he is merely following orders. What should I do with my husband? Should I throw myself into his arms and scream, "Romeo, I am all yours"? Or maybe meet him with a kitchen knife in hand and explain who the boss is? Rat poison might be another option… No, never. Miranda…

Remembering the blue of her daughter's eyes tamed her anger. Lily sighed.

Marriage without love? Could be worse! We will find a common language. People have gone through worse things. On the contrary, am I not a woman after all? I am a woman! I have a hundred-year-old experience behind me. I can make anyone fall in love with me.

Hans watched the change of expression on Lily's face, from baldly rebellious (*'to Maldonaya with him'*) to surprisingly complacent (*'I've got this!'*). It was strikingly familiar.

"Lilian?"

The woman looked at her friend.

"Hans, report back to your superiors that the countess agrees."

"Do you really agree?"

"I don't want to get on his bad side."

She said it in such a tone of voice that it made Hans pity the earl. *On the other hand, Jess Earton had asked for it himself.*

‍ॐ☐ℭ

It all began with Hans' report.

"My Lady, Douglas Faymo and Anvar Rockrest had a meeting."

"What of it? They are relatives, after all."

"That's right, only for some reason they didn't meet at home, but in a private room."

"Did you have a chance to listen to their conversation?"

"No. But the boys swear that Douglas came to the office with money, and left without it. The amount was large."

"So what? Maybe he decided to invest money in a business. Maybe it was his savings."

"What business? The same night Anvar hired ten killers in a port tavern."

"What for?"

"Here comes the most interesting part. They plan to ambush the road to Taral."

"Suiciders?"

"Oh, no. Do you remember those toys with liquid fire that the Virmans use so successfully?"

Lily shuddered.

"Do they own any?"

"Yes, and in great quantity."

"That means we have a chance. Fire, arrows—"

"We will surprise them right at the crime scene."

"When?"

"My boys are on watch for them. I suppose tomorrow or the day after."

"Can you let me know, so I don't ride Lidarh when it happens?"

"My Lady, you don't need to be present!" Hans looked angered. "You are not going anywhere."

"Oh, really?"

"Leave it to the men to fight. We will choose someone from amongst our men, put a wig and a dress on him—"

"What if they run away?"

"What if you get hurt? The king will skin me alive!"

Lily nodded. The king's wrath had no bounds.

"Fine. I will remain at home on one condition."

"What is it?"

"All the weapons with liquid fire are mine. I need them for my experiments."

Hans agreed immediately, only to keep her out of it. He valued and respected the countess. He even loved her—not romantically, but as a friend. She wasn't a bad woman, although she was a bit strange, but everybody had their idiosyncrasies.

However, when Lily meddled in his affairs, Hans wanted to howl. Her ideas were often great; they were intelligent and interesting. But sometimes she didn't see the realistic side of things. This world had been forever strange to her.

ಡ ೞ

It was an ambush just as Hans presumed. The wolf hunted the hare, and the hunter awaited the wolf. There were not that many convenient places for an ambush, and Hans arranged his secret traps there. As a result, two dozen bows were aimed at the killers. They surrendered without playing heroes, especially after being told that they could wait for the countess as much as they wanted—she wasn't coming. Hans reported back to the countess that they had captured the villains, but there was zero point in it. They could capture Rockrest, maybe even Faymo. Both were good at keeping their mouths shut, at least for a while. Loren Ivelen would come and claim that he was slandered, that the money was not his…in short, he would claim innocence. *Who would question the word of a count?*

Lily contemplated.

"The duke is able to refute all allegations. We need to catch him red-handed."

"The question is, how?"

"I have an idea." Lily was not a professional, but anyone involuntarily picked up information from watching the news in the twenty-first century, not to mention reading detective stories and thrillers. Centuries of human history enriched Lily with knowledge that was inaccessible to Hans.

"We cannot detain them legally, right?"

"Yes, My Lady."

"What about illegally?"

Hans raised his eyebrows, but in an instant, it came to him.

"Are you saying that if the Ivelens always act through Faymo—"

"It means that they don't have their own contacts in low society."

"Oh!"

"If we get rid of Faymo and Rockrest, they will have to look for other ways. He could resort to dagger and poison."

Hans shuddered.

"We could try. Kill them?"

"You are so cruel, Hans." Lily hadn't even smiled. "Who would give testimony if we killed them? No way. Do we not have any hidden place to keep them for a little while?"

Hans smirked.

"We have many of them."

"Great then. They will get notified that the ambush failed."

"Who by?"

"Alicia."

"I will get ready then."

Lily encouraged Hans with a nod and asked Lons to let her know as soon as Alicia arrived.

☼ ☐ ೞ

The old viperess arrived the next evening, and Lily bombarded her with information as soon as they sat down to dine.

"Alicia, my dear, I would like to ask you for a big favor."

"What is it?" The viperess operated her cutlery skillfully as if it was her long-life habit.

"The Ivelens—I would like to reconcile with them."

"Last time it didn't go quite so well."

"I hope that Amalia has forgiven me."

"Do not even hope for it. Amalia tiptoes around her huge offspring like he is made of gold."

"It is still worth trying. I have found her children awfully spoiled."

Alicia immediately picked up the subject.

"You cannot even imagine the extent of it! The only request that their parents would fail to fulfill would be to get the moon from the sky."

Lily suddenly realized that the Ivelens had three children. The youngest one though had been born with serious issues. She didn't speak, couldn't perform any tasks besides eating, moaning, and creating a mess.

Lily shrugged. Her specialty was surgery, not the treatment of psychological disorders.

"Maybe we could show the girl to Tahir."

Tahir, who was also present at the table, put his head down slightly.

"I can offer them help," nodded Alicia. "It is possible…"

"I apologize terribly, but although we fixed the boy's nose, how would he join the army being so spoiled?"

"Amalia dreams about a career at court for him."

"He has to know how to defend himself all the same. Take only the other day!"

With these words and round eyes full of terror, Lily blurted out the convenient version of the story: how they had tried to hunt her down yet again. They may have succeeded if it weren't for Leis who had run into them. They had struggled against the plotters who were soon defeated. Lily said she was very annoyed because she had wished to learn who ordered the deed before destroying them.

"Treacherous villains!"

Alicia also sighed and groaned. She promised to go to the Ivelens right away.

"By the way, dear Lily, could you maybe let Miranda and Prince Amir visit Angelina and Joliette? Without any fuss and pompous ceremony."

Lily generously gave her permission.

ಶ ಛ

At first, the Ivelens met Alicia with discontent. But the viperess knew how to manipulate people. She started apologizing, oohing and aahing, and rolling her eyes. In short, after an hour of moaning and suffering, Amalia accepted Lilian's invitation and agreed to show her daughter to Tahir Djiaman din Dashar. She invited Lilian and her family for a visit.

Alicia accepted the visit with a sigh, informing them that they would need to be escorted by a lot of guards.

"Why?" inquired Loran.

In reply, Alicia told him a heart-breaking story about the ambush on the way to Taral. Poor Lilian was worried about not having found the people behind it. *An utter nightmare!*

The Ivelens politely agreed. They said it was terrible to realize that the land was swarming with such villains who would make attempts on the life of the most delightful countess. After all, she does so much for the Crown and is the epitome of benevolence, they said.

After Alicia agreed on a visit and left, the Ivelens started discussing the matter.

"Where did you find these idiots?"

"S-sir..."

The man who was accountable before Ivelen was scared to blink. He might have even looked presentable in other circumstances, but not now. His fat body seemed to droop, and cold sweat ran down his face. His master felt no pity toward him.

"The Countess of Earton will pay us a visit tomorrow. On her way back, I want you to—"

"Y-es, Sir..."

"If you fail this time, you will not escape my rage. Get out of my sight!"

As soon as he let his servant go, the man poured himself a glass of wine and gazed outside. *Well, well, it is getting more serious than ever.*

He had no choice and could not abandon what he started. There was no way out now. It had all started ten years ago. However, a quick coup was doomed to failure. Now the king was tired and old. Richard was too young, involved head to toe in his books. The army was more or less reliable, and Yerby could always infiltrate his agents. Bribing a sensible colonel was enough, he didn't even need a marshal; he would do anything to rise up in the ranks. Ten people in total were enough.

The coup had to be immediate. If he managed to eliminate Edward and Richard, he would be left with only the two princesses. They could be given in marriage to his trustees. He already had more than one candidate. The Aldon would be unhappy, but he would eventually give in. After all, Ivelen could blackmail him too.

Sadly, Edward and Richard had to die—and Jerisson, too.

It was useless to send the killers now. The prince had to die here, in front of everyone. Otherwise, impostors would flood in. It was better to do it before he got married.

It was a gift from heaven that Richard had remained a bachelor for so long. As for the countess, he'd had his doubts for quite a long time, especially after having met her in person.

She was a gem of a woman. She was smart, unpredictable, and dangerous. That was why she needed to die before she met her husband.

Miranda would be an extremely useful asset—an orphan with a good dowry. *I owe a certain person some money; why not pay him back with a marriage contract?*

As for Lilian...it was a pity she had to die, but there was no other option. She had escaped all his blows so swiftly, as if Aldonai warded off danger from her. He could accuse her of being a shilda. However that was almost impossible; she was too benevolent. She treated everyone with the same dignity. She had also been completely faithful to her husband. *Maybe she does love him, after all.*

The Earl of Earton was famously promiscuous. Ivelen had to get rid of him immediately.

What can a woman do when you take away the man she loves? She could do a lot of evil. He knew it like nobody else. He resolved to kill Jerisson's wife as soon as possible. Earton had to be left without an heir.

ဆ ☐ ଔ

They called him Ratty for being agile and invisible. Ratty guarded the gates of Laveri. He was part of the Tremain Squad. No longer did the street boys need to beg, rummage through piles of garbage in search of food, hide from the adults, or struggle to feed their families. They were now happy and satisfied with their lives. They had a job, which paid them at least one copper coin a day. They could take the money home and not be scared that someone would take it from them. Anything they could get during their tasks was also theirs, as long as it did not negatively affect the affair.

Ratty's sister Martha was also put to service at Lilian Earton's place. She worked as a student with the lace-makers. The rumor went that the king was to establish the guild of lace-makers and that Martha would be part of it. Last time Ratty saw her, she looked tidy and happy, wearing a clean dress. She said they valued her there; they complimented her skillful fingers and sharp wit. Once, he went to check up on her. She lived in *that old castle called Ter— Tar— Taral.* The wench had her own room that she shared with three other students. She had her own bed, wardrobe, and even shoes—two pairs of them: one for every day and the other for special occasions.

Flipping good!

His own job was somewhat different. He was small and agile. They wanted him to run around the streets and spy on the people the leir pointed out to them. This was an easy job for the lad, providing that he already had a different job secured for when he was older—he would either be a soldier or an apprentice. They would make sure he was well settled. To make sure his source of income did not disappear, Ratty began teaching his younger brother his trade. Although his brother was not as nippy as Ratty himself, he could improve.

Their mother was very happy with him now. *How else?* Since the death of their father, she had slaved away as a laundress. She could now relax a little. Her employer was none other than the Countess Lilian

Earton. She told everyone that the countess paid well. Their family did not disclose any details about their jobs. They did not gossip or show off. Poor and miserable people could be trusted to be very silent if they were given a helping hand. Ratty would sooner cut himself to pieces than say a word about either the Countess of Earton or Leir Tremain.

The boy squinted. Mounted on a horse, a man approached the gate. He was evidently the one. The boy whistled with two fingers, calling for reinforcements. One of them would run to Leir Tremain, and the other would keep the watch together with Ratty in order to report where the fat guy on the chestnut horse went.

The work began.

☙ ❦

Douglas Faymo felt terrible. His heart was beating, sweat was running down his body, and vomit went up his throat. He had one last chance. Otherwise, no one was going to stand on ceremony with him, his daughter, or his son-in-law. They were now happy and content. His son-in-law's affair had promise and was flourishing. He really wanted to set the horse in the direction of home, leave forever, and forget about this business. At first, his tasks had been little: to bring this or that, to talk over matters with someone, to find the right people... The nature of his tasks had soon changed. Douglas was terribly frightened when he realized what it was all about, but his master did not give him any say in the matter. He simply said that Douglas would either serve him or part with his life. Douglas was convinced.

He did not know what that terrible man was capable of, so he was now going to see his son-in-law. Fortunately, Anvar was in his office. The two men did not suspect that they were being overheard by a boy who conveniently lay on the roof above the open window.

"Your hired guns have been captured."

"And?"

"They are defeated and beaten up. Where did you get such idiots from?"

"I wish you saw how much they charged me," snapped Anvar. In reality, they did not charge a lot, but Anvar had stolen half the money. Ever since he realized what his foolish father-in-law had gotten him into, he had begun saving for his escape. If it so happened that everything failed, he would quietly start a new life in Elvana or Avesterra...It did not matter where. The most important thing was to get as far away as possible. He could even abandon his wife for, provided he had money, he would be able to find a new one in no time.

A quiet knock on the door alerted the men.

"Are you waiting for anybody?"

"No. I let everyone go. Are you?"

The door opened with a quiet squeak.

"Good evening, gentlemen."

Hans Tremain was smiling.

"Are you going to put up a fight or will you follow me voluntarily?"

"Who are you?" Anvar held onto a dagger. Hans waved his finger.

"Don't. As a royal representative—"

Anvar turned deadly pale. Douglas turned out to be less sturdy as he sank into his chair.

"I can tell that you understood me well. You aren't going to yell in indignation, are you? That's better. I know everything anyway. Erik!"

The Virman completely blocked the doorway.

"My friend, could you please lead this couple to our modest little house?"

The Virman smiled in a way that made Anvar forget every thought of resistance.

Two hours later, Anvar and Douglas found themselves in a cozy cellar. They repented so fervently that it was impossible to make notes of their words. They were almost not aware of anything; they were mere executioners, but knowing that they had paid for the countess' murder was enough. At first, they were to poison her by order of Anvar. Soon after, they had tried to kill her by any and all means. The reason for it remained a mystery. The Duke of Ivelen had given the order. His son, the marquess, had nothing to do with it.

❀ ❁ ❦

When Hans reported this back to Lilian, she did not express any interest. *To hell with the duke, we knew of his involvement from the very start. It would have been better to know of the motivation behind the crime.*

"My Lady," Hans hesitated, "Douglas overheard something strange on several occasions."

"And?"

"He did not give the exact phrase. Something along the lines of 'the royal blood' and 'Richard is a secondary heir to the throne'.

"Who did our duke speak with about it?"

"With his son."

Lily sighed.

"Hans, correct me if I am wrong, Edward has only two sons—Edmund and Richard from Imogene of Avesterra and two daughters from Jessamine."

"Perfectly correct."

"The elder son died—"

"To be more precise, the story is very dark. Your father-in-law, by the way—"

"What about him?

"About four years ago, not long before your wedding, Jyce Earton and Prince Edmund were found dead."

"Did they kill each other?"

Hans hesitated. "There was no investigation."

"Hans?"

Judging from Lilian's tone of voice, she was not going to give up. Tremain sighed heavily.

"Lilian, I implore you—"

"What?"

"It should remain between us two."

"I promise."

"I was there."

"Hans! Tell me! I beg you! It is very important..."

Lily would keep it a secret; he could see it from her face. Hans began telling the story.

"By that time, I was already ten years in the royal service—even longer."

The past stood before Hans' eyes as he spoke. He had gone to the castle to give the king some securities. He had just left the study when a butler with disheveled hair came running.

"Your Majesty, they are dead!"

It was so unexpected that Hans unwillingly slipped behind the curtain, the secretary jerked, and the king deigned to reply.

"Who?"

"Prince Edmund and...the Earl of Earton!"

Edward went pale, his face changed, and he stormed out of the study. Hans followed him—not out of mere jealousy, no. Although, he knew Earton and the elder prince. He was ready to hide away as soon as the latter was made king. He treasured his life.

The fire burned in the red living room. It was warm and cozy. The room was one of the calmest and most private in the palace. It was located in a tower, on the third floor up the staircase. A soldier guarded the way up to prevent unwanted visitors from coming to the study. *How did the butler end up there? The answer was simple.* The prince had asked him to bring up a good dinner for two, which meant that in any case, he had not planned to die.

The fire was burning now. There was a bottle of wine and two glasses on the table with a tiny bit of wine still left. When they gave it to the dog, it died.

"Was there poison in both glasses?"

"Yes."

"The same kind of poison?"

Hans looked at Lily with surprise. Somehow, this question had never occurred to anyone. Poison was poison.

"I am curious if they had poisoned each other or one of them poisoned both drinks—or maybe there was someone else?"

"It is unlikely that there was someone else."

"Why?"

"First of all, because the king would not have covered up the scandal if that was the case. Secondly, the prince ordered the wine to be brought beforehand and sent the servant away. The servant swore that the bottle was sealed. Moreover, the poison was in the glasses, not the bottle, that is for sure."

"Edmund was prepared. Could he have hidden the killer?"

"No. The tower is arranged so that there are no secret niches and passages."

"For sure?"

"I myself examined the latter out of curiosity."

Lily nodded. She trusted Hans. If he said no, it meant there were none for sure.

"So, it was impossible to hide anyone. What about going past the guards?"

"There were two guards, and no one passed them."

"Could they be lying?"

"Impossible. We interrogated them. In a word—no."

Lily nodded once again. *One would admit to anything under torture, but apparently—*

"So, that servant was the only person who entered the room."

"Correct. He entered and stormed out as soon as he saw them dead."

"That means that a third party wasn't involved."

"It was done by one of the two."

Lily shrugged.

"It's possible, but people are usually not very likely to kill themselves—although I agree, it depends on the case."

"They looked almost the same. They were both sitting in chairs and had calm expressions on their faces. That meant that the poison was painless. They did not throw up and had almost no traces of foam on their lips."

"You said almost—meaning that there was some foam, after all?"

"Yes." Hans liked to listen to the countess reasoning. There was something peaceful in her voice, full of contemplation.

"Was it of the same color?"

"I think so."

"Did it smell of anything in particular?"

"The window was ajar, and the wind carried away the traces of any possible smell."

"I see."

"The king nearly lost consciousness."

Edward froze in the doorway, refusing to believe the facts before finally entering the room. He walked up first to the friend and after to the son; he closed their eyes. Hans saw the tears streaming down his face.

"Try to remember! Did he come up to the friend first?"

"Yes, and that is not a surprise."

"Why not?"

As it turned out, the whole court knew that Edmund and his father had had a strained relationship for the previous ten years. Edmund remembered his mother and was not at all happy about the king replacing her with some royal whore. He called Jessamine even worse things. The king slapped his son in the face, whipped him, and lectured him, but nothing helped. Jessamine cried; Edward got angry. The idea of a happy family was failing in practice.

Richard had a calmer disposition; although he did not take Jessamine for his own mother, at least he treated her like a sister. He was ready to accept her if it made his father happy. Lily approved of that principle.

In a word, Edward was in love, but his elder son did not share his happiness and fought against it with all his might. He tried to turn Richard against them, offended his stepmother and squabbled with Earton's children.

"Were Jess and Amalia educated at court?"

"At first, they were brought up by their father with a bit of help from his sister. When she married the king, she insisted on Jyce bringing her nephews along to court."

Hans knitted his brows. He did not like the way Lily was biting her nail. She was clearly thinking, and it was unlikely that the results of her brooding would please him.

"All right. His Majesty shut the eyes of his friend and his son, what next?"

"He turned around and, upon seeing me, asked to be left alone for a while. They shortly called me back in."

"If the poison was there after all—"

"We cannot determine who put it into the glasses, that's right."

Lily hit the table with her little fist.

"Did they carry out an investigation?"

"No, Lilian. The king ordered to drop the case."

The woman nodded.

"This case is bad."

"Indeed."

"No, that's not what I'm saying, Hans. Think! Let's say, an ordinary nobleman comes back to his house and sees his son and his friend dead. Wouldn't he want to investigate?"

"Of course he would, but it might cause a great scandal."

"Would you not have managed to avoid the scandal?"

"I would."

"And I would do anything to avenge my loved ones. Damn the scandal! One could just conveniently arrange for someone to 'fall from a horse'. By the way, were there any sudden deaths among the high-ranked shortly after the incident?"

Hans took a long time to think. He then shook his head.

"One duke had a stroke, but he was already over seventy."

"Yeah, the age…"

"There was another duke whose wife stabbed him in his sleep. Everyone knew that he had been severely abusing her for years."

"Let's not count barons and leirs. They're too low in status. We need to look for someone more significant. Were there any financial cuts in the embassy?"

"No. If it were not for this, the year would have been incredibly peaceful."

"That means that it was either Jyce or Edmund."

"What do you mean?"

"If we exclude the strangers, and we are forced to do so, we are left with them. I would personally bet on Jyce," Lily noted simply.

"Why?" Hans also thought along similar lines, but he was interested to hear the countess' thoughts.

"Because the earl knew that the prince could not stand him. Just imagine: the man who hates you invites you…to talk. Your actions?"

"I would put armor on,"

"Would you take the poison with you?"

"I don't know. Only if I always carried it with me."

"Instead of salt?"

"I would take a dagger."

"And I would take poison. It is possible that Jyce would, too. Edmund was younger and stronger than him. There was no chance for Jyce to beat him in a fair fight. Poison was his only option."

"It is ugly and undignified for a nobleman."

Lily winced.

"So is trading. Jyce Earton was a tradesman, too."

"True. But still…it is one thing to trade extravagant goods and another thing to poison a prince."

"Extravagant goods you say?"

"Do you think he might have gotten hold of some exotic poison, which he left for himself to…try out on someone?"

"If let's say I managed to get hold of a ring with poison—which I know exists—I would have never let go of it. Hans, we are incredibly lucky for you to remember that evening so well! Aldonai is with us. Tell me this—when you came back in, did you find the dead unchanged?"

Hans pondered and shrugged.

"I think they did change. However, I wouldn't be able to tell you what exactly changed."

"They remained seated, right?"

"Yes."

Lily nodded.

"Most likely. Was there any change in the arrangement of their clothes?"

"I think not. Either I didn't pay attention, or the changes were not striking."

"The king searched them. I assume that he had his own theories and suspicions."

"What theories?"

"Here comes the most exciting part. What if Jyce Earton poisoned the prince and then killed himself? Could that be the case?"

"Why would he do it? Of course, in theory, he could have done it. However, every action has a motive behind it, doesn't it?"

"It does. Well noted, Hans. So, what could have been the motive for him to do it?"

"It is clear why the earl might have poisoned himself. Too many people knew of his meeting with the prince."

"So he did it to avoid public execution and so on—"

"It is possible. But why did he poison Edmund?"

Lily bit her nail once more and eventually made it break. She was too focused to even notice it.

"I have an idea, and I wish to test your reaction. Tell me if I am foolish. But first—"

The woman rose from her seat and took out a little box. It contained all the letters that Jessamine wrote to her mother.

"Have a read."

One by one, Hans skimmed through each letter. When he put aside the last letter and lifted his head, Lily recognized the question in his eyes. It was the same question that she was asking herself.

"Is it possible?"

"Quite so. Edmund could have blackmailed the earl, which drew the latter to commit a—"

"As far as I comprehend, Jyce was ready to do anything for his sister and children. It's not surprising. Would Edmund have the material for blackmail?"

"A nurse maid's confession or something similar? Even so, nothing was found. My Lady—"

"Hans, I hope you understand that this conversation and its result must remain between us. You are aware that this knowledge could kill us."

Hans understood it perfectly well. The fact that Lily also understood it and would keep quiet made him sigh in relief.

He knitted his eyebrows.

"No, the story about the Ivelens doesn't add up."

"But Amalia—"

"So what? She is not a legitimate heir. On the contrary, such a thing would not have happened here—"

"What if Edward married Jessamine before Imogene?"

"This sounds like an utter impossibility! Even so—Jess is the heir, while Amalia is nothing. The people would have started a riot."

"Exactly! They already tried to leave Jess without an heir. They wanted to kill me. They would have killed him too, if he wasn't out of the country."

Hans shook his head.

"No, My Lady. Something doesn't seem right."

Lily sighed.

"What is it? If only I knew!"

"I suppose that only the king knows the truth."

"Alicia must also know."

"It is unlikely that they would tell us anything. If something comes out—"

"They would rather bury us alive than let it happen. I understand. I will keep silent."

"Me, too."

Hans met Lilian's eyes. They were on the same page. There was no proof, and to meddle in the secrets of the Crown was a sure way to get killed. Their death would be swift and sure. Neither of them was keen to die.

"Still, something doesn't make sense."

"Think about it, Hans. I will go to see the Ivelens tomorrow and look at their child."

Hans smiled. The countess did trust him. Otherwise, she would not be so open about her activities. He had long realized who the true miraculous doctor was in the pair Lilian— Tahir Djiaman din Dashar. He kept his mouth shut. It was not a good idea to talk about it. He worked for this woman and immensely benefited from it. In a word, being voluble wasn't worth it. One might be surprised to see what miracles a person is capable of for the sake of self-profit.

ಬಿ ◻ ಜ

Lily was not happy about her visit to the Ivelens. Although they seemed polite, smiley, and courteous on the surface, she could not make out what they were thinking. As for herself, she was terribly furious.

Ungrateful beasts! Bastards! That's how my kindness is repaid. I rescued Amalia and helped to deliver her babies. I even had to remember the much-hated obstetrics that I despise with all my heart. I would have liked to see how she could have survived if I had let the midwife cut her open with that dagger.

She did not get any pleasure from thinking of Peter either. Although he loved his wife, he was a real slug. She remembered him crying with a runny nose, unable to help his wife. Compared to Peter, Jerisson Earton seemed even likable to Lily, for she did not like or respect men without character. *Alas.*

She thought Loran Ivelen a snake and imagined fangs behind his radiant smile.

Your attitude toward certain people changes incredibly quickly when you find out they paid for your murder.

They received Tahir quite warmly and immediately directed him to the patient. The man refused and demanded that Lilian come along with him. She was his student, period. She had to be present. Otherwise, he would leave.

Tahir behaved so arrogantly that it made the Ivelens invite both of them to the tower. Lily snorted and thought it an ugly custom to hide the unwanted in a tower. The thought amused her.

When the doors to the small room opened, Lily became serious.

On the bed in front of them sat a charming girl. She was a nice, plump little doughnut. Lilian thought that she looked familiar. Her hair was light, and her eyes were gray. The elegant face bore no expression—half-open mouth and dripping saliva.

"Can she walk?" asked Lily in a simple voice.

Amalia shook her head.

"She barely walks or speaks."

Lily asked a lot about the child and concluded that she was most likely mentally deficient. It was a hard case of oligophrenia, close to idiocy. The symptoms were slow development, an inability to eat anything except liquid food, and learning difficulties. This was not the result of wrong handling, but an inherited gene. Although it was not common for such children to survive in the Middle Ages, they had nursed her well, for she was the marquess' daughter.

"The girl is mentally deficient," Tahir uttered meaningfully. "What do you think, Countess?"

Amalia did not know that Lily had already given Tahir a sign of 'incurable'. The countess nodded and began to chatter like an exemplary schoolgirl.

"The disease is incurable. The girl will always stay like this. You might be able to potty-train her, but nothing more."

Strictly speaking, Lily had nothing against oligophrenic children and admired the people who raised them. But who in the Middle Ages would bother with a handicapped child? This society was like a wolf pack;

it complied with the law of natural selection. It was cruel and rational. The girl could become a mother to healthy children, but that was not for sure. The choice would fall on Sessie and Jess. *But why does this girl look so familiar?*

Lily glanced at Peter and Amalia and almost swore.

Blue-eyed and black-haired Amalia... Peter with his dark hair and eyes...What recessive gene is responsible for the birth of a gray-eyed blonde who is also mentally disabled?

Unlike many people, Lily was sure that some diseases were genetic. While some thought that oligophrenia was due to the mother's age, Lily considered it to be a gene mutation. She could have been wrong; she was no Gregor Mendel after all.

I'll think about it once I'm back at home!

Lily carefully examined the girl.

No, there's nothing we can do. The child is kind, affectionate, isn't afraid of contact, but will remain a child forever. Lily turned to the marquess.

She said that they could raise and feed the child—they could try to teach her. The result might be either positive or negative. There was no guarantee.

These words were like sharp knives to Amalia. Peter was evidently concerned for his wife. As for Loran, he did not even show up.

Peter cares for his wife alone; he doesn't give a damn about his daughter. Besides, her grandfather doesn't care a bit! Is that normal?

The pieces of the puzzle were falling into place, but Lily could still not see the complete picture. Something was missing.

Amalia kept asking Tahir the same question—if it was true that nothing could be done.

The doctor confirmed, and the woman's face dropped. It seemed that she was blaming herself for something. Tahir found it necessary to comfort her.

"Your Grace, you are not to blame for this. The Heavenly Mare moves in mysterious ways."

Amalia suddenly burst into tears.

"No! If anyone is to blame, it's me! It is all my fault!"

With these words, she flew out of the room, having greatly frightened the girl.

Lily began comforting the girl, meanwhile giving instructions to the servant who was looking after her. Peter apologized and followed his wife out of the room.

Lily considered the options in her head.

Light hair, gray eyes... Who does the girl remind me of? Falion? It's possible, but such looks are all too common. Take only His Majesty!

Lily bit her finger.

His Majesty? Impossible! But I've got no other thoughts. Something is missing. I need to speak to Hans—and review genetics. Perhaps, genetics wouldn't be of help. I have seen those eyes before...only they bore a completely different look. They weren't senseless, no, but capricious and arrogant. Where have I seen them? Earton? No, however, it was definitely in a gallery of portraits... Capricious and arrogant...not Earton. Eartons are blue-eyed and black-haired. Falion? Alexander never showed me any portraits of his relatives. Perhaps the answer is here?

Lily knew that she would not have peace of mind until she remembered. She would stay here longer and look over the portraits again. It was like a pebble in a shoe, like a song stuck in her head, like a needle in a seam. She could not ignore it; she had to trace it back as soon as possible.

The Ivelens returned after about five minutes. Amalia was tearful but firm. Peter stroked her head.

Tahir took his leave and promised to think on the case. He repeated that they should just bring the child up, while keeping in mind that she would forever remain a senseless creature that could not even recognize her own mother. The child was forever a clean slate.

Thank God Lily managed to let Tahir know they needed to stay overnight. Tahir, who was ready to do anything to make his beloved teacher/student happy, immediately stated that it was necessary to examine the patient again at dawn so that the grace of the Heavenly Mare touched her. The Ivelens did not object. When one has a sick child, one believes in any god, be it the Heavenly Mare or the Moon Hare.

At dinner, Lily brought up the ancestry of the Ivelen family.

"Say, the Eartons are also an old family, but the Ivelens must be even older!"

Loran Ivelen was pleased to dwell on the subject, adding that the Ivelens even had royal blood in them. Lily gasped in admiration, and the discussion gradually reached the topic of family portraits. After dinner, Lily was invited to have a tour around the gallery— in place of a bedtime story. She immediately accepted the invitation and spent three fascinating hours with the elder duke. Communicating with him was frankly unpleasant. At least she received the information she wanted. Medieval portraits, for all their peculiarity, possessed one benefit. They were one hundred percent realistic. They were not of Cubism or Impressionism that this world would not know for ages. If the eyes were painted blue, they were blue in reality, not red or green.

❦

They reached the house without any incident. Hans Tremain was not at the estate, and Lily asked to invite him to the office as soon as he arrived. Meanwhile, Lily sat in her study with a dozen sheets of paper and asked not to be disturbed.

A couple of hours later, Hans knocked on the door and was immediately bombarded with questions.

"Come in, sit down."

Hans came in, took from the chair a sheet with weird formulas (AaBb x CcDd and inscriptions "dominant," "recessive," 75% and 25%), and sat down carefully.

"Lilian?"

"Hans, I cannot understand anything!"

"Regarding what?"

"I saw the third daughter of the Ivelens."

"Is something wrong with her, My Lady?"

Lily frowned, letting Hans understand that she didn't like formal titles.

"She is mentally deficient."

"Things like that happen, My Lady."

"Listen. She is blonde with gray eyes."

"So what?"

"Do you not make any connection? Well, why do I expect you to know? So! A child inherits the eye color of one of the parents. Is that clear?"

"But what if..."

"No, if one of the parents has blue eyes, the child could have gray, such cases are possible. However, Amalia and Peter could not bring such a miracle into the world."

"Why not?"

"In order to get a gray-eyed blonde we need a dominant…in other words, there are fewer people with light hair than there are with dark."

"Right,"

"In short, a child inherits eye and hair color from one of the parents—maybe grandparents. But even then, the child inherits the genes that come up more often."

"That is, dark hair…"

"Yes. Such a beautiful combination —blonde hair, light eyes, and white skin—is not a coincidence. It is a hereditary stamp. Here is the thing. Eartons are all dark-haired and blue-eyed. I looked at the family portraits. They all look related. Their looks have very distinctive attributes. Amalia's twins are also blue-eyed. I'm not sure about the hair color.

"Her elder ones also look similar. They have very strong genetics. That is, you can overpower them only if… I don't even know!"

"Do you suggest that the child is not Peter's?"

"At least one of them. I deliberately stayed overnight!"

"You risked your safety."

"They wouldn't poison me in their own house, would they?"

"One can't be sure."

"Exactly! I needed to make sure that my assumptions were correct. I kept silent. Hans, there were a couple of blonde Ivelens in the family—dating a hundred or hundred and fifty years back. This gene couldn't have survived for so long. Besides, all of them have dark hair and skin."

"The Ivelens are from the South. There were cases of mixed blood in the family…"

"Yes, I've heard there were a few Khangans. In short, it is unlikely that the dark gene comes from their bloodline. They all look alike! All of them are dark-haired and blue-eyed."

"Who might the father be then?"

"We'll get nothing if we don't question the duchess."

"We might be left with nothing if we do."

"What do you suggest?"

"We should go to the king, My Lady."

"WHAT?"

"We have no other choice."

"But Hans!"

"My Lady, I hope you understand that this might be a conspiracy against the Crown!"

Lily nodded.

"If we don't report it, we will be accused of cooperation. Faymo and Rockrest, by the way, know enough…"

"Why do you think we should report?"

"The truth is that the butler is a complex individual. He hears one thing, imagines another… Our Virman friends are very good at it."

"And?"

"It's a serious conspiracy. He doesn't know all the details, such as that the Ivelens have someone who has rights to the throne. There are documents and people, everything is ready."

"Why did they not begin?"

"Because of Richard's departure. If they plan to overthrow the dynasty—"

"It has to happen here. Even I understand it. What forces do they have?"

"About twenty people, but they all hold key positions at court. There are a couple of good mercenary troops involved."

"Why was I not aware of this?"

"Because these killers are not the Ivelens', but his accomplices'. Let me tell you everything, My Lady."

Lily nodded and was told a lot of unpleasant things. As is known, it is the "foreign friends" who benefit from rebellions inside the country, in particular—Avesterra. He provided the Ivelens with men and money. The Ivelens got another two dozen nobles involved in the conspiracy. Although they weren't the most influential of aristocrats, their sort was the most dangerous, for they strove to topple the existing order. Besides, the Ivelens were short of money, so they required getting rid of Lily so that Jess' sister could gain custody of Mirrie and they could use her money as they pleased.

Lily bit her nail but listened carefully. They had planned to get rid of her before the arrival of the crown prince. Jess was going to die during the coup, for the Royal Guard obeyed him. Although he didn't have a splendid reputation, it was dangerous to underestimate his power. For what it was worth, he was a good leader.

There were a couple of killer squads. Soon, the ships of Avesterra were going to enter the harbor. As soon as Richard arrived (and he was travelling by ship), they would try to intercept him and blame it on Virman pirates. If that plan failed, they would get him in Laveri. The king would soon move to his summer residence outside the city. Its location was quite convenient for the plotters. The castle itself was more of a luxurious house than a fortified building, and it was in close proximity to the land owned by the Ivelens.

Lily looked at Hans.

"What do we do?"

"First, we need to report everything to the king. Secondly, Erik is already at sea."

"Erik?"

"Yes. Our friend enjoys authority in his circles. On Virma, his title is less than an earl, or even a duke. I asked him to take at least five more ships and meet the embassy."

"I see!"

"I also handed him all the explosives from your laboratory."

Lily nodded.

"Good job. What about—"

"Jamie went with them."

"Hans! What if he gets into trouble! He is only a boy!"

"He is old enough. It could be a great chance to confirm his title."

Lily shook her head. The eternal feminine desire to take everyone under her wing had no place in the Middle Ages. Here every boy grew up quickly.

"Do you insist on talking with the king?"

"Yes."

"When?"

"Tonight."

"I don't want to go to the palace." Lily wrinkled her nose. "It's been too often...I don't want to."

The palace! For some reason, she associated the face of the poor girl with the palace. *A beautiful, bright, young lady of the court...*

Lily squeezed her temples and moaned.

"Whereabouts have I seen her? Where?"

"Is everything alright, My Lady?"

"Hans! The daughter of Amalia is a copy of someone I've seen before. I cannot remember where I've seen this person. I can't think of the place!"

"Perhaps in the palace?"

"Yes, yes—but where exactly? Whose portrait was it?"

Hans sighed. *What conundrum is she trying to solve this time?*

"Do not torment yourself, My Lady. It is only a—"

"It's important! But where?"

"Take a breath, My Lady." Hans took her hand almost by force. If he couldn't distract her from thinking, he had to help her. He wanted her to cool down so they could discuss this "important matter."

"You have to remember. This woman in the portrait, what was she wearing?"

Lily concentrated. Her visual memory was magnificent. She, like many other doctors, constantly improved it.

"The woman is blonde—in a purple dress—scarlet and gold—beautiful—arrogant... She is sitting in a chair, her hands free—with a straight, confident look."

"Incredible. What is the arrangement of her hair?"

"Her hair is up, with a couple of curls reaching down to her shoulders."

Lily closed her eyes and saw the portrait coming to life before her. *An arrogant blonde painted against a gold and white backdrop, in a gorgeous dress... Her gray eyes staring decisively, a deep cut reveals her beautiful breasts.*

"Is she wearing any jewels?"

"Yes—diamonds. A small diadem made of diamonds, a necklace, a bracelet and a couple of rings—"

"Is it a diamond bracelet?"

"Yes."

"On which hand?"

"The same as mine," Lily said, remembering the portrait.

Hans unclenched his fists.

"My Lady, you will have to go to the palace with me. And another thing—this portrait was not in the palace gallery?"

"I haven't ever been there. It was somewhere in the palace."

"You saw it while walking along the corridors?"

"Yes—and it struck my eye," Lily swung her head, and her heavy braid stung painfully on her bare back.

"I was lost and wandering along the palace corridors, when suddenly I saw this portrait. It seemed to come out of the darkness as if it had deliberately been put out of sight—"

Hans bit his lip. Unlike Lily, he knew whose portrait the king would be willing to hide.

"I think I know which portrait you are talking about. In case I'm right—you will not accompany me to the king."

"What about an alibi?"

"Do you trust me, My Lady?"

"Yes."

"In that case, trust me to the full."

Hans didn't say more. He knew that only the royals had a right to a wear a diamond wedding bracelet.

ഐ ☐ ൽ

Edward opened the note and frowned. He trusted his servants. A royal trustee was an important source of information. The king selected his trusted people very carefully.

Hans Tremain was one of the best. It astonished the king to see what ingenious plots he managed to bring to light. He had been faithful and stubborn since his youth—since the very moment when Prince Edward, the future King of Ativerna, had helped him out.

What urgent matter could bring him to me if he insists on attending this evening? He was asking for the king's audience today, as soon as possible. He said in the note that it wasn't very serious. It was something about the Countess of Earton and her daughter.

Well…if the matter concerns Miranda, it cannot be put off. She is my granddaughter, after all. Edward had no clue that Hans had deliberately lied in the note. He had to get the audience of the king as soon as possible at all costs. He wasn't going to postpone this matter, for it was not the kind of matter that could be put away until better times. If Lilian Earton was right, then the kingdom was in danger, and the king had to know about it.

The note said it was about Miranda. That was to discourage eavesdropping. No one cared about children in this world.

 ෴

Alicia Earton received a note from Lily.

Her daughter-in-law had asked if she could pay her a visit. Lily would come to the palace to meet with Alicia in private, so they could sit and talk about Miranda.

The countess pondered for a moment. She then resolved that everything was not as scary as it sounded.

Lilian Earton is a smart young woman. Why not spend time with her? We could meet and sit down to talk… Why does it have to be this evening? I suppose there is nothing to be surprised about. With her mad routine, she must be too busy during the day.

 ෴

"Home soon."

"Yes, very soon," Richard grinned.

"The ships are ready, and our things are loaded. We will raise the sails in three days."

"I am sick of remaining in Ivernea."

"It's your own fault. You could have a good time here if you wanted. We have bought a lot of scrolls, which would otherwise be destroyed here. We talked to the merchants and made some of them see Ativerna in a more favorable light. We went through the shops. It felt like all the rare things came from us. The Mariella Trading House, a beautiful name."

Jess turned the golden pen in his hands.

"Yeah. I wonder who came up with it? The owner must be a smart lad."

"I'm also extremely curious. We have to find out upon our return."

"We also have some news to bring to the king."

"The princesses are due for a visit. There will be a couple of receptions, I will soon marry Anna, and everyone will be able to breathe freely."

"Everyone except you."

"Alas…"

Richard wasn't excited for the future.

ಬಾ ▫ ೞ

Lily and Hans rode in the carriage and looked at each other gloomily. They didn't want to talk. They had already discussed everything they could think of. They had even managed to quarrel and reconcile a couple of times. Lily tried to find out from Hans who this lady was. Hans was silent as a fish. He told her that if his guesses were right, she would find out soon. If not, it wasn't worth messing with her head. Nevertheless, it was a must for her to see and identify the portrait. Any information was useful. Lily suggested that she could go to the king with him, but Hans dismissed it. It was better for her to stay away from that snake swamp—the vipers would be safer. Lily hissed no worse than a snake. She declared that Hans was her own trustee above all. She said that the state secrets were extremely life threatening. She was a countess, after all, but he was a simple royal representative. They would not have mercy on him.

It didn't take long for Hans to lose his temper. Lily was told that if every royal secret endangered the life of one royal representative, there would be no one left to do the job. They would most likely take mercy on him. After all, it was his job to keep secrets. He couldn't be so sure about the countess.

Thus, they fought, disagreed and reconciled. There was no time for arguments. Lily rode in the carriage and thought that the eye of the storm was no metaphor. It was her destiny to attract hurricanes.

Is it wise to go to the king, if it puts Hans and me in danger? Maybe it is best to agree with the Ivelens, let's say, in exchange for getting rid of Jess? I can be useful for any dynasty.

This thought tickled Lily's mind, but she immediately rejected it. It was good to have a strong and powerful monarch on the throne. At least Edward was a fair ruler. He guarded the kingdom's peace. *Would the Ivelens manage to provide peace and stability for the kingdom? It is one thing to put one's ass on the throne, and quite another to pass it down to the family.*

The False Dmitrys had their minute of fame, but neither of them managed to preserve the throne. If no one had supported the Godunovs, there would have been no Time of Troubles and no Romanovs on the Russian throne. Gee, they would have avoided the big hemorrhoids!

Lily supported legitimate rulers. *After all, Edward is different from Nicholas the Second, who strove to bring happiness to all, but lost a couple of wars, as well as his own country. No, Edward is a good, serious man. He is not afraid of tough decisions but is also not drowning in a pool of blood. He manages to keep everything calm and cozy. What if the Ivelens failed to keep the throne? It would bring a new Time of Troubles, cause bloodshed, war, and revolution. Nobody needs that, especially not me. I have lived through that hell and borne the consequences of Perestroika back in my own world. Let the lovers of change go to hell and not provoke the greatest of sins. After all, not every murderer gets his deserved punishment.*

Alicia met them at the entrance to the castle. She gave Lily a very serious look.

"Lilian, what is this secrecy for?"

Hans waved his hand, dismissing all her questions.

"My Lady, I implore your forgiveness. I asked the countess to remain in the castle just in case. I wanted her to stay around you. His Majesty might want to see her."

Alicia shrugged.

"If it's so necessary—"

Lilian nodded.

"I trust Leir Tremain. Let's go?"

"Yes, only one thing—"

Hans confidently stepped inside the darkness of the corridors. The women followed him. Lily did not look into the darkness very far. *Besides, what can I expect to see in the dark?* Old portraits, old armor. When they stopped, the dancing candlelight separated from the darkness the beautiful face of a woman.

"My Lady," asked Hans and froze. He realized that his guess was right.

"It is that very portrait I have seen before. Who is she?"

Hans remained silent, but Alicia couldn't resist.

"It is the king's first wife. Her name was Imogene of Avesterra."

Lily inspected the surroundings. It was that very place where she had once found herself after the reception with the king. Back then she didn't know the palace too well. Her knowledge of it hadn't improved since.

"Who put her picture here?"

"It was the king's order. They put it in a central spot to preserve the queen's dignity. However, almost no one comes this way."

Lily nodded. *It's difficult to spot the similarity between the sick child and this woman, but damn it! The resemblance is certainly there. If the girl wasn't sick, she would have been the queen's spitting image! Those eyes...their shape and color. That could be attributed to Amalia, who is after all related to Edward. But why does the girl look so much like Imogene? The same nose and lips...Damn it!*

The pieces of the jigsaw pulled together so suddenly that it made Lily flinch.

"Countess?"

Hans became genuinely worried when Lily's green eyes flashed in the dark.

"Everything is fine, Leir. It's just —it finally came over me."

"Let's go then?"

She realized that she wasn't the only one who understood.

"Leir?"

"Yes, Countess. Your assumptions seem right..."

"But it is nonsense!"

"I'm afraid that it's true."

"Hans, you shouldn't go to the king alone. It could be—"

"This is not a good time to argue, Lilian." So metallic was his voice that it gave Lily shivers. "Right now you have to put your trust in me."

Lily sighed and nodded.

54

"Fine."

"Would anyone care to explain what's going on?" Alicia was slightly annoyed and didn't think it necessary to hide it.

Hans and Lily simultaneously shook their heads.

"No."

"Really?"

Lily raised her hand.

"Alicia, darling, I will tell you everything later. Such trifles are not worth our time right now."

Soon, everyone went their separate ways. Hans hurried to the king, Lilian followed Alicia.

Edward was waiting for the guest in his study.

"Leir Tremain?"

The man bowed.

"Your Majesty, I am grateful for your generous—"

"No need for eloquence, Leir. What happened to the countess and Miranda?"

"They are fine, Your Majesty. I wish to apologize in advance for misleading you. There was no evil intention behind it."

"Is that so?"

"Your Majesty, I deliberately didn't write about the true purpose of my visit."

Edward nodded in the direction of a chair.

"Well. Sit down and tell me, Leir."

Hans bowed, sank into the chair and spoke softly.

"Your Majesty, I must inform you that the Duke of Ivelen is plotting against the Crown."

"Really?"

"Yes, Your Majesty."

"And how did you find out?"

"They first tried to assault the Countess of Earton—"

"There she is again!"

"It all began with her, Your Majesty. I apologize for the bad news which I brought you."

"Go on, Leir."

Hans told him everything. Edward got progressively gloomier. The plot wasn't too complicated or ambitious. Only some twenty people were involved, but all of them were of high rank. Everyone had their own problems. Some had debts, others, children, and the rest were either cuckolds who saw it as an opportunity for revenge or held an inherent grudge against the Crown. Except for the Ivelens, there was not a single duke among the plotters—only earls and barons. Some captains, some maps…all had been planned quite well.

The whole thing began around three years ago. It was then that the Ivelens began writing to Avesterra; when being very offended by Edward's treatment of Imogene, Leonard helped them; Richard added to his offense when the former rejected his daughter. With Leonard's help, the Ivelens hired a lot of killers and engaged many other dissatisfied individuals (there were always plenty of them).

There was never much money. Having been financially strained, the Ivelens decided to kill Lilian once they found out that she was pregnant. They planned to murder Miranda afterwards because she had a right to inherit. As for Jerisson, they planned to get rid of him long ago, together with Richard and Edward. As a result, Amalia would inherit everything. They could always give Mirrie into marriage with someone trusted but decided not to risk it. Killing her was easier.

"The Ivelens, you say. Sounds delightful! Does the countess know about it?"

"No, Your Majesty. She knows some things, but not everything."

"What does she know about?"

"She knows there is a conspiracy. She knows that the Ivelens are involved. She doesn't have to know everything."

"Good. Amalia, Amalia…"

"They were out of the spotlight. No one ever suspected or checked them. That left them enough space to weave their spider's web and recruit allies. There are not a lot of them. However, the capital is also not particularly armed?"

"We only have the archers and the guards."

"Don't trust the Shooters Squad," Hans said. "They have long been bribed by the Ivelens."

"How do you know this, Leir?"

"Every crime leaves a financial footprint," Hans grinned. It was not worth mentioning that those words belonged to the countess. "Even cash doesn't come from the air. One could always talk to tailors, artisans, and peasants about how much tax they pay; the servants could tell you about their mistresses' dresses; the armorers are quick to complain about how much they are owed—"

"How did you manage to investigate this so quickly?"

"I got a couple more representatives involved," Hans honestly admitted. "As soon as I realized that there was more to it than the attempt on the countess' life, I didn't trust myself to work alone. We joined forces. Our intelligence office and the Virmans were the additional support. You can order to execute me, but if I hadn't involved them, I would have never found out even half of the truth. As soon as the whole picture became clear, I hurried to Your Majesty."

"Did you come alone?"

"The rest trusted me to report it to the king."

"What do your people know about the Ivelens?"

"Nothing, Your Majesty," gasped Hans. "Be it in my power, I would have kept the countess out of it. This whole affair is not fit for a woman."

"Fine." The king waved his hand. "Let's agree on the following. I won't tolerate the hassle around it. I will give you the special squad. Will you be able to put everyone to the Stonebug?"

"Everyone?"

Edward frowned.

"Everyone including the Ivelens. Loran, Peter... Amalia..."

"What about the children?"

"Only the elder ones."

"Your Majesty..."

"Do it!" Snapped Edward. "The sooner, the better. Write an order, and I will sign it."

"Yes, Your Majesty."

Hans obediently jotted down a few lines, not without appreciation for Lilian Earton. Her invention of the pen was extremely handy. The king couldn't wait for the ink to dry, quickly signed the order and put a stamp on it.

"Go."

"I'm sorry, Your Majesty, but I must tell you something else."

"Is there something else I should know?"

"Yes, Your Majesty. I beg you to forgive me—"

"Leir!"

"Your Majesty, do you remember that day when your friend and your son..."

"Yes, I do. Why are you talking about this now?"

Edward assumed that the story wouldn't bring him joy, but he had to listen. He was the king; it was his duty.

"Your Majesty, I ask you in advance to forgive me for all the ill-considered words that might hurt you. I apologize for those questions that I'll have to ask. I do not want it. However, I do not have a choice either."

"How interesting. Ask me. I guess I will be able to answer."

"When they found Jyce and Edmund dead—I will refer to them as such, with your permission and for the sake of convenience. It was Jyce who poisoned both the prince and himself, right?"

Hans looked straight into the king's eyes. Edward reluctantly nodded.

"Yes. How did you know?"

"I guessed. If it hadn't been so—not that you would have hidden the truth—the investigation would have concerned the prince, his motives and the nature of the poison. As for Jyce—you protected your children. You did everything to avoid the erupting scandal. You found the supposed murderer—a butler—and executed him."

"I let him leave in secret and gave him money in return for his silence. I didn't want to kill the innocent boy. He was even younger than Edmund."

Edward arched his back and shoulders. The weakness was momentary. He straightened his back and pierced Hans with a glaring look. Hans wasn't self-delusional. His own life was at stake.

"Children?"

"You heard it correctly, Your Majesty. Jerisson and Amalia, your children from Jessamine."

"How do you—"

"I've been to Earton. The countess kept some letters."

"What letters?"

"She wrote to her mother. Before the birth of the children, she implored her mother to forgive her for the sake of her great joy. She said that having children always gives happiness, whether they are born in a marriage or not. I compared the dates and made assumptions. I made inquiries. Alicia Weeks—medicuses and relatives said she was a barren woman. All of a sudden, she receives a marriage proposal and gives birth to two children. Amalia was born prematurely, her mother never cared for her. She didn't care for Jerisson either. The children were taken to the palace and became the princes' playmates."

"I must pay tribute to your ingenuity. Does the countess know?"

Hans shook his head.

"She is not as involved in the affairs of the royal family to be able to spot the truth. Besides, she doesn't care for it."

"Do you?"

"I tried to understand, to figure out the truth—and it shocked me."

"What are you going to do with your understanding?"

"I'm going to keep silent for the rest of my life. The secret will die with me."

The king's look slightly softened.

"Keep your mouth shut. Otherwise—"

Hans touched the medallion in shape of the sign of Aldonai through his shirt.

"I swear by Aldonai, Your Majesty. Let the way to his kingdom be forever closed for me if I'm lying."

Edward sighed and decided to explain better—or maybe he only wanted to get it off his chest.

"The pregnancy was accidental. We tried to be careful, she took a potion from one witch, but such herbs are dangerous if taken continuously. I was out of the capital for a long time. Jessie decided to take a break when my father unexpectedly called me in. We were careless, but also madly in love," he said.

"It was Jyce who pushed the idea of pretending that the children were his, not his sister's." Hans wasn't asking; it was a statement.

"Correct. Jyce loved his sister immensely. He was loyal to Jessamine with all his heart and was ready to kiss the ground on which she stepped. When she fell in love with me, he became my most loyal friend, just to stay by her side. If they had only been cousins, he would have married her. He was ready to do anything for her—kill, die, betray, lie... She realized it well."

Hans nodded.

"Amalia and Jerisson don't know about it, right?"

"They know nothing."

"This question kept me thinking at night! May I ask you—did the poison belong to Jyce?"

Edward nodded and took off the ring with the big blue stone. He turned it carefully, and the stone opened, revealing a grayish powder inside the ring.

"I found this on Jyce's hand. We gave this poison to the dog, and it killed the bitch."

"So far, everything makes sense. Here is a tale. Five children were growing up together. Peter Ivelen was Edmund's age and frequented the court."

"Yes."

"He was his highness' playmate—a very simple task, which causes some to advance to new heights and others to fall painfully. I have no doubt about the strength of their friendship."

"Yes, Peter is a good young man—"

"Except he is easily led. He was always second best to the prince. Edmund was your firstborn child. He was jumpy, sensitive, and adored his mother. He also hated the Eartons. Jessie took his father from him, and Jyce was the one who helped her. I don't know if it was Imogene who turned the son against the Eartons or whether it was the boy himself. Imogene didn't know about the children either, right?"

"We had terrible scandals," His Majesty sighed. "No matter how wild and disgusting our arguments were, she did not reproach me about the children once. She would've done so if she had known. We did everything very fast as soon as we found out that Jessie was pregnant."

"Jyce had surely prepared in advance. I remember him, he was very clever."

"Yes."

"So, the children grew up together. Upon realizing that he would become the next king, Edmund was planning to get his revenge on the much-hated Eartons. Amalia was only a year younger than him and Peter. I don't know how, but I am sure that Amalia and Edmund fell in love with each other."

"What?" gasped Edward.

Hans shrugged.

"They didn't know that they were related, so they felt free to do anything. At the same time, Edmund hated all the Eartons. Amalia was born into the hated family. Now the sad part—your grandchildren Sessie and Jess Jr. I am more than convinced that they are Edmund's, as well as Amalia's third daughter. Have you seen her?"

"Only in her infancy."

"It is not surprising. The baby is the spitting image of her grandmother, only the eyes are yours."

"Jessie?"

"No, Imogene. They realized it and hid the daughter well. They made a mistake when they called Tahir to see the girl, who refused to go without his beloved student. The countess saw the girl and told me."

"Does she know?"

"No, she only made a joke that the little girl is a copy of Queen Imogene."

"How does she—"

"Seeing the portrait once was enough. It suddenly struck me. If the children were Peter's—forgive me, Your Majesty, but the girl would have been at least your copy, but not the copy of Imogene! Incredible!"

Edward slouched.

"But why—"

"I was surprised when they decided to show the girl to the mediduses," sighed Hans. "Maybe something else provoked such a rash decision. Tahir is a Khangan, he cares nothing for our courtly intrigues and will forget them as soon as he leaves. As for Lilian, her husband tried hard to create an appropriate reputation for her. She is known to be a fool and a cow, am I right, Your Majesty?"

Edward drew his eyebrows together, but it no longer intimidated Hans. He laid his cards on the table, hit or miss. The second option seemed more likely, but the card was already on the table.

"For once, this has played into our hands. No one expected any trick or comprehension from Lilian. Imogene and the girl look identical. It suddenly occurred to me that the Ivelens had decided to claim the throne. Amalia is your daughter; the Ivelens have a connection to the royal dynasty. When Lilian told me about the child, she said that it could only happen if Amalia was a bride to someone fair."

Edward straightened in his chair.

"A bride?"

"Yes. My assumption is that although they were never officially married, Amalia and Edmund... When was she betrothed to the Ivelen?"

"He asked for her hand in marriage himself and insisted on a wedding. Amalia didn't object either."

"Meanwhile Edmund was away, right?"

Edward pondered, calculating something in his head.

"About a month before the wedding, I sent him away to the border for offending Jessie."

"Presumably the events developed like this. After the departure of her beloved, Amalia realized that she was pregnant. Wild horror overtook her senses when a third person got in her way. It was Peter Ivelen, who had loved and tenderly admired Amalia since childhood. The young man was happy to get her, even that way."

"What way?"

"She became his wife. It was a matter of formality and not the real state of affairs. She was already married to Edmund. I don't know if Loran Ivelen was aware of it."

"He wasn't happy at the wedding."

"Did the couple leave for the estate straight away?"

"Yes."

"It was easier to hide the length of the pregnancy. I suppose that was the reason why Jess Jr. was a full-term baby, unlike Amalia herself."

"Do you think that—"

Edward looked aged as if he wasn't fifty but two hundred. It was scary to watch, but Hans could not remain silent. He had sworn an oath of loyalty.

"I'm sure of it. Edmund returned, but the scandal did not break out. You wanted to get him married, so he had to remain silent."

"I tried to arrange his marriage, but he would find ways to refuse. He slipped through my fingers!"

"What else? He already had a wife and three children, what would he do with another bride?"

"It's unthinkable."

"It's unbelievable! Only think about Jyce's reaction if he found out that he had a different son-in-law—Edmund; that Amalia had given birth to three of his children; that they loved each other and were going to make a public announcement."

Edward bent his head slowly.

"It must have turned him mad. I understand why he poisoned Edmund."

"Me, too. Alas! Jyce hastily made a terrible decision. Edmund tried to establish a good relationship with his father-in-law. He knew that it was important for Amalia. He offered to make peace. Jyce was astonished. Incest, although involuntary, was a continuous affair. How would he stop them? He could speak to him, tell him everything… What if he didn't believe it? I wouldn't have believed it myself. What proof could he give?"

"I would have said that—"

"Would Edmund have believed it? Or would he think that you were trying to separate him from his beloved?"

Edward considered his words for a while.

"It's possible."

"Jyce had to make his decision in seconds. He chose the simplest option. No person, no problem. Edmund didn't suspect anything and took the poisoned cup from the hands of his father-in-law. As for Jyce, himself, he either poisoned both cups out of loyalty, or he decided that death would wash away his shameful act. I don't know…"

"I think it was the second."

"You know better. It has muddled my brain to think about it for so long. Something didn't seem right. People don't willingly jump from a cliff. It is perhaps the doom of our age, which makes so many willingly throw themselves against bare rocks. I couldn't understand the web of blood relations. Suppose the Ivelens had a certain third aunt who was somehow related to the king."

"The Ivelens had royal blood on both sides."

"Even so, it wasn't enough to claim the throne. Amalia is a bastard child. If she promulgated her true ancestry, it would make her life unbearable. No one would see her on the throne."

"The people wouldn't have accepted her either way."

"Yes! But the Ivelens created such a tight network of usurpers that it seems they found valid proof to claim the throne."

Edward sighed.

"Why are you telling me everything now?"

"I swear on my life that I don't intend to spread royal secrets. My life is also at stake. If it weren't for the plot against the Crown, I would never have made a sound or sign of my knowledge. But things are getting worse. I would be the first one to die, followed by you, Your Majesty. I want to live."

"Who doesn't?"

Edward knew. Peter Ivelen was Edmund's friend. Once they were old enough, Amalia and Jess were always invited to the palace. Alicia never took care of the children; Jyce and Jessie brought them up together before she was made the queen. It was useless to argue. He had only himself to blame.

"You can go, Hans."

"Your Majesty, do you want me to invite someone else to your study?"

"Call my valet in."

"Yes, Your Majesty."

Hans rushed to call the squire. The king had only one valet, old and trustworthy, he had served him from the king's very childhood. He treated the king in a quite peculiar way, like an old uncle to his silly nephew. Seeing the king in his underpants every day, he couldn't treat the royals seriously. Meanwhile, Edward sat at his desk and rubbed his forehead.

What do I do now? Execute my royal representative? Could do to keep the secret. Still, even if I punish Hans, I wonder if Lilian Earton knows or not. She probably does, but surely not everything. She might know a tiny bit.

"Your Majesty?"

The valet and Leir Tremain entered.

"I have issued an order, Leir. You may proceed."

Hans took his leave and disappeared. Edward rubbed his chest—it had lately been giving him much pain—and nodded to the valet.

"Help me undress, John."

"Yes, Your Majesty."

Edward was going to lie down and rest. He wouldn't be able to fall asleep.

"Give me some mulled wine with honey and spices."

"Of course, Your Majesty. Shall I call anyone in?"

Edward didn't want to see his official favorite.

"No."

"It's for the best. They say that the baroness spreads her feathers and beats her beak before the dukes and earls."

"Is it my favorite or your chickens you are talking about?" grinned Edward. He gave the old man a lot of liberties.

"She's a big hen, your lady!" The valet unlaced the dress and helped the king take off his tunic.

"A big, stupid hen! Let me help you take off your boots, Your Majesty!"

Edward surrounded the servant's hands. Little by little, the cozy grumbling calmed him down. As soon as he put his head on the pillow, the pain soothed. He wouldn't be able to sleep, but at least it would help him let go of the pain.

ಙ ♢ ಚ

Even though Hans was extremely busy, he found time to visit Alicia Earton. Lily was sitting on the chair chatting.

"—to go to the shipyards. Why not? Father would be happy."

"My Lady?"

"Leir Tremain!"

Lily almost jumped from her chair and grabbed her friend by both hands.

"Is everything alright?"

"I am going to the Ivelens now. Promise to stay here, My Lady."

"Fine."

They exchanged a serious look. "Did it work?"

"I do not know yet, but it's better to remain silent."

"I will not say anything. Alicia?"

"Tell them I'm glad of the truth."

They were silent, but sometimes words weren't needed. A thin thread of understanding stretched between them. Some might take years to achieve it, but not them. They thought the same thing, felt the same way, they were almost one.

As soon as Hans left, Alicia looked at Lilian with a question.

"What happened?"

Lily briefly retold the story of the Ivelens. She didn't mention royal relations and many other things, such as their suspicions and letters. She told Alicia that the Ivelens were plotting against the Crown and that Lily happened to be a by-product between millstones. If the plotters managed to kill her, they would get her money and maybe her shipyards.

Alicia shook her head.

"A conspiracy? Aldonai, the king will simply get killed."

"The main thing is to ensure that the king will not kill Leir Tremain."

"Lilian!"

"Those who know state secrets don't live long."

"Lilian, Edward is a clever and merciful ruler."

"I would like to think the same." Lily sighed. "As for now, I have nothing else left but to worry."

Her own experience showed that those in power seldom sided with justice.

Chapter 2
Anagnorisis

Alicia's room was exemplary to the strictest of monks—narrow bed, tall wardrobe, a couple of chests, simple strict draperies and a table. When Lily asked why her mother-in-law had not settled there, she only shook her head.

"I don't need much."

The two women sat and waited. Hans had asked Lilian to come to the palace for a reason. He had taken the Virmans with him and couldn't ensure the countess' protection during the time he was away. He could ask Leis' people, but it was risky. Hans didn't want to put the life of his lady (and his friend) in danger. Therefore, the women were going to spend the night in Alicia's room. It was unlikely that the killers would come to the palace, at least not that night.

The main problem of the Middle Ages was the slow spread of information. Hans left two Virmans at the palace dovecot. No message would reach any addressee before dawn. Everything would be over by the morning.

Lily knew about the plan. She sat in a chair and drank soothing tea. Although it was bitter and mucky, it calmed her down.

Alicia paced the room.

"I still don't believe that Amalia—"

"I would have never believed it myself. What do we know about her?"

"She is my—"

"Daughter. What about the rest?"

"She is a wife and a mother. Peter adores her."

"What about her?"

Alicia paused.

"I think she does, too."

"How does she show it?"

"What do you mean, Lilian?"

Lily sighed. She didn't know how to explain it. It was like a veil of happiness hanging in the air. Lily remembered how her father returned home and her mother met him and kissed him, their eyes glowing with love. They turned to their daughter who also ran into the corridor and smiled, and the air was filled with warm rays of sunshine. It only took the breath of sweet air that filled the house to realize that everyone was happy there. One could spray their house with Chanel, only the smell of happiness was impossible to fake. Happiness was like fireflies floating in the air. It was everywhere—in a gesture, a smile, a glance, a touch. Lily didn't feel this happiness in the house of the Ivelens.

Ingrid and Leif had it three thousand times stronger. *It is different for Peter and Amalia,* thought Lily. *He worships her, and she takes it, no more. How does everyone fail to see it?* Perhaps they were good at keeping up appearances, but Lily showed up right when it all started crumbling. No one considered Lily clever or dangerous, thanks to her husband.

"I didn't see happiness. They had a home, Peter's love, and calm stability. Why is it so, Alicia?"

"Are you talking about Edmund and Amalia?"

"Yes."

"I don't know. I can easily believe that Edmund, who passionately hated the Eartons, didn't believe himself when he fell in love with Amalia."

"They could have come to the parents and explained."

"Do you suggest he should have come to his father whom he hated?"

"He could have come to Jyce."

Alicia began thinking.

"Lilian, maybe you just fail to understand how much Edmund hated the Eartons. He would never have come to Jyce or me for help."

"What about Amalia?"

"Would you go up to your father with a statement that you love a man, carry his child, and want to marry him?"

Aliya Skorolenok would go to the president with such a statement. As for Lilian…

"I doubt it."

"He would have simply killed you."

"I hope not, but—"

"There would have only been one way—to kill the child and send Amalia to the monastery."

"Amazing. We can make as many guesses as we like, but only Amalia knows the answer."

Alicia rolled her eyes.

"Do you understand the danger you are exposing yourself to?"

"What danger?" Lily looked naive.

"You know it yourself now."

"About the conspiracy? Yes, I know. So what?"

"You mean you—"

"Alicia, I am going to keep silent. You should do so as well. Hans would never admit that he told us. No one else will find out. As for those who dare to discuss the king's private affairs—are we short of executioners?"

Alicia burst into laughter.

"You are right, in some ways. Only how should we deal with the Ivelens?"

"We could set up an unfortunate accident," muttered Lily. "Are there any other options?"

"What about the children?"

Lily scratched her nose. She hadn't thought about the children.

"I don't know. The younger girl is certainly out of the question. She wouldn't be able to give birth to healthy offspring and would not last long."

"What about the elder ones? Jess? Sessie?"

"It depends on how much they know."

"Do you think that…"

The women exchanged serious, somber glances. Lily sighed.

"I don't know. I wouldn't want to be in the king's place."

ಜ ೮ಜ

Edward would have gladly swapped places with someone else. There was a dull pain in his chest, his temples were on fire; the pain seized his shoulder and his right arm. It wasn't the first time, but he was strong, he could cope.

Edward lay on his bed and stared at the wall. He wished he could raise the alarm, recruit the guards, and reinforce the palace. There was no way he could do it. If he raised panic, the plotters would either run away or strike first. It wasn't wise to ring all the bells. The best way was to quietly take the Ivelens, interrogate them in Stonebug.

Deprived of the key figures, the plotters would involuntarily get into a fight. They wouldn't have anyone who was important enough to claim the throne. That would win him at least ten days. Right now, time was their most important asset.

Hans had made a sound suggestion to create a Royal Division of Assassins. The king was dealing with people whom he could not leave alive, but it was dangerous to let him leave. *What should I do? Either set up a tragic accident or a duel. Who would do it? I need special people. That could be one of the children from the Tremain Squad. Why not? Is it too vile? Those young boys and girls would have otherwise died on the street. Instead, they would be paid a good salary and work for the benefit of the state. They could even get a title.*

Hans should definitely be made into a baron for his work. He deserves it. Is it inhumane to kill the people who plot against the state? There are some who must be killed—Aldonai forgive my soul—for if they stay alive, more blood will spill. Why did you do this to me, daughter?

⚜

That night Lily stayed with Alicia. She lay down on the hard bed, generously offered by Alicia and covered herself with a cape (the blanket was somewhat dirty). Nanook fell heavily at her feet, warming them. Her job was done, and she would leave the fighting to the men. *Hans must take the blow. Maybe the king will make him a baron. Hans is a good man. If Jess had his personality, we would be soul mates.*

⚜

Hans Tremain was left to his own devices. The Virmans and the royal warrant did wonders. The warrant was a golden badge, lavishly decorated with gems. There were only three of them in the kingdom, and they were all stored in the royal palace. It was impossible to fake them. Showing this ornament turned Hans' words into the words of the king as if His Majesty himself gave out the orders. Hans used it eagerly, but solely in the interest of the Crown. With the help of the Virmans and Leis' people, he started with the Royal Guard.

"You are under arrest, Captain."

The plot had to be nipped in the bud. The sooner, the better. He did everything without noise and hassle. He stunned the victim, tied him down, put a gag in his mouth and threw him into the carriage to Stonebug. He wrote letters to the commandant, ordering that the villains be thoroughly questioned. He also wrote letters to several of his...friends. The royal trustees weren't friends in the ordinary sense of the word; however, there were people who they trusted more and people who they trusted less. Hans sent notes to the ones he trusted, ordering the arrest of several criminals or setting up their murders. *Is it too ruthless? Am I taking too much on myself? It doesn't matter! It is an ulcer that must be burned with a hot iron as soon as possible before it breaks through.* The birds flew; the messengers raced. Meanwhile, Hans set his way to the Ivelens. *Every conspiracy has a head, and if we chop it off... In any case, I must capture them and put them in Stonebug. First things first.*

ೞ ☐ ೂ

Amalia and Peter sat by the open window. The twins gave their mother a hard time. Usually, the children were sent to a different wing of the castle, but Peter could not part with the babies. They suffered from colic and other sicknesses, which made them scream heartily. Because of the heat, all the windows were open wide, making their cries spread far and wide. Exhausted, Peter went to the wet nurse, then to Amalia, and stayed there.

The woman looked out of the window and gazed at the stars.

"What are you thinking of, my dear?"

Amalia seemed to not have heard him straight away and responded with delay.

"Vengeance, Peter."

"So many years have passed,"

"How many?" Her blue eyes flashed with anger. "How many? They took away my beloved husband, they deprived my children of their father and killed your friend. This crime has no age."

Peter sighed.

"It doesn't."

He loved his wife but strongly suspected that she didn't love him. She didn't love him in the same way that she loved Edmund. Back then, Amalia had been on fire. Now, he was left with ashes. *Is it painful? Perhaps.* Peter hoped that Amalia would become herself once everything was over, and would even be able to love him—perhaps not as strongly as she used to love Edmund. That wasn't important to him, because his love was enough for two.

"Everything will end soon, and I will breathe freely. Justice will be restored."

Amalia clutched her pearl necklace in her hand. It was Peter's present for giving him children.

"What is it? Torches?"

"The Royal Guard?"

Peter peered into the darkness.

"No, I wouldn't say so. There are only five people."
"Who is there? We need to come down."
"You're not dressed. I will call servants."
"Go down as well, okay?"
"Maybe we should wake father—"
"I don't see the point—only if it's important."

As it turned out, Loran Ivelen was not asleep either. He and Peter met each other downstairs and exchanged glances.

No, they hadn't expected failure. It wasn't natural for a person to admit that others might be smarter. Besides, everything was well hidden. They thought perhaps it was something else.

Hans used this to his benefit. He had a letter sealed by one of Lilian's rings with a short note inside it. The Virmans who talked to Alicia determined that there were around twenty guards at the estate. If they started the fight immediately, the Ivelens would have time to run away. Hans decided to come with around five people, informing the Ivelens about the successful murder of the Countess of Earton and Alicia's request to arrive as soon as possible. The main squad was waiting nearby. If someone gave the alarm, they would come to the rescue. It was a military stratagem.

When Hans banged on the gates, they were let in immediately. Five people couldn't pose a serious threat.
Leir Tremain greeted the duke, kissed Amalia's hand, and began explaining. He looked so convincing that they believed him. He had red eyes, a tired face, shaking hands, messy hair, and dirty clothes.

"What a terrible thing! An attempt on the life of the countess!"
"Aldonai!" gasped Amalia.
"What happened?"
"She was shot. We didn't get hold of the murderer. The arrow pierced her lung. The countess lost a lot of blood, she is not well. Tahir said that it is unlikely she will survive past the dawn. My Lady, she implored me to bring you and the count. I beseech you."

Hans dropped to his knees, and Peter hastily lifted him.
"Why does she want to see us?"
"Because of Miranda, My Lady. Lilian cannot die in peace until you come. She knows that you will look after the girl."
Hans was inspired by his own lie, under the effect of adrenaline. His words sounded so genuine. *Who else would Lilian ask? The old viperess? Alicia is the last person Lily would trust with her child.*

Amalia sighed.
She didn't want to go and couldn't refuse such a request at the same time.

"Maybe in the morning."

"My Lady! The countess is extremely unwell!" Hans dropped to his knees again. Big tears came down his cheeks. *How else?* He banged his knees against the marble floor very hard, and it hurt. In all fairness, Hans was firmly convinced that no one would follow him anywhere, but that was just what he needed. His aim was to make the Ivelens believe in his lie and make them host him and his people for the night. So it happened.

Hans suffered. He implored the Ivelens to go with them and was promised that they would leave first thing in the morning. Once everyone went to sleep, the Virmans dispersed over the territory. It wasn't difficult for the five professional soldiers to open the large gate and let the firing squad in.

ಯ ೞ

Leif looked around. Hans' people were put in the stable. Well, at least not in the pigsty. All the warriors sighed and wiped their manly tears, telling of the countess' suffering. She was supposedly dying and had asked them to bring her relatives to say farewell. The men looked genuinely frustrated, although they didn't have much of an audience—only the stable boys. Leif waited until all the lights went out in the big house and then signaled to his people.

"It's time."

The stablemen plunged into a deep sleep, having each received a blow of the fist to the skull. The fist of a Virman was as large as a pumpkin. Even the horses didn't stir. There weren't any fatalities, blood, or screams—nothing. The only difference was in the number of people awake, which reduced from nine to five. Nothing critical, the stablemen would come to their senses.

It wasn't difficult for the three wolf-shadows to silently slip into the yard, look around and quietly get rid of the sentries. Contrary to popular belief, the Virmans weren't a wild screaming crowd with axes who smashed anything that moved. Not quite. Leif's team was exceptional at spying, sneaking up, and slipping through. Such skills were useful both on Virma and on the continent. Erik would have done a better job, but he was away at sea.

The four sentries were shot in the twinkle of an eye. Two of them were killed without a drop of blood, the other two, who stood further away, were stabbed with throwing knives. A couple of quiet rales and all was silent again. Two men slipped into the barracks where the Ivelen soldiers slept peacefully. The Virmans contemplated whether to kill them or wake them up and allow them to putt up a fight. Their aim was to keep everything quiet and peaceful.

When Lily had realized what she was dealing with it made her curse the day she was born. The countess was contemplating.

Datura, maldonaya seed, something else...

The Virmans held the secret recipe precious. It was stored on Virma. It was something like sleeping gas, although it couldn't put a healthy person to sleep, it would make a sleeping man fall into the deepest of sleeps. Even a cannon wouldn't wake him. The side effects were horrid—drowsiness, vomiting, and nightmares.

Why make noise if the Virmans could just put a couple of burning clay censers inside and let the guards take in the smell? What a lasting impression!

Moreover, the barracks at the estate were built traditionally, out of wood. The roof was low and heavy, with only a few windows on top. They only had to wait a little while, and the whole room full of guards was defeated.

Three Virmans slipped out to the side gate. Opening the central gate with a military alarm wasn't necessary; the squad fit perfectly through the little side door. The Virmans' manly pride didn't suffer from a little walking.

Twenty people were enough to capture the Ivelens. This was a small capital residence where the family stayed before their visits to the king. It would have been much harder to capture the familial castle. Nobody thought it necessary to overprotect the small estate in the suburbs. According to Loran's logic, if the king found out about the plot, nothing in the world would save them from his wrath and vice versa; the Ivelens trusted the king to protect them from an enemy. They didn't consider riots and rebellions, for they were too rare and unpredictable, like avalanches in the summer.

With this in mind, the Ivelens had built a big house with two wings and a balcony. The cries of children directed them to Peter and Amalia. As a rule, the younger children had to be in the opposite wing. The shadows slipped into the patio and dispersed themselves according to the plan. Hans Tremain was already waiting for them on the porch.

Two people went to Loran Ivelen, the other two went for Peter, one to Amalia and another two went for the children. Hans wasn't going to leave anyone out. He would capture everybody and take them to Stonebug.

If their suspicions about the plot proved correct, they had to handle the operation with great care. All youngsters, including the infant twins, had to be captured. They should be able to find them a wet nurse there. No one would die of hunger. As for Hans himself, he would exchange a couple of words with Loran, something like a cross-examination. Everything went smoothly. The Ivelens were taken aback. Wearing only nightgowns, they weren't able to put up a serious fight. Peter was hit on the head with a heavy fist as a safety measure. Even the sick girl had her hands tied.

Cruel but necessary. There had already been cases where such tender creatures had stabbed a soldier in his throat, and Hans forever remembered that lesson.

Each in their room, the servants remained as quiet as mice. One of the Virmans had prudently blocked the doors to their room with two massive tables, one on top of another. Only one butler tried to escape and got hit on the head. He resolved to quietly rest in the corner and refrain from violent language.

Hans took out a dagger and approached Loran Ivelen.

"Where are the papers?"

"Do you have any idea of what you're doing?" whispered the aristocrat. "I will—"

His later words weren't of much interest. Hans had regularly received hundreds of similar threats. Printing them on parchment would have made the biggest library in the kingdom. A nod to Leif, a gag, and the flash of a dagger—the ear of one of the noblest of aristocrats and most famous of dukes separated from his skull. There was a lot of blood and Loran crouched in pain. Hans waited until Loran regained his senses and waved his ear before his eyes.

"I won't stop at this. I will go down. I will cut your fingers and toes. I will cut your wiener in three goes. Do you not understand? Lay your cards on the table." Hans borrowed this expression from Lilian. "We know everything. If you are stubborn, I will order your grandchildren killed. I will cut them before your eyes—slow and sure."

Ivelen tried to put on a proud expression but miserably failed. Hans reached for the crib.

"I am talking about your real grandchildren—not the bastards. Do you think that we don't realize whose children they are?"

Those words touched him for real. Amalia went so white that it seemed that her black hair separated from her skull and floated above it. Peter was still slow to follow the events; they had hit him hard. Loran looked worse than a dead man.

"I will take the gag out. Don't you dare make a sound! Remember that this is about the safety of the Crown. The law is on my side." He thrust the golden badge into Ivelen's face.

"I could hang you if I wanted to and set your estate ablaze with Maldonaya's fire."

Loran barely managed to lick his lips. One could tell by his eyes that the duke was contemplating something. Hans outdid him and spoke first.

"Leave your vulgarity. Don't offer me money. The only thing we can bargain for is your quick death instead of a slow and painful one. Or do you think I won't dare to burn your infants with a hot iron before your eyes until they meet their death?"

Hans was frightening. He stepped over the superiority of the rank and rose higher than the duke. Ivelen broke down after they cut off his second ear and three fingers. As a result, Hans got hold of all letters, receipts, contracts and, most importantly, the marriage certificate of Amalia Earton and Edmund of Ativerna, who had gotten married seventeen years earlier. Everything was proper—the pastor, the stamps—and another paper with a handwritten testimony from the same pastor, describing the marriage ceremony and naming of children. Both Edmund and Peter had given their consent.

Hans sighed.

The mad countess was right all along. How did she find this out? Only Aldonai knows, although the child is a copy of Imogene. Lilian is smart, but only when it comes to business. Alas! There are certain things she doesn't understand. She stayed with the king in the castle and ensured me that everything was under her control. On the other hand, what if she really did have everything under control? No, it cannot be...

Worried so, Hans could not wait until morning and took the whole party to Stonebug that night. The Ivelens were simply loaded onto horses like bags of grain, except Amalia and her children, whom the Virmans watched closely. It was impossible to escape. They reached Stonebug by dawn.

୨୦ ␣ ଓ

Edward winced and rubbed his chest. It hurt. The pain was severe, sharp and recurring. It surged and retreated, and it wouldn't let the king sleep. *How did I overlook it? How did I not notice? How? My daughter! Although she thinks I am her uncle, we are a family! How could she hurt her relatives? What did she lack? Money? Power? Or was it maybe to avenge Edmund?*

The pain only intensified at the thought of his son. He was his firstborn, his own child. The king could barely think of incest. Edward blamed himself. *Who else do I have to blame for my carelessness? Jessie? Being a queen was hard labor. She was only allowed to see her children once a quarter. Jyce? Although he had done everything he could, he remained a bad keeper of maiden secrets and didn't have any authority in the eyes of Edmund. It seems that Jess doesn't have any secret marriages, but one can never be sure,* thought the king. *I will need to check.*

The thought of Lilian Earton made the king frown. *Does she know about the plot? It's unlikely. Hans isn't a fool and won't tell a lot to a woman—even a woman like Lilian. Although she is clever and serious... No, he wouldn't.*

The king had no idea that it was Lilian who had solved the conspiracy.

What do I do with Hans? There are a lot of traitors and very few loyal people. The king wasn't going to get rid of Hans. *Why would I? Hans is a clever lad fit for his job. He will bring a lot of good to the kingdom, if not now, then during Richard's reign. His ideas go in line with my thinking. No, it would be a mistake to kill a person like him.* The aching in his chest got worse.

There was a slight creaking of the door.

The old valet quietly walked around the bedroom. He put out the candlelight and saw that the king was not asleep.

"Your Majesty? Do you want anything?"

Edward paused.

"Walk quietly to Alicia Earton and invite her in if she is not asleep. Do it quietly. You shouldn't be seen or heard."

"I'll do it now, Your Majesty."

The faithful servant disappeared behind the door. The king rubbed his chest. It was better to talk than to lie and think—a sure way to lose his mind.

ಖ ☐ ೞ

When someone tapped on the door, His Majesty was already in his dressing gown sitting in a chair.

"Come in."

Alicia Earton looked empathetically at the king.

"Your Majesty?"

"Do come in. Sit down."

Tair, bring us something—maybe wine?

"Would you like me to call Lilian Earton as well?"

"Is she at yours, Countess?"

"Yes. She came this evening with Leir Tremain."

The valet left.

"Is it because of the plot?"

"That's right, Your Majesty. Hans took all the guards with him and didn't think it safe to leave the countess at the estate alone."

Edward thought and concluded that Alicia was one of the very few people who saw him as a human being, not as a king. As for Lilian Earton, it seemed that she saw him as a human being only and often forgot that he was a ruler who could execute her at any moment.

"And Miranda?"

"She is at August Broklend's."

"Perfect. And the countess—"

"She is sleeping. She said that she wants to use the opportunity to get a good night's sleep while she can."

"What about at home?"

"At home, there's her child, her work—it sounds strange."

"Why strange?" It wasn't that Edward was particularly interested, but he wanted to distract himself.

"She talks about the child and about her work with an equal amount of pride. Your Majesty, what will happen to Amalia now?"

Edward sighed.

"Interrogation first."

"What next? Execution?"

"If our guesses are correct, her future will depend on her loyalty. You know what I mean, Countess."

"I understand—either execution or the nunnery."

"To the nunnery only under constant watch."

"What about the children? Sessie? Jess? They haven't done anything!"

"That's right. Therefore, I am sending her to the nunnery and nothing else! Incest and plotting against the state!"

"Will you make it public?"

"No!" Bellowed Edward. A sharp pain pinched his heart. "No promulgation or other nonsense. Edmund didn't have any wife or children. If anyone decides otherwise, I'll introduce them to the hangman!"

Alicia nodded.

"Does Lilian know about my children?"

"She knows about the plot, but she doesn't know about your children."

Alicia wasn't a hundred percent sure, but she did not intend to betray the woman either. *What does it matter if she knows or not? She is clever enough to keep silent. If not, she would be the first one to suffer. There is no need for him to know.*

"Are you sure?"

Alicia didn't flinch when she met the king's gaze—nothing of the sort.

"Only Aldonai could be truly sure. I am only a weak woman."

Edward smiled. Alicia thought that Lilian was perhaps the only one who tried to give her at least some warmth. Jessamine was constantly jealous of the children—Amalia and Jess—and preferred to take care of them herself. Alicia didn't see her grandchildren often. Lily, on the other hand, accepted her unselfishly, and so did Miranda. For the first time in her life, Alicia felt part of the family. There was always August Broklend.

No! I will fight for my happiness. Even with the king!

The conversation seemed calm on the surface, but in reality, both of them sat on pins and needles. They weren't surprised to hear the quiet knock on the bedroom door. It was the valet.

"Your Majesty, the secretary wants to see you…"

"Let him in."

The secretary was pale. He himself was not involved in the conspiracy but rather was in line to be killed—for being one of the king's closest servants. Being aware of this, the man was somehow agitated and dreamed for the plot to fail.

"Your Majesty, Hans Tremain sent a pigeon. They are in Stonebug. Everything is well."

Edward sighed.

There was no way to let the prisoners be released from Stonebug, but his Majesty wanted to question the villains personally.

"Order a coach. I will go there with a minimal escort."

The secretary bowed and disappeared behind the door. Alicia looked at the king and decided not to ask stupid questions like "why?" She was clever and took her leave.

Edward sighed, looked around the room and called the valet.

"Get dressed, immediately!"

Stonebug—a gray stone spire-tower. The people said that it was built by one of the first kings and it had served a distinctive purpose. He had wanted to imprison his wife, who had cheated on him. Since the man did not waste his time on trifles, he built a massive tower before realizing that his wife didn't deserve such honor. Therefore, he resolved to put the tower to use and expand the field of activity.

Its first residents were, of course, noble-blooded. He couldn't put dukes in the same catacomb with thieves, beggars, prostitutes, and murderers for they would be cut to pieces. Therefore, he made sure that Stonebug had individual cells, an excellent cook, affectionate commandant, and the best executioners, who were all deaf and dumb—skilled above hearing.

The elder Ivelens were handed straight to those guys. Amalia was treated with some care for she was a noble lady. As for the rest, Hans ordered them to be treated harshly. The executioners of Stonebug knew working methods for exposing the truth.

Hans sent a pigeon to Edward and began looking through the papers. He needed to know who he would execute and pardon. The commandant of Stonebug happily let the royal representative use his private study. He owed him for clearing his name from the murder case of a rich relative. Hans asked for wine and water, or an herbal brew and started working. The pieces of parchment piled up in separate sections. Contracts, obligations, promissory notes, letters, and the structure of the plot crystallized into something concrete.

Avesterra is heavily involved! Bastards! Why can't they be happy with what they have? They always wish to ruin their neighbors! Richard made the right decision when he didn't marry their ratty daughter.

Hans was so busy with the papers that he noticed the king only after he had entered the study and quickly jumped to his feet.

"Your Majesty."

Edward nodded graciously. The pain in his chest was stronger, but there was no time to pay attention. He would later call the medicus or that Khangan. *Why not?*

"What have you got there? Tell me."

Hans sighed.

"We have letters with names and the moves of the plotters. In general, we were correct in our guesses, Your Majesty."

"Avesterra?"

"Sadly, yes."

"What about Amalia?"

Hans sighed again with a sad countenance. He took out a heap of papers from his bosom, which he had hidden from public sight.

"Have a look, Your Majesty."

Edward extended his hand and Hans noticed his trembling fingers. The story got worse and worse; one wouldn't wish it on his worst enemy. Incest, murder, conspiracy, parricide—there was little joy in what was happening.

Edward quickly looked through the papers.

"Is this pastor still alive?"

"He is." Hans knew it for sure. Pastor Vopler had lately been popular. As a result, a lot of churchmen flocked to him, including the one in question. It was hard to forget such a big turd.

"Get him to Stonebug."

"I've already sent for him, Your Majesty."

Edward looked up.

"Did you know what was written here?"

"I suspected," Hans admitted honestly.

"Are they here?"

"Yes, Your Majesty. What is your order?"

"Interrogate and execute, what else?"

"Do you mean—"

"I mean both of the Ivelens. As for Amalia… I need to talk to her."

"What about the children?"

"Depending on what they know… If they know nothing of their royal descent, let them live in the monastery under watch."

"What about the twins?"

"Someone has to inherit the barony, but I will think on it."

Hans nodded. Edward mechanically rubbed his chest.

"Take me to Amalia."

The woman sat on a rough straw mat. The interrogation chamber was quite tidy. Her dress was torn, and she had a couple of bruises. However, there were no traces of rape or serious torture. Edward opened the door and entered. Hans followed him without asking for permission. He dismissed the executioners and the scribe and didn't flinch when His Majesty flashed his eyes.

"Your Majesty, I will leave if they chain her. Otherwise, I know everything."

80

Edward waved his hand. *Damned, be the pain! This face... She is almost a copy of Jessie, only my features in place of her softness. My daughter!*

"Why! What for! What have I done to you?"

Amalia sat up. Her eyes flashed brightly. She wasn't going to attack the king but held herself with pride.

"For Edmund. You killed him!"

"Not me."

"My father never did anything without the royal order. I know!"

"I didn't give him such an order. I swear."

The woman took a step back and cast down her eyes. She believed him.

"I loved him. We were married. You would have never let us—"

"You never even asked. Why?"

Amalia sighed. *Why didn't we?* The haze of memories marred her sight.

She remembered being a little girl and being invited to stay in the palace.

A harsh comment from Queen Imogene had left Amalia crying in the corridor.

"What are you crying about?"

She remembered how a serious boy with gray eyes approached her for the first time. That boy was Edmund.

"It's none of your business!" retorted little Amalia.

"Don't cry. Do you want a lolly?"

Amalia timidly nodded, and a large striped candy fell into her hand. Her blue eyes met his gray ones for the first time.

"Thank you."

Another memory. She was twelve and Jessamine was the queen. Amalia was often invited to the palace. She walked along the corridors and looked through the halls and paintings.

"What are you doing here?"

"Ambling around."

"You aren't allowed."

"Why not?"

"Because you are an Earton!"

"So what? At least I am beautiful!"

"Who told you that nonsense?"

"Father and mother." Alicia never told her that, but that was an innocent lie. "Am I not beautiful?"

"Are you an Earton?"

"I am Amalia Earton. So what?"

"I hate you all!" screamed the boy, leaving Amalia with a feeling that she had lost something important.

She was fifteen. She was one of the girls who helped the queen with little tasks. Her mother, Alicia, was close to the queen and they attended court often. She passed Edmund in the corridor but pretended not to see him. She noticed how the boy with brown eyes who followed the prince looked at her admiringly but said nothing. Suddenly Amalia slipped and fell. It wasn't deliberate, not done for attention. She slipped on some apple core and, falling, let out a short scream. Edmund returned.

"What happened?"

Amalia had fallen very badly on her back, and it had winded her. Edmund was the one to help her. He gave her wine and rubbed her chest to make her recover her breathing. She gradually came to her senses, and the past enmity disappeared. Edmund carefully concealed his feelings but spent time with Amalia without resentment. Very slowly, step-by-step, they were enclosed in the embrace of first youthful love.

Peter Ivelen, Edmund's best friend, was always by their side. He was forever the third, a loyal friend and comrade, a good reliable lad, who also looked into Amalia's blue eyes with admiration.

Another memory: the screams coming out of the king's study.

Amalia remembered hearing the exchange between the son and father.

"Your whore—!"

"Get out of my sight!"

Edmund left the king's study and headed in a random direction. Without thinking, Amalia rushed after him. The young man was sitting on a garden bench that was sheltered by thick bushes of ivy. His eyes were downcast, and his arms were hanging loose. Amalia noticed the subtle trembling of his shoulders. She slowly approached the young man and kneeled next to him.

"Edmund?"

"Go away! You are the same as your aunt! Whore! Prostitute!"

Two glistening trails of tears crossed his cheeks. Impulsively, Amalia leaned forward and embraced the boy.

"Don't cry! I love you."

Edmund's eyes flashed, but he had no time to respond. The next moment Amalia was kissing him ineptly and timidly, and Edmund had nothing else to do but to answer the kiss. That was a turning point and the start of a new life. The lovers hid their feelings from everyone but Peter, who was inseparable from Edmund. Amalia's father took notice of the young man and thought Peter Ivelen a perfect match for his daughter.

Amalia remained indifferent to everything around her, for she had Edmund—his shining gray eyes, the dull gold of his hair and a tender smile.

"I thought I would always hate the Eartons."

"I could always cease to be an Earton."

"I would marry you, but right now I can't go against the will of my father. Will you wait?"

"I will wait."

"No, we shouldn't wait. I won't risk losing you! I won't let it happen."

"Me either. It is better to die at once."

The next day, they went to an abandoned church, and the pastor joined their hands in marriage. The pastor was young and ambitious. He realized that Edmund would become the next king and didn't want to miss an opportunity to side with him. Aldons always relied on kings.

The couple was happy for a while, until Edmund forgot his place and publicly called Jessamine a bitch. His hatred was boundless, and it spilled out from all the cracks. It couldn't be tamed.

That time, Edward didn't forgive his son and got seriously angry. He banished him for a year and sent him to the border. His anger would soften later, but for now, her beloved husband was leaving. They could not announce their marriage yet. Marriage against a father's will was a serious offense. Both of them could be sent to Stonebug or Royhe—banished, executed, poisoned, and so on. After a couple of weeks of silence, she fainted.

She was found by an old wet nurse and brought to life, only to immediately throw up.

"You are expecting," said the old woman in a calm voice. Amalia rose and realized that the woman was right.

"I will have a child by my beloved!"

"You are an unmarried girl."

"I am married!"

"Well, well."

By Aldonai's mercy, Peter Ivelen happened to be in the capital. Amalia rushed to him with the news and Peter replied, "It's bad. We need to get married."

Amalia nearly fainted.

"I am already married, Peter."

"Your marriage was a secret, Amalia. What would happen to you and Edmund if the secret came to light?"

"I don't know."

"We will simply announce our marriage. I fell in love and you couldn't refuse. We ran away and got married."

"What about your father?"

"I have a man who can fake any document; he can fake our marriage certificate."

"No, I will try to speak to the king. If it fails—"

"I am here for you, Amalia. I understand that you love Edmund. I also love him; he is my best friend. He is like a brother to me. I don't hope for anything. I only want to be by your side."

Amalia lowered her chin.

"I will try to speak to the king."

"I will be there for you. You can rely on me."

ಐ ☐ ಛ

Amalia did try to speak to the king, but her habit of eavesdropping and spying didn't play to her advantage. That evening, Edward got drunk with Jyce and said that he hated Edmund's guts. Although Edmund was an heir to the throne, Edward impulsively suggested it would be cheaper to hire killers and make three new heirs to replace Edmund.

After a good night's sleep, those thoughts vanished without a trace. The next morning, the king didn't even remember what he had said the previous night. His comments were a trivial complaint to a friend about his children and meant nothing. Even a goat would realize it. However, a goat is a clever, intellectual animal, not a snotty girl suffering from toxicosis— hormonal and brainless—with one hell of a problem.

The result was more than predictable. Amalia went to Peter in utter shock. She agreed to the secret marriage and moved to his estate the next day.

Loran Ivelen, who at that point wasn't aware of anything, sent the naughty children to the estate, away from the scandal—just what they needed most.

They wrote to Edmund once they got to the estate. The prince arrived, heard Amalia's story and nodded in approval. He thanked Peter for saving his wife but said that in that case, he couldn't immediately pronounce his marriage to Amalia. Meanwhile, he would take care of the formalities, and Amalia would remain under the guise of the Marchioness of Ivelen until Edmund found a solution. Peter had nothing left to do but agree. The situation lasted for several years. Edmund writhed like a slug in salt in his attempts to shake off numerous marriage arrangements. The issue became so acute that Edmund resolved to act.

Jessie had died, so the father-son relationship was newly unstrained. Besides, it was easier for the son to understand his father once he was in the same situation.

Edmund decided to speak to Jyce Earton first. He thought that if Jyce took the news well, he would speak to his father.

Instead, Jyce was truly in shock. His brain went numb with rage. As a result, two corpses sat in the tower. Amalia simply lost all ability to feel. She died together with Edmund, and her only wish was revenge.

There was another thing on her mind. *Jess, my boy. He deserves his father's throne. He must become the king.*

With this thought in mind, Amalia sheltered the boy from all hardship. He was growing up in a golden basket, and he realized it himself. As a rule, such an upbringing spoiled children. This happened to Jess.

ಊ ⎵ ಐ

Edward listened to Amalia's revelations with a stone-like face—and thought himself a blind fool.

"When did Loran Ivelen find out about everything?"

"After the birth of the third child. She is a copy of Imogene."

Edward had a burning in his chest. He thought that Hans was right.

"I see. Do the children know?" He read it in the glimmering blue of her eyes.

Yes. They know everything about their birthright and origin. The ground was swimming under Edward's feet, but he made an inhuman effort, turned around and left.

He had nothing else to discuss.

She was his daughter and a madwoman at the same time. He saw it in her every movement, every gesture, and every glance.

She was no longer a human, but a dangerous, poisonous snake. He saw only one way out.

Hans met the king with a worried look.

"Your Majesty?"

"Hans, you have the arrest warrants. The Ivelens must be executed painlessly."

"Everyone?"

"You can leave the twins alive. They're still too young."

"What about—"

"I said—everyone. Loran, Peter, Amalia, and the three elder children. Is that clear?" The roaring set his chest on fire.

"Your will is law, Your Majesty."

"And let nothing leave the walls of Stonebug, do you understand?"

Hans silently nodded. He saw the burning fireplace. From the folds of his shirt, he took out the marriage certificate between Amalia Earton and Edmund of Ativerna. The flame burned brighter. Edward nodded in approval.

"Stifle the conspiracy. You can do it; you have the authority. Come to me in the evening with a detailed report. Try not to make noise in the capital."

Hans nodded.

"Yes, Your Majesty."

Edward nodded once more and went to the exit. He would still need to get to the carriage and home. Some animal instinct led him on. Like a sick and wounded animal, the king tried to hide in his hole.

ଓ ⌐ ଔ

Lily was held in the palace by the bored princesses. Lily was telling the little girls about the ways of the water drop in nature. Alicia looked at this idyll and went to the king's chamber. If the king had left in his carriage, he would order his men to leave him by the Rose Passage, the shortest way to the palace.
It was not hard for the old palace dweller to meet with the king. She waited for him by the passage and gasped upon seeing him in person. Edward looked worse than a dead man. He made a sign to Alicia, asking her to follow him to the chamber, paying no attention to the courteous bows of the servants along the way.

He collapsed on his bed as soon as he reached his room.

"I am not well. Call the medicus, Alicia."

Alicia nodded in a frenzy and rushed on. Since she thought the court doctor a fool and a charlatan, she went to find Lilian Earton.

"Lily, my darling."

"What happened?" stirred Angelina.

Alicia dropped in a curtsey.

"The king urgently asked to see the Countess of Earton."

Lily nodded, took her leave from the princesses and left the room. As soon as they were alone, Alicia grabbed Lilian's hand and whispered wildly.

"Call Tahir! The king is sick."

"What's wrong?"

"I don't know. He said he wasn't feeling well."

Lily grabbed her bag—a fashion item in which she carried important things. A purse, a handkerchief, a little something, but the most important item was a small first-aid kit without which she never left the house. The kit contained several sachets with powder.

"I will send a note to Tahir as soon as possible and meanwhile attend to the king."

"Are you out of your mind?"

"Don't argue with me. Can you lead me to him? Show me the way!"

Lily's tone was so commanding that Alicia obeyed. *What if she could really help the king?* The valet, wringing his hands by the royal chamber, did not say a word against it. The king gave an order to let the Countess of Earton pass—no one else but her. The rest should be told that he was busy with state affairs, no more, no less. They would have never let Lilian in if it weren't for her splendid reputation at court, her friendship with the Khangan doctor, and her miraculous knowledge. Everyone had long been aware of the fact that the court doctors were not only poorly qualified but also angry at the king for his orders concerning the guilds. Lilian Earton was a safer bet. She had a good reputation.

ಬ ಛ

In ten minutes, Lily was kneeling by Edward's bedside. His Majesty opened his eyes.

"You?"

"Save your voice, Your Majesty. Any unnecessary effort might harm you right now. Let me feel your pulse."

Most of all, Lily was afraid of it being a heart attack or a stroke. The king wasn't a young boy, after all. If his heart suddenly failed, his family would be left with nothing but a doughnut hole. *What would happen to the country?* She had a word for it, but she was busy counting the pulse. The pulse was encouraging—a hundred and ten, too little for a heart attack. Any student could register such a pulse before entering an exam. It was neurological. Now she had to figure out what was hurting and not let the patient pass out in the process. *Get to work*, Lily said to herself. She unfastened his jacket hooks, untied all the strings and carefully undressed the patient. *You can do it!*

At first, Edward tried to resist but then gave up. *Does one care about formalities when one is ill?* Edward suffered from physical and moral pain, and he unbuttoned himself a little. Above all, Lily behaved like a doctor with a sick patient before her. *A king or a peasant, a Virman or a Khangan—all of you are equal when sat on the potty or splayed across the operation table!*

Edward entrusted the countess with his life. She acted with confidence, like a true professional.

She remembered that the patient was always more scared than her. Lily confidently carried out palpation, percussion, and repeatedly sighed with relief. She kept asking questions.

"Don't speak. Blink once for a yes. Otherwise, keep your eyes open. It will hurt to speak."

Lily was right.

"It hurts here and here. The pain changes when you inhale or move or put pressure. The pain isn't static."

Edward was blinking and feeling more at peace.

I hope it's not death? I cannot afford to die now!

Lily also regained her self-assuredness. She would create a tonometer when she had time, a primitive one. A Riva-Rocci, for example, she could do that. She knew the history of medicine well and took an interest in it.

The king's symptoms reminded her of intercostal neuralgia, a disease that was curable. It wasn't the best thing to have, but it didn't pose any direct threat. It was easy to confuse with a heart attack. To endure so much pain wasn't a pleasant experience.

The more she questioned the king, the more she was sure about her diagnosis.

On top of everything, does he have a cold? Most probably. His back is always painful, there are drafts in the palace and no hot baths to warm up the bones. It is as clear as day. As for the treatment, I've got everything necessary—my healing ointments and anesthetics.

So the king was examined, given medicine diluted in mulled wine and wrapped up in rags. Lily became his nurse and remained by his bedside. She would never trust this patient to anyone.

Having heard about the prospect of swift recovery, Edward sighed in relief only to taste a bitter medicine. He had to remain in bed for the first few days. Like it or not, humans hadn't yet learned to perform Aldonaian miracles.

The king did not object. He called for his secretary and ordered him to cancel all receptions in the following five days and all important documents to be delivered to his bedroom. The old servant immediately passed the order to the valet. He looked at Lily with a certain reverence, for he realized that she wasn't just another woman with a title but a certified doctor who knew her trade.

The king resolved to receive court visitors in his bedroom in small groups.

Let them see that the illness is a slight whim of the king and that his wrath is still terrible! Lily expressed no objection but demanded that the king take an anesthetic and preferably remain under her watchful eye. The king was happy with this arrangement. Alicia watched Lily with recurring feelings of doubt and terror. *A housewife wouldn't know how to be so professional and practical, even if she learned from the famous medicus! It doesn't add up*, thought the viperess. *There is something incomprehensible about Lilian, something strange and rational. At least there is no enmity in her behavior, thank Aldonai.*

Alicia's hopes exceeded her fears. *If Edward died now, it would have been a disaster with Richard still on his way and in the face of the conspiracy disclosed. No, the king has to be on the throne. His death would cause chaos and rebellion. I pray for Aldonai's mercy.*

Lily had similar thoughts. She asked Alicia for a scroll from the palace library and sat at the king's bedside, reading.

Tahir arrived shortly and brought her joy. Lily received a couple of ointments and anesthetics and nodded.

"This will do."

"Your Majesty." The valet tapped on the door.

Edward nodded.

"Your Majesty, the medicus has arrived."

Edward looked at Lily.

"If you want, you can listen to what they have to say." Lily smiled. "Only do not agree to bloodletting and enemas, for in your condition it will do you more harm than good. Besides, has it ever been effective?"

Edward shrugged and nodded to the valet, asking him to let the medicus in. When he entered, he looked more like a parrot than a doctor. It was a unique sight. He wore a green tunic embroidered with a great number of gems, his trousers were light blue with ribbons, and he had a huge pink bow around his neck. The most amusing addition to the costume was a yellow bow nestled on his flour-powdered hair.

"Your Majesty, as soon as I found out about your illness, I hurried to drop at your feet! I promise you, you will be bouncing around in no time!"

Lily conveniently hid behind the bed. *Dusty!* She smirked. *At least ask what the patient's complaint is, smart Alec!*

Smart Alec grabbed the king's hand and began studying his nails. He turned the hand over and studied the palm in the same concentrated manner. He asked the king to show him his tongue, to spit in his palm. The king stoically endured while Lily kept silent.

After studying the spit, the man compassionately said,

"The color of saliva is uneven; it has got a blueish tint. This marks a dysfunction of the cerebrum gland. I suppose we couldn't avoid bloodletting."

Uneven blueish saliva! Idiot! I gave the king a drink from wild blueberries to ensure that his digestive functions are all right, given he is suffering from a lot of pain already. Let him at least go to the toilet effortlessly. It would be good to put him on a proper diet. His royal habits are harmful to his health. Improper nutrition is a cause of all diseases! Constipation, diarrhea, digestion problems...the rest follows.

"I don't need any bloodletting." Edward was confident.

"Your Majesty! What about the gland! It is evidently inflamed! In that case, let me give you an enema, it does wonders!"

The saddest part is that it does help some in cases where one is pissed or can't shit, pardon my language. To add nausea and vomiting to neuralgia is to create the worst suffering.

"Shove it up your—"

Lily nearly whistled. The king's popular lexicon turned out to be quite rich.

"Shoo! Get out of my chamber—and out of court. You are fired!"

"Your Majesty, but you have an inflammation!"

Lily stepped out of hiding like a ghost. She couldn't stand his nonsense and was sorry for the king. He was struggling to keep his countenance, and it wasn't worth arguing with that fool of a doctor.

"It is a sin to go against the will of the king, you cur!"

The medicus jerked with surprise and yelled something about dumb women and their witchcraft.

Lily wasn't going to get her hands dirty. She called for the valet, who made an immediate appearance.

"His Majesty ordered this idiot out of his chamber," informed the countess in a poisonous voice.

The servant glanced at the king, caught his approving glance, and rang the bell furiously.

A pair of guards appeared out of nowhere. They grabbed the medicus by his shoulders and pushed him out.

Lily sat closer to the king.

"Everything will be fine, Your Majesty. I promise you that you will recover, only don't agree to bloodletting."

Edward lowered his eyelids once again.

"Now you should sleep. I promise to wake you up in the evening, three hours before the setting of the sun." Edward nodded.

Strong hands grabbed his shoulders and put him in the least painful position. They raised him above the bed and adjusted the pillow to make it more comfortable.

Edward closed his eyes.

"Are you still here?"

"I promise to remain by your bedside until you wake up." Lily looked at the chair. *Comfy. It will do.* "Time to sleep, Your Majesty. Sleep tight."

Hmm! She overestimates the need, but some rest will help me get well.

Edward closed his eyelids and fell into a heavy, dreamless sleep.

"Let His Majesty get enough sleep," Lily turned to Alicia. And she flinched. *She looks so—*

"Who are you?

Lily understood everything but did not intend to surrender.

"Lilian Earton. Brocklend in girlhood."

"I don't believe you. You're different, you're kind of odd—"

"We'll talk about this later. I'm the same Lily. I can describe what you told me when I married Jerisson, I can remember your every dress, and my father would have never accepted an impostor!"

"But you—"

"I am Lilian. People change. Who wouldn't? I was almost sent to the Aldonaian kingdom."

Alicia shook her head but did not object. *She won't escape my questions but not in front of people. She will tell me in person.*

Edward woke a couple of times, and Lily gave him herbal tea with honey that plunged him back into his heavy sleep. Hans arrived in the evening with a report. Lily, who would sleep right in the royal chamber, went to meet him herself.

"It's good to see you, Hans."

Hans kissed her hand.

"How is His Majesty doing, My Lady?"

"With the mercy of Aldonai, he will be better very soon."

Lily didn't understand why she was allowed to see the king so easily. The answer was quite simple: no one dared to contradict the king, especially in times of chaos, when the guards looked particularly unfriendly. Kings in sickness are no worse at beheading than healthy ones. The valet let a couple of people peep into the slit. The king was asleep, the countess sat reading a book, sometimes adjusting his blanket or pillow. Rumor had it around the palace that the king had a cold but would recover quickly, so the courtiers refrained from disturbing him.

Only Baroness Ormt, who tried to break into the royal chamber, was sent off by the valet. He paid no attention to her yelling, as she threatened to "behead" and "imprison" the valet for being such an "impudent creature." The king had a whole bunch of flamboyant characters like her. She was regarded as a stupid hen, and nobody cared about her. The baroness strolled before the guards, and her theatrical extravagancy disappeared. The princesses could have helped her, but they weren't going to. Richard wasn't there. As for the rest, they told her to not bother the king, or else she would go to Stonebug.

The Aldon was not at court, although his appearance was a matter of time. As for the courtiers, nobody wanted to risk it. Hans waited for the valet's permission and followed him to the royal chamber. Edward was still lying in his bed, but with his eyes open. Lily took charge of him. She helped him to sit up and fixed the pillow.

"Is that better?"

"Yes. Where have you learned this from, Countess?"

"I promise to tell you everything, Your Majesty. In the meantime, you have Leir Tremain waiting to bring you some news."

"Are you making use of my illness?"

"I wouldn't dare, Your Majesty!" Lily looked at the king with a cunning smile. "Once you're seriously angry with me, only then will I conclude of your full recovery!"

Edward replied with a weak smile.

"You speak like a real medicus, Countess."

Lily silently dropped into a curtsey.

"Leave us alone, Countess."

"If you happen to feel worse, let me know immediately, Your Majesty." Lily looked stern and uncompromising. "Promise me."

"Have you forgotten that I am your king?"

"Right now you are my patient."

"You forget your place, My Lady."

"The liveliness in your voice tells me you are feeling better. I obey you."

Lily took her leave and disappeared. Edward looked at Hans.

"Report back, Leir."

"Your Majesty, I questioned all three. It *was* a conspiracy, after all."

"Avesterra?"

Hans spoke so silently that not even a fly could hear. It was only for the ears of the king. He confirmed the king's every suspicion. After the death of Imogene of Avesterra, Leonard had put a bet on Edmund and made him a certain offer. It got Edmund interested. He was the crown prince. He didn't hate his father but rather thought him confused. He despised and hated the Eartons, although not all of them. He was never going to commit parricide. The options he considered were imprisonment or abdication.

Edward smiled crookedly. *How long do imprisoned kings live?* They either fall on a spear or choke on a pillow. Edmund was the first one to realize it. He didn't mind destroying Jessamine. It was he who ordered her two attempted murders and the final successful one.

"The third one?"

"It was not a disease. It was poison."

"Who did it?"

"The medicus you kicked out."

"Find him and execute him without making a fuss."

Hans didn't object. He would find him and finish him off.

"As you wish, Your Majesty."

The year after Edmund's death, Amalia existed in a kind of stupor, and the Ivelens took it to their advantage. The situation was like a pebble in the shoe of the eldest Ivelen. Loran realized perfectly well that as soon as everything came out, heads would roll, but there was nothing he could do.

Peter was so in love with Amalia that even if Aldonai himself had forbidden him, he would still have done anything to be near her. After Edmund's death, he tried to somehow entertain her, support and enliven her spirits, and his efforts were successful. Around two years ago, they secretly got married—this time, legally—which made the youngest twins his legitimate heirs.

"I will soon sign the order to divide the Ivelen lands between them, let them have it."

"Your will is law, Your Majesty."

For a year after Edmund's death, everything was relatively peaceful. Jyces' trick even did a service to the Crown. The Avesterras thought that Edmund's conspiracy had been disclosed and went into hiding; they didn't want to be pulled out by their mousy tails. Time went by, and people started to forget about the incident. Then the emissaries of Avesterra paid another visit to Loran. He was presented with the same offer, only this time it was Jess Jr. instead of Edmund.

Unlike the conscientious Edmund who hadn't wanted to step over the corpse of his father, Loran Ivelen didn't suffer from any pangs of conscience. Besides, his personal motives played a big part.

As it often happens, fear before the Crown transformed into aggression. The man was tired of being scared, so he attacked.

Or maybe the fact that Amalia was coming out of the crisis played a significant role. She was eager to avenge her first husband. There were no psychologists after all, and the only people who could explain to the woman that she was the cause of her own suffering were the pastors, whom the Ivelens forbade to come near. They feared that the foolish woman would go mad.

"I wouldn't spare her," admitted Edward.

The Ivelens suspected danger and realized that the secret was doomed to be revealed. Provided that the third girl was the spitting image of Queen Imogene, anyone who saw her face would see the truth. The Ivelens accepted Avesterra's proposal, and Loran began to prepare. Amalia was lured into the conspiracy for another reason. In her eyes, her son was entitled to his father's place on the throne.

"She still knew—"

"Yes, Your Majesty."

"Why did they make attempts on Jerisson and Lilian?"

There was a simple answer. If Amalia was Edward's daughter, then Jerisson was his eldest son. It didn't matter that he was a bastard. He loved his uncle, although he had no idea that he was really his father. Now, he was a talented commander. Loran didn't need turmoil in the kingdom. There were enough people who were loyal to the Crown, and they had their own troops, not to mention other candidates to the throne who considered themselves more entitled to wear the crown. The hardest task wasn't seizing power but retaining it.

Loran Ivelen took care of everything. He found supporters, bribed, built intrigues…

The main issue was the lack of money. Although Leonard was a king, he was terribly greedy. There are three things needed to organize a revolt: money, money, and again money. Therefore, they also decided to get rid of Lily and Miranda first and then Jerisson in order to fix the family affairs. If Jerisson died first, Lily would take Miranda to her father, and it would be difficult and time-consuming to get her out, not to mention the tumult it would cause which was so feared by the Ivelens. Conversely, if Lily and Miranda died first and Jerisson second, his business and money would go to his only beloved sister, as was stated in his will.

As soon as the Ivelens received the fake letter about Lilian and Miranda dying, the plotters made an attempt on the life of Jerisson. Indeed, the countess deceived her enemies well, and they were shocked to see her in the capital.

Edward became progressively gloomier.

Loran Ivelen worked like a hamster in summer and dragged anyone and everyone into his hole. At that point, he had the support of around thirty people. They were neither the noblest nor the poorest. As for honor, the lawful right to the throne belonged to Jess Jr. Nobody was going to mention the incest and the familial ties between Amalia and Edmund. There was never going to be such an announcement. The main question was what to do with the troubled nobility. As soon as the Ivelens were destroyed—

"Have you not finished them yet?"

"Only Loran and Peter."

"Why not everyone?"

The look in Edward's eyes frightened Hans. Before him was the king, albeit sick and angry; he was a ruler who put the interests of his kingdom before his own. The Ivelens were a threat to his state, and Edward was going to get rid of that threat. *Is it strange that he is dealing with his daughter and his grandchildren? No, it is frightening to have a kind and amicable person having to destroy his loved ones. There is no other way. Otherwise a mad rebellion, civil war, where life and death have little worth. It is easy to preach about good and evil, but what about the lesser of the evils?* The king had to buy out the lives of many thousands with his own pain. How easy it was to judge when one didn't have any responsibility. It was an odd feeling for the king to realize that his decision would be backed by the thousands of lives of his people.

His gray eyes sparked with comprehension.

"Kill them."

Yet Hans still hesitated.

"Maybe spare the children?"

"I spared the twins. As for the rest—"

"Exile to another country, monastery, imprisonment—"

"—Avesterra, escape…no. Do it."

Hans nodded.

"Yes, Your Majesty."

Hans thought about his Tremain squad. The Ivelen children were no different than his boys and girls, who were freezing and wet, who risked their lives, starved and robbed. Some were born in the sewer; others were born to a duke's family. *If the first kind died, why does the second kind have to be more fortunate? Is it a sin to kill them? Aldonai would forgive; Maldonaya wouldn't judge. It is a terrible sin.*

"Your Majesty." Hans drew back his shoulders. "I must tell you some terrible news. Having received the note from Lilian, the Ivelen family decided to pay her a visit to give their condolences and show their ill daughter to the Khangan doctor. Unfortunately, on the way there, the horses got frightened by something and charged off. The carriage fell off the cliff, and no one could be saved apart from the twins who miraculously survived."

"And whom the Countess of Earton will take with her."

"But Your Majesty—"

"Do you expect *me* to take care of them?"

Strangely enough, Edward felt better.

"Next, I propose to announce that the news made Your Majesty ill and forced you into bed. After that, I will catch the remaining plotters without making a fuss."

"Do you suspect they will make an attempt on my life?"

"It's possible, I suppose."

"Should I just lie in bed and wait for the killers?"

"Oh no, Your Majesty. You have light hair, gray eyes, and a good physique, and I have an idea. Fortunately, the royal chamber has a secret pathway out."

Edward listened to the idea and approved it. All the same, it was necessary to catch all the conspirators—the sooner, the better. Not a word would get beyond the walls of Stonebug. The Virmans and the royal representatives realized what they were risking. Still, the secret's existence was inversely proportional to the number of people who held the knowledge of it. For this reason, they had to either strike as early as possible or let the plotters strike first to catch them red-handed—a piece of cake.

Had they asked Lily's opinion, she would have told them that the plan wasn't too original. Back in her own world, a long time ago, a certain tsar by the name Ivan the Terrible had practiced this tactic. He successfully caught all the plotters and died a natural death. But the men discussed the matter alone.

                          ಣಿ ☐ ಣಿ

Edward regarded the door that closed behind Hans. He was sickened. He had a vision of Jessamine's blue eyes glaring in the darkness of the room.

"How can you be so cruel, my golden prince?"

I can be cruel, my queen, my bright sunshine. Yes, I sentenced my daughter and my grandchildren to death, but I wasn't the first one to start this feud. I am not guilty of Edmund's death, for Aldonai oversees my ways. Amalia resolved to seek revenge. Fair enough if it concerned me alone!

Alas! Any king, above all, is a king before he is a man. Dirty, bloody, and cruel decisions were the king's license.

The main thing is to make sure that my descendants and I will exist and to ensure the future of Ativerna.

                          ಣಿ ☐ ಣಿ

Lily waited for Hans by the entrance to the royal chamber, and they immediately bombarded each other with questions.

"What happened to the Ivelens?"

"Will the king live?"

"How are my people doing?"

"How soon should we expect the king to recover?"

The man and the woman exchanged glances and simultaneously snorted. Lily ruffled her hair and gave him feedback.

"He will live. Although his illness causes him much pain, it is not particularly life threatening. The main thing is to not let it progress further. In that case, he will be back on his feet in ten to fifteen days."

"Is he able to move?"

"Of course. However, it would be better for him to always take an anesthetic and have someone who can help him. It is best to stay in bed for the first few days."

"Hmm!"

"What about the Ivelens?"

"No mercy, everyone will die. You will be trusted with bringing up Roman and Jacob."

"Me? How? All executed?"

Hans looked at the countess with surprise.

"My Lady, would you prefer a revolt?"

Lily covered her face with both hands.

"But the children—"

"You know everything yourself."

Lily sighed and turned away. Hans caught her dropped hand.

"My Lady."

Hans saw the countess' face, and it seemed very worn out and old.

"Don't, Hans. I won't do anything. It just hurts to think about. Let go—"

ೞ ☐ ೞ

An hour later, the king's valet, a personal trustee of the king and a keeper of royal secrets, found the Countess of Earton crouched on the windowsill behind the curtain.

The woman looked worse than a corpse. Her face dropped. The tiny wrinkle between her eyebrows and the trails of tears on her cheeks were strikingly noticeable.

"My Lady, the king wants to see you."

Lily moved lifelessly from her spot and attempted to fix her dress. She couldn't help but ask the valet a question.

"Do you think that cruelty is the privilege of kings?"

The old servant wasn't surprised. He had heard a lot of things during his long life at court.

"I think it is the main trouble of all kings, My Lady."

ೞ ☐ ೞ

When Lily entered the room, Edward gave her a piercing look. *Well, well, has she been crying? Her hair is messy; her eyes look sick and red.*

"What's the matter, Countess?"

"It's all right, Your Majesty."

"Are you sure?"

Lilian knelt beside the bed.

"Your Majesty, will you let me go home to Earton?"

"Why?"

Lily was silent.

"Countess, I want to know what is—"

He said it in such a harsh tone of voice that Lily gave in.

"Amalia and her children, they are... I spoil everything! I bring trouble everywhere! I do not want so much power anymore! I wish I were dead!" yelled Lily as she burst into tears.

Edward frowned.

"No, Lilian, no."

"If it weren't for me..."

Lily cried and cried, drying her tears with the back of her hand and wiping her nose with a towel. Her tears were unfeigned. Her soul suffered at the thought of Sessie the youngest, Jess, and the sick girl. She thought herself an utter fool for worrying over her husband and their failed marriage. *Twice a fool!* As long as everyone was alive and well, everything could be fixed, glued together, sewn up. On the contrary, the fate of the Ivelens was unalterable. She was guilty of their death, it happened due to her foolishness.

The king watched this dramatic show in silence. Edward was not only a good ruler, but he also knew that a woman should be left to cry. She would come to her senses herself, whereas comforting her could make her hysterical fit last for several hours. His Majesty's wisdom had proven true. In around fifteen minutes, Lily blew her nose into a wet towel and nodded.

"Forgive me, Your Majesty."

"Make me feel better, countess. We can talk about it later. Only remember that it wasn't you who started it. You only defended your life and the life of Miranda."

Lily became seriously embarrassed for sobbing instead of helping her ill patient who was suffering in pain.

So! Pillows, anesthetics, pulse... I could have determined his blood pressure using a needle and a ruler. But the trouble is there is no standard! It's good when there is a metric system at hand. What now? What is the length of the meridian here? Bugger! Why am I such a fool, why did I neglect physics and not attend astronomy lectures? Silly girl.

ಲ □ ಆ

Edward was slowly falling asleep. He could hardly feel the pain even though the countess warned him this was temporary. But even so, it was better than nothing. *To let her go to Earton... Well, well. Maybe it's better. It will be easier for her at Earton than at court, but if I want her to remain safe for the Crown, she must remain the Countess of Earton. Knowing Jerisson, Lilian's mere presence has trampled on his reputation so many times already. Their first meeting must happen under my watchful eye. Otherwise, it might go terribly wrong. I also need her to look after my grandchildren. I trust her with taking good care of them. Miranda's awe for Lilian is reassuring.*

There is so much to do! No time for dying.

೩೦ ౡ

Hans, too, felt ugly, especially after visiting Amalia's cell. He couldn't let someone else do it.

"Madam, I must inform you that you have been sentenced to death for an attempt on the lives of the king, the Earl of Earton, and the Countess of Earton, for preparing a coup, and so forth."

Amalia nodded and got up slowly.

"What about my children? Will they live?"

Hans remained silent. Amalia thrust her body forward.

"I beg you! I will do everything! They are guilty of nothing!"

Hans was silent, and so was the executioner behind him. It was the king's order—no poison. Death must be unquestionable, and poison was the least charitable and reliable of all known methods. Poison didn't always work the way it should. It caused a slow, painful death that was worse than being quickly strangled by the skillful hand of a killer.

"Leir Tremain!"

Amalia dropped to her knees. Hans shook his head.

"Not all your children will die. The thought of it should be consoling."

"Who? Jess?"

"The three elder ones."

"NO!"

Amalia's blue eyes filled with pain.

"Not them! I am begging you! I'll do anything you want!"

Hans shook his head.

"This is the king's order."

"They're his grandchildren!"

"Twice grandchildren," Hans looked sad. He did not want to do this at all.

His words greatly surprised Amalia.

"T-twice?"

"You, too, are His Majesty's daughter. Did you not know?"

"N-no—" Amalia opened and closed her mouth. What could be said? She hadn't known it until now.

"You are his illegitimate daughter, whom Jyce Earton took for his own child. Prince Edmund was your half-brother."

Amalia turned pale as a wall.

"No no no—"

She had fully realized that Hans wasn't lying. The whole picture came together at once. Her father would never have poisoned her husband without a reason. There had been one.

Aldonai, wherefore lie your righteous ways?

Hans nodded to the executioner. The large man quietly slipped behind Amalia's back and threw a snap on her neck. Hans watched until the end. When there was no life left in the frame of the beautiful woman who lay before him, he took her hand and inspected her pulse.

Dead. Vile? He prepared for something much worse.

ಐ ೞ

An hour later, Hans went out of Stonebug into the fresh air and wiped the sweat from his forehead. He felt morbid. The way they looked at him made the man hate himself. He knew that the feeling would never go away. He also knew that he would leave Ativerna, he couldn't stay there. *Should I ask the countess if I could stay at Earton? Only to never experience this again!*

Now, he understood the state in which people lay hands on themselves. He was sick from his own heinousness. *No, the children didn't suffer. Poppy brew is a strong thing.* They drank it and fell asleep. It was fiendish, heinous, ugly—all this for the future of the kingdom.

Aldonai forgive me, for I will never be able to forgive myself.

Chapter 3
Black pawn, white pawn

"They say that the Ivelens were crushed in a carriage…"

"And the king fell ill with grief…"

"And the younger Ivelens are constantly with him, in his chambers…"

"The Countess of Earton and her Khangan medicus almost moved into the bedroom of the king, I heard it from a servant…"

"You think…?" The lady made an intricate figure with her fingers.

"No, it's unlikely. The king is really bad."

"Even the baroness is not allowed to see him."

"Is she angry?"

"Like a wild lioness."

The gossipers exchanged glances.

"The Countess of Earton is becoming the king's new favorite."

"It's hard to tell. We will see. Our king prefers the blonde ones."

"But his previous ones are all silly, which isn't true of the countess. Besides, Jerisson is the king's nephew—"

"So there will not be any scandals."

"But what if there will be?"

The man who overheard the conversation spat through his teeth.

The Ivelens are dead. Catastrophically dead! The Crown is safe.

In any case, the chances for success were still there.

༺ ༻

Erik looked at the horizon through the telescope. Nothing had happened so far.

The embassy ships had to pass through the strait between the continent and Virma, through Viriom, and reach Ativerna.

Erik trusted Hans' suspicions about the assassination, so he had taken the route through Viriom to the shores of Ivernea. If anyone wanted to attack the embassy ships, it would have to be there. They could blame the attack on the Virmans, meaning the end of diplomatic relationships between Virma and Ativerna and the success of the plotters. Not that Erik was that worried about Ativerna's fate. As for the kings of Ativerna, they used to be all the same to him until recently, when relations began to improve and showed promise for a potential alliance. He wouldn't let a bunch of amateur plotters destroy that. Let Hans provide peace and order on the land; he and his crew would manage to protect the seas.

All that was left for the Virmans to do was to move on, scan the seas through the telescope, and wait.

ഓ ര

It was time to go home. Not that Jess was particularly excited, but at least he would be able to figure everything out and would finally have a long-overdue meeting with his wife. Richard watched his friend and sneered. He had already written from Ivernea to his father about the agreement with Gardwig. *He was pleased. Of course, I will have to marry, but after all, not a crocodile!* Anna seemed quite sweet and easy-going.

The brothers left Ivernea peacefully. They were heading right along the shore to get home. Three ships from the embassy and six escort ships; Bernard didn't give them more. No trouble, they would manage without.

"Richard, we are approaching the first port—Altver. Shall we stop there?"

Richard nodded. *Why not?* They had to stock up on provisions and repair the sails destroyed by a recent storm. Bernard's ships were also not in their best state. It strongly offended the Ivernean Brat that the marriage with Lydia hadn't taken place, and he took revenge in his own way. The Ivernean ships would escort the embassy to their border, no further. *How much are you worth if you cannot guarantee your prince's safety on your own territory?* Bernard had said. His logic was impeccable; there was nothing to complain about. *Why quarrel? Everyone understood everything; only no one could prove it.*

ഓ ര

Torius Avermal didn't fail. Thanks to the trade with the Countess of Earton, Altver had become a fairly visited port. The governor made good use of it. He enlarged the port, strengthened the walls, paved the streets with stone, as advised by Lilian, and imposed a cobbles tax. Anyone who wanted to enter the city must pay one cobble per man and one cobble per horse. The stones would be taken away in the evening and used to pave the streets. That way, they didn't have to pay for bringing the stones in. Everything was done almost for free. *The countess has a golden wit, pity she is a woman!*

Torius made an effort to give the prince the best welcome reception. He sent his eldest son away and organized a luxurious feast in the town hall. When he found out that the Earl of Earton would also be there, he began throwing out compliments about the countess. What surprised Jess the most was that Torius didn't praise her beauty as was the custom, but instead complimented the subtlety of her wit, her comprehensive nature, and original ideas. In short, by the end of the feast, Jess was seriously wondering who had gone crazy —him, Torius or the countess. He concluded it was all of them together.

Pastor Leider was also present at the reception. He didn't harbor tender feelings for Lilian, but the word "profit" greatly softened his heart. Therefore, he held back his accusations of heresy but reproached Jess for neglecting his wife and giving her spare time to invent odd objects.

"It would be best if she didn't invent anything," implied the pastor.

Although Torius discouraged the conversation before it could develop further, the Earl of Earton figured that the pastor's every word about Lilian was true.

What a wife! She hangs around with the Virmans and the Khangans, involves herself in trade, invents peculiar objects! And now her uncle is praising her too! What do I do?

Jess had no idea. The only thing that struck him was that everyone described Lilian as a very pleasant woman, not a pink haunch in ribbons.

What is happening?

෴

"It's time."

"Let's strike when they depart from Altver. We would be asked to provide escort either way."

Torius knew nothing of the plot, but the commander of the second fleet of Ativerna, Count Schaltz, did know and was even involved in it. He was married to the sister of Loran Ivelen, and this made him naturally become part of the plot. It wasn't difficult to choose loyal commanders and fire those sailors who were particularly honest. It was easy, provided he didn't have to use his own ships. Furthermore, the operation was done in parts. Altver was one of the few ports close to the border. The Ivernean ships escorted the embassy up to that point and handed them over to the

Altverian fleet. The next day or the day after, the embassy would depart for home, accompanied by ten ships of the port fleet. All those ships had loyal commanders, only their own commander was not the king. The embassy had two galleasses and a nave. He had four military galleys and one naval flagship—a clear advantage. In the absence of cellular communication, the commander didn't yet know that the operation had already failed, so he hoped to advance rapidly for eliminating the prince.

The time was near. After two days, the embassy lifted anchors and left the port of Altver behind. Baron Avermal beamed. He managed to please all his guests—the Crown Prince of Ativerna, the Earl of Earton, and the Duke of Falion, not to mention the other courtiers. He made useful connections, which meant an increase in the flow of money, provided the mayor already had some "hypodermic fat" and tripled it with the help of the Countess of Earton. Only one thing surprised the baron. *Why does the Earl of Earton react so strangely to every mention of his wife?*

☙ ❧

The sea, seagulls, the smell of salt water—Richard enjoyed the journey. He accepted the invitation of the commander and switched to the galleass, followed by Jess. The men chatted about trifles, enjoyed the view of the sea, looked forward to arriving home. Meanwhile, Jess counted the minutes. He wished for the shore to disappear in the haze and to be left alone at sea.

One cannot say that the commander was an avid conspirator, but he was an ambitious man and couldn't stand to be "one of the many." King Edward wasn't going to let him advance. Ativerna was a marine state, and the royal fleet was its key power. The king had to comply with the fleet, his ruling principle for his kingdom being "divide and conquer."

Nevertheless, the commander wanted even more power.

Richard and Jess felt so safe that they even left their swords in their cabins and only kept their daggers. If anything happened, they would have time to arm themselves. Even if they stumbled upon pirates, there would first be a rapprochement and maneuvres—and only then a fight.

They didn't regret leaving the weapons anyway. A single sword wouldn't help against thirty armed sailors.

Almost twenty-four hours passed calmly. The ships slowly moved toward the capital. The commander was preparing, sending out messages to all the ships. The young brothers were highly surprised when they saw the commander waving the white flag.

Everything had been planned in advance. Richard and Jess found themselves in a ring of swords. A scarlet flag flew up on the mast, and the remaining ships began enclosing the embassy's galleys into a ring, unequivocally aiming guns at them. The commander looked triumphant. It was his moment of undivided power. The right to execute and pardon was in his hands, and he would take advantage of both.

"Gentlemen, I must tell you that you are our prisoners. Resistance is futile."

Jess grinned and drew out his dagger. Richard followed his example.

"Try to get us!"

"I won't even try. Drop your weapons, or else I will—"

There was the whistle of an arrow. Jess jerked away from the howling air close to his ear.

"Will you kill us?"

"Not yet."

Richard interposed.

"What does this mean, commander?"

"What's so incomprehensible? Sometimes power changes. Those who would come in your place promised me more."

"So you chose to become a traitor for money? Bastard!" Jess replied spitefully.

The commander smiled.

"Well, it depends on how you look at it. Didn't your father poison the lawful heir to the throne, His Majesty Edmund?"

Jess turned pale as a canvas, a mixture of impotence and rage. Everyone suspected that the incident was untoward, but kept silent about it. Edward's wrath was quick, for no man is without sin.

"If you were a man, I would have made you swallow those words!"

"We'll talk about swallowing later, when I have time for you," grinned the man. "If you don't surrender peacefully, we will dissect your body with arrows. In the meantime, to the hold!"

The prisoners had to obey.

"Attack the galleasses!"

A black flag flew up on the mast. At once, the embassy ships were peppered with a rain of burning arrows, among which stood out the large arrows of ballistas.

            ☙ ❧

The ships of that time were poorly armed. Small ballistas, catapults that could throw "liquid fire" and so on. Those weapons were enough to cope with a galley that did not expect it.

The basic plan was to set the ships on fire, make them sink by hitting their sides, and leave—not immediately, of course, but after had they destroyed all potential witnesses. They only had to wait an hour or so before they could raise the sails, put oars into the water, and head to the capital. One could even consider the commander a merciful man. Freezing water was sharper than arrowheads, and less painful, too.

            ☙ ❧

Richard and Jess were helplessly sitting in the hold, knee-deep in dirty water. Both were blazing with anger, but there was nothing they could do. They were tied with ropes so hard that it was impossible to tear them with teeth or hands. The villains had prudently put them apart. The only thing they could do was talk to each other.

"Who would have thought?"

"We need to escape." Jess was more practical.

"How? By making a hole in the ship with your teeth?"

"No. But if we could bargain with the commander, ask to talk to him—"

"One on one? He is not a fool."

"But it could work—and then we put a rope around his neck."

"Bad idea."

"There will be no other chance. Do you understand that they will kill us?"

Richard understood that perfectly well, but he also did not doubt the commander's intelligence. He was a bastard and a piece of scum, but not an idiot after all.

"I doubt that he would risk that. If he took this step, he thought it through."

"We have got no choice."

"I am curious as to what he got promised and by whom?"

"Me, too. I'm afraid we won't find out before we reach the capital."

"If only my father were alive."

"If there is a mutiny—"

Jess didn't finish the sentence, but Richard understood him anyway. The prospect of mutiny reduced their chances of survival to zero, and they wanted to live.

"Wait, what's that?"

The boys fell silent and listened. Judging by the noise, there was a battle going on outside.

But why? And how?

⊰ ⊱

The ones responsible for the "whys" and the "hows" were Erik and the Countess of Earton. The former for his efficacy, the latter for her telescopes that allowed the crew to see three times farther. Consequently, the Virmans spotted the plotters before they could be discovered themselves, but did not approach any closer. Although they had the king's order, it still wasn't crystal-clear if they would be taken for friends or enemies. If they approached, they risked their ship being destroyed before they could start negotiations. After all, the crown prince was on board. If Erik were in place of the commander on the embassy ship, he would have done just the same. Therefore, the Virmans decided to follow the embassy ships unnoticed. Their sails would occasionally emerge on the horizon, but in the sea, no one would open fire without an evident reason. A passing ship was expected to pass.

Erik's watchmen reported seeing something strange—the escorting ships enclosing the galleys of the embassy and firing at them. Erik didn't hesitate to act. *Decent people would never act this way.* As a result, no one would reproach him for dealing with these noble villains as he pleased.

"The oars!" roared Erik. "We advance! Get ready for a fight! Wear armor! Raise the red shield!"

The crew on the Virman ship enlivened. The ships turned around and slowly headed toward the embassy ships and their escort.

"Olaf! Go around from the other side and see what's up with the embassy!"

The ship of Olaf Redbeard slightly changed its course to show that he heard Erik's order.

The catch is promising! The Virmans never refused prey.

⊰ ⊱

That day, the stars favored the Virmans.

The commander had not expected to enter into a fight. He got slightly carried away firing at the helpless ships. *We must leave soon.* The main prey was already in his hands. He didn't care for the fate of the others. The black-flagged ships slowly turned away from the perishing galleys, ignoring all cries for help. Erik's appearance wasn't a surprise. The commander had seen the Virmans from far away but didn't think that they defended the interests of the Ativernian Crown. Once the commander saw the Virman ships swiftly heading toward them with the scarlet shield on the mast, he clenched his jaw.

"Get ready for battle!"

He first tried to raise the black shield as a plea for a dialogue. *Yes, it is humiliating. The Virmans are pirates, robbers, the wolves of the seas.* The commander desperately wanted to live. *Everything had been going so well up until now. We could put up a fight, but not with such a valuable treasure in the hold. Our forces are approximately the same. We risk losing both our lives and our prisoners!*

A flying arrow whistled across the sea, stuck in the black shield and defiantly fluttered its red plumage.

There will be no talks!

෨ ⃞ ෬

Olaf's ship was slowly dragging itself past the sinking galleys. Long ropes dropped into the deep waters, fishing out the ones who had escaped the arrows. The Virmans didn't do it out of their kind hearts; they wanted to know what had happened there.

The Duke of Falion was lucky to be the first man saved. The duke had spent a lot of time on deck, and when he realized that the ship was being attacked, he managed to escape the first blow. Realizing that the traitors would not take captives, he grabbed a piece of wood that had broken off after the blow and jumped overboard. He wanted to live and realized he had more of a chance for survival in the water than on the ship. He had had just enough time to take off his boots so they wouldn't pull him to the bottom. He also noticed the Virmans and cursed everything. He didn't want to become a slave at his age. Although he could trust his son to redeem him, only Aldonai knew when. Meanwhile, the Virmans came in between the sinking and attacking ships and dropped their ropes. Falion, who was nearly frozen to death, decided that the pirates were better than the sea-tsar and swam to the Virman ship.

No one was going to tie him down or chain him to the mast. Instead, they handed him a piece of cloth and a jar with strong wine. A pleasant wave of heat went down into his stomach, and it made him dizzy. He heard one of the Virmans speak. It was Olaf.

"What is happening here?"

Why do you Virmans care for the prince, Ativerna, the embassy? But the diplomat was used to taking all chances.

"I am from the embassy of Ativerna. I am seeking help."

The Virmans weren't even surprised. *Did they know? Did they spy on us?*

"Where is the prince?"

"He was on the embassy ship, but the commander invited him to his galley. I don't know what happened to him there."

"I doubt they killed him. So, it is treason! Gar, take the flags and inform them that the bastards sank the embassy ships and hold the prince captive—"

"The prince and the Earl of Earton."

Olaf's lips curled into a malicious smile. Falion didn't understand.

"He is the spouse of our lady. We need to help him out."

Falion sank low to the ground. His legs didn't hold him.

Their lady? Help him out? I don't understand.

The boy flew up the mast and began waving the flags, as agile as a monkey.

Lily had also suggested the flags. At first, she remembered Morse code, then about the flag alphabet. It was not just used at sea. When children played in garrisons, they played spies and partisans. They transmitted messages, wrote coded notes, and signaled with their handkerchiefs. Leif and Erik made the countess create a local directory of signals. It didn't fit everything, but brevity was famously the sister of talent.

It was easy to recreate Morse code, guided by its general principles. As for flags, red stood for letters, green, for words. One could use flags to say *our lady, husband, captured, prince, attack, theft, offense,* and so on.

Gar managed to fit the message into three signals. *Enemy. Hostage. Value.*

What else does one need to understand? An enemy has a valuable hostage on board.

"Let's fight them!" yelled Erik.

※ ☐ ❧

"Bastards!" muttered Schaltz. Swearing was of no use, so he sent the galleys toward the Virmans. He didn't want to join the fight; he would rather leave. But Erik, too, was dangerous. Two Virman vessels, which obeyed his orders transmitted by a flag boy, rushed after the commander's ship without getting into the fight.

The battle flared up. The people from Ativerna tried to pepper the Virmans with arrows, but they obstinately hid behind their shields, trying to come closer and engage in close combat. Their success was limited. Erik had eight fresh Virman ships—or dakkars as they called them—while their opponents were already exhausted from the previous battle. The reserve of arrows and stones was also limited, so the "hail of death" wasn't as powerful as intended. One dakkar was finally set on fire, and the Virmans desperately cut the boards, throwing themselves into the water to survive for at least some while or swim in the direction of help. Olaf's dakkar drifted around the marine battlefield, fishing out the survivors.

The dakkars collided with the galleasses in desperate combat. The Virmans jumped on the enemy's decks, and the fighting ensued. Both parties had nothing to lose, so neither took prisoners. Except for one.

※ ☐ ❧

Erik watched Schaltz's galley with the gaze of a predator. *We will get to you, my darling, wait a minute.* Bjarni froze beside him with a hefty shield in his hands, ready to cover his leader, and the arrows flew up in the sky. Erik noticed one arrow before it landed, another was reflected by the boy's shield.

"Ballista!" someone shouted from the mast.

Erik's smile was the smirk of a predator.

"Arrows! Go!"

Several guys under Elga's command stepped forward.

"Two fingers up, hit to the left!" bellowed Elga. He was a natural archer. The arrows flew at his command as if he put them in by hand. The two men near the ballista shook and dropped dead. Another person didn't fall but was evidently wounded. The dakkar quickly overtook the galleass. The target was too big for one ship, but Boar's dakkar caught up with them, preparing to encircle him. A couple of arrows fell very near the boat. The enemy managed to use the ballista again, but its arrows also missed.

Erik waved to the captain, but the man didn't need a signal to realize what he should do.

He aimed to break the enemy's oars into pieces with the body of the ship. Schaltz tried to swerve, but the chances were slim. The Virmans showered the galleass with arrows, not giving any chance for escape, trapping the enemy ship in their tight grip, like two wolves that had cornered a forest deer.

Everything got mixed up in the chaos of the battle. There was an archer on the enemy's mast. Erik threw a spear with such force that the shooter did not even fall; the spear nailed him to the wood, dead. The grapplers flew aboard, tightly locking the ships together. Another dakkar came from the opposite side of the galleass and was also shooting at the enemy.

"Ahead! Go!"

The uncontrollable wave of Virmans spilled onto the deck. Erik chopped like a woodcutter. The axe was flying in his hands like a feather. It was no place for a civilized fight. Everyone hit with what they had—axes, shields, arms, legs. You hit the enemy even if he was standing with his back to you, and moved on. The Virmans fought desperately and won.

"Climb to the top! Hit the archers!" roared Erik.

Björn rushed forward. In one dramatic move, he jumped onto the face of a shield and onto the upper deck. A sweep of his axe was followed by painful yelling and the splashing of blood.

The Boar's team came on deck and joined in the fight—this time with more calculation. A man in expensive armor tried to resist but didn't stand a chance. He was simply clamped between two shields and finally received a fatal blow to the head. After his death, the overall resistance fell flat. As the Virmans finished off the rest of the crew, Erik overlooked the battlefield.

It wasn't a clear win, but it was definitely a victory. Two out of eight sunken dakkars still burned in the water. Two out of four galleys had already gone to the depths of Poseidon. The other two were fine, and they would be enough to reach Ativerna. On the bright side, the Virmans now had enough resources to replace the sunken ships with the new. Erik looked around and grabbed his signalman by his collar. The youngster had not been able to resist joining in the fight. He was turning into a man.

"Up the mast, you go! Tell them to collect the trophies."

Meanwhile, he took care of the commander.

※ ☐ ☆

Schaltz was shabby and beaten up. His shoulder had been broken in the battle, and he held up his arm with his other hand. His armor was taken off with brutal force and put in the pile with the other trophies. This did not affect the manners of Erik. He couldn't get it into his noble aristocratic head that the "Virman scum" could cut him into pieces and feed them to the fish if they wanted to.

"Do you realize what you are doing? Your island will be destroyed."

Erik smiled at him, carelessly playing with an axe.

"Where are the prince and the Earl of Earton?!"

The answer was a proud silence. Erik nodded to one of his men, and without further ado, he kicked the commander in the face. Schaltz jerked back but didn't have time to open his mouth. The same Virman placed a hand on his shoulder and began squeezing where it was broken. The man yelled at the top of his lungs, forgetting aristocratic dignity.

"Where? Should I begin skinning you alive? I am very good at it."

Erik looked scary—big, covered in blood—and Schaltz's spirits broke.

"In the hold! They are in the hold!"

"Alive?"

"Yes."

Erik silently nodded to his people, pointing in the direction of the hold.

"Get them out of there."

Two Virmans leisurely proceeded with the order.

※ ☐ ☆

Richard and Jess had spent the previous two hours in complete ignorance. They heard the battle noises and screams coming from above, but had no idea who was attacking or who had won or what it meant for them.

There were more questions than answers, and the waiting was extremely painful. Therefore, when the cover of the hold opened, and a huge Virman jumped down, Jess could not believe his eyes.

"Your Highness? My Lord?"

The questions were purely rhetorical. The man freed the prisoner's hands and pointed at the rope.

"Can you climb up?"

Jess would have climbed onto the moon to get to freedom, not to mention a rope, but his hands hadn't yet recovered, so he began actively moving them, ignoring the unpleasant and painful tingling.

"Where are you from?" he asked.

The Virman squinted. He didn't like Jerisson. He had begun to dislike him much earlier, disapproving of Jess's treatment of his wife. The man would have happily said something nasty to him, but one doesn't get to hell ahead of the commander.

"We are the people of Erik Thorsson. Our commander will explain better. Are you all right?"

"Quite so."

Richard looked calm; Shaltz and his men had only wanted to kill them. Things like that happened. They were saved—all the better. Now, they needed to warm up their arms in order to get out of that prison.

"That's good. Will you let me help—"

The Virman began helping the prince. In around three or four minutes, Richard felt fit to climb up. The soldier hurried them on.

"Get out of here. This bowl of a ship is decently destroyed and might soon go down."

He didn't have to invite them a third time. Jess was the first one to climb out; he looked around and saw corpses and blood—and a couple of Virmans, smirking. A devastating sight—nothing made sense and no one was going to give an explanation. One bully with an axe especially stood out.

"Earl Earton?"

"At your service."

"Your Highness?"

"Yes, yes. And you? What is going on here?"

Erik stood straight.

"We are at the service of His Majesty Edward the Eighth. The ships over there are the Virman Embassy. We were asked to meet you and escort you to Laveri. As soon as we saw what was happening, we intervened.

Richard shook his head, trying to somehow put together what he was hearing with reality.

"You are—"

"Erik Thorsson. At your service, Your Highness."

"Richard of Ativerna," Richard bowed properly. "I express the deep gratitude of myself and my father for saving us."

Erik squared his shoulders even more.

"Your Highness, any honest man would act this way."

Richard answered something eloquent. Everyone was pleased with themselves. Jess looked around. The Virman ships, the remains of the embassy cargo in the water.

"What about the people?"

"We managed to rescue a few. As for the rest…"

The movement was quite eloquent. Jess clenched his fists.

"Bastards! What is the matter with them?"

Ivar smiled.

"You can ask this nit."

He stepped to the side and revealed Schaltz. Ivar barely managed to hold back the highborn earl. Otherwise, the young lad would've destroyed the commander in the blink of an eye. They needed the commander alive for interrogation. With this in mind, the Virmans stopped Jess, calmed him down, and examined him for bruises. They asked the young man if he wanted to speak to the rescued, as well as give them first aid, or at least take their armor off them.

In a word, Jess was given a task and promised that the villain wouldn't escape him until the time of interrogation. In the meantime, they would tie him up and put him somewhere comfortable. Those reptiles often tried to commit suicide to avoid execution. Schaltz did not have such a prospect. The Virmans were experts at capturing prisoners.

༄ ༅

In the evening, Richard tried to question Erik. The Virman ships temporarily landed on the shore, and everyone settled down for the night on the comfortable beach. They made a fire, fried some meat, shot a couple of birds. The prey was tiny, but having just come out of the battle, the men wanted entertainment. Erik rolled out a couple of barrels of wine—enough for several swigs each, but too little to get everybody drunk.

Richard and Jess were given the best spot around the fire, and the men quietly talked about their own business.

"Schaltz is a nit! So many people died!"

"Yeah. Only twenty of them were saved."

"Including Falion. Pikes don't drown in water, even the old ones."

"He is grateful to the Virmans now."

"Me, too. After all, we owe them our lives. My father will treat them better now."

"He already does. It was him who asked them to keep an eye on us and escort us to the capital."

"True! How does he do it? I wouldn't have managed!"

"My uncle is still strong, you'll have time to learn."

Richard shook his head. Erik sat beside him.

"Your Highness, My Lord, how do you do?"

"Call me Jess, leave out the titles," said the earl. "After all, I owe you my life."

The Virman hesitated but eventually went for a handshake.

"Erik. A free captain."

Jess nodded. A ship captain, especially of the old type, was on par with any nobleman, equal to a leir or even a baron.

"It was providence itself that led you to us. I am forever indebted to you."

"Providence is only our foresight and our actions." Erik smiled. "We create our own destiny."

He really wanted to drag the earl's grimacing mug over the rocks, for everything good and bad he had done and hadn't done for his wife. But he couldn't. That would make it worse for Lilian, so he kept quiet.

The crew also knew about everything and kept silent.

"Aldonai is watching over our fate."

Richard smiled. He could see that his words had nothing to do with theology. Erik answered with a smile.

"Sometimes I feel sorry for your Aldonai. Our gods divide responsibility between each other, but yours has to do it all alone. It must be hard for him."

Heresy? You bet! If Erik dared to say that in front of a pastor, his words would be met with the yelling "anathema" or a two-hour lecture about religion. Pastor Vopler was particularly annoying with the latter. But the Virmans endured. The man wasn't evil; he was harmless and believed in what he was saying. *Why kill him for it? Let him drizzle on.*

Richard appreciated the Virman's honesty and grinned.

"Leave the Aldons to argue about the gods. We are the Earth's children. I once more express my gratitude to you."

"Erik," Jaimie never stood on ceremony with people when it was about medicine. "Where are you?"

"Can't you see?"

"Order your men to let me see Schaltz! He is wounded, but they wouldn't even let me close to him!"

"And rightly so. He'll be fine."

"What about blood infection? Do you want to deal with a man in delirium? I don't!"

"I don't need him at all! It's the king—"

"You will explain it to the king, uncombed savage!"

"Shut up, you toddler. You still have milk on your mustache," retorted Erik without a trace of malice. He appreciated Jaimie and didn't pay attention to his rude remarks. It was clear that the lad was asserting himself. *Why not? A quarrel here, a lesson there—that's the making of a man.* He was a promising doctor. Richard raised his eyebrows when he saw the baron sapphire around Jaimie's neck.

"Excuse me, and you are?"

"James, Baron of Donter, Your Majesty. Forgive me my rudeness, but the patients come first."

"Donter?" Jess raised his eyebrows, but Jaimie went on.

"My Lord, I also ask you to forgive me. I will speak to you later after I attend to the wounded. Will you let me see Schaltz, Erik?"

"Go on. My men will go with you. And don't you dare unchain the creature!"

"What if I need to dress the wound?"

"Think with your head, Jaimie! He will soon die anyway when His Majesty finds out all he needs from him. Why waste your time on him? Make sure he's alive, that's all."

The man sighed. Erik was right. The Virman wasn't going to let him dwell on his mental torment. He called forth his men and sent them off with Jaimie to the commander.

"Is it possible to interrogate him now?" Jerisson was impatient. He was curious as to why they had carpeted them.

"It's best not to," Erik said. "Everyone is tired and angry. What if they get carried away? Leave it to the executioner, he will give him a shake and find out what we need."

"Do you know anything about the conspiracy?"

Erik shook his head.

"People say that Leir Tremain uncovered it. I am only carrying out his orders." The Virman was good at putting on an act of ignorance.

The Duke of Falion approached Jess and Richard. "Your Majesty, I am happy to see you well and alive."

"Me, too, My Lord. How do you feel?"

"To be honest swimming in the freezing water at my age left me expecting the worst. If it wasn't for Jaimie... He rubbed me with some ointment and gave me a peculiar potion. It tasted like wine but ten times stronger. I feel great, only not without a little headache."

"Have you tried to question anyone about the conspiracy?"

Falion shook his head negatively.

"I thought it could wait. We still have a long way to Laveri. But now everyone is worn out and tired. There are a lot of wounded; the Virmans suffered heavy losses."

"That's also true," the prince admitted. "We will have time. Who else survived?"

৪০ ০৪

In the morning, Richard and Jess decided to bombard Jaimie with questions. They were disappointed. The ships had enough wounded to keep Jaimie busy. He was constantly running around and had no time for chatting. The only thing they managed to find out was that Jaimie wasn't a medicus but a student of the famous Tahir Djiaman din Dashar, as well as information about his legitimate barony. The rest was a mystery.

Richard and Jess weren't stupid and saw that the Virmans were hiding something from them. They were tormented with questions.

Erik noticed this but had no intention of enlightening them. He considered this harmless moral terror a kind of punishment for the way Jess treated his wife. As for the prince, it was better to stay away from the crowned individuals. The tiniest mistake of etiquette could be costly. *No, thank you! We did our job, we rescued the prince, and now we back off.*

The lads weren't happy about this attitude, but all the cards were in Erik's hands. The ships were heading at full speed toward the capital.

৪০ ০৪

Funerals are always dreary and tiresome, even if the dead are strangers, let alone those I once knew. Let's face it, they died at my hand— the Ivelens. Loran, the Duke of Ivelen; Peter, the Marquess of Ivelen; Amalia, the Marchioness of Ivelen; Cecilia, Jess, and the youngest girl. Lily kept forgetting her name.

It is painful to read it, so much PAIN! If it weren't for me...

Yes, as hard as it is to admit, their blood is on my hands. I played Sherlock Holmes and forgot that life is not a game. Their death is my reality.

The faces of Loran, Amalia, and Peter were deformed by pain. The faces of the children were calm. Lily hoped that they had died a peaceful death.

And yet, she was Lady Macbeth. "All the perfumes of Arabia will not sweeten this little hand." Lily looked at her hands.

"My Lady."

Lily smiled at her friend.

"Hans, I am so happy to see you! At least one dear person…"

Hans looked at her with sadness. The choir sang. The nobles who had attended the funeral whispered to each other. The Ivelens would soon be put into their caskets and laid to rest in a familial crypt in Ivelen. The funeral service was held publicly, to destroy any doubt about their deaths.

"Where are Roman and Jacob?"

"We are looking after them."

Lily sighed. She had no idea what to do with these two little worms. They squeaked, they demanded. *But what do they want?* As it turned out, the solution was easy. Two were enough. However, Lily did not stop at that and made all medical students do infant practice. They had to learn to feed, bathe, and swaddle them. *Why not? As for me, I have no maternal feeling toward them. I don't even find them cute! They will get all the care in the world. They will have teachers, get a proper education, but not my love.*

"I feel guilty," Lily quietly confessed to Hans.

The look in his almond-colored eyes was calm.

"Me, too. We weren't the ones who started it."

"No."

"It wasn't you who forced the Ivelens to betray, intrigue, and participate in conspiracies. You were a victim and were forced to swim out of the whirlpool. As for me, it's my job to defend the Crown. Why should I feel guilty?"

"Because we are alive, and they are dead. Because children suffered…"

The singing stopped. Hans squeezed the countess' wrist in a friendly handshake and let it go.

"Let's talk in the evening."

Lily nodded and went to say goodbye to the Ivelens. She and Alicia were among the only relatives at the funeral. Jerisson was absent, and the king was unwell, so the two of them attended instead. They had to put a small cypress branch on each coffin, make the circle of Aldonai before they closed the lid, and listen to condolences uttered without any special feeling.

Lily wasn't grieving, and the same went for Alicia. Those who had come along for the gossip were aware that there would be none. Everything was proper and peaceful. At the sight of the peaceful face of the youngest girl, the surging guilt overwhelmed Lilian once again but retreated soon after.

ഋ ോ

"No, the children did not suffer. So what?"

Hans settled comfortably in the armchair by the fireplace. Lily and Alicia were sitting beside him. There was no one else there.

"They were just children. They weren't guilty of anything—"

"Is that so?" Hans's eyes turned into slits. "They weren't ordinary children, but the legitimate heirs to the throne, who benefited from the conspiracy to become successful. Do you think that if Jess Jr. was asked to choose between Miranda and himself, he would choose her?"

"It's wrong to judge like that."

"I am telling you the truth. These children were already poisoned by the chimera of power. Believe me, they have died their best deaths."

"They died!"

"Fine, what would have happened if they had stayed alive?"

"They would have grown up, gotten married—"

"And sooner or later would have been found by the emissaries of Avesterra, who would have made an offer they would not have refused. Devastation, war—how many other children are you able to sacrifice for the lives of these children?"

Lily covered her face with her hands.

"It's inhuman, Hans."

"Life does not always allow us to remain human. Sometimes we have to get dirty to protect the safety of those we care about."

"This dirt can touch our own children."

"It can, but not necessarily. I did my duty, and so did you. Don't try to look for justification."

Lily cast her eyes downward.

"Amalia was my daughter, but that didn't stop her from sentencing you to death, along with her brother and her niece." Alicia looked calm. "Do you think she would have spared me?"

"She loved Edmund."

"I also loved Jyce. But I don't have corpses around me. There is a line that one mustn't cross. Otherwise, the fire would consume them. Those who seek revenge are the first ones to die."

"The children—"

"Roman and Jacob are alive. If you want to expunge your non-existent guilt, take care of their good upbringing."

Lily sighed. Hans' look showed that the man sided with Alicia.

"I will try."

"You can do it, Lilian."

"I hope I won't have to inform my husband about everything."

"Don't worry." Alicia's smile was poisonous. "There will be a lot of those who will inform him—in fact, too many!"

৪০ ⬜ ೂ

Bit by bit, Edward recovered. Lily didn't have to watch him day and night by his bedside anymore. The medicuses were outraged, but couldn't do anything. The king had created an alternative guild for Lilian. It was Lilian and Tahir who saved the king, not the guild medicuses, who tried to cure him with pumping and bathing. *Let them taste their own medicine until the end of their days!*

Life returned to normal. They hadn't caught all of the plotters yet, but they would sooner or later. Loran Ivelen turned out to be a very resourceful individual. He had stored materials for blackmail on every participant of the conspiracy. Overall, there were around twenty people involved, mainly from the upper-middle class. There was one duke, a couple of earls and a few barons, who had a lot of ambitions but very little money and brains.

The gentry was composed of complex structures—relationships, connections and money ties—like one big fungus. Lily didn't even try to figure out its intricacies. As for Hans, he was a royal representative and swam in it like a fish in water.

Should we reveal the truth to the public? Never! The Ivelens died as the result of an unfortunate accident. That's it. Only what do we do with the rest of the plotters? If we execute thirty people without any explanation, there's bound to be a riot. Should we throw them in prison? What about "innocent until proven guilty"?

Therefore, they had to act gradually, slowly, smoothly. As Hans explained, they would eradicate the conspirators one by one. Some would die in an accident, others from illness, and the rest would be taken to prison on other charges. *Should we expect the conspirators to openly start a resistance?*

The Ivelen family was at the heart of the conspiracy, with legitimate royal blood. The whole success of the plan had depended mainly on them. Now that the Ivelens were dead, all that was left for Avesterra to do was to find another pawn among the conspirators. There was no such person. Besides, even if he succeeded in taking over power, his triumph wouldn't last long. Avesterra knew this. The best plan of action for the conspirators was to escape. The king would let them savor freedom up to a certain point. They had a long-established hunting mechanism. Sooner or later, the plotters would be caught.

Lily waved her hand as if shaking off the memory of yesterday. *Let them go far away! I need to come to my senses and prepare for a meeting with my husband. Edward did promise that he wouldn't let anyone hurt me, and yet... Jerisson Earton is my legal husband.*

Lily was afraid, terribly afraid. Everyone comforted her—August, Alicia (who was noticeably more lively in the presence of the shipwright), and Miranda who insisted that her papa was a wonderful man.

Lily could hardly believe it. The meeting was approaching.

‪ༀ ☐ ༀ‬

Alexander Falion jumped off his stallion and threw the reins to the servant, who obediently led the horse into the stables.

The man looked around the house.

Hmmm ...How happy had I once been, that time when I first came here with my young wife. How wonderful it was to see my daughter growing up!

And now, all my dreams are in shreds. My wife is insane, and my daughter is likely to inherit her disease. My bloodline ends. I don't hope for a miracle.

This was the very moment when Falion resolved to take his life into his own hands. One would sooner die than receive help from Aldonai. But he had hope for a better life, and it bore the name of Lilian Earton.

She is charming, intelligent, with character, completely healthy and knows medicine, an important asset to possess. She will give birth to healthy children.

Alexander would happily marry her. There was only one thing. Lilian was Jerisson Earton's wife, and nothing could be done about it. The only way was to have Jess push her away himself.

He is not a fool; he is a womanizer. As soon as he sees her, he will cling to her. That's for sure. It's not just her dowry, but her beauty and her mind as well. What a wonderful woman!

Hoping for a divorce was useless. The king wouldn't allow it. Sometimes, it was best to not ask the king. It was also useless to hope that Jerisson would turn out to be a fool. Falion had to prepare the ground himself. He shook his head and grinned like a wolf.

Lilian Earton treated him as a good friend. If he was lucky, he could make her fall in love with him. He could deal with Jerisson and the king after.

My father will be home soon. I will need to speak to him and start preparing. The Falions never miss out on their luck!

Chapter 4
A solemn arrival

"Your Majesty, the embassy from Wellster has arrived to see you."

Edward glanced at Tahir.

"Will you let me meet the ambassadors?"

Tahir bowed low, hiding ironic sparkles in his eyes.

"How can I object, Your Majesty? Who am I to argue with Your Highness?"

"A doctor," sighed Edward.

Over the past few days, the king had come to terms with the mild tyranny of Lilian Earton's doctors. They were all convinced that health came before everything, even before duty. He imagined the doctors' nagging him. *You can argue and fire us only once you are cured. You will have to endure our rules for as long as you are ill.*

Only five people in the kingdom knew about intercostal neuralgia. Although Edward argued with the doctors, his health deteriorated without their help. The king's only wish was to recover. He realized that it was best to let the doctors do their job—for his own benefit. The Khangans were extremely polite.

The countess, on the other hand, hissed and yelled, but that didn't offend the king in the least. It was her way of taking care of him. Sometimes she did it awkwardly, forgetting the norms of etiquette and not thinking about the consequences. Nevertheless, she acted with his best interests in mind. For instance, she got really mad when the king tried to leave his bed. She was very "polite" about it.

"Your Majesty, you can kick me out with a stick—once you recover. As for now, let me cure you! Otherwise, all our efforts will go down the drain, and we will have to start over. Do you really enjoy being ill?"

If Edward were healthy, he would have her guts for garters for such words. But the cruel pain persisted. *No, no. It's better if she finishes her curing. I can attend to business even while in bed.*

He could listen to all reports lying down and dictate his answers to a scribe. He was a king, not a workman, and his job wasn't to dig trenches. Although the king was physically unwell, his mind remained sharp, especially after Lilian decided to stop giving him anesthetics that marred his reason. The doctors cut the doses, and that left him with a perfect mind.

"Your Majesty, you may obviously meet the embassy, but only if you let us take good care of you after the meeting."

Edward nodded.

He would have to endure his body being rubbed with smelly ointments and swallow nasty powders. *Oh well, I will spend an idle evening, but at least I will make a terrible appearance before the embassy in the afternoon.* Everyone at court should remember that his wrath was great.

"With your permission, I would like to accompany you—"

"Accompany me where?"

It was Lilian Earton. The royal valet omitted her formal introduction. He felt gratitude and awe toward the countess for her healing powers. The old man was utterly devoted to Edward and recognized that Lily sought no self-interest. He called her a "real lady," incomparable to these "wax dolls" and gave her unimpeded access to the king's chamber. Edward didn't mind. Furthermore, she was the wife of his nephew.

As for her manners, what could one expect from a shipbuilder's daughter? It's good she doesn't wipe her nose on the curtains!

Tahir and Lily exchanged bows, and the Khangan began rapidly speaking in his own language. The king managed to understand a few things. Lily squinted and nodded.

"Your Majesty, you ought to meet the embassy. I won't give you any strong painkillers, but I beg you to take good care of yourself as soon as the meeting finishes."

Edward smiled.

"Will you agree to be my companion at the meeting, dear Countess?"

"Really?"

"Why not? You have the full right to accompany me. As for the rest, they should be aware that you are the wife of my nephew!"

"What about Baroness Ormt?"

Edward snorted at the thought of his "favorite."

The woman had tried to sneak into the bedroom a couple of times, but the valet was given strict orders to chase her from sight. *Neither her fluttering eyelashes nor her crocodile tears can soothe my aches and pains! Send her to Maldonaya,* thought the king.

"The baroness will get the hint. So, will you agree to remain by your patient's side?"

Lily sighed. Edward was a handsome man. He reminded her of a leopard—a nice, fluffy kitten with fangs and teeth. *If you tickle him with a finger, he will chew your arm up to the shoulder!*

"Your Majesty, what will I tell my husband? It will cause a lot of gossip!"

"A little gossip would do your husband good after all the suffering he brought down on you. Besides, I'll talk to him myself. Trust me, no one will dare take you for my mistress."

"I obey your will, Your Majesty."

Edward grinned with playful, innocent malice. He felt at ease with the countess. She didn't know about a lot of things, but that wasn't surprising, considering she first lived in her father's home and then in the wilderness. Both places did little to encourage royal behavior. Despite all that, it was clear that the countess treated the king with respect, as one human being should treat another. *Isn't that the most important thing?* Edward was never a stubborn tyrant.

Meanwhile, Lily looked at her dress and sighed.

"Your Majesty, I am not appropriately dressed for a reception."

"It doesn't matter, dear Countess. You look charming. But if you are still worried about it—"

Edward touched the bell, and when the valet appeared, he asked him to bring the Countess of Earton golden-coated pearls. The servant nodded and disappeared. Lily looked at herself once again.

She was dressed in a simple, beige, empire-style dress decorated with lace. Her hands were covered with lace gloves. Although she didn't look bad, her clothes weren't elegant either.

She felt a surge of confidence after she put a couple of gorgeous strands of golden pearls about her neck and hair. After all, she wanted to rise to the occasion.

૪૦ ෫ଓ

The embassy wasn't a magnificent place. The Khangans beat its opulence in all respects. Still, it sought to impress the guests. The usher drove everyone mad with his long list of titles and flamboyant figures of speech, half of which meant nothing to Lily. It bored her to stand behind the royal throne imitating the king's favorite, tenderly touching his hand from time to time (even though she was only feeling his pulse). To pass the time, Lily observed the embassy.

There were around thirty people excessively dressed up, among whom stood out a man wearing a small crown and a young girl standing beside him. Like any woman, Lily first inspected the man. It was His Majesty Gardwig.

He was handsome and evidently smart, around forty years of age, with bright lively eyes. There was something wrong with his leg. He refrained from treading too heavily and leaned on a walking stick. He had the face of a man who coped daily with pain and would sooner die than surrender.

I wonder what happened to him? Back in his youth, the man must have looked dashing. Even now, he is tall, fair and blue-eyed. Wasn't his nickname the Lion of Wellster? He deserves it!

Looking at him now made Lily lick her lips.

Stop this surge of pheromones! Had he been at least ten years younger, I wouldn't think twice about becoming his favorite. His habit of re-marrying is evident. What a handsome man!

The girl next to him was different. She was short, dark-haired and dark-eyed. The look in her eyes reminded Lily of a silly fairytale about a silly goose.

She was giving her a diagnosis: many words described the symptoms, but only one term was correct. Anna wore a thin tiara, a lot of jewels and a pompous dress. Lily couldn't help but notice her dirty neck, a deceivingly innocent look, and a naive smile.

Men were usually deceived by women like her. The women next to her either tried to look even more innocent and tremulous or chose to get angry. Lily belonged to the second category. Anna let men solve her problems, whereas Lily took everything into her own hands. *We won't get along. Poor Lons!* Lily genuinely doubted that this lassie would exchange her royal life and diamonds for a love shack in the wild. She wasn't that type of girl.

Anna looked up under the weight of Lilian's gaze, who barely had time to cast her eyes away. One second was enough for Lily to spot that Anna's look was that of a snappish, cornered rat.

How could nobody see it? Poor Lons!

One of the men who came with Gardwig opened his mouth and gave a twenty-minute speech. Edward nodded, expressing his admiration. After that, the kings exchanged letters and assured each other of their mutual loyalty.

Edward invited Gardwig to a ball in honor of his charming daughter, who "lit up the entire palace with her radiant charm." These words made Lily bite down on her tongue hard to refrain from snorting. One royal secret was enough for her.

The parties agreed on the date and time and took their leave. Edward ordered the usher to dismiss the courtiers and leaned back in his throne. He was covered in sweat, and his pulse was racing, but Lily didn't show indignation. She simply called the royal valet and, with his help, transported the king back to bed.

"I hope you'll come to the ball, Countess?"

Lily nodded. How could she refuse?

"Your Majesty, Miranda wanted to visit her cousins. The princesses said they would also be happy to—"

"Let her come. I'll instruct the guards."

ಲ ಐ

Ten days after the sea battle, Eric's ships anchored in the port of Laveri. Without further ado, everyone went to the palace. That evening there was a ball to mark the arrival of the Wellster embassy, the Lion of Wellster, and Anna Wellster.

Every year at around the same time, the king organized his famous masquerade ball—a whole month of preparation, making costumes, sending out invitations, choosing a date. This year, the ball was named in honor of Wellster to please both wolves and sheep.

Lily didn't care to prepare for the ball. She only needed to find a costume and spend an hour there to please the king.

I will survive! No one will dare make an inappropriate comment to the "royal favorite."

Although the thing about the "royal favorite" wasn't even true, Lily knew that her "judges" were the irritable ladies who would happily lie in all poses in front of the king, as well as the men who were eager to arrange it in return for dividends.

Yuck!

Edward treated Lilian like his niece, and Lily addressed him like he was her proud uncle—with due respect but without unnecessary flattery. The benefits of this included security and protection from her husband's anger.

Why couldn't this reptile of a husband disappear somewhere?

Lons rushed to the ball to see his beloved Anna. Lily thought a little and decided that it would be best for she and Lons to be dressed as Khangans.

We will get a stick-on beard for Lons from the barber. Why not? The Khangans are also invited.

As for Prince Amir, he can be a caravan guard in a familial dress. He's a prince, after all, he can do what he pleases. It will look rather exotic.

Unfortunately, the Khangan ladies had no suitable fancy dress for Lily to borrow. Everything was either too big or too small.

What to do! There is too little time to fix a dress!

Marcia was devastated. She wouldn't let her mistress show up to the ball like a pumpkin.

Never!

Lily sighed and decided that the classic costume would always be a win.

A bat—or a vampire?

She had a black dress. To make a black satin mask took only a minute. *As for the cape, easy!* She could sew in short splinters to shape it into bat's wings.

Quite decent! Only what do I do with my hair? I will leave it down and entwine it with black ribbons and black pearls.

August had generously given his daughter a ton of jewels, enough to decorate a Christmas tree.

Perfect!

The girls fixed the cape in no time and even embroidered it with red beads. Lilian's dress was ready.

It wasn't difficult to turn Lons into a Khangan. A black beard made him look exceptionally scary, and the first sight of him nearly made Lily jump. She reminded him of their agreement.

"Do not dare tell your beloved where you live and who you serve. You can tell her only if she agrees to run away with you on the very same day. Do you understand?"

Lons nodded, but that did not dispel Lily's doubts.

Meanwhile, Amir got very upset because he couldn't take Miranda with him. Lily frowned and dragged the young man to her study.

"What are you saying?"

"What do you mean?"

"What are you getting Miranda into? She is still a child!"

"Why?" Amir didn't understand. "Girls her age are already engaged! In some five years, she will be able to get married. She is already a grown-up."

Lily frowned.

"Are you a potential candidate?"

"Why not?" the Khangan Prince didn't give up. "I've been contemplating it for a while."

"Since when?"

"Since I came to Earton. Miranda is beautiful, clever, being around her is always fun—"

"Are you going to lock her up in a harem and shut her away from the world?"

"I don't know yet. I will try to make the custom more flexible."

"What if you're not able to? You and Miranda have completely different upbringings and mentalities."

"Women in your culture don't have much freedom either! They sit at home or visit their friend's houses."

"You preach two different faiths!"

"So what? A woman can keep her own beliefs. The Khangans are allowed to marry overseas women."

"Miranda doesn't love you."

"It's only a matter of time."

Lily squinted.

"My husband—"

"As if you ever ask for his opinion," Amir decided not to stand on ceremony. "Miranda is your daughter."

"She's the daughter of Jerisson. I am only her stepmother."

"It doesn't matter. I am a very good match. If it's so important to you, we can have a traditional Ativernian wedding. Why not?"

Lily sighed.

"Amir, she is still a child."

"Not forever."

Ugh!

After two hours of bargaining, they agreed on the same thing. They would ask Miranda. If the girl didn't mind, they could sign a preliminary contract. If she was against the idea, it was forever out of the question. They would forget about the contract for at least ten years. The only thing Lily allowed before the girl turned sixteen was an occasional friendly visit. They could get married once Miranda turned fifteen (Lily insisted on seventeen, but Amir had the upper hand). When the time came, the decision to marry would depend solely on her.

"And another thing," said Lily, "if Miranda wanted to use contraceptives, you would have to comply." The prince turned red but had nothing to say.

The last thing Mirrie needs is to have a child every year and become an old woman at thirty. No way! She should choose when to give birth and to how many children.

There was one husband who had famously brought his wife down to the grave. *She met her death in childbirth, and he built her the Taj Mahal, only who uses it—her? Love is love, but one should also have some brains!*

ಠ╵ಙ

Amir was left quite pleased. *Even if I cannot have four wives, a man can still have concubines! Any son could be an heir, provided he was smart and strong. Miranda is a good match. She already knows a lot and is able to do a lot.*

The Khanganat would profit from women who could weave lace; blow clear, smooth glass; heal people. Besides, Miranda was related to the king.

Lily understood that. There was nothing she could say. She knew Amir; the young man was smart, had good manners, and was not much older than Miranda. The king wouldn't object to this marriage. Until then, Miranda would live at home.

ಠ╷ಙ

"Is something bothering you, Momma?"

It was Miranda. She quietly came up to Lily's armchair and stroked her cheek.

"Yes, my baby."

"Why? Because of Papa?"

"That, too. But mainly because of you."

"Why?" her blue eyes looked surprised.

"Prince Amir asked for your hand."

"Amir? My hand?"

"Yes. He wants you to be his bride when you are of age to marry him—when you turn fifteen or even seventeen."

Mirrie was puzzled.

"Does that mean I'll have to go to the Khanganat?"

"I'm afraid so. You will be able to visit, but you won't be able to live at home."

"Will you come with me?"

Lily ruffled the girl's hair.

"Baby, at that age you will not need me anymore. I will knit booties and caps for your children and pass them to you on occasion. Sometimes, I will visit you."

"I would be sad without you."

"Me, too."

"Is there any way out of it?"

Lily sighed.

"There's only one way out."

"What is it?"

"To say yes now, so they don't give you in marriage to someone else. We will see to it when you grow up. Amir is a clever young man. If you happen to fall in love with someone else, he will let you go."

"Do you think so?"

"The king is interested in this marriage."

Miranda sighed like a grown-up.

"I cannot go against the king's will. I am scared, Mother."

"What are you scared of?"

Miranda climbed onto the woman's lap and snuggled with her.

"I am scared of finding myself in a loveless marriage, like you and Papa."

"Why do you think that?"

"Momma!"

Her voice was struck with pain. Miranda was already a grown-up child. Children grew up faster in this world.

"Okay, you are right. But your life will be different."

"You really think so?"

"Yes. I hadn't seen your father once before we got married. It will be different for you, I promise."

Mirrie clung to her mother.

"Do you give me the Countess' word?"

"I give you my word."

"Let's play backgammon!"

Of course, Miranda agreed to marry. She was too young to make decisions herself.

Lily had a great desire to slap his Majesty the Prince, but she remained silent. *Life would put everything in its right place.*

The masquerade ball was about to begin.

Jess wanted to go straight to his house in the city, but Richard wouldn't let him.

"Wait. Let's first head to the king, and afterward, you can start looking for your wife. Otherwise, you will look foolish."

Jess didn't think himself foolish, but it was wise to test the waters. The palace was bustling and noisy. The king's servants welcomed the prince and the earl and led them straight toward the carnival. The Virmans stayed outside. The king despised them, and they could not help it.

Richard went straight to his father. Edward was sitting in his study. He looked a little paler and thinner, but so dear.

You realize how you miss your loved ones only after you leave home!

Richard could not resist and rushed to embrace his father. He felt the trembling in his hands.

"My son."

Jerisson also received a big hug from the king.

Edward ordered the servant to bring herbal tea and wine for his children and closed the door.

"Tell me from the beginning, is everything okay?"

As if! Richard told his father how the Virmans had saved them from death. Edward only shook his head. He told him of the Virman's lion hearts, of their bravery, of the ones who were saved and those who were lost. The king sighed.

"I will ask for them to be rewarded immediately. I shouldn't have been angry with them; they saved my boys."

Richard agreed passionately and suggested rewarding the Virmans with Broklend ships. Edward shrugged, implying that August's ships were quite advanced. The king would rather give the Virmans something more precious to equate their venerable deed.

Richard inquired about the conspiracy, but Edward brushed him off.

"Conspiracy?"

"Yes, there was a big one. The Avesterras tried to put the false son of Edmund on the throne."

"Whose son was he?"

"Some servant girl's in the palace. They faked the marriage certificate and blackmailed the Crown. This is not the worst thing though.

The whole Ivelen family died in the aftermath of the plot, leaving only the two youngest twins alive."

"How did that happen?"

"It was bad. We suspect it to be an attempted murder given off as a mishap. Yes, we also grieve, but what can we do? We can seek revenge for the poor girl and her family. Although I was never fond of the Ivelens, I am deeply sorry for their misfortune."

His Majesty would have revealed to Richard the entire story, but he did not want to tell Jess. He wanted him and his wife to sleep soundly at night. Edward decided to wait.

"We have our annual masquerade ball tonight. I hope you remember."

You bet! Jerisson loved the annual ball and enjoyed it heartily.

"Today?"

"Did you mix the dates when traveling abroad? Yes, today. It coincided with your return. I hope you will both be attending."

"We've just arrived."

"The court tailors will help you. Jess, your presence is compulsory."

"Why? I want to go back to my home."

"Because your wife will also attend."

"My wife? But she is—"

"Have you not yet realized that she has little in common with the pink cow you picture her to be? Lilian Earton is a good, clever woman. I will give you a piece of advice, Jess. Watch her at the ball. I will point her out to you. Richard, go to the court tailor and ask them to fix you a costume."

"I have a better idea. I will ask the Virmans to lend me some of their clothes, to mark the peace treaty."

Edward nodded.

"Good. As for the Earl of Earton, I wish to have a word with you, my boy."

Richard winked at his friend and left the room. Jess slouched in his chair. Edward didn't attack him, he only glanced at him and sighed wearily.

"Leave it. I am not a fool. What do you want to say to me? That your wife seems to have become an entirely different woman?"

Jess nodded. *This too, but not only—*

"I would like to hear what you've got to say first. I feel like everything around me is crumbling."

"I've known your father my whole life. I remember you as a little boy. You're a clever young man. Right now you are also mad at your wife."

Jess shrugged.

"Not anymore. I cooled off a bit."

"Good because I need your marriage to last. Lilian is a clever woman. I am going to give her the title. Either your second or your third son will become the Baron of Broklend, depending on who inherits the trade. Lilian asked me. If I am to give her the title—and I will—the Broklend family will become hereditary nobles."

Edward touched his delicate lace cuff.

"Don't be that surprised, dear nephew. Cases like yours have occurred before countless times for as long as my memory serves me. There are only two paths: either divorce—and I stand by your wife's opinion and decision—or you will have to step on your ego. Tell me honestly: did you commit adultery?"

Jess didn't even try to deny it.

"Did you give any jewelry to your mistresses?"

"Her jewelry?"

"Who else's!"

"Erm—"

"August gave you her jewelry. What have you done with it?"

"I don't remember. But I gave her all the Earton jewelry—"

"And gave a couple of her rings to your mistress! August had to buy his deceased wife's ring from a stranger. He was in a rage! They barely managed to restrain him."

Jess whistled in apprehension. He understood August's anger. The incident must have come across as a serious insult. Even though Jess hadn't committed it out of malice, it would be difficult to believe that. The door creaked.

"Your Majesty."

"Come in, Countess."

Alicia Earton slipped inside the room. Jess stiffened.

What's happening? Did they invite her on purpose or did she come herself? What does all this mean?

Alicia bowed to the king, waited for his approving nod, and approached her son.

"My darling son, I am glad to see you."

"Mother."

Jess performed the entire court ritual of greeting under the cold look of Alicia's eyes.

"I am glad you are alive. How was the voyage?"

"If it weren't for the Virmans, my body would've been freely drifting across the seas, and Richard's, too. Who would have known that Schaltz was—"

"Nobody could have suspected it. Amalia didn't know either. It was a serious conspiracy that aimed to destroy all my relatives and put Tyson on the throne."

"Earl Tyson?"

"He is not a simple earl. He has the kinship to the Crown. On top of that, he has strong ties with Avesterra," noted Edward, naming one of the noblest of the plotters.

"But that's not enough!"

"It would have been if there was no one else."

Jess understood.

"What now then?"

"We'll see. They started with the Ivelens. You and Richard were next. I was kept for the end. They could've made me abdicate and given one of my girls in marriage to the villain."

Jess clenched his fists.

"Uncle, why did they start with Amalia?"

"Because the Ivelens have more right to the throne than these Tysons. And because you and Richard are friends, and Amalia is your sister. Avesterra wanted to destroy the most powerful families before they even started the riot. He destroyed the Ivelens, the Lemargles…"

Edward was lying about the Lemargles. His agents had set their house on fire from eight sides and made sure that nobody escaped. The official reason was fire by negligence.

"Bastards!"

"Precisely."

"I was also at risk of being poisoned. If it wasn't for your wife—"

"How?"

"Tahir Jiman din Dashar. Does this name mean anything to you?"

"He is a medicus from the Khanganat."

"Absolutely correct. Your wife brought him to the palace when I fell ill. She spent days and nights by my bedside; she even changed my pot."

Jess's eyes bulged with surprise and made him look like a crab.

"Yes-yes, don't be so surprised. Lilian is not the woman you described her to be. I am genuinely surprised that you failed to see her for her true worth. Your mother can confirm…"

Alicia smiled.

"I happily call Lilian my daughter-in-law."

Jess thought that that wasn't the best compliment.

"She is clever, beautiful, she loves Miranda. Is that not enough for you?"

It was rather too much for Jess.

"What are your intentions regarding your wife?" asked the king. He gave Jess a piercing look.

I must be careful with my answers.

Jess spread out his palms.

"I don't know. At first, I wanted to rip off her head. I wanted to lock her up in Earton. But now, I only want to talk to her and go from there."

"You speak like a man. What are you going to talk about?"

Jess's spirits rose.

"First, I will ask her how she is doing since we last saw each other and thank her for looking so well after Miranda. I also brought her some amazing presents—"

"What's so amazing about your presents?"

Alicia couldn't resist asking.

"What exactly have you found? I'm sorry to interrupt, Your Majesty!"

"It's absolutely fine, Countess. A woman knows what another woman wants."

"Luckily, we managed to rescue our belongings from the sinking ship! I suppose that the Virmans took a lot of things from Schaltz."

"Too little a price for saving your lives," assured Edward. "So?"

Aldonai be merciful! I owe Richard a dozen bottles of my best wine. If it weren't for him, I would've been left with nothing now. Thanks to him, I don't look like a fool.

Jess chided himself. *Get yourself together. Reply only to the king. Pay secondary attention to your mother.*

"Your Majesty, I understand that it will be extremely hard to get my wife to forgive me!"

Edward and Alicia exchanged glances.

"Go on," the king's voice was passionless.

"Due to certain circumstances," (*them being Lilian's cowishness,* thought Jess) "I was undoubtedly not very keen on seeing my wife so often. As a result, I put her life in danger. And not only hers, but also the life of my daughter. Considering the ways she had to deal with those problems, my guilt grew to unimaginable heights."

Jess measured the "unimaginable heights of guilt" against the sum of money spent on presents. The guilt might have been unimaginable, but like any immaterial value, it faded against the ingots of gold. Jess almost winced at the thought of the expense. Most courtiers would be left penniless. *Is it too much? No. It will give me security.*

"I will certainly try to have a word with my wife, but mere words wouldn't be enough. Judging from your letters, I decided to ask you to make a preliminary evaluation of some of my presents to my wife. Fortunately, as I have learned, you communicated with her more than I have ever done over the whole course of my family life." Jess congratulated himself on the eloquent phrasing. In his address to the king, he managed to give mention to his mother, point out his regret, and cover his guilt with a plain request.

"How did this thought occur to you in the first place?"

"Richard instructed me."

"He told you to act this way?" The King's voice was deceivingly calm, but Jess gave himself an imaginary beating—with an axe on the head. "No, Your Majesty. He was surprisingly not very voluble about it."

"Stop speaking in riddles, Jess."

Observing the slightly shifted poses of his interlocutors and noting a change in the king's tone, Jerisson realized that he could let himself speak more freely. His uncle would not get too angry.

"The only thing that Richard did was make me stop pacing around the room and start thinking."

"Very interesting. And how did he manage that? What did he say to you?" Alicia asked unexpectedly. Jess almost fell. The fact that his mother spoke without asking the king's permission showed that they had primarily agreed to skin him to the bone together. Alicia's silent scorn wasn't accidental; everything was much worse. For a moment, Jess was overwhelmed with a slight panic. *Thank Aldonai, the conversation is going well.* His fright soon receded.

"I am also curious, Jess," said Edward. "As your king and your elder relative, I would also like to hear these magical words." The king's tone was imbued with mockery (not to mention the double-meaning that could be appreciated by only two people in the room). Jess didn't dare throw a joke back, although his answer might have come across as a joke.

"Actually, I don't remember word for word what he said, but it all came down to an offer to bang my forehead against something heavy to make me think. Oddly enough, it worked well, and I began to reason out loud, as suggested by Richard."

"I congratulate you on your son, Your Majesty," Alicia addressed the smiling Edward.

"Fine, Jess, I am curious what presents you have chosen. I hope you will not disappoint me." Although unsaid, the word "again" was implied in the sentence.

Jess opened a chest and began revealing the gifts.

"To begin with, it would please any woman to receive jewelry. For example, here is a set of multi-colored amber. Earrings, brooches, even this ferr— futo—" Jess stumbled and murmured silently to himself that one could break his tongue with these female things.

"Excuse me, Your Majesty, this is a decoration which is meant to be worn over your head, with a droplet which hangs over your forehead. I am not a great expert on jewelry but, in my mind, the jeweler who invented this is just a genius. I would also like to know where he got this colored amber from. If these droplets are not rare, the place of extraction is a gold mine! I even dare to suggest that your people should try to find this gold mine. I saw some of your ladies wearing these headpieces and they look just wonderful!"

Alicia interrupted Jess with a strange expression on her face.

"Well, in any case, it is good that you put consideration into your choice of presents. This, of course, is not a jewelry set but individual ornaments. However, you managed to combine them well."

Jess could hardly hide his surprise. His mother wasn't standing close enough to be able to determine that it wasn't a proper set. *How?*

"Yes. At first, I only bought earrings and—"

"This is not important," said Edward with a wave of his hand. "Continue."

"A cutlery set. Since Lilian loves to eat... Well, I decided that she might like it," Jess said awkwardly.

The corners of Alicia's lips twitched slightly. "Cutlery? How interesting! Is it from Ivernea or Wellster?"

"No, this is the work of master Leitz." Jess shrugged. "It seems to come from here, from Ativerna."

Edward nodded.

"A painted fan—a recent manifestation of fashion. Provided they have a skill, women use it to—"

Jess lost his thought because the king cleared his throat in a somehow strange manner.

"Enough about the fan, we are aware. We already have them at court. Anything else?"

Jess put the fan aside and carefully unpacked another bundle.

"A magnifying glass—a recent invention—it allows one to examine very small objects. Since Lilian loves embroidery, I thought she might find it useful." Jess was about to continue, but the king interrupted again.

"Move on." The king's voice had strangely stiffened.

"A mirror—not a metal sheet but some glass. It needs careful handling, but the reflection is significantly improved. It turns out that glass makers are as good as jewelers. It is, however, not too big, just the size of a palm, but everything is so visible in it! Metal could never reflect an image so well! And the frame is luxurious! Lilian will love it."

"I'm sure she will," Alicia's voice quivered slightly. "Whose production is it?"

"I don't know."

Since their shopping trip had been rushed, Jess just hadn't had time to find out the maker. Luckily, it had a stamp—a Red Cross.

Jess remained silent, waiting for further questions. With a wave of his hand, the king asked him to present the next object. Both the king and Alicia were acting strangely.

"As far as I've understood, it's a new game which came to us from the Khanganat. I am not sure that the women will enjoy playing this logical game, but it could also be used as an eccentric decoration."

The king's chuckle made Jess stop again.

"Are you all right, Your Majesty?"

"Yes, I'm fine," said Edward in an unnatural voice. "I haven't been so well for a long time. Continue."

"Here is lace. The seamstresses learned to make wide bits of fabric from lace. I specially chose Lilian's favorite color—pink." These words made Jess wince and lose the thread completely because he noticed their shoulders twitch from laughter.

"PINK!" Alicia yelled hysterically. "Your Majesty, I can't—"

Jess shifted a confused glance from Alicia to the king. They couldn't contain their laughter. *What in Maldonaya's name?* For a moment Jess couldn't believe his eyes and ears. He soon realized that their laughter was completely genuine. He'd never seen them laugh so hard. They laughed wholeheartedly, crying with joy. The curious sight didn't add up with the king's brilliant ability to maintain his control and Alicia's coldness.

"What is going on here? Maldonaya, take it all!" Absolutely confused, Jess silently looked at Edward and Alicia, absorbed in their fit of laughter.

"It's nothing, Jess. You'll be laughing yourself when you find out. However, maybe I am wrong. As for the rest of your presents, aren't they going to be something like a kaleidoscope, or maybe a telescope?"

"Y-your M-majesty, how do you know?" Jess's speech was a confused stutter. "I mean, yes, er, no, well, umm, only a kaleidoscope, I didn't buy a telescope. I mean—"

A new burst of laughter.

"Good. Imagine if there was also a telescope!"

"I don't have a telescope! It was worth a terrible amount of money. Lilian would treat it like a mere toy, and it's too much…" continued Jess in a lifeless voice. Hesitating a little, he added, "but as a matter of fact, I did get one for myself. It can be used at sea, for maritime affairs—"

His Majesty couldn't stop laughing for about ten minutes.

"Jess, you are something!" he finally squeezed out before another burst of laughter, ignoring the tears running down his face. "Did you come up with this yourself or did someone advise you?"

Jess was embarrassed.

The second time they had walked around the capital of Ivernea they had met some charming ladies who had told them about these novelties. They had shown them the way down a lovely path and treated them to other pleasantries. It wasn't proper to mention this to the king. For a moment, Jess stood hesitating, but Alicia rescued him.

"Your Majesty, don't be so hard on the boy!"

Thank you very much, mother, thought the old, bulky "boy." Alicia smiled at Jess' plain face imbued with an unhidden emotion.

"First of all, my little boy clearly wanted to impress his wife and Your Majesty." She couldn't stop herself from making a light joke. "So he went to the most famous shop. His chances of finding a decent present no worse than what he had already gotten were simply miserable!"

"Yes, that's true. What's the second thing?"

"Secondly, he was running out of money," declared the heartless "viperess" invoking another wave of embarrassment in Jess and another laughing spree in the king. "Very few of Your Majesty's subjects can afford such presents." Jess was silent and utterly lost. He decided against joining in the conversation.

Edward shook his head. "Jess, you are something else! You say you brought us novelties, the most expensive and fashionable things?"

The earl blinked. *They are very fashionable and very expensive, so what? It's painful to think about how much money I spent on each piece of cloth, each useless trinket!*

"What's the matter?"

"The matter is," the king's voice was poisonous, "that the artisan Leitz works for your wife. He simply brings her ideas to life—apart from lace. It's made by the weavers who work for your wife."

"And mirrors," Alicia's voice resembled sobbing. "Lilian came up with them herself. Everything you bought was made under your wife's supervision and following her ideas!"

These words hit Jess like a whack on the head.

"But—"

"Yes, son. Your wife…" Alicia was more or less composed, "She handed all her inventions over to the kingdom."

"Not for free, but it's copper coins compared to the estimated gains in pure gold," said Edward with a smile. "By the way, where is her rightful share of the money?"

"Um—" Jess lost all his speech. "I sent her money to Earton. You can check."

"The overseer in Earton stole. I understand now wherefore he accumulated such sums of money! But that's not your fault. Let's move on to discussing other matters. As it stands, Lilian has nothing against your person. Her medicus poisoned her. Did you not realize? It's not surprising! He lies without shame."

"Have you found out who was behind it?"

"Do you think that the attempts were made on Amalia's life alone?" Edward had a lump in his throat. It was still hard to think about Amalia. "The Yerbys—you know them—are responsible for it."

"Bastards!"

"It's your own fault. You should've chosen your workers more carefully. Your principle is 'out of sight, out of heart.' Have you ever worked with August, Jess?"

"I have once."

"You should learn from him. He's a professional."

"The only thing is that he cares too much about his workmen."

"Get used to it. Your wife Lilian is the same. She furiously defends her people."

Jess shook his head. He could hardly believe it.

"Does she get hysterical?"

"I told you—she was poisoned."

The Earl of Earton sighed heavily.

"What do you want from me?"

"Well, well," Edward's look was hard and cold. "Look more closely at your wife at the ball tonight. I will soon organize a meeting. You will have a chance to talk, to think… I am sure that you will like her. If I like your behavior, I will help you. Otherwise…"

"You should've seen the courtiers licking their chops," smiled Alicia. By the way, she will be wearing a Khangan dress tonight."

It hurt Jess's pride to hear that someone dared to encroach on his wife. *No way! She is mine!*

"As soon as Richard returns, you will head straight to the court tailor. I want you to have some rest before the ball. No woman could resist your charm. Aren't you capable of seducing your wife?"

Jess had no doubt about his virility and charm.

"And another thing, take a seat. Have a look at this."

Edward took out a big trunk from his table. He placed a small key into the lid.

"Interrogation protocols. Enjoy your reading."

"What about—"

"We will talk about everything else later. Alicia, could you lead your son to the small salon and leave him alone? He needs some time to think on his own."

Jess awkwardly stood up from his chair, bowed and followed Alicia.

What a moron! Pity he is nothing like me, thought the king.

ℬ ☐ ☯

It took Richard some courage to enter his father's study, but Edward looked warmly at him.

"Sit down and tell me."

Richard only shrugged.

"There is nothing to tell, really—"

"Is it Anna or Lidia?"

"Anna."

"Not bad!"

"Didn't you prefer her anyway?"

"Yes, I did," confirmed Edward. "We need to stay on good terms with Gardwig."

"And so we will. What is this conspiracy about?"

"Have you realized that all was not so simple?"

"Yes. Do you not want Jerisson to know?"

"You will tell him nothing, understood?" said Edward.

"Why not?"

"Because Edmund's son wasn't from a servant. He was from Amalia."

"For goodness's sake!"

"Exactly."

"Now it's clear why uncle Jyce poisoned Edmund."

Richard went silent.

"But who? How?"

Edward took out a second trunk. It was smaller than the first one and had a special seal that meant "royally confidential."

"It contains protocols. I want us to take turns in keeping them. Jess should never find out."

"It will be a shock to him."

"It won't be, because it never happened, never!" Edward raised his voice slightly.

"Your word is law. Fine. I will see to it today. And what of Jess's wife? I suppose that's also not so simple."

"Are you curious?" said Edward with a smile.

"I cannot even emphasize how much! Can you imagine being in a different country and not being able to trust the privacy of letters! On the one hand, I couldn't risk discussing private affairs. On the other hand, there were so many rumors of the countess hiring the Virmans, sympathizing with the Khangans—"

"Those rumors were quite truthful."

"So what happened, after all? I am curious!"

"Jess has all the papers about it. You can also have a look. In reality, not everything is that frightening and mysterious. There had once been a girl, Lilian Broklend. She lived in the wilderness, spoke solely to her father and suddenly found herself married. She was scared at first, then shocked after her father sent her back to the wilderness, out of everyone's care and sight. Although Lilian blames herself, she couldn't do anything. Jess didn't want to cast his eyes on her."

"True."

"They began poisoning her. She was on the verge of death after having lost her child. The villains thought that she would die anyway and stopped giving her poison. One of her servants nursed her, and she recovered. She is a smart woman with a strong personality who refused to accept death."

Richard shook his head.

"An iron lady?"

"Oh no. Lilian is a very charming and gentile woman. However, there is something else. She is nice, polite, knowledgeable…but something doesn't add up."

"I don't understand."

"She doesn't want to rule. She cares nothing for power. She doesn't even spend money on herself. Any other woman would have bought herself a lot of dresses, trinkets, but not Lilian. She teaches the children of the poor instead. She feeds, clothes, and takes full care of them. It is to make them into loyal servants of the Crown, as she explains, instead of replenishing the city's ghettos."

"Does she do it for the Crown?"

"No. She does it for the children themselves."

Richard shook his head.

"It sounds strange."

"I also thought it strange, before I figured out the cause of it. She is the third generation. August's father was an excellent military man. August himself is a born carpenter who makes incredible ships. Lilian is even more interesting. That blood is thicker than water."

"I guess. It's like she is a different person, you know?"

"It's impossible. She was always surrounded by servants. Who could have done it?"

"A neighbor, someone else—"

"Her father recognized her."

Richard shrugged.

"It's like she's come from a tale about an old outcast who suddenly went to fight dragons."

"Life can sometimes be more interesting than fantasy."

"True. What do you think about Jess?"

Edward's eyes went cold.

"Let him understand that I am not very pleased with him. If he doesn't do the right thing, he will have to suffer the consequences."

"What if he ties himself up in a knot?"

"I will burn the rope."

Richard went to his study, and after two hours, returned the documents to his father and went to see Jess.

ಖ ☐ ೞ

Richard found the Earl of Earton sitting in a stupor with a box of documents next to him. Richard took in the sight and began pouring wine.

He was thirsty and wanted a drink. Jess downed the glass of wine as if it was water. His blue eyes were sad.

"Richard, am I an idiot?"

"No."

"I feel like one. There is so much I have missed. It makes me crazy!"

"What are you going to do now?"

"I will go to the masquerade ball."

"What about your wife?"

"I don't know. Richard, can you sell me at least half of your scrolls?"

"Why? Didn't you get her a lot of presents?"

Jess's cup flew into the wall.

"Are you kidding me?"

"No. Tell me what happened—or do you need more time on your own?"

"If I stay on my own for any longer, I will go mad. Besides, His Majesty told me to ask you the rest. Aldonai be merciful! How they laughed at me!"

"Who laughed? At you?"

"Yes! Your father and my mother. Thank Aldonai nobody else was there. Did you know?"

"That Alicia would be there? No. Hmm. Two against one! I bet they planned to give you a lot of lecturing. Why did they laugh though?"

"You won't believe, and you will probably join them in mocking me. And you dare to call yourself my friend! What an insatiable curiosity!"

"Calm down, friend! All curious ears are already in the ground. I shall be silent as a dead man."

Jess began his story. His sense of tension loosened and replaced itself with a healthy self-mockery. Jess cherished the possibility that he would be able to pour his heart out to a friend. He jumped around and acted out the events of the story for Richard's entertainment.

ஐ ෆ

"I show them another gift—lace fabric, and I tell them that I specifically chose the pink because my beloved wife loves it. This was when mother had a fit, she howled 'Pink!' Only then did it dawn on me that they had been laughing at me all along. After I mentioned the color, mother could barely stay on her feet. Their laughter was louder than all the neighing from my army horses. I understand about the rest, but do you have any idea as to why they reacted so strongly to the color pink?"

Richard tried to be more considerate than Edward and Alicia. He tried to contain his laughter during Jess' dramatic performance, and his lips were all bitten. At last, he couldn't keep in his laughter and chuckled into his fist.

"I understand them! The mention of pink destroyed them!" Then he suddenly became serious. "Although in reality, the root cause is not funny at all. They, of course, didn't think about it at the time."

"Maldonaya take you! What's wrong with pink?" Jess was genuinely confused.

"Your wife can't stand pink—not anymore!" Richard said when Jess tried to object. "There are a lot of contradictory rumors about it, but your mother says that Lilian started hating pink after she lost the child. I am very sorry for your loss, but Lilian wouldn't thank you for the pink presents. You would have made it worse."

Jess grabbed his head.

"Oh, Richard! At first, I thought it a wonderful idea to show the gifts to the king. Later, I knew it was utter nonsense. Only now, I realize how bad it was"

"Yes. It's for the best. So what's next?"

"Next? I wanted to tell them about the presents I got for Mirrie, but the king asked me about the telescope."

"And?"

"I was foolish enough to admit that I bought it for myself."

Richard burst into laughter.

"I can imagine their reaction."

"You bet! It's easy for you to imagine the anger that was directed at me. What killed me was Alicia's ice-cold smile and her question about whether I knew that Mariella is my wife's creation under the protectorate of the Crown! Turns out that Lilian is a boss there, but it's kept in secret."

"How did you react to that?"

"How could I have reacted? Like a real man! I nearly fainted, my eyes bulged, and my mouth opened. I must have been a pathetic sight."

Jess became somber.

"I couldn't stand it anymore. I exclaimed, "Your Majesty! How could this cow"—"

"You called her a cow?" Richard grimaced.

"The word slipped out. I always used to call her that—and especially now, when they were making fun of me…"

"You're a fool, Jess! I've told you this before. You've never called her anything but a cow! She was probably aware of it. If a person is continuously told that she is a slug, for example, it will eventually push her to prove otherwise and roar with all her might!"

Jess looked at his friend with surprise.

"You won't believe it, but the king gave me the same example, only he said that a chicken would eventually cluck. Are you relatives, by any chance?" quipped Jess.

"You won't believe it!" Richard mocked back. "Don't get distracted, go on with the story!"

Jess shuddered.

"It's you who's distracting me," he said without enthusiasm. "I was so unhinged that I didn't even realize where I messed up and went on digging a hole for myself. I declared that she was only a woman, a silly woman, and if she seems to be good at something, it is because someone else is standing behind it. I said I desired to know who the person was, make him bleed to death and let his blood fill all the wine-jugs of Ativerna!"

Richard let out a whistle.

"You couldn't have made it worse even if you'd wanted to."

"I know! I lost my temper. Their mocking maddened me so! I immediately realized my mistake and explained that I had said it only because I've always seen my wife as stupid, whereas, in reality, she was not in her right mind because of the poison. I said I rationally knew that she was a clever girl, but haven't yet felt it with my heart. My eyes told me she was a total freak. When she came to herself, I was already away. I spoke badly of her only because I couldn't contain my emotions from spilling out. It took me around three times to repeat this thought in different ways before I realized that I was going around in circles."

"Did they believe you?"

"I think so. But, of course, Edward remained greatly displeased with me."

Richard thought to himself that Jess had better things to worry about, but kept silent so as to not interrupt his train of thought. So Jess continued.

"But he believed me. Otherwise, his answer to me would've been different."

"What was the answer?" Richard realized that Jess was going to continue his story anyway, but he wanted to keep the appearance of a dialogue.

"Lilian Elizabeth Mariella, the Countess of Earton, is under my own protection. Be sure that I will stand by her side even if she ceases to remain an Earton. She will get another name. As for the man who stands behind her deeds, you have nothing to worry about. We have sifted it through the finest sieve. There is nobody. How she endured everything still amazes me to this very day." That's what he said. His words made me sweat. He added gloomily that he was terribly upset that Lilian didn't have her husband by her side, although he ought to be there."

"Oh yes. Such phrases would unhinge anybody. What did he say next?"

"It gets much worse. Edward became silent and let my mother bury her claws in deeper. Why did he let her do that?"

Although the question was rhetorical, it wasn't left without an answer.

"I will explain to you in detail after you finish," snickered Richard.

"Hmm, you've got me interested. Okay, so..." Jess remembered the conversation.

"At first, he listed all the people who've lied to me or betrayed me. Two governors, two village elders, a mistress (whom she called ugly names) and her cousin, Baron Donter, the medicus whom I invited, Miranda's nanny, her teacher, one of the soldiers. There is proof of their disloyalty; there is either a confession, a testimony or both, or confessions from the people I've hired! That is not the worst part though. One of the rings that I gave to Adele belonged to Lilian, just as you suspected. Moreover, she inherited it from her mother. As it turned out, August bought out all the jewelry that was paid for hiring the killers. I wouldn't have paid so much; he paid way more than it's worth,"

"That depends."

"Yes. Mother also said that, as a present, that ring is more precious than all the things I bought together." Jess frowned. "Do you know how much I've bought?"

"More or less. Alicia is right, and you know it yourself, only you do not wish to accept it."

"I *did* not wish to, until they laid all the evidence before my eyes. Before, I had only been told what happened in those interrogations briefly. But here, for the first time, the king ordered food for them and a tall pile of documents for me. Those secret reports could leave the walls of the palace only in ashes, so I don't have any illusions. Two candles burned down before I could finish."

"Considering your reading speed, that's too many."

"You bet! I only had time to read half. I skimmed through the papers, paying particular attention to the ones Alicia pointed out. She was so sarcastic! She said that I seemed more like a complete idiot than the poisoner and murderer of my wife. She asked me to read carefully the report about the servant in Earton with whom I had an affair. It turns out that that fool decided me throwing her around a couple of times and whispering a few compliments meant something more serious. This tart," swore Jess, "turned out to be the one to blame for the miscarriage. She was even worried that Lilian had survived."

"Jess," Richard couldn't resist making a remark, "have you tried wearing a chastity belt or asking an herbalist for some medication against sexual arousal? If you didn't like your wife no one would blame you for starting an affair on the side, really, but not in Earton and not with a servant! Goodness me!" Richard stammered, realizing that he shouldn't have snapped. A painful silence suspended over them.

"Well, never mind," Richard's voice wasn't entirely genuine. "I was only scared that since you chase everything that moves, it would be safer for me to stay out of sight."

Jess forced a smile. The joke was bad, but both friends pretended to laugh.

"Don't be hard on me," said Jess finally in a tired voice. "I am having a hard time as it is."

"I'm sorry."

"It's fine, I'm just... Maldonaya take it! Let me tell you what happened next."

Jess was relieved.

"Tell me, and afterward, I want to explain why it was Alicia who spoke to you and not my father. Maldonaya take that silly maid. Go on!"

"The second document that my mother told me to inspect was about the Baron of Donter. It gets worse. Together with the nanny, this bastard tried to kidnap Miranda. He was going to take her to his estate. Whatever it is he had planned to do with her, it makes me angry. Given we found out about the sins of this bastard, his premature death was for him a blessing in disguise, especially since no one got hurt."

By "no one" Jess meant Miranda. All the dead, of course, meant nothing to him.

"The official story is that the baron (who, by the way, turned out to not even be a baron) was stabbed during the fight. That's what Lilian says, and the rest, including the king, pretend that this is what happened. In reality, though everyone had a chance to find out that Donter was caught alive. Lilian ordered her Virman guards to punish him as they punish child theft on Virma. Hence they—"

"Don't!" Richard stretched his arms forward. "I know their customs. Although I entirely support this way of dealing with criminals, I'm going to pass. I guess that my father did you a tremendous favor by ordering you to keep celibacy. Maybe if you try very hard, your wife will forgive you. If you let your member loose now, I doubt you will ever be able to have it up again."

"What do you mean?"

"Your wife will chop it off with a blunt knife—in five goes! Even worse—in twenty, and with a very blunt, very rusty sword, too!"

"Very funny!" remarked Jess with a tinge of uncertainty.

"Maybe. But if I were you, I would not risk it. Judging from how she tamed your mother and my father, they would both swear that you were born a woman—only they needed an heir, and so you had to wear a codpiece. But one day it suddenly went off because of excessive emotions!"

Jess gave out a nervous giggle.

"Don't make jokes like that! Otherwise, it will give me nightmares."

Richard thought himself very witty but didn't say anything. Jess continued.

"Besides, I myself became a bit wary of her. It turns out that I did not know my wife at all. Can you imagine that Lilian led the pursuit of Baron Donter? I don't know what she did exactly, but the soldiers and the sea wolves…golly! Such authority must be hard earned!"

Richard grunted.

"Don't whine! Look at yourself. Not like your wife is any better."

"She's my fiancée, not my wife. Go on, continue."

"In short, some parts I read in full, others only briefly. Not everything is so boring. Mother asked, "What do you say now?" I had nothing to say and spread my hands instead. What else could I do? Say, "You're right, Your Majesty. I am not a murderer, I am an idiot!"?"

Jess paused for a while, then continued.

"My mother started looking through the things I had bought. At first, she asked if I remembered the stamp on the table set. 'How could I forget it,' I asked. There were two hallmarks. One of them was a bit more intricate, the second one was quite simple, although I still can't figure out how they got that particular red dye. One by one, mother began showing me my purchases—they were all marked with two crests. One of them was always the same. She then asked me if I was ready to find out a big state secret. That's when I suddenly realized, but it was of no use. Until that very last moment, I harbored the sweet hope of getting a normal explanation, a believable explanation! I begin to realize that I hoped in vain, that I was done for, but the hope didn't go away. Please please, please! Tell me that I've made a mistake in my judgment, tell me that the guilds went on a riot! Anything that is not related to Lilian!" Jess almost broke into a scream. "But no."

"Should I be afraid to hear it?"

"Don't be mean. First of all, you already know it. Secondly, I specifically asked about it. The only people I am allowed to discuss it with are my mother, Edward and you. No one else. Oh, I forgot Lilian, if she wills it."

"So, they explained to you that all the presents you brought back are your cow's creation?" asked Richard, hiding his cunning eyes.

"Why do you call her a cow? How could a cow... Oh, wait. Are you joking at my expense? Or maybe you're testing me?"

"Both!" confirmed Richard.

"Well, I have clearly passed that test!"

"Calm down. I am only trying to entertain you!"

"I know. Do you think that we'll keep having such conversations even after you become king?"

Richard flinched. "Aldonai let my father see the day when his son inherits the crown."

"Is this your answer?"

"It is. I could lie to you and say that everything will remain the same. I don't want to lie to you now; I'll save it for worse times. Certain things are bound to change. Let us remain good friends, for Aldonai's sake!"

A cozy silence befell them.

"You know my mother! She is... I, of course, knew about her being referred to as the Ice Viperess, but I never really understood why. Yes, she's cold. Yes, our palace is a nest of vipers. Her name combined the two together. Ice or cold, who cares? For Maldonaya's sake! Suddenly it dawned on me that 'cold' and 'ice' meant two non-synonymous things. I've always thought that her attitude toward me was cold indifference. Now, I realize that her attitude was almost pure love."

Jess was too immersed in his memories to notice Richard's sad smile.

"It seems somehow unexpected for you to realize this after so many years. Hmm!"

A pause.

"Mother told me everything about Lilian—how useful she is for the Crown and how much profit she makes. The profit! And the digit was only a rough estimate! Mother then asked me to count how much more profit I brought to Lilian with my reckless spending at the salon compared to the worth of my marriage presents."

"And you couldn't tell!" Richard's tone was affirmative.

"Of course not. Like a pile of gold next to nothing. Take only that ring! Alicia's words hit me harder than stones."

"She's a mighty thing. You should calm down."

"How do you know? Have you already discussed it with her? Of course you have, why do I even ask?"

Richard remained silent.

"Mother also told me about the rest of Lilian's ideas. Take sea salt for instance. We used to buy it before, too. Ours was only good for the pigs. The people of course used it, but it's a crime to spoil our normal food! I found out only scraps of information, but couldn't believe it, couldn't quite put it together. Speak only of medicine! That Khangan doctor is a dime a dozen! They treated the heir of the Khanganat. As far as I have understood, although Tahir is a famous medicus and Lilian is his favorite student, it was her who found the cause of the disease. As for my sister..." Jess banged his fist against the table. "Mother said that the medicus guild could soon cause some trouble. Edward intervened again and said that he didn't give a damn about all the medicuses. He said he would try to avoid blood, but if they cross the boundary, he will order them all drowned in memory of Jessamine."

"I can see why."

"Yes, I remember what you said to me in Wellster. Do you think that if they got their hands on you, you would—"

"Almost certainly."

"Hmm. And then Edward declared that..." Jess sighed deeply. "'It's good that Lilian follows the covenants of Aldonai and keeps her marital bed chaste, even though it might not be worth it.' Those are his exact words. He then said that if it occurred to Lilian to ask him for a divorce and a new husband, he would only ask when and how many husbands she needed. And if there is any Aldon who is against it, he's got Gardwig as an example to back it up."

"Aldonai be merciful!"

"Well, it was clearly a joke. He said it with a smirk. But the mere fact! I had nothing to say. Well, he finally said that was probably enough learning for one day. He said that he wouldn't mind me speaking to you in private. Lilian was also among the trusted, but she should not find out about his last words, neither from me nor you. It would have been a crime not to take advantage of her patience."

"Obviously not! I'm not a fool."

"Well, I'm only passing on his words to you. Although I understand you'd keep quiet anyway. Can you explain to me, Richard? I see, I hear, but I don't understand! My wife and all... She is different! Fine, I know she was poisoned. But still, it's not Lilian. It's a different person, or rather a different crowd of people! It cannot be! Everyone says she is beautiful, but every time I remember her, it makes me gag! It could either be mockery or a compliment. I never paid too much attention to it before the conversation with Alicia and Edward. Does this mean that all the unbelievable rumors about her are true? I want to bang my head against the wall, or better—to finally wake up. I keep pinching myself, but it gives me nothing but bruises. I don't wake up! I don't un-der-stand!" Jess didn't even take a breath.

"Maybe they poisoned me and not her? Lilian this, Lilian that... The ruler of the Khanganat worships Lily, Gardwig asks me if Lily will come, where she got that dress from, if it was me who got her such beautiful jewelry, could I make Tahir come and see their relative because he doesn't go anywhere without Lilian! Lilian is everywhere!"

Richard nodded sympathetically, letting Jess talk his heart out.

He continued. "Edward forbid me to meet her in person! Do I have to spy on her to figure it out? She seems to be everywhere! I will be peering around the corner only to have her come from behind out of nowhere! I will turn around, have a heart attack, and she will just evaporate! She won't be guilty of my death because the moment I pass away, she will have an alibi! She will have proof of being in five places at once, all of them five hours away from each other on her Avarian horse! She would get her presence confirmed by those whose words cannot be disputed!"

Jess sighed heavily. "I never used to understand those who suffered from insomnia. I always thought they were making it up. Aldonai has punished me for my disbelief!"

"Jess, you seem to be slightly exaggerating. Lilian is only a woman, although not very ordinary."

"She's not a woman! She's a mixture of a racehorse with a tornado! I will sooner believe that a shilda got into her after she lost her child."

Richard noticed that despite Jess's joking voice, his eyes expressed a certain worry.

"Let's consider the option with the shilda."

"It's only a joke, Richard," Jess nervously replied.

"Let's do it anyway. Don't interrupt me. I listened to you."

"It's silly to interrupt a jester, you will get less laughter," murmured Jess. Richard pretended that he didn't hear him.

"Thank Aldonai I am not a pastor, but I know a few general things. First of all, shildas are lustful. They cannot contain it. As far as I know, they studied Lilian's life and background. They found nothing and no one at all apart from you, which was a long time ago, a couple of times a year, without any particular excitement from her. By the way, considering your appetites, a shilda sooner entered you than entered your wife. We need to ask the Aldons to check you."

Richard pretended to start leaving.

"Do you think they would believe us?" Jess' face became curious.

Richard dropped back into his chair.

"The problem is that even if they believe you, you'll find yourself on the gallows or in a monastery. They cannot hang you because you are related to the Crown. As for the monastery, only women go there. It would be too much if they put you there."

Jess stretched his fingers.

"After everything Lilian did for the church, a Maldonayan shilda would burn to ashes. Thirdly, no one noticed any change in her appearance—such as her pupils becoming squared or her running around naked—apart from that she lost some weight, of course."

"Some weight!" murmured Jess. "Well, you also promised to tell me why it was my mother who questioned me and not Edward. Now seems to be the best time for you to tell me."

"I was just about to. But I warn you, no one should know it."

"Richard, I think you know that I would never—"

"I know. You told me the same about Lilian, remember?"

"Ah!"

"Oh!" Richard became silent. "I am glad that you realized it yourself. It makes it easier for me. Do you realize Ali— your mother's role for Edward?"

Jess pondered.

"I think I do, but I am not sure."

"I guess you can call her his real favorite—a secret one."

"You are saying that they—"

"One day, I will really hit you in the face! There's only one thing on your mind. Who cares about their private life! It's of zero importance. Favorites for bed are a completely different thing. Even if they were lovers, would you judge Edward or your mother for it?"

"I wouldn't judge anyone. It's their business."

"So why do you ask such a silly question?"

Jess went silent, and Richard continued.

"I highly doubt that their relationship is anything beyond professional."

Richard remembered his father telling him that Alicia put so much heart into state affairs that it left her children deprived of love. It made the king feel guilty before his nephews. But Alicia's talents were much too useful for the Crown to refuse them. Richard wasn't going to tell Jess this. It would've been one thing if Jess realized it himself, but to hear such concerns from someone else was too much.

Of course, Richard didn't recognize the double meaning of Edward's words, but it didn't make much difference. It was entirely true that Alicia substituted the palace intrigues for her private life.

"Father has control over men. He can speak directly to counts, dukes, barons, merchants and so on, but not to their wives or their daughters, which is a big drawback. Take only that fool Cradies. She was as silly as a goose, but that didn't stop her from ruling the county, albeit badly!"

Jess shook his head.

"I've never thought about it that way. You say that my mother—"

"Yes. She adds a female touch to his politics, and does it quite well, too. By the way, tell me, is August Brocklend only a good shipbuilder, or is there something more to him?"

"August is a genius," answered Jess, surprised by the sudden change of subject. "Only a genius can create ships that can survive the most severe storms while suffering from seasickness on the same ship in a flat calm. Why do you ask?"

"Because. You'll understand soon. Have you figured out why it was mainly Alicia who spoke to you during the reception?"

"Wait," pleaded Jess, "don't jump from one topic to another so frequently. I myself get motion sickness from it!"

Richard smiled. "It's necessary. Fine, I will explain to you what I think I understand myself. If my father was lecturing, you would stand dumb and only nod your head. He's the king, you're his subject. You would pretend to agree with everything. You would return to your original course as soon as the storm passed, provided that it didn't rip your sails and jam your wheel."

Jess said nothing.

"If your mother tried to lecture you alone, you'd never take her words seriously. You would either listen to her out of duty or change the subject. You'd ignore her advice or instantly forget it. Considering that you perceived your mother as an ordinary court lady—an ordinary woman."

"Yes, I already realized how 'ordinary' she is," grumbled Jess.

"Let's get back to that later. My father and Alicia foresaw this. Therefore, your mother was the one who spoke, and my father was the one to make sure that you didn't run away. You'd never dare to ignore your mother in front of the king."

Jess stared at Richard in slight horror.

"Wait, do you suggest that they predicted my behavior and tried to deliberately catch me off guard?"

"Of course. It was to make you seriously consider your behavior. One thing they didn't expect was your presents."

"In that case, we're even," snorted Jess. "Yet there is something in your words that makes me... Edward didn't need Alicia to make me open up, only it would require more time and more cruelty. Instead, he chose to reveal Alicia's role. It's clear why they so carefully conceal her position. I would've figured it out even without your help. But why would I bother?"

"I emphasize that it was you who told me about Alicia's presence, and it made me think about why. Go on, let's compare our conclusions."

"Bastard!" exclaimed Jess without malice. "It hurts me to think so much."

"Maybe that's what thinking does to you. As for Edward, Alicia and me," sighed Richard, "it's necessary. I suppose your wife must entertain herself with daily doses of thinking too."
"It was a joke."

"Your jokes have gone too far."

"I wasn't the joker, quite the opposite. I was laughed at. Don't talk when a pure-blooded earl is thinking!"

Richard grunted, got up, and stretched his arms. While Jess sat covering his eyes, he took out his brand-new pen, ink, and paper, and began to write something down.

"Is it a private or business letter?" inquired Jess.

"Don't talk when a pure-blooded heir tries to arrange his thoughts," Richard answered absently.

"Isn't it a waste of parchment?"

"It's not parchment, it's that paper that they showed you in the store."

"Don't tell me that Lilian invented this paper."

"As you wish."

Jess and Richard fell silent. He shut his eyes again. Suddenly, it dawned on him, "What? You're trying to tell me that she—"

"Me?" Richard replied theatrically. "Maybe I tried, but you asked me not to. I also won't tell you that apart from the paper itself, she found a way to not only copy the text but PRINT it as well. Don't worry, she handed it over to the Crown and the Church, except medical books and books for children."

"Ugh!" summarized Jess. "My daughter will be laughing at me, too!"

"At least she will not be crying."

"Yes. Or me crying for her." Jess frowned.

"Right. Didn't Alicia talk about paper and books to you?"

"I don't know," answered Jess honestly. "I was so confused by the end of her speech. She might have said something about it. There was a lot to absorb anyway."

"Understandable. All right, what have you come up with?"

"Oh yes. First of all, I am a king's servant. Sometimes it's even best if no one knows about how often we meet. Since you are a crown prince, communicating with you would still draw attention, whereas nobody would find a relationship between a mother and her son suspicious."

"Yes. And yet, I would've put it differently."

"Also, they wanted to show that Lilian is extremely important for the Crown and the Crown protects her vehemently."

"I also thought about that, although I consider it a consequence, not a cause. What else?"

"Well, they wanted to show that they still trust me despite all my love adventures, which is good and bad at the same time. I'm not sure if I would want to know if I had a choice."
"Trust, check. What else?"

"And the rest is a mess," Jess answered honestly. I understand that there are still a lot of pitfalls, but—"

"Too few of them. On the other hand, you've been pushed too hard today, although that's partly your fault."

"What's wrong? Wait, I know. Because I got angry and wasn't trying to analyze?"

"Sounds about right. You also said that if Edward was stricter, he could force you to open up to him without Alicia's help. Yet, maybe he didn't want to take you by force. He wanted no resentment and bitterness from your side."

"Do you think so?"

"It was you who mentioned trust. One follows from the other. Trust and violence are incompatible."

"How are you so eloquent, Richard?" asked Jess. "And without a word of swearing. Amazing."

"It's practice. Moving on. They wanted to show you that Alicia is clever."

"I can see that."

"Why didn't you say so then?"

"It somehow stands as it is."

"You could have named it, made a conclusion. What do you think?"

"What of it?"

"I'll help you. Alicia is very clever… Alicia is a woman…"

"Well, if she is my mother, then I, too— Yes all right, I understand."

Richard raised his eyebrow but wasn't going to insist on a more definite answer.

"Fine. Let's discuss August the genius. As we know, you didn't have much contact with Lilian, and when you did, she was not herself for different reasons. Can you draw a conclusion from that?"

"Let them go to Maldonaya!"

"Say it, it's important!"

"Ughhh! Well, they showed Alicia's role, she is a woman. A woman can be clever, even very clever. This I still don't understand. A woman has to be… she can't be—"

"Stop! You understand everything but refuse to accept it. You need time. Remember the conclusion we've drawn and let's move on."

"Okay. August is a genius. Therefore, his child can also be a genius, even if she's a girl. Hmm! I'm an ass!"

Richard responded in quite a common way.

"Congratulations, Jess. Let's drink to it. They have just sent me a very good bottle. Pour me some."

"Why? Because I'm an ass?" Jess asked ironically, pouring a glass of brandy.

"Because you are a male march cat. I've already told you. No, let's simply drink to drawing conclusions."

Jess poured the brandy and rubbed the glass in his hands.

"So, let's drink to conclusions and their consequences!"

ঔ⃞ca

Richard couldn't stay for long. They had to literally drink the brandy on the go. Left alone, Jess started pacing around the room. The conversation wasn't enough. So, the choice was simple: he had to either fix the relationship with his wife or the relationship on the border, somewhere in a shithole. *What's good about the second option? Preserving my pride. But knowing the king, he would get me even there. What's good about the first option? I will have to submit to my wife's ways. Judging from her letters, she would not demand too much. As for the rest, you are young, clever, handsome. Will you not be able to make your wife adore you? Easy. Even if someone stands behind her, I will have to find him and finish him off to subject this cow to myself. Why not?*

Despite everything, Jess couldn't believe his wife's business abilities even with every piece of evidence. At the same time, there was no need to take chances.

He had to choose what to wear. He wouldn't have enough time to choose a full costume. He already had a mask.

What color? Green or black?

"Papa!"

Jess turned around and caught a small bullet, which knocked against his chest.

"Miranda!"

"Papa!"

Miranda was visiting the princesses at the palace. Together, the girls wrote down stories about Sherlock Holmes. As soon as they realized that the prince returned, Miranda realized her father had returned, as well.

Jess had his own rooms in the palace, and Mirrie had decided to check them out.

"Papa! I am so happy! Lou-Lou, sit!"

Some ten minutes passed before the child let go of her father's neck. Jerisson looked closer at her and did not recognize his daughter. He left her a pale, delicate aristocrat and found—he wasn't sure what.

Although the girl was short, she held herself with royal dignity. She was dressed in an unusual fashion—a blue skirt and a navy vest embroidered with beads, a white blouse with a gorgeous lace collar and a wide belt decorated with a knife in a beautiful sheath.

Miranda has a knife?

She also had a huge gray dog, evidently a Virman shepherd. The dog bared its teeth and growled at the sound of Jess' voice. Miranda had changed a lot. Her tanned, happy face looked more mature. Her black hair was braided with golden and pearl ribbons. Her lips were smiling.

"My little girl has grown so much!"

"I know! Lily says it often. Papa, this is Lou-Lou."

"Lou-Lou?"

In Jess's humble opinion the name wasn't suitable for such a huge gray beast. "Flayer" or "Nightmare" would suit him better.

"Yes! Lily gave her to me. Isn't she beautiful?"

"Lily?"

"I mean mother!"

"MOTHER?"

Jess didn't expect his daughter to call a strange woman her mother.

"I mean Lilian—your wife and my mother."

"Miranda, do you remember that she is not your real mother?" Jess carefully clarified.

Mirrie winced.

"Not the mother who gave birth to me, but the mother who brought me up. I don't remember my first mother. Lily is nice, and we both missed you!"

"I also missed you, Mirrie. I brought you some presents—"

Mirrie happily shrieked and rushed to open the box with presents. In five minutes, she returned to her father with a question.

"Papa, did you know that we produce all of this in Laveri?"

"I did. Do you not need any of it?"

"It can be useful in the household or as a dowry."

Jess almost choked from hearing such a statement.

"Are you going to the ball?"

"I am. Is Lilian going?"

"She is. But I don't know what she's wearing. She didn't prepare a dress and planned to borrow something from the Khangans."

Jess nodded.

"How do I look, my munchkin?"

Mirrie looked closer, walked in a circle around her father, and wrinkled her nose. "You smell, dad!"

Jess inhaled the air around him. *She is right. I traveled on the deck of a Virman ship and didn't have any change of clothes. Even so, I don't smell that bad.*

"I don't think I need to—"

"Papa, every person is required to have a shower at least once a day, every day! You should wash your clothes more often," said the child. "Have you dirtied me?" Miranda looked at her dress. "Luckily I can't see anything. Otherwise, Marcia would tell me off."

"Marcia?"

"Our dressmaker. She keeps telling me off for staining my new clothes."

Who dares to tell off a Viscountess?

"Does she tell you off? Who is this dressmaker, how does she dare?"

Miranda frowned.

"She's a human being. She worked hard to make my dresses, whereas I dare to rip or stain them out of mere carelessness. It's not good."

"So what? You are an earl's daughter!"

"A countess doesn't mean a pig," snapped the beloved child at her silly father.

Jess only muttered, "I just came down from the ship…"

Miranda contemplated.

"I can ask the servants to bring you clean clothes and a hot bathtub."

"I have clean clothes."

"But you can't put them on until you have a bath! Sit down, have some rest, and I'll talk to the servants."

Jess nodded, and his daughter stormed out of the room. The noble earl dropped heavily onto his seat and sighed. *Who's gone crazy? Miranda, the world, or myself?*

ಬ □ ಜ

Fifteen minutes later, someone knocked on the door. A few lackeys and a huge bathtub appeared in the doorway (it was a big wooden barrel and buckets with hot water). They rolled it in, placed it in the center of the room and poured the water inside.

As soon as the men left, they were replaced by two maids. Giggling, they helped the noble earl take off his clothes and sit inside the tub and began rubbing his body. They joked and laughed; slipping their playful fingers in places they shouldn't touch.

"What's going on here?" Miranda's clear voice echoed across the room.

"Uh," stumbled Jess.

"Get out!" shouted Mirrie like a grown-up.

The servants lifted their skirts and left. Miranda gave her father a reproachful look.

"I guess they entered here by accident. Bathe. I am going to see Angelina and Joliette."

The door slammed. Jess winced.

How did I manage to let Mirrie catch me out like that! I hope she doesn't tell Lilian. Goodness! My daughter, she is so different! She holds herself with royal dignity. How did my wife manage to teach her that? Although it wasn't just her; I raised my daughter, too. It's most likely that Mirrie inherited it from me. She must have!

Jess finished bathing and got dressed.

Ball? Perfect! Why not look at my wife from a distance first? We can solve our issues later. They say she is friendly with the Khangans—right. If Lilian is so precious to the Crown, it's better not to get on her bad side.

Although Jess was quick-tempered, arrogant and haughty, he wasn't a fool. He would test the waters before going into action.

A masquerade ball was a large, royal celebration. All the guests came wearing masks and costumes. Every sign of title, including titular bracelets, was to be taken off. Those who came without a partner were paired right at the entrance. The ballroom was full of wine, dancing, and flirting.

Edward liked balls. He and Jessamine used to adore dancing when they were young. The carnival ball gave them a sense of freedom. Now, it was his children's time to enjoy themselves. His dancing days had long since passed, and so he sat at the end of the ballroom. His royal corner had comfortable armchairs and a table with various foods. It was lit by candles that created a pleasant atmosphere. From there, the king had a full view of the Royal Hall. On that night, His Majesty Gardwig joined him.

Although it was against the royal code, nobody dared to object the will of the king, or rather two kings.

Given that the kings were soon to become relatives, they had a lot of things in common: both of them wore masks, both liked talking and neither liked dancing. For that matter, Gardwig was the only person Edward could call his friend. There was something in his biography that Edward found similar to his own.

Both of them had experienced a loveless marriage. Gardwig had turned out to be stronger than Edward, perhaps due to not having had his father as a king. He had come to the throne when he was just a boy and had been forced to survive.

Edward had felt genuinely upset that Gardwig did not have a son. Now, he was happy that the bloodline would continue, which was most important.

Edward made himself comfortable. At first, Tahir Djiamin din Dashar remained standing behind the king, but then Edward invited him to sit in the corner chair.

"Let's agree that I'm letting you sit in my presence tonight. The ball will last a long time. I don't want you to flake out by the end of it."

"As you say, Your Majesty."

"I suppose the countess will arrive a bit later?"

"She will arrive together with the Khangans, Your Majesty."

Amir Gulim is only a prince, but he will soon become king of the Khanganat. I need to establish contact. It would be perfect if he got married to one of the princesses, either Angelina or Joliette. As for his faith, why does it matter when it comes to the welfare of the state? The union between Ativerna, the Khanganat and Wellster will scare away the vultures of Loris!

Gardwig arrived second. He settled in his chair, glanced at Tahir and with a careless wave of his hand sent off his whole retinue except a couple of trusted servants.

"Your Majesty."

"Your Highness."

They bowed slightly to each other and smiled from behind their tiny masks.

"How do you feel, my friend?"

Edward lowered his eyes.

"Since I put Tahir in charge of my illness, I am feeling much better. How is your foot?"

"I guess I will need to ask you for permission to invite your medicus to mine," Gardwig said with a smile.

"Of course. Sir din Dashar!"

"Your Majesty?" Tahir stood and bowed hastily.

"I hope you will extend my friend the courtesy of inspecting his sore leg. Your Majesty Gardwig—"

"Your Majesty, I am your guest and your will is my law. But without my student—"

"I will give her permission," nodded Edward and briefly explained to Gardwig. "The Countess of Earton is the wife of my nephew and the main reason why Sir din Dashar hasn't gone back to the Khanganat yet."

"Why is it so?" Gardwig raised his eyebrows.

"Because I promised my mistress to teach her everything I know, Your Majesty. I keep my word."

"Do the Khangans keep their word when it is given to a woman?"

"To any creature, even if you give your word to yourself. The Heavenly Mare reads it in your heart. She would trample the heart of a liar and a traitor."

Gardwig shrugged. He viewed them as barbarians who didn't know Aldonai. *What can I say?*

"I will be glad to see you and your student."

Tahir bowed low and stepped back into the shadows. It seemed like another interesting case was coming. The crowd kept arriving.

৪০ ෆ

Lily arrived with Amir's retinue. She strongly suspected that she would not be left alone. Therefore at first, she pretended to be wearing a Khangan dress and mask. Beneath the blankets decorated with Khangan ornaments, however, was a different outfit.

It was a long black dress with a cape. She had sewn the strips of fabric in such a way that they created the illusion of wings.

It was easy to get rid of the blanket and slip into the room as someone new. She even changed her mask from white to black. She gave everything else to Amir's servants. That way, nobody would recognize her, and she would be free to have fun, dance, and flirt. She was a woman, not a workhorse. She must at least try to relax.

৪০ ෆ

The "Virman" Richard and the "Aldon" entered the hall in a free manner. They were immediately chosen as partners, and the men led the ladies around the room in a dance, then dissolved into the crowd. Any courtier knew the art of disappearance. Richard headed toward his father.

He saw the turban of some Khangan, and saw there was a serious conversation going on. Jerisson decided to walk across the ballroom and look for his wife. *Alright, where are the large ladies?* Nobody bothered to tell the Earl of Earton that his wife was not fat anymore, but only plump instead. He couldn't find the haze of pink in the crowd. He shifted his eyes from one lady to another, admiring their seductive cleavage, round hands, and brilliant eyes.

Jerisson got bored strolling around the room and decided to dance a little. He would continue his search later.

☙ ❧

"Lilian,"

Lily turned around so abruptly that her braid knocked the glass out of the hands of the Marquess Falion.

"Marquess!"

"I am glad to see you, Li—"

"No-no," Lily waved her hand in the air. "Tonight is a masquerade. A carnival! Don't say my name out loud."

"But what do I call you then? My queen? My goddess?" It was too much.

"You can call me Mousy, but only tonight!"

"You don't look like a mouse!"

"What about a flying mouse?"

"A bat?"

Falion smiled.

"All right, in that case, you can call me Alex tonight."

Lily gave him a smile.

"Do you want to dance, Mousy?"

"Alex, that's not how you invite a lady for a dance."

Black lace wings floated in the air. Lily danced poorly, but it was pure bliss to dance with a partner like Falion. Alexander led her confidently and calmly, prompted her steps, smiled from the corner of his lips and made jokes.

The evening was suddenly starting to live up to expectations. The hall was dirty, sad, and stinky. *Enough! No one will entertain you! You have to amuse yourself. That's the only way to enjoy the local crowd.*

Three steps, a spin, a walk, and two more spins.

"Alex, you dance very well."

"Mousy, aren't you adorable!"

"I am really about to fly up in the air!" laughed Lily. "I feel so light!"

"You look charming tonight."

Common empty talk—she would blame the dance for the fast beating of her heart, her spinning head, and the floating stars in her eyes. *The dancing is to blame.*

Lily didn't notice the tall brunette in a mask. She passed him once, then twice…

☙ ❧

Jerisson leaned against the wall, sipped wine from a tall glass, and looked at the dancing couples. He couldn't find his wife. He just watched, rested, and enjoyed his life. He was alive. *Is that not a good enough reason to enjoy myself?*

Musical laughter struck his ear.

"Mousy—"

Falion?

Although they weren't particularly close, Jess and Alex were friendly with each other. Jerisson recognized the sound of Falion's voice. He was surprised to see the son of the Old Pike laughing with a woman, for he was known to treat his women coldly and with indifference.

Jerisson carefully inspected his old friend's companion. She was a beauty, no doubt. He couldn't see her face, but her body looked gorgeous.

She had a stately bust and long legs, like a noble virmaness. Her hair was fair and long, with strands of black pearls woven into it. The dress she wore was just extraordinary.

Should I try to speak to her?

Jess didn't consider Falion a close friend, therefore he could easily steal his woman. *It's already happened a couple of times, why not do it again? Although no, it isn't worth it.*

He had to find his wife and take a closer look at her. It was a bad time to start running after other women. *I need to take a walk outside or sit on a bench. I wonder where that cow could be?*

☙ ❧

"The cow" dutifully accepted a few dances from Falion and decided that that was enough. She had to get outside to the garden and breathe fresh air. As much as she tried to enjoy herself, dancing wasn't her favorite thing.

People sweat a lot when dancing. The hall smelled of sweat, perfume, dirty clothes, and rosewater. *No, thank you! Spending a night in a pigsty is better!*

Lily fanned herself and went outside. Falion wanted to keep her company, but a little fat man distracted him, and Lily slipped out onto the veranda.

Whether the garden was a pleasant space was also questionable since it was full of waste and excrement. Thus taking a walk meant risking her new shoes. They weren't of perfect design, but after much painful effort, she got something similar to what she wanted. This world was still too far from high heels and wedges, but she had managed to convince a local artisan to make her something of the kind. *Why not? High heels make a woman more confident. I remember seeing a little arbor with a bench somewhere around here…*

When a female figure appeared in the entrance to the arbor, Jerisson was genuinely surprised. He didn't have time to swear or send the lady away.

"I'm sorry," uttered the lady. "I didn't see you inside."

A fair braid against black fabric. Jerisson recognized it.

It's the woman who danced with Falion! Is she too large a prey?

No, I would not do it inside the ballroom. But here…it would not lead to anything serious. It's only flirting!

"Madam, your company is my pleasure. Please. I suppose you were also bored inside the Royal Hall?"

The woman bowed her head slightly.

"I suppose. Thank you for your kind invitation."

She took a few steps inside the alcove, touched the bench with her fingers, took a handkerchief from her pocket, wiped the bench with it, and sat down.

"Thank you once more." She threw back her head and closed her eyes. Silence fell inside the alcove. Lily didn't feel like talking. Jerisson couldn't think what to do next. *This is strange, women always run after me themselves…*

༺ ༻

Anna of Wellster danced, laughed and enjoyed herself as much as she could. *Aldonai is gracious! How wonderful it is being here!* Everyone bowed before her. *I am a princess! The shine of jewelry, the rustle of silks…Yes, I want to be a queen! I am made for it!*

A Khangan with a black beard bent his face over hers and held a hand to his heart. Anna accepted the invitation to dance. *Why not?*

The music sounded louder and louder, when suddenly…

"Anna, my sweetheart."

Anna was lucky they had managed to move apart from the crowd. When she started to faint, the Khangan caught her, and he ran to one of the alcoves. He patted her cheeks and put a vial of smelling salts to her nose.

"Anna, darling, it's not the right time for fainting!"

It took no less than five minutes for Anna to come to her senses.

"Lons?"

"It's me, darling."

"You—are alive!"

"Yes. I am alive and well. I came here for you."

"For me?"

Anna's head was spinning. He had come for her. *Lons is not a dead man; he's a living catastrophe! He won't leave me alone. He could spoil everything. I won't pass the tests from midwives, even despite all my witch remedies. What does he want?*

"You are my wife, and I've found us a place. Almost no one goes there. It's peaceful; quiet. We will be governors there. My master—" Lons remembered to keep Lilian Earton's person a secret. "He is a good man. He understood everything and will accept my wife in his household."

"You want me to come with you?"

"You are my wife! Why not? Do you not love me anymore?"

Anna hastily nodded. *Yes, Aldonai, yes, don't start a scandal!*

"I do. But, how? How are you alive?"

"I was lucky. We need to leave immediately…"

Anna shook her head in denial.

"We cannot leave right now."

"Why not?"

"Because," Anna had already recovered, and her tongue began weaving verbal laces. "Our embassy came here to sign a contract. Everything has already been discussed. I am to become the prince's wife. I need to be here now. If I run away, we will never be able to leave the capital."

"We will. I know how."

Lons hesitated. He hadn't thought of how they were going to escape to the harbor and find the ship. The Virmans could help, but only once the tide came in the morning, by which time the rest would have noticed her disappearance. The Virmans would do anything for the countess, only he wasn't the countess. He paused, thinking about putting Anna on a ship without her belongings. Anna felt his hesitation.

"They are going to look for us. Besides, we will need money."

"Yes…"

"I can take my jewelry,"

"I love you even without jewelry."

"Why not take it? If not for us, at least for our children."

Anna looked so innocent.

"Anna, I can't live without you."

She put both hands on his chest.

"Pull yourself together. If they see us together—"

"When am I going to see you? How?"

Anna contemplated.

"I am a guest in these parts. I don't know anything here. Do you come to the palace often?"

Lons nodded. He could come in the company of Lilian or Miranda Earton.

"I can come to the palace, but it would be better if we met in the church near here. Go there for the morning service."

Anna nodded.

"I won't come tomorrow, but I will come eventually. I promise."

"I will let you know when everything is ready. Do you agree to leave with me?"

Anna nodded.

"Yes. Get ready."

Lons kissed her hand.

"Sweetheart—"

"I love you, too," said Anna. "Leave now. If they see us together…"

Lons nodded and disappeared behind the curtain. For at least ten minutes, Anna sat still. It was a miracle that no one noticed her absence. It was so easy to lose sight of a mentee in the hustle and bustle of the ball. The most important danger had been eliminated. She wouldn't need to run away immediately.

How do I get out of this? Who did Altres Lort advise me to speak to? Not now, not at the ball but… I am not going to run away Maldonaya knows where with a resurrected husband! Not when I am about to become the Queen of Ativerna! Lons died, end of story. He shouldn't have shown up alive. Now I have no choice but to send him back to the dead.

Getting fresh air after the overcrowded ballroom had an intoxicating effect on Lily. She sat with her head thrown back and almost floated. The feeling was good. The man opposite her was silent and didn't make any efforts to get closer. *The better! I need some rest, not flirting.* But alas, men are not perfect, and the silence was quickly broken.

"It's strange that such a beautiful lady should be alone. If I was your date, I wouldn't leave your side for one minute!"

"What makes you say that I'm beautiful?" Lily retorted lazily. "Maybe my whole face is covered in warts!"

"You have a wonderful voice!" said Jess staring at her breasts.

I ought to react and snort, but I am so lazy...

"And a wonderful pair of ears, don't I?"

"Ears?" flustered Jerisson. His long practice of enticing women had taken a toll on his charm. "I am sure that you're beautiful inside and out. Every part of your body is—"

"Undoubtedly beautiful."

There was a triple dose of malice in her voice. Jerisson sighed with repentance, changing his tactic.

"How can you laugh at the unhappy man smitten with your beauty? You have a cruel heart!"

Lily sighed. *Another gigolo! I'm so fed up with this!*

"The lady is grateful for shelter. Goodbye now."

Lily wanted to stand up and leave the alcove, but Jess blocked her way.

"I beg you don't get offended. I didn't have any bad intentions."

Lily sighed and explained. "You will start apologizing now. I will accept your apology, and we will continue our pleasant evening. You will then start flirting again, I will want to leave, but you will restrain me once more. This will last until one of us gets bored. Consider that I already am."

Jerisson blinked in confusion.

"Is my company that unpleasant?"

"Like any stranger, you are of no importance to me."

"In that case, let me introduce myself to you. Jerisson, Earl of Earton."

Lily nearly collapsed.

"Jerisson?"

The earl was surprised to see the masked face change to a deathlike pallor. For a second, it seemed like she was going to fall. She took a deep breath instead and straightened. Lily was really taken aback.

Although she had found his voice familiar, she didn't recognize her husband with the mask on. When he introduced himself, it was like a punch in the stomach.

"Do we know each other? I can't believe it. I would have never forgotten such a beauty!"

Yeah, we've met a couple of times—in our marital bed!

The woman shook her head in denial. *Keep calm, take a breath... Devil! What now? Hello, dear husband? Yes, I am your wife, you prick? No. It's better not to dispel the magical confusion of the evening. Long live Lily the Mouse!*

"I didn't know that the embassy had already returned."

"Yes, we arrived this morning."

"And went straight to the ball?"

"His Majesty's wish is law."

"Did Your Majesty invite you here for a reason then?"

"It's a secret of the state."

Lily raised her eyebrows.

"In that case, I won't question you. I know your wife, by the way. She is a most charming woman. Is she here?"

The mask couldn't hide Jerisson's grimace of disgust.

"Y-yes, she is inside."

Lily had already realized that Jess didn't recognize her and so decided to take advantage of the situation. She couldn't let herself throw a fit as Lilian. But now, in the twilight and with a mask, she could let herself go. Either way, it was useless to reveal herself and settle marriage disputes.

"Send her my greetings. A charming woman! You are a lucky man."

"Y-yes, of course."

"She is such a talented medicus! It's so unusual for a woman."

"How long have you known her?"

"I can't say exactly, but she has already managed to impress the courtiers. My friend said he understands you well. Such a woman should be kept in the wilderness, out of sight, or else someone might steal her. The capital is full of temptations."

"Yes."

"Will she not be jealous about us being here together?"

"N-no. She is with the princesses now," Jess managed to come up with a sound lie.

Of course she is, thought Lily.

"I've heard that it was you who told her of Baron Holmes, or did she hear these stories as a child?"

"Baron Holmes?"

Jerisson reminded himself of a parrot, a silly parrot. He had to put an end to it.

"Will you introduce yourself to me, madam?"

"Oh, no," she answered him with quiet laughter. "It's a masquerade, and I am in a hurry. You also shouldn't leave your wife alone for so long."

Jerisson grimaced again. He didn't want to leave this woman without having found out about her.

"Will we ever see each other again?"

"Obviously. I am a frequent guest at court."

"I meant something more private."

Lily clenched her fists. *He has a wife and no shame!*

"Your wife is waiting for you. Besides, I am married, too. Let me pass—"

"But will I recognize you if we meet again?"

Lily grinned and took a little black pearl from her ear. It had been made by master Leitz.

"Take it as a memory of me. Be sure that you will recognize me by it."

She heard the sound of gravel. For a moment, Jess was distracted, and Lily pushed past him with such force that the noble earl nearly fell over. He wouldn't dare to grab onto her clothes to keep steady.

The woman slipped past and flew out of the arbor like a rocket...and just in time. She saw Falion walking down the pathway. The woman rushed to him and clung to his sleeve.

"Get me out of here, quick!"

ಬ ಆ

Jerisson watched his beautiful stranger rush toward Falion. He frowned. It didn't seem like the two were in a close romantic relationship. Otherwise, Falion would've hugged her instead of taking her by the elbow. Although he did it with great care, there was a certain aura that distinguished lovers from friends. Jess twisted the little earring in his fingers. *An expensive item! I will get another chance to see her. Next time, the conversation will be different.* Although he would have to dedicate some time to his wife, the beauty in black left a deep impression.

‎ಌ ಐ

Holding onto Falion, Lily was thinking the same thoughts. Alexander noticed the woman was shivering tremendously. Therefore, he didn't go back to the hall. He left Lily for just a moment and returned with a glass of wine.

"Drink."

Lily obediently took a couple of sips.

"What happened?"

"It was my husband."

Lily wasn't going to lie. Besides, the wine added to her honesty.

"Jerisson Earton?"

There was no surprise in Falion's voice, and it made Lily angry.

"Did you know of his return?"

"My father returned, meaning that your husband returned, too. I thought you knew."

Lily shivered.

"Yes! I know now!"

"Drink some more wine."

The cup flew into the wall. Lily didn't want to live. She recalled how she had flirted and laughed with Falion in front of her husband and it made her want to die.

"Take me to the carriage."

"Lilian—"

"I want to go home. Take me to the carriage, please." The last phrase seemed to break into a wail, and Falion gave in to the lady's whim.

"Can I accompany you?"

"Yes! Just faster, please."

No one noticed their departure.

ಌ ಐ

Jerisson danced, had fun, talked, and couldn't believe his ears. Many people said many different things about Lilian, sometimes in too much detail. Some scolded her for arrogance, others praised for her knowledge of medicine. There were people who were convinced that she was the king's favorite, others thought that Edward treated her as a daughter. People talked a lot, and all their different opinions still agreed on a few things: Lilian was beautiful, smart, charming, and it was good to be her friend. Except for Baroness Ormt, who persistently tried to be her enemy. While the king was sick, she had begun to spread gossip about Lilian Earton. When the king recovered, she flew out of the court faster than she could spread her lies. His Majesty made it clear that he would not tolerate disrespectful gossip behind his back.

Jess approached the king and bowed down. Edward nodded and waved his finger asking Jess to come closer.

"Are you enjoying yourself?"

"I tried to find my wife, but I cannot see her anywhere."

Edward looked around the room and called the master of ceremonies. He asked him something in a whisper and frowned at the reply.

"Indeed, your wife was here, but she left for home a couple of minutes ago.

Pity! She must have left while I was speaking to that beautiful stranger, thought Jess.

"I hope to pay her a visit tomorrow."

"Impossible."

"Your Majesty?"

"You will be at the palace tomorrow. I will invite Lilian here. I want your meeting to happen before my eyes."

Jess looked offended.

"Do you not trust me?"

"No, I don't," replied the king in a calm voice. "I don't trust either of you. Feelings, passions, insults—you will get into a fight, and I will be the one to sort everything out! It's better if you speak in my presence."

There was nothing Jess could say in his defense. He took his leave and dissolved into the crowd. *Since my wife is gone, I can let myself join the dancing.*

⊗ ⌐ ⌑

As soon as Lily found herself in the carriage, she curled into a ball and huddled in the corner of the seat. Memories of the former Lilian filled her head, and they were far from pleasant. When one loved and was separated from one's lover by the blows of fate, he or she still retained the feeling of self-affirmation. The unfortunate fatty had found herself in a situation where her love was met with cold indifference. Her love might have been silly, hopeless, hysterical, but at least it was love.

If Jerisson had expressed a bit more love, care, attention, and understanding... had he sent her at least one flower... It wasn't only the attempts that killed the fatty, but also the absence of love. Having lost the only thing that connected her to her loved one, she had lost all her will to live.

Lily was split in two. The former Lilian Earton still loved, she still trembled from the mere sound of his voice. She dreamed of seeing warmth in the blue of his eyes. As for the new Lily, she preached one principle: *Anyone who doesn't love me can go to hell. I have my Alex.*

Breathe in, breathe out. Keep calm.

"Stop the carriage," exhaled Lily.

Falion banged on the door of the carriage with all his might. The horses slowed down, and Lily almost fell out onto the road. She would have dropped onto her knees had Falion not caught her. The woman threw up. Her reaction to nerves was severe vomiting until she had dry, painful spasms. Alexander stayed with her. He supported her with both hands, wiped sweat from her forehead, and even tried to give her water. After a few sips of water, the vomiting intensified. It was no less than an hour before she even slightly came to her senses. Falion held her in his arms and looked at her with genuine sympathy.

"Lilian, Lily…"

Lily buried her face in his shoulder and closed her eyes for a moment. She wanted to feel protected and loved, at least for a little while.

"Everything will be fine."

"Is it because of…him?"

Lily nodded.

"I will kill him."

"Stop it, Alexander. Don't." For the first time in a while, Lily was calm. "It won't change anything."

"You will be free!"

"The king won't forgive you. Don't."

"Your one word will be enough for me to do it."

Lily was silent. If a man was capable of this—of bringing a woman to her senses, seeing her unfortunate and crippled, it meant that…

"Alexander…"

"You can always count on me. Always."

Lily sighed.

"I would really want to. Oh, Alexander."

For a while, Falion was silent. Finally, he touched her forehead with his lips.

"You know."

Lily squeezed his hand.

"Let's go, Alexander. I need to go home." Falion obeyed without a word. They sat in the carriage and remained silent. The silence was louder than a hundred words.

"I will do everything to make you happy."
"I will not let you put yourself in danger."
"I will decide myself."
"Don't sacrifice your happiness for mine. Aldonai will help."
"Aldonai helps those who help themselves."

Late that night, Lily looked at the sleeping Miranda. As ever, the girl had climbed into her bed. Having snitched the blanket, the dogs lay at her feet. Lily took a deep breath. She was calmer now and could think straight. She carried out a logical analysis.

Do you still love your husband or is it a physiological reaction? A defense mechanism? It was most likely the second option, which made it better already. *Do you need such a womanizer in your life?*

Lily bit her lip. The answer was unequivocal. She still needed him but on her own terms. She would be happy if he agreed to them; if not, he could go to hell. She could divorce him and find a new husband. *Hold on, you aren't in the twenty-first century where you can divorce six times a week,* thought Lily. *They will eat you alive for it. Or will they choke?*

Either way, she had an advantage. The first thing was that he had no conscience. Being at the ball where his wife was present, he dared to flirt with a strange woman. Secondly, she was now warned about his return and could prepare for his visit. *Hold tight, Earl of Earton, lest you end up falling from your saddle!* With Falion, things were more complicated. He loved her. Otherwise, there would've been no such intensity in his eyes and deeds. *Do I love him back? Or maybe it is a desire for protection, a desire to be weak?*

If so, it was bad. She was strong and clever. *What would happen to me if I became weak? I wouldn't survive a day.*

And Falion, is it love or mere want? I don't know, I don't understand!

She looked at the peacefully sleeping girl. Lily continued her internal monologue.

There is one certainty in this life. Miranda loves her father. No matter if he's good or bad, it's worth giving Jerisson Earton a chance for the sake of Mirrie. The fact that he chases after any woman gives me an opportunity to appreciate that I don't love him and will help to judge his actions pragmatically. If I loved him, it would hurt me to know about his behavior. As it is, I can laugh in his face. I will try to fix things between us for the sake of Mirrie. God help me in this noble task.

☙ ❧

In the morning, Lily decided not to go to Taral. *What difference does it make? I am unfit to perform at my best.* That day, everything dropped out of her hands. She ripped her belt and nearly poked her eye with a hairpin. At least Mirrie was pleased and happy.

"Papa has arrived!"

If it weren't for Mirrie's love for her father, Lily would never agree to make up with her husband. Yet Amir was right. She should speak to Edward and create a marriage contract to protect Mirrie in case she and Jerisson had an irresolvable disagreement. It was important to ensure her well-being. The woman looked at herself in the mirror.

Perfect. Green skirt-trousers, green shirt (white trimmed), simple jewelry (the bracelet and the ring were compulsory, plus a pair of earrings). The only luxury in her dress was a pair of white lace gloves. Even reincarnation couldn't save her from the vile habit of biting her nails.

"My Lady, receive the messenger from the king."

The messenger bowed, knelt, and handed her a scroll. Lily broke the seal and skimmed through the text. *"To attend the court immediately, upon receiving this scroll."* If it says immediately, she should obey. *Why so urgent? Because of the earl's arrival.* Lily would've been more surprised if His Majesty didn't supervise their first meeting.

"I will ask them to prepare the horse. It will be quicker that way."

Lily nodded to the servant who was standing at the door, and he ran to the stables. The woman fixed her dress and faced the window. She took a deep breath and repeated in her head.

Keep calm, Lily, your heart is pounding like mad. If you throw up again (on the earl!), you will surely not come up with a compromise. Breathe, easy!

☙ ❧

A small cavalcade made up of six people—the messenger, Lilian, and four guards—wheeled across the road, splashing mud everywhere. Lily was glad she had chosen to wear dark green, almost black clothes. Although there were not many puddles on the road, her clothes would certainly get dirty. The stains were luckily invisible against the dark fabric.

Lidarh slowed down, and the woman began to calm down a little. Lily spoke to herself.

It's fine. You've got this. Get yourself together.

You've been preparing for this meeting since you learned of the existence of a husband. All the power is in your hands. The king is interested in keeping you satisfied. You have friends. You are the center of this small, but very unique society. You have your own production. If your husband decided to lock you up in some tower, he would get a pretty good ransom, only to keep you free.

Miranda loves you. Alicia respects and values you.

No one would dare to intervene in your family affairs. Yet, it's the same as in the twenty-first century. A lot of things are forbidden, but if you need something badly, you can find a way.

Our first conversation needs to go so well that my husband won't change the status quo. In a way, I have to downplay my strengths. For any man is like a spring—if you put too much pressure on him, he will bounce against your forehead. But if you do it slowly, neatly and politely, you will get your way. This method is known to any surgeon. Very carefully, very neatly; no surgery is carried out otherwise. There are chances for success.

And what's easier? To give in or to explain? If I'm being honest, I don't want any marriage with Earl Earton, or, in fact, any kind of relationship. But one needs a compromise. So! I will be polite and gentle. The most important thing is not to forget to bat my eyelashes.

ℬ ☐ ℭ

Jerisson was comfortably seated in the royal study. Edward looked serious.

"Jess, I want you and Lilian to find common ground."

Jess rubbed his temple. He hadn't overdone it the day before, but it seemed the stress and tiredness negatively impacted his well-being, for he had a little tingle in his temple.

"I will try. What are your plans for my wife, Uncle?"

"What?"

"Half of the court thinks that she is your new favorite."

Edward didn't even start to object.

"Moron!"

"Uncle!"

"I have been your uncle since you were born. I respect and love your wife as a beautiful and clever woman. Do you want me to swear with my memory of Jessie that I have no other intentions for Lilian? You don't? Good. You can consider it my order. Try to fix your relationship with your wife. Do it at least for your daughter."

Jess was about to lose his temper, but the mention of Miranda was like a bucket of cold water poured over his head. Indeed, Miranda loved her new mother, and would not forgive him if he used her beloved Lilian. The earl understood this already. Besides, spending time with Lilian did her good. She had turned into a real princess and grown more mature. Jerisson was ready to do a lot for his daughter.

"The Countess Lilian Elizabeth Mariella Earton."

His Majesty nodded to Jerisson, pointing to the corner of the study and ordered them to invite the countess in.

ഹ ൽ

Lilian entered Edward's study and curtsied.

"Your Majesty."

"Good to see you, Lilian. Please."

"I am also glad to see you." Upon casting a quick glance from under her eyelashes, Lilian discovered that Edward was beaming, and she returned a radiant smile. "How do you feel?"

"I feel like a burden to you. Tahir also doesn't leave my side."

"I am glad, Your Majesty, but I also hope that you remember to follow the regime—"

"Tahir keeps telling me the same. Lilian, I invited you for a reason."

Lily raised her eyebrows but remained silent.

"Your husband has returned."

"I am glad, Your Majesty."

If Lilian hadn't bumped into him the day before, she would've been very shocked to meet him. Right then, her adrenaline was low. Adrenal glands weren't made of iron and couldn't produce it in industrial quantities.

"Is that all you have to say?"

"It depends on what my husband says."

"Jerisson!"

A dark shadow rose from the corner of the study.

ഹ ൽ

To say that Jess was shocked was to say nothing. He expected to see Lily as anything—except the golden-haired beauty with a royal demeanor and a slight smile on her pink lips. She wore a gorgeous dress, expensive jewelry, and had an elegant gait. Her every word and every gesture was endowed with confidence. At first, he could not even move.

Pink cow? I wish she looked like that before! Someone said Earton? Such women should be hidden with maximum security—inside the husband's bed without the right to leave. There must be a lot of people who want her. What a woman! What a body! Yes, she is slightly plump, but she doesn't look like a cow at all. A softness of figure, a smooth floating goddess!

His complete admiration for her figure was natural.

And this—is my wife? I cannot believe my eyes!

If Jess had seen such a beautiful woman at court, he wouldn't have been able to walk by. He'd have wooed her. And this woman was his wife.

Lilian, Countess of Earton—even then, she held herself like a queen.

It was true Lily was in complete control of her body. Everything that happened the day before was a thing of the past.

She dropped in a low curtsey and stretched out her hand, just like Lons taught her.

"I hope you had a pleasant voyage, dear Earl?"

"Erm, yes…"

Lily refrained from a snort.

A superman, a heartbreaker and—a rudderless dummy!

He looked just like one, with a bewildered and astonished facial expression.

"I am glad to see you're well and safe. I hope that Jamie delivered his best?"

"J-Jamie?"

"Jamie Meytl, he is also the Baron of Donter. Tahir Djiamin din Dashar taught both of us, and the young man went to work as a healer on the Virman ship."

"Oh, yes, if it weren't for him, there would've been plenty more dead."

Jess remembered how, swearing violently, Jamie had cleaned the Virmans' wounds, disinfected them, bandaged them, and changed the dressings.

"Have you seen Miranda today? She is not in the palace, but I will free her from her studies today so she can spend time with her father."

❦

Edward snorted, not caring about dropping his royal dignity. Those two didn't seem like they were going to kill each other right away. *What else do I need? If they fight later, I won't be able to stop them.* From what he could see, Jess was confused. He hadn't expected such a turn of events and was starting to devise a new course of behavior.

Oh, Jess, you will have to run after your wife!

Lilian was obviously having a little fun. Perhaps someone had let her know in advance, and she had prepared for the meeting. *Who was so clever as to do that? I will need to send them a royal thank you!* She was now calm and serene on the surface. Even Jess wouldn't be able to get to her easily.

"Jess, take your wife home. You have a house in the capital, go there and spend time with your wife."

"Yes, Your Majesty," said Jess mechanically.

Lily bowed in a curtsey and took a step toward the door. Jess suddenly realized that he ought to follow her and take her by the elbow. Although Lily didn't pull out her hand, it was as if Jess was holding a wooden doll.

❦

They walked in silence along the palace corridor. Jerisson was trying to come to grips with such change. He left the cow behind and took in the queen.

Maybe the air in Earton has miraculous powers?

He wouldn't have recognized her on the street.

How do I behave in front of her?

She was calm. She walked, smiling to her own thoughts, replying to greetings.

What is there for me to do? Argue? There seems to be nothing to argue about. Besides, it would be silly to argue in the palace. We'll speak once we get home. She is truly a beauty, and holds herself like a royal!

༄ ༅

If Jerisson could read Lilian's thoughts, he'd be much surprised. The beautiful woman wasn't calm at all. On the contrary. There were two persons inside her, the former Lilian and the new Lilian, who felt contradictory things. Everything was pretty clear with the first Lily: unhappy love, lawful rape, and a staged suicide. It was, of course, the killers who made sure she was dead, but the reason for her death was clomping next to her as if nothing had happened.

One could understand the former Lilian. One couldn't take away the fact that Jess was handsome. His face was attractive. He wasn't Leonardo di Caprio, but Lily never liked sweet-looking boys. *Leave their faces for decorating chocolate bars!*

Jess looked like a real man. There was something charming in him. On top of it all, his body was excellent. He wasn't quite as large as Erik, but his muscles were big. She could understand her former self. It was easy to fall in love with such a handsome man.

On the other hand, no housewife could ever have as many cockroaches in her kitchen as the amount of ill-wishers the earl had.

His diagnosis was clear: reluctance to cut off his whims, selfishness, and self-admiration in aggravation and a deep disregard for women. His main advantage was that he loved Miranda, or maybe that Miranda loved him. The rest were flaws, apart from the pretty face and the earldom. *I wonder what they think about separate habitation here?* The answer wasn't positive—only if a couple had children and mutually agreed to live separately. They needed to make children, after all.

Lily contemplated. The earl's animalistic instincts played to her advantage. He licked his chops at the very sight of her. He wanted her like a cat wanted a bowl of cream. Even then, he was ogling at her breasts. It wasn't a bad sign. She wanted to be honest with herself. She had had to leave her boyfriend, Alex, in another life. She hadn't had any man in this world. She was a healthy, young woman, and her instincts were also healthy. She knew she couldn't allow herself to start a personal relationship at work. It was her sacred rule to keep work relationships professional.

Any sex, any love affair has to happen outside of work, the hospital or the factory, even if your office is a hut in the tundra. Otherwise, you risk creating an impression that any man can ash his cigarette in your ashtray.

Jess was, after all, her legal husband. *How do I become his one and only and make it last forever?* There is so much written and said about it, but there is no answer to this question. Every woman had to find the answer for herself. She would try to find that answer, too.

☙ ☖ ☗

While Lily was contemplating her husband, he also thought about his wife and admired her. *Her gait, her smile, her form! I would happily drag her into some secluded corner!* Jess had altogether forgotten about the beautiful woman he had met the day before. *I have my own beautiful wife! Only she doesn't need me.* Jerisson was very good at recognizing the signs that told him when ladies liked him. They tried to draw attention to themselves, batted their eyes, tried as hard as they could…

His own wife was indifferent to him. She walked beside him as if he were an old, impotent man.

I wish I knew what she was thinking. Her hands are covered in delicate lace, her eyes are calm and downcast, her lips smiling… Everyone wants me, everyone but her! It's a shame, gentlemen!

A hunter's instinct slowly arose in him, replacing resentment, anger, and irritation. Such is the world where men happily forgive a beautiful woman any sin. Lily broke the silence only at the exit.

"I arrived here by horse. Are you in a carriage?"

"No, but I suppose I could find a horse."

"I will ask one of my bodyguards."

"Bodyguards?"

"After the attempt, my people don't let me go alone anywhere."

It was clear from her voice she wasn't lying or exaggerating.

"There is always a horse for me in the royal stables."

"I will wait for you on the road then."

Lilian turned on her heel. A couple of Virmans waited for her, one of them holding a gorgeous Avarian horse by the reins. Jess could immediately tell the breed. He was purebred and cost a lot of money.

"Is it yours?"

"Meet Lidarh."

Upon hearing his name, the horse proudly bent his neck. Lily patted him on his gorgeous mane.

"He's truly handsome, isn't he?"

Jess nodded.

"He's splendid."

Jess said this looking at the woman, not the horse. Lilian gracefully saddled her horse.

"We'll be waiting for you."

The servant needed at least ten minutes before he could find Jess a horse. All the while, the earl tried to find a common language with Lidarh.

Alas, feeling his mistress' mood, the horse's behavior was far from exemplary. He snorted, turned away, refused to take the apple, and almost bit the earl's shoulder. *Aren't horses herbivores? Someone must have forgotten to let Lidarh know about that.* Finally, the earl was given another horse, and the party left the palace grounds.

ఎ ⌐ ఆ

Alas, that day, the stars decided to mock the earl. A combination of several factors proved fatal. First, Miranda decided to head to the earl's house in the capital, to see her father. Her father was away, and Miranda decided to use the opportunity to go to the stables and play with Shallah. The Virmans who guarded the girl's safety followed after her to the stables. Second, having found out about the earl's arrival, Baroness Ormt decided to pay a visit. She wanted to discuss his wife's behavior with him. *I, the poor baroness, was shamefully pushed away, out of the king's favor, the place that I've been warming up for myself so diligently! If only the earl could give his wife a beating or lock her up at home, the place next to the king would free. The old love was better than the new.* For some reason, many ladies didn't like the countess.

Miranda jumped out of the stables for a moment to see to the noise outside and saw a gilded carriage from which emerged a lady in a luxurious dress. As for Mirrie herself, cleaning the horse wasn't the same as sitting in the living room. Her wide and dirty apron securely covered her clothes. No one would have recognized the Viscountess of Earton with her hair tied up and her face covered in dirt. The lady looked around and saw a dirty boy standing in the yard. She demanded imperiously, "Hey, you! Come here!"

Mirrie wouldn't even think of obeying.

"What do you want?"

She wasn't scared. The Virmans were at her every beck and call. They wouldn't let her get hurt. It never occurred to Mirrie that someone might cause her harm.

The baroness flew into a rage. *What on earth is going on? How does this low creature dare to be rude to me?!* The woman nodded to her coachman.

"Bring him to me! Now!"

Mirrie didn't even have time to squeak. Struggling against the cruel hands and overwhelmed with indignation, she forgot about everything—about the knife in her boot, about how to free herself from the grip, about the Virmans in the stables. The former favorite of the king watched her with evil eyes. In her opinion, everything was just. *A couple of lashes will teach the boy. It's unlikely that Jerisson will get angry over it—only a street boy.*

"You, little rubbish, must obey instead of asking questions! I will order you beaten in the stables!"

"Let go!" yelled Miranda. "Let go now!"

The lady squinted and raised her hand. The only reason the baroness stopped was that she didn't want to get her expensive gloves dirty.

"Jean! Give this midget ten lashes immediately!"

Jean grabbed Mirrie's waist, and the girl screamed, loudly and desperately. She forgot to call for help; instead, she was calling for her mother.

ဆ ☐ ၄

Lily would hear Miranda's cry ten miles away. Luckily, they were already close to the estate. It was a desperate, loud cry, and it made Lily forget everything. Her daughter was calling her. *She is close by, but where?* Lidarh flew into the courtyard like thunder, justifying his name. The Avarian was a weapon, especially since he'd been educated. Miranda was struggling in the hands of some big bloke with a great royal whore next to her. Lily wouldn't have remembered the baroness even in her most terrible nightmare. Right then, her only worry was Mirrie. *Where are her guards? It doesn't matter! Everything, later!*

"Let go of her!"

Her order came out so patronizing that the coachman unwillingly flinched. This tiny movement was enough for Mirrie to break free. The sight of Lily restored Mirrie's senses, and she bit the hand that held her. She tasted blood, rushed away, and nearly got hit by Lidarh. Lily jumped off the horse, picked up the girl, and held her close.

"I am here my baby, everything is fine."

"I got so scared, Momma…"

Lily held her daughter tight.

"There, there. Everything is fine now. No one will hurt you again, kitten, I promise you."

The girl let out a sob and grew calmer.

"Mother, who is this?"

Lily handed the girl over to the Virmans who arrived shortly at the scene, their eyes seeking revenge. Lily gave the baroness an evil look, pulled a whip from her belt, and took a few steps forward. She was furious. She wouldn't think twice about killing the woman who dared to hurt her baby girl.

Did you say your morning prayer, Desdemoron?

So terrible was Lily's face that the baroness tripped backward. Only fangs would have made her more menacing.

"You louse, are you going to raise your hand to my child?"

Lily almost roared.

"But I didn't know!"

Lily wasn't reassured.

"If you had known it, I would've killed you altogether!"

"What's going on here?"

Jerisson Earton finally arrived. The picture was deceiving: furious Lily, pale Baroness Ormt, a Virman with a 'boy' in his arms. Jess looked at Lily with genuine indignation.

"What happened, Countess?"

Lily hissed like a cat. One more minute and everyone would receive her wrath. Jess would be the first one to receive a whip across his charming grimace. Mirrie saved her father.

"Papa!"

She let herself free of Leif's hands and rushed to Jess. Only then did he recognize his offspring and pick his daughter up into his arms. It became clear how similar they both looked. They had the same dark hair, the same blue eyes, and the same chin with a dimple. Lily sighed.

Her inner voice spoke to her. *Don't kill him, Lilian. Easy. At least he loves his daughter. Besides, he didn't see what happened.*

"Miranda Catherine Earton, did you clean the stables with your clothes on?"

"No, Papa! I cleaned my horse. He's a foal! His name is Shallah. Lily says he will grow up to be a strong, fast horse, like a real Avarian! She also says that I have to take care of my own horse by myself."

"You do," agreed Jess who realized very little. Lily inhaled again. She could finally bring herself to speak without the fear of accidentally using vile language. That's how much she was infuriated by the incident.

"Explain to this whore, my dear husband, that it's not fit to boss around people in someone else's house, and unthinkable to try to harm my daughter."

"Your daughter?"

For a few seconds, Jerisson was taken aback. The situation was unfolding too rapidly. He would think of an answer, but Mirrie interrupted.

"Let go, Papa! Momma, what is a whore?"

Great, the girl repeats everything I say.

"When boys are scared to sleep alone, and their wife is far away, they invite a special woman to their beds, so she warms them up and entertains them. These girls are called whores," explained Lily to Mirrie, who broke free from her father's arms and ran to her.

"Yes?"

"Of course."

"Papa, why did you not take Momma with you if you were scared?"

Some sixth sense told Mirrie that Lily was in danger. The girl tried to protect her as well as she could. She was affirming Lily's status.

This is my mother. Don't touch her. I love her!

Jerisson realized it. Vile language froze on his lips. He looked at the angry Lily, at Baroness Ormt who was about to become hysterical, the Virmans who were genuinely enjoying the scene, and Miranda, who now clung to his wife so tightly that even three people would've struggled to separate them.

"My dearest wife, would you be so kind as to take our daughter and wait for me inside while I deal with the incident?"

Lily slightly bowed her head and pulled Miranda's hand.

"Come on, baby."

She turned on her heel, and her braid spun in the air. She picked up Miranda and arranged her comfortably in her arms. Jess heard part of the conversation.

"Miranda Catherine Earton, what did I teach you?"

"Momma…"

"If your hands are free, hit with the knife! Where was your dagger?"

"It got lost."

"Got lost? I'll make the training tomorrow an hour longer, so you can practice how to avoid being captured!"

Jess refrained from spitting on the ground.

"What's happening here?" he asked the baroness. "What Maldonayan urge sent you?"

He received the answer immediately. Having quickly realized what she had gotten herself into, the baroness swore that it was a mistake. She didn't have time to see the dear Jerisson and decided to pay him a visit on her way somewhere else. She saw the stable boy in the yard and didn't recognize the viscountess. When 'he' began to answer back, she took it for a great offense. She would've never touched the viscountess.

Jerisson believed her. He came to realize that his future depended on his present reaction to the incident. If he behaved correctly, his wife would not only forgive him but would also become his ally. If not, he would destroy the last opportunity of reconciliation with his own hands. Jess smiled maliciously and headed to the house. He already knew what he should say.

ಬ ೂ

Lily sat in the living room and comforted Miranda. She also reprimanded the girl for walking around on her own, without even her dog.

"Was that kidnapping not enough for you?"

Jerisson Earton appeared in the doorway. The noble earl listened at the door for a few minutes like he was a servant choosing the moment when to come in. He dropped into his chair as soon as he stepped inside the room.

"Lilian, I understand everything, but this should never happen again."

Lily squinted at her husband.

"I agree."

"I understand that we lived apart for a while. I understand that you have every reason to be angry at me, but this must stop. Due to the ambiguity of our status, people spread a lot of unflattering rumors about our family, which can negatively affect our daughter."

"What do you suggest?"

"I suppose that a few public appearances and living together would help to shut the gossiping mouths."

Lily gave him an incredulous look, but the secret weapon of Earl Earton played her part: Mirrie shrieked with enthusiasm.

"Papa! We will all live together!"

"Only if your momma doesn't mind," assured Jess. *What an insolent and nasty man,* thought Lily.

"I won't object."

What else am I left to do? I can only seek revenge.

"Mirrie, tomorrow morning, I'm waiting for you to do a warm-up. I'll ask Leif for more intensive training."

"Can I come as well?"

"You can."

Jess noticed a sarcastic grin on his wife's lips, but it did not scare him off. He was already thinking about moving.
Bad choice!

ಬಿ ೧೫

The next morning, the earl's dignity was significantly damaged. It was six o'clock, and someone banged a copper basin with a ladle. It was none other than his own daughter, with a disgustingly cheerful and contented expression on her face.

"Papa! It's time to wake up!"

"What?"

"Rise and shine! The water for washing your face is already here. We'll be waiting for you in the backyard." She hit the ladle once more and vanished. Jess leaned back on his pillows with a moan. The day before, he had gone to bed past midnight, and now everything was a torture to his senses, even the sunshine. *Less brightness, please!*

Did Lilian say anything about the training yesterday? I need to have a look at least.

Jess pulled on simple leather pants and a shirt, splashed some water on his face, tied his hair back into a ponytail and went to the backyard. He froze in astonishment.

A couple of Virmans, under the command of a big man called Leif, performed various exercises. They stretched, lifted stones, a couple of men ran around in a circle. Among them ran two small persons— his daughter and his wife.

Jess closed his eyes. He shook his head wanting to dispel the vision. *Alas, it isn't a dream.* Wearing simple clothes from coarse, unpainted material, in loose shirts and blue skirts (or pants?), his daughter and his wife ran around with the Virmans. Jess saw them watching his wife in a way that made him want to murder them. His wife had a lot of virtues, and they expressively swayed with her every move. It didn't even occur to the Virmans to turn away. *I will kill the bastards!* If it wasn't for Mirrie, Jess would have done terrible things.

"Papa, you came! Join us!"

"Breathe properly," whined Lily at her daughter.

ಬಿ ೧೫

Two hours later the noble Earl of Earton slipped into the tub and groaned.

He was swept off his feet, his hands were shaking, and his head dropped. Jess exercised with a sword and considered himself a trained aristocrat. Yet there was a big difference between an aristocrat and a warrior. The first spent more time at court, led a certain lifestyle, and could let himself skip a couple of trainings. The warrior, especially the Virman one, had to keep fit for staying alive. For this reason, the Virmans trained a couple of times every day, without pity or compassion. Sparing their sweat would mean losing their lives. They trained the Countess of Earton in the same fashion, not suspecting that ladies needed less pressure. Miranda was taught as a boy. Lily didn't mind; Miranda was happy.

Jess felt absolutely shattered. His wife even had energy left to go to the Aldon. *Not now, after breakfast.*

🙰

Porridge depressed Jess even more. Loyal to his decision not to get angry at once, the noble earl only meekly inquired whether the cooks had made a mistake and confused the count's high cuisine with the dishes for the stables. Mirrie answered his question with laughter.

"Papa, it is good for your stomach!"

"Really?"

The greyish-yellow mass invoked words that wouldn't even take form. Mirrie put the spoon in her mouth. "And tasty, too."

Jerisson's wife took pity on him and nodded to the servants. In a few minutes, they brought him a huge plate with eggs, roasted meat, cheese, and salad.

That's better!

Jess looked at his wife with sincere gratitude and set about destroying his breakfast. Later, Mirrie grabbed her father's attention, whereas Lily decided to head to the aldon.

"Momma, do you really have to go?"

"Yes, sunshine."

"Will you come back soon?"

"I will try to make it quick."

"Stay, Lilian!" Jess used all his charm, but it worked badly.

"I promised."

"I understand that I've just arrived, but we need to spend more time together. Maybe we could go riding outside the city? They need to see us together."

Lily sighed.

"Can we do it when I return?"

"I would be glad to." *Glad? What does he think I feel?*, thought Lily as Jess added, "We don't know much about each other."

"Not surprising! Back then I was severely poisoned." Lily sighed. "I remember almost nothing about myself from the past. Everything is covered in a haze. It's scary to think about."

"It's my fault that you got poisoned." The subtext of his words was, "*It's obvious that you will forgive me. Women don't stay angry at me for longer than ten minutes*".

"You are not Aldonai to be able to foresee everything."

"I had to take care of you." Jerisson's hand covered Lily's palm. The woman freed her hand and moved a lock of hair away from her face. She wasn't pushing him away, but she let him know that she wanted to keep a distance.

"Yes, it was part of the contract. But it's too late to talk about it now."

"Why?"

"Because the past is in the past. You're alive, I'm alive, we are more or less in good health—I mean your wounded hand and the consequences of my miscarriage."

"Is it anything serious?"

"As the medicus says, I can't have children for at least a couple of years. Otherwise, I could die with the child."

The only medicus Lilian trusted was herself, but she wasn't lying. Her health was far from perfect, plus she needed to get in shape before another pregnancy. A woman is not a stamping press. Jerisson vigorously expressed sympathy.

"Hmm! A couple of years is not long."

Lily shrugged.

"We'll see. Do you know about the theory of relativity?"

"When something is carried somewhere?"

"Almost," giggled Lily. "If you spend the night with a beautiful woman, it will fly by in an instant. If they put your naked bottom on a hot frying pan, an instant will seem like an eternity to you."

Mirrie laughed. Lily kissed her nose and asked her if she could tell the servants to prepare the horses. The guards needed time to get ready, too.

Miranda ran off, and Jess decided to ask his wife, "What does your theory have to do with our family? If you wish, I can ask to dispose of all frying pans at once!"

Lily felt more freedom without Miranda.

"Relationships can be built in different ways. Some people make an eternity seem like an instant, others make a minute seem like an unbearable eternity."

Jess understood the hint.

"I hope we will not tire and annoy each other."

"What about cheating?"

The question was very blunt and acute. Jess gritted his teeth but restrained himself. It was his own fault.

"I won't," the earl said calmly. "There is no need. Any woman looks ugly next to you."

"Lady Wells would say otherwise. She made several attempts to kill me."

Lilian rose from her seat and paced around the room.

"I don't blame you for what happened. Let's admit, I was nervous before the wedding, and I wasn't myself. After the wedding, everything started to go wrong. It happened so quickly! It was hardly possible to find attractive the woman who was just a piece of meat. As for reason, mine was marred by datura. What about now? You had a mistress, and I don't want to be a part of your love triangle."

"Calm down," Jerisson almost forced the woman into a chair. "If you understand everything yourself, please don't. Why would I need a lover if I have such a beauty at home?"

Lily squinted.

"A beautiful woman who should wipe away a crystal tear and fall into your arms?"

The irony in the melodious voice surprised Jerisson. *What's wrong? We're married, I'm attractive, and she's attractive. Why waste time?*

There was so much offense in Lily's voice that Jerisson unwillingly smiled to himself. *Women are so strange! They can forgive anything except being with another woman.*

"There will be no more women." Jerisson did not even doubt the power of his charm. Lily, who had started to cut through her husband's character, did not even think to put pressure on him. She was suffering. She already realized that any attempt to put pressure on her husband would end à la the Stone Age—hitting a woman with a bat on the head and pulling her to bed. She didn't want to get into the same bed with Jess. *Not just yet. The earl is terribly attractive. One should give him that. So what? I will show him how to run after his own wife!*

Love? Lord, what are you on about? If Jerisson Earton takes me for Lilian, I passed the test. There will be no suspicions on account of my identity. If not, they might kill me. If I reject the earl, he will definitely start a wave of unpleasant questions, suspicions, reproaches...

Lily realized well that the Crown protected her only because she made a lot of effort for it, and the king favored her because she treated him. Second, her artisans could pose serious competition for the guilds. Everyone had begun to realize it. The king gradually realized it. Before, Edward hadn't had an alternative. But now he had an opportunity to crush the guilds. *Why not use it? He would agree to a treaty with Maldonaya, not to mention with Lilian Earton.*

"How many women have you been with apart from me? Every second lady grins after I pass."

"Forget them."

"Do you think it's that easy?"

After about twenty minutes, the spouses agreed they should attend court together more often to make everyone shut their mouths. Jerisson swore he wouldn't run after every lady. Lily looked at him with disbelief but acted out something like Tatiana Larina from Pushkin. *Onegin, I was younger then, and it seems like I was better, I used to love you.* Lilian did say something that sounded like a love declaration. She described her sufferings after she came to her senses. *The child is lost, the castle is destroyed, the husband started going from woman to woman. I loved you, I suffered, how could you have caused me so much pain?* Tears streamed down her cheeks. Men shouldn't believe women's tears if they aren't from cutting an onion. Any woman can cry on request. If not, she's a man in disguise.

Yet, Jerisson relaxed. Everything fit into his scheme—a weak woman, a fragile creature, nerves, jealousy. The thought of her production didn't occur to him once. *Production? So what? The earl couldn't take a woman seriously. He doesn't perceive me as a real owner of the business.*

"—Taral castle was in ruins, I did everything I could, but then my father sent a governor who sorted everything out—"

"—Production? Father helped. He sent me his people. Taris Brock is his trusted person—"

"Doctors? I found them by accident. If they had been around earlier, our child would have stayed alive. Our poor child! Will you ever forgive me for his death? If only the medicus Craybey hadn't poisoned me when you were away—"

"—What! The Virmans? Father helped them with the ships. When he found out about what happened—"

"—I couldn't hope for your protection, you were so busy! Your guards did a good job—"

"—The Khangans? My friendship with them is purely accidental. I was looking for the best doctor to make sure that the thing with Craybey doesn't happen again."

Lily carefully studied Jerisson. The earl didn't think it necessary to hide his emotions. Therefore, it was easy to guess what to say. He would've done otherwise had he expected a trick, had he taken women seriously. *What's the easiest way to put any person off guard? One should say what's expected of him.* Lily simply credited her father for her own success. It convinced Jerisson that Lilian didn't have a lover. A father had the right to help his daughter, especially when her husband was away.

ఐ ⌷ ౧

Lilian's sophisticated perfidy did not occur to Jess. It was not unusual. Every representative of the stronger sex was firmly convinced that a woman was a tender, fragile creature. It was hard to explain to men that this tender creature could stop a horse with only her gaze. The gentle creature woke up at five in the morning to make breakfast and feed her husband, get him ready for work, feed her children, get them ready and take them to school. She went to work, went grocery shopping during her lunch break, rushed home after work, and the scenario went round in circles: dinner, husband, children, homework, mother in law, husband, washing, cleaning, cooking. If a decent horse followed such a schedule, it would have been exhausted long ago. Women, though, ran around in this manner year in and year out.

Lily sobbed, showing her weakness. She talked about her broken heart. Jerisson comforted her. He didn't put pressure on her just yet. He was of the opinion that any woman could be pulled into bed. It wasn't worth rushing. He never raped women; they themselves jumped into his bed. Jess wasn't going to become a rapist. A little earlier, a little later, she'd eventually give in and fall into his arms.

He had in front of him a stranger; he didn't know this new Lilian. *If only I knew what she's like...*

Jerisson asked himself questions. *How would I have behaved if I had seen this Lilian at the wedding? I would have definitely not gotten that drunk. I also wouldn't have sent her away into the wilderness.*

Jess was angry at himself and at his wife. Lilian gave Jess nothing he could use against her. She did reproach him, but only with her tears. There was no malice and no anger. She didn't shout "scoundrel!"

Instead, she said, "I suffered so much, I wanted to die, you did not write to me at all."

The complaints were similar in nature but very different in form. Lilian balanced on a very thin line. If he put too much pressure, she would explode; if he didn't put enough, he risked remaining on a long leash. He took every step almost blindfolded; every move was like walking on ice. It was scary, but he had no choice.

Lilian didn't get a chance to continue her play-acting. Someone tapped at the door (as much as a Virman managed to tap).

It was Olaf. "My Lady, you wished to go to the aldon today. He will be waiting for you."

Jerisson flashed his eyes, but that was like bananas to an elephant. The woman grabbed her head.

"Oh, Aldonai! I'll make everyone wait! My Lord, my dear husband, I need to run."

"Can I keep you company?" The earl didn't expect to be rejected, and rightly so.

"Of course. I have no doubt that Aldon Roman will be happy to see you. He already tried to speak to me about our family life."

༄ ༅

Lily hastily pulled a mirror out of her purse, looked into it, wiped away her tears, and blew her nose. *A little breeze will make my face look brand new!* Although she was a blonde, she was lucky to have thick skin. Some women couldn't allow themselves to cry. After five minutes of crying, their thin skin would look terrible. Lilian had smooth, thick skin, and in some twenty minutes, there would be no trace of her recent performance. *Or maybe it's due to the better environment? Oh, never mind!* After the mention of family values, her husband evidently changed his mind. He followed his wife with his eyes and went to deal with the Virmans.

༄ ༅

Lily warmed up her horse, leaning against his disheveled mane. Lidarh raced with the wind, but that didn't dispel Lily's disquieting troubles. She thought about the earl. Jerisson was definitely leaning toward closeness. *Am I ready for it?* A ghost of memory came over Lily.

She saw herself as Aliya Skorolenok at sixteen. Alex Satin was an army conscript, a couple of years older. Later, they would study together. Back then, they were still two young children who sledded down the hill together with joyful laughter. He was on his army leave, she had school holidays, and they were both happy together. Pine trees swung over their heads, the snow rose like a silver blanket. Their eyes shone. The sleds slowed down as they looked each other in the eyes with the brightest look of love. This radiance of love that is described in novels, plays, and movies, is different in reality. You look at someone and see your life in them. It's empty, dark and cold without them—nothing less. This is what happened with her and Alex. *As for Jerisson, is it possible to reignite the fire of love?* Lily didn't know. Deep down, the splinters of the first Lilian moaned and whined. *Try it, see what happens! Maybe it will work out!* Lily wasn't sure. Miranda was her only bridge over the abyss. She loved both Lily and Jess. They both loved their daughter. *Maybe it's worth trying for her sake?*

What if Jerisson, fed up with the novelty of their relationship, decided to have a bit on the side? *That's who he is. I won't be able to hold him back. To be a cheater's wife? First, I'll be ridiculed behind my back. Second, I'll get diseases. There are no antibiotics here, but there is syphilis! Do I need such a life? No, thank you. Children? Fine. Jess's children will be good, but they will need to be educated!*

She could see the result of Jerisson's education. She had barely managed to save Miranda from turning into the first Lily. *Will he let me raise my own children? With his conceit, he might refuse me such an opportunity.* Lily wasn't going to leave her affairs. One way or another, her husband was going to stay in a secondary role. An intelligent man wouldn't be offended by this. Lily knew one such family. She was a businesswoman; he was a colonel soon to become a general. Such was their working tandem. The husband accepted the fact that his wife was a talented economist and was even proud. *My wife is a strong, clever woman! There's no one better than her, be jealous!*

Will Jerisson be able to accept such a deal? Lily wasn't sure. *What do I lose if I try? Nothing.* She had Miranda and a title. It didn't matter that she had problems with her husband. *What could I do? Drop at the aldon's feet?* His Majesty promised to give her a title, but their deal was written on running water. That meant that she would need to immediately find herself a new husband, one who would "please the crown." His Majesty would surely want to select the new husband himself, it was not a question of love. He would choose two or three candidates at the most, to create the appearance of choice. *Will I survive this? I will even chew it up.*

If it was still going to be a marriage of convenience, it was easier not to bother. The present candidate was at least handsome, and it would make the former Lilian happy.

Lily touched the pocket with the single pearl earring and cunningly grinned.

Well, dear spouse, I will give you a month to see how you react to my everyday life. If you prove yourself to be a smart man, great. If not, I will take a hard approach. I need to start thinking about it now. There was yet another dilemma. *Should I give in to sex or not?* On the one hand, it would be better not to. You never know what STDs he picked up during his trip. On the other hand, she could ask Jamie for a contraceptive pill. It was fine to share a bed with Jess as long as she was married to him. She wasn't a nun, after all. Sex was just another need of the body; love was out of the question.

Sex is necessary, at least a couple of times, to restore my hormonal balance. I am not going to deprive the husband of his legal marital rights. Although I wouldn't throw my arms around his neck with the cry "honey, I want you" either. Everything should happen naturally. If he gets what he wants, he might finally start to show his true face. I'll be able to conduct a "crash-test" early. Am I going to take action today? We'll see. Perhaps I wouldn't even need to do anything. Her cunning smile widened.

To get what he wants, he would first need to free the bedroom of Miranda, the two dogs, and the ferret. I will give him a big thank you for it!

The male ferret, Tash, had gotten into a habit of sleeping on Lily's head.

To see a ferret loins first thing in the morning isn't very pleasant!

ಠ ಥ

The construction of the beauty center was well underway. The walls were already standing, and the builders were about to begin the roof. Lily was pleased. Soon, the salon would open its doors to visitors.

If only they could build it faster! I cannot wait!

Tores Herein reported back to the owner, and it left her satisfied. They went through the planning once again. The summer hall had a veranda. The winter hall had big windows and a huge fireplace. The shop had ten fitting rooms, seven on the first floor and three VIP rooms on the second. Staff rooms, storage, workshops…there was just enough space to fit everything.

"What if we buy more land, My Lady?"

Lily counted her cash in her head. The Eveers had eagerly gotten down to business and the interest had slowly accumulated. The girls laboriously spun lace. On top of it, there were mirrors and glassware.

"Get it! It will soon be as valuable as gold."

Herein pleasingly rubbed his hands.

"Should we, after all, create a garden there?"

"We'll see."

Lily liked the idea of creating a park. They could create a playground for children there, both for summer and winter. She would make little pathways here and there and cut the bushes in different shapes. She could put in swings and so on.

Mariella Fashion House. Sounds good!

ಠ ಡ

Aldon Roman flipped through the freshly printed "Word of Aldonai." Thus far, a dozen pages, a single copy, but only for the time being. He rose to greet Lilian and even slightly inclined his head to her. Lily immediately dropped in a curtsey, went down on her knee and created a circle of Aldonai.

"Your Grace!"

"Rise, child of Aldonai!"

Lily liked that the local priests addressed everyone as "child of Aldonai." All of them were his children. Lily didn't like being addressed "my child" by priests of her former world. There were no "slaves of God" like in her previous world, only "children of Aldonai." The difference was huge.

Lily obediently got up and sat down in a chair. She took a sip of blueberry tea. The aldon had learned by now that Lily didn't drink alcohol.

"I've heard your spouse is back."

"That's right, Your Grace."

"I suppose you met him with great joy like a wife should meet her husband."

His words had a clear implication—*What did you do when you met him?*

Lily lowered her eyes.

"Jerisson Earton is my husband."

"And you will obviously be happy together. I will pray for your shared happiness."

The word "shared" was emphasized so much that it made Lily smile.

Of course, the aldon didn't give a damn about Jerisson. It was Lily he needed, for Lily knew paper-making and printing. She could also bring new ideas. No one had invented etching yet, and Lily remembered its principles. *I will keep it in my sleeve for later.*

She was glad to have the church on her side. The monastery wasn't the best place. And yet, it depended on how one accommodated it. Many scientists were priests, and many monasteries concealed brothels.

"Let Aldonai hear your prayer."

The aldon nodded and slowly moved on to his topic of interest, namely paper and its production. Nettle, hemp, other fibrous plants—some were bought, others sown. They still had to arrange a factory and make equipment. Some things were already in Taral. They had also decided on the ingredients of ink. Lily had a hard time making the ink water-resistant. Such ink existed before, but it was rough and poor quality. She filtered it and added a little alcohol. Lily knew her little tricks, and they were useful. It was amazing how many tricks one learned to use in the twenty-first century.

It wasn't fit for the countess to get busy with making paper and ink and hiring workers. Only educated monks could be trusted with such a task. They were much more intelligent and educated compared to the local nobility. Such was Lily's opinion, and it made the aldon put on airs. Lily praised the monks so extensively that it was almost as if she was ready to buy and sell them for their weight in gold. The monasteries were indeed the centers of cultural life. She saw to choosing the pioneer heroes of book printing. They practiced with already existing letters and would soon begin to adapt to the new set. The first texts in line for publishing were already announced. Along with the "Word of Aldonai," the lives of saints, royal orders, and the "Book of Families," one could spot two new titles: "Alphabet Book" and "Arithmetic." Lily insisted on their publication. She argued that children should at least know the basics and that they should learn to read and write. After much consideration, the aldon agreed. His Majesty wasn't even going to object. *Why would he? He was the one receiving all the benefits from my labor.*

☙ ❧

Lilian was in for a surprise at home. Although she didn't mind, the extent of her surprise was too much. Jess greeted his wife with a crooked smile and a bruised cheek. For the sake of symmetry, the other part of his face was also purple. The man moved around the room sideways. Lily clapped her hands to her cheeks.

"What is that?"

"Things happen," smiled the noble earl.

"Did you get attacked by a shilda?"

All healthy parts of his body expressed confusion.

"You must have walked past them, and they flew out and started mocking you."

Jerisson looked so pathetic and confused that Lily became ashamed and nodded to the door to her bedroom.

"Let's go."

She started rummaging through her wardrobe and pointed at the bed.

"Get undressed."

Jess, the eager womanizer, didn't remember the last time he felt so indignant.

Is she serious? I don't mind, I am very keen, but NOT NOW! His ribs and his stomach were in pain.

With the medical kit in her hands, Lilian turned around, read the thoughts on the bruising face, and stomped her foot.

"Get undressed, mister! I will inspect you for broken bones."

Jerisson looked quite frustrated but got undressed without a word. He lay where she pointed. Lily started inspecting the patient.

It looked like he had gotten into a drunken fight. *But when?*

"Did you get into a fight with someone, dear Earl?"

Jess sighed. He didn't want to admit to it, but Lily looked decisive. She would find out one way or another.

"The Virmans and I… had a little discussion."

"All of them together?"

"Not all."

Lily sighed. This was predictable. The alpha male found a whole herd of strange animals in his pack. It enraged him, and he went to show them who was boss, but considering his temperament…

"Was it a draw?"

Jess smiled with his broken lip. He couldn't say that he had it easy, but at least the rest had begun to respect him. Jess didn't have any illusions in this matter. He knew that the question had to be reopened, but at least the process was underway.

While Lily professionally tended the abrasions and scratches, she couldn't resist admiring his abs. Some people had to build them, but Jess's body was a gift of nature. He was a warrior. It was a pity that this gorgeous body was now covered in bruises. He would have to walk sideways for at least three days. His ribs were fine. Although he had bruises, he had managed to avoid any fractures. Lily dressed the injuries and applied a tight bandage. Jess watched his wife and kissed her hand when she finished.

"I thank you, Countess."

"It's my duty."

"Your duty as a doctor or as a wife?"

"As a merciful woman," said Lily.

Jerisson's healthy eye looked at her with slight cunning. The second one was totally mashed up.

"May I invite you for dinner, hoping for your mercy that wouldn't let you refuse the heavily injured man?"

"You may. Only I don't eat in the evening," admitted Lily.

Jess got lost, having remembered Lily's former preferences.

"But—"

"Let's go to bed," suggested Lilian honestly, "I am so tired today, I only wish to get my head to the pillow."

Jess nodded but tried his luck once more.

"Would you care for a walk around the garden before going to bed?"

Lily sighed but did not refuse. She promised herself to try to patch things up with Jerisson.

"Let's go, My Lord."

An hour later, the Countess of Earton floated into the arms of sleep, stretching out on the clean bedsheets, and hugging her little daughter who climbed into her bed.

The earl turned out to be a good companion: reasonably witty, helpful, serious, and attentive. *Perhaps this trial period won't be as bad as I imagined! We'll see.*

Miranda was already sleeping soundly; the dogs would no doubt come climbing into bed at midnight. Being on the brink between sleep and wakefulness Lily sensed something warm nestling on her head. *Damn ferrets!*

The earl planned to continue seducing his wife the next morning. His ribs hurt less now, but there was one other problem. He simply couldn't catch his wife. She woke up at dawn, went to the church service, had a word with the pastor who was soon to become the aldon, played with Miranda a little and fled to Taral.

Jerisson woke up much later, from a wondrous sensation. The noble earl had had a dream that he got hit by a tree. When he tried to push it away, the tree bit his arm and said "arrr." As much as Jess wanted to continue sleeping, he had to open his eyes. In his bed next to him, he discovered two huge dogs. Without the slightest intention of moving, both dogs settled among the bedsheets and put their muzzles and paws on Jess's body. They looked at him with reproach, as if asking, "What's wrong? Isn't it nice lying down together?"

Jess had to push them off by force. He rang the bell that he found next to his bed. The maids flew in and received a question. "What are these beasts doing in the noble earl's bed?"

Alas. The beasts turned out to be the personal watchdogs of her ladyship Lilian Earton and the Viscountess Miranda. The two huge beasts, Nanook and Lou-Lou, walked freely around the house. They were used to sleeping with humans. After the case with the murderers, the countess always let them into the bedroom.

The beasts were kicked out and a large basin with water brought in. The servants asked if the earl wished to have breakfast in the room or downstairs. He said he'd go down, and the maids began helping him get dressed.

Jerisson asked them about his wife and was told that after her morning prayer, she left for business at Taral Castle.

"Will she come back soon?"

"In the evening, My Lord."

Jerisson quickly got dressed, had breakfast, and set off for Taral. He stopped in the courtyard as if struck by lightning.

A few dozen children were playing a strange game. There was a circle drawn on the floor, and children threw daggers at their feet, after which they drew new circles. Among them was Mirrie. She was happy, cheerful, dressed in something dark, and holding a real dagger in her hands.

"Miranda!"

The daughter noticed her father and waved to him.

"Papa! I'll come in a second! I need to win first!"

After a couple of throws, she shook a boy's hand, who stood inside a circle, and ran up to Jerisson. The earl picked the girl up in the air.

"Ugh! You're such a calf!"

"A chick," corrected Miranda, not in the least embarrassed. "I am a woman."

Jess snorted.

"What is your game, woman?"

"A game of knives."

Mirrie briefly explained the rules. Jess asked her to show him the knife and was astounded at what he saw. The knife wasn't a children's toy. It had a good blade and a handle covered with shark skin. Such a knife could easily kill a man.

"Yes, it can," confirmed Miranda. "Therefore one should be very careful with it. It's not a toy but a military weapon."

Jess was going to say the same words and choked at hearing them from his daughter, who knocked him on the back.

"Are you okay, Papa?"

"Yes, I'm fine. Who gave you this knife?"

"It's a present from Uncle Erik! Don't worry, Momma knows."

"She lets you play with it?"

"On the condition that I learn to handle it. Who knows what can happen. If I had been able to use the knife back when the Baron of Donter kidnapped me, I would've definitely killed him!"

Mirrie climbed out of her father's hands, looked around, and pointed at a couple of wooden poles.

"Look!"

The knife whistled through the air and stuck in the wood. *Not bad for a little girl.* Jerisson only shook his head. He had nothing to say. It was true about the kidnapping. She should know how to defend herself next time.

"I will speak about it with your mother."

"Have you brought me anything of the kind?"

"You're a girl, a viscountess."

"So what? Does that mean that I have to walk around defenseless?"

Jess sighed. In light of the recent kidnapping, any argument against having a weapon sounded unconvincing.

"You do have to know how to defend yourself. Who were you playing with?"

"Mark, he's Pastor Vopler's son."

Not the best company, but it passed the test of rank. Jess couldn't object much. "Should he go to Taral? Why not?"

☙ ❧

"My Lady, I spoke to Anna."

"Judging by your radiant face, she didn't send you away?"

Lons frowned.

"I am glad for you, really! Only think about it yourself. Edward really wants a union with Gardwig. They seem to be decided on that."

"What about Ivernea? His relationship with Gardwig is already good."

"Did Anna tell you?"

"Y-yes."

"Lons, you come to the court often and have heard a lot."

"My Lady, if we decide to run away—"

"You would either be received at Earton or in the Khanganat. Amir will hire you as his secretary, but on one condition. When are you going to run away?"

"I will meet Anna in the church."

"Will you speak there?"

"Yes."

"Lons, my condition is that Anna shouldn't know a word about me. Do you understand?"

Lons nodded.

"By honor."

"And one more thing. Do you understand how much you risk if your ex-wife is fooling around with you?"

"My current wife, My Lady!"

"Your Lady is only saying that if your lovely Anna is lying to you, you'll most likely get killed," retorted Lily.

"Anna is not like that! She is kind, tender, naïve—"

"Do you understand that Anna will choose the future king before you?"

"She loves me."

"She's buried you once already. My second condition is this: sit down and write."

"Write what?"

"Write down your whole story in your own hand. I will call the pastor, he will sign it, seal it, and we'll keep it hidden."

"What for?"

"If something happens to you, I will at least know who is responsible."

Lily gave him a sad smile.

Aldonai be merciful! How could female tenderness and fragility produce such an effect! Does one necessarily need to pretend to be a helpless fool in order to play a man? Unbelievable!

"My Lady," Lons said with a frown.

"Write. If everything works out, I will burn it with my own hands."

ಇಾ ಚ8

As soon as Lily left Taral, she went to His Majesty. Despite the king being busy dining, the Countess Earton was immediately invited in.

Lily dropped in a curtsey, smiled at Tahir, and took her seat next to the king. She thought she had accidentally stepped on someone's foot. *It doesn't matter! The rest can move.*

Gardwig and his daughter weren't present at the dinner. That evening, they stayed in the embassy. Richard had to go somewhere to check up on the Ivernean diplomatic mission that was to arrive at any moment. The courtiers squinted, grimaced, and smiled 'kind' jealous smiles at Lily. They seemed to be taking her for the king's new favorite.

Idiots! The king could sleep with anyone, but to find a good doctor was far more difficult. After dinner, Edward beckoned the countess with his finger.

"My Lady, you will accompany me on a walk."

Lily frowned. She knew what a royal walk meant. It was long and tiring. He should've taken a nap instead. Yet, it turned out that the king cut the walk to half an hour.

"I follow your recommendations, dear Countess," teased the king.

Lily smiled.

"How can I impose authority on the king?"

"I suspect that both you and Tahir are terrible tyrants, My Lady!" Edward was clearly mocking her. "How are things in Taral?"

"Everything is in full swing! Fifty days, and we will start producing if nobody gets in our way."

"Did anyone make any efforts to get in your way?"

"The Virmans caught a couple of strange people, who really wanted to stay by the fire, at night, on the shore. They all had an inflammatory liquid with them, in a very convenient form for throwing it inside the Taral courtyard."

"Is that so?"

"Yes, Your Majesty."

"Who were these criminals?"

"Hans Tremain is in charge of the investigation."

"I can see you are getting along very well with him, Countess."

"He is very clever, Your Majesty." Lily suspected that Hans could see through her, but she was useful for him and could give a lot, so he kept silent.

"What about your husband, Countess?" His gray eyes looked cold. Lily didn't flinch.

"My husband is at his best. We are trying to fix our relationship, but it needs time, Your Majesty."

Edward nodded.

"I hope you will find a solution together."

"I hope for the same, Your Majesty. I do it for Miranda."

The king nodded. He didn't care much for the reasons. What he cared about was the result.

"Have you shown your husband what you do?"

"Not yet, Your Majesty."

"I will speak to Jerisson and will ask him to accompany you to Taral. Let him see how significant you are for the kingdom, let him see your business grip."

"Thank you, Your Majesty."

"Don't thank me. Especially since I'm glad to see you for another reason as well."

"Your Majesty only has to issue an order." Lily curtsied.

"Countess," Edward paused in choosing his words, "I am very pleased with your help. I thank Tahir. But my crowned brother, His Majesty Gardwig, is in bad health. Yesterday, he asked to see the famous doctor from the Khanganat."

"What?"

"Tahir, in his turn, declared that he never goes anywhere without his student. Without you, Countess."

"Are you against it, Your Majesty?"

"No, Countess. Sooner or later, Tahir will leave for the Khanganat, and you will stay. We need at least one good doctor at court. Besides, there is also your project about creating a school for children."

"Tahir will be glad to help."

"I have no doubt about it. He is loyal to you, which is very strange considering that he's a Khangan. He calls you nothing other than Lilian-jan."

"It's a mere sign of respect."

"A woman in the Khanganat is considered on par with a beautiful flower. It's difficult to respect a flower—"

"Tahir has always sought knowledge. Having recognized that I have the same desire, he didn't pay attention to whether I wore a skirt or a pair of pants."

"Are you trying to be disrespectful right now, Lilian?"

"I would've never allowed myself such a liberty, Your Majesty."

"You would. You have the Virmans and the Khangans to protect you."

Lily answered with an innocent smile. It wasn't that the king wanted to annoy the countess. Such jokes during a serious conversation allowed him to test her reaction. He expected her to get annoyed and nervous and lose her temper—and maybe give off some important bits of information she might be hiding.

To the king's great surprise, Lilian remained completely undisturbed. It was as if the conversation was about embroidery and not about business. *Good. Both Lilian's father and her grandfather were remarkable people. It would have been strange if she hadn't inherited their temper. A lot could be explained by her education. She was raised in a shipbuilder's household; she was bound to acquire some extraordinary knowledge.*

Edward remembered the royal library. *Who knows, if the mice haven't eaten it up, it might still contain a lot of interesting things. Her knowledge could be explained.*

Where on earth did she learn to tame and use people like that? No school could have taught her that. It requires talent, a certain skill, and by Aldonai's grace, a full commitment! She could've simply used those people, but they are loyal to her. Their loyalty comes from the bottom of their hearts.

Her friendship with the Virmans might be a mere accident, but how did she manage to find a common language with those sea wolves?

The king saw the ships with black shields on their masts arriving at the royal harbor—a rare sight. The people who got off those ships were ready to tear apart anyone who dared to look at Lilian in a disrespectful way.

Their loyalty could be explained by some sort of mutual benefit, no doubt, but any loyalty has to be earned. What about Hans? His blood and soul belong to the king. Nevertheless, he watches and protects that strange woman. Tahir, the Khangans... She cured the prince, and they wagged their tails at her feet. They are devoted to her. But why?

"I recognize the servitude of my people, Your Majesty. I also pay them back with my loyalty. They are ready to do as much for me as I am ready to do for them." Lily looked straight ahead. "I helped them. I gave them an opportunity to survive and to advance in life, I offered them support and help. I receive the same things in return."

"I'm beginning to envy you, Countess."

"Don't envy me, Your Majesty. It's the same hard labor as yours, only it's easier for me. I am responsible for several people, whereas you are in charge of the whole country."

"For some reason, I don't observe the same loyalty toward my person."

"Your Majesty," her tone of voice was clearly reproachful, "don't look at these..." A careless wave of her hand enclosed half of the court. "What about your royal representatives? My husband? I don't appear at court very often, but I know that there are always people who are loyal to their king and the country. As a rule, they live in the parts where they prove loyalty with acts not speeches. Take only Baron Avermal. He works hard for the kingdom without even hoping to become part of the court."

"Countess, you will soon make me ashamed."

"Your Majesty, may I—"

"Yes, you may. Take Tahir and depart to my crowned brother immediately."

"Your will is law," Lily dropped in a curtsey. "Only what do I do with my husband? I wanted to spend time with him this afternoon, but it turns out that we will see each other only in the evening."

"Is it so tricky for such an intelligent woman to find something to do with her husband in the evening?"

Lily sighed.

I guess it's inappropriate to ask if the bastard is kidding.

"I will immediately—"

"No need to rush. Better tell me how Roman and Jacob are doing. I've seen Miranda recently. She is happy and cheerful. What about the young Ivelens?"

What does he expect me to say? A shadow came over Lily's face.

"I found them a wet-nurse, Your Majesty. She is a Virman. One woman happened to give birth recently, and we asked her to—"

"Is that a reasonable decision?"

"At least they keep themselves clean," Lily said roughly. "I wouldn't let fleas near the babies."

Edward snorted.

"As you wish, Lilian."

"I'm sorry, Your Majesty! But hygiene is important."

"I remember. By the way, hot baths are indeed good for the bones."

Lily smiled contentedly.

"Your praise is a big honor, Your Majesty."

"Tell me more about the children."

"They cry, piss, sleep, eat—"

What else could one want from babies who are less than a month old? Certainly not logarithms.

"Are they in good health?"

"Aldonai will see to it."

Lily made a circle of Aldonai.

"Have you seen the Aldon?"

"Yes, Your Majesty. We agreed on the list of printed literature. Is it wise to give book-printing fully into the hands of the Church? Maybe it makes sense to—"

"Let's organize at least one publishing house. If everything works out, we will open a few more."

"Yes, Your Majesty."

ಲ ೞ

The Wellster Embassy was impressive. Actually, Lily didn't see the embassy itself. As a rule, the ambassadors rented a big country house close to the royal palace. But since the king and the princess arrived as well, the king gave them one of his own summer houses in the countryside called Terein Castle.

It was a beautiful castle made of white-stone with thin spires, which were now crowned with flags. There was a crowd of people, a luxurious garden, and the same distinct smell. There was nothing one could do; noble counts and dukes saw nothing wrong with pooping behind the bushes.

Lilian didn't have a big retinue with her: only four Virmans and Tahir. Yet, her pocket was pleasantly weighted down by a letter from the king. The secretary of the king furtively mentioned that her visit was already approved and expected by all principle figures of the embassy. The diplomatic protocol was usually very strict, but if the two kings at once didn't mind breaking it, no one would argue with them. Especially with Gardwig, who chopped off heads like summer grass.

Lilian dismounted at the main entrance and was immediately greeted with a whistle from a couple of men. She threw the reins to a servant who came running and made an arrogant announcement: "Dearest sir, report that her Countess Lilian Earton together with the Doctor din Dashar arrived at the request of His Majesty Gardwig."

This sentence was enough for everyone to start moving. Whether the king was sick or healthy, he trained his servants well. Lily saw how the look in the servant's eyes became more respectful. In a few minutes, a very dressed up man showed up.

"My name is Thomas Rayton. Leir Rayton. I am the king's servant. Let me show you the way."

"With great pleasure, Leir." Lily gave him a beaming smile, and he answered it. His title wasn't the highest. He worked hard for it, only dukes and counts would always look down on him. Lily wasn't going to swagger. She held onto his obedient elbow, and he took her gliding across the castle corridors.

Lily arrived just in time. His Majesty's leg was hurting more than usual. The mediocuses had drawn his blood and planted leeches on the king's limb, which had put him in a bad mood.

⊗ ⌐ ☙

"Get out of here, you dunce!" Gardwig snapped at his daughter.

Anna dropped a piece of cloth and stormed out of the chamber, crying.

She had to take care of her father's leg despite nauseating disgust; she had no choice. For all her efforts, they had sent her away and offended her, and she had gone away crying.

Yet there was another reason for her mood. She had had no time to speak to the trustee of Count Lort after the ball. She had spoken to him the previous evening instead, and the memory of the conversation made her shiver.

"He's alive."
"Who?"
"Lons Avels. My—"
"I know. Where is he?"
"He approached me at the ball. What do I do?"

"Does Edward know?"

"No, Lons managed to escape without anyone's help. Aldonai, have mercy on me!"

"Keep quiet. You don't want to ruin yourself."

Anna stopped wailing and clutched lace handkerchief, bringing it to her mouth. She bit the fabric so hard that she had to spit out its threads a minute later. Meanwhile, the man contemplated.

"What did you agree on?"

"To meet in the church and run away together."

"Good girl. When you see him in the church, you will pass him a note. You'll write what I tell you. The rest is not your concern."

Anna went pale. Yet she saw no other way out of it. She had already made the choice between becoming a queen and remaining a village girl.

"Why not now?"

"Because it's not Wellster. To do things here will need time. Go about your own business and keep quiet."

Anna obeyed.

Presently, she was running to her chamber and wondering whether that scary man had come to see her.

Lilian walked into the chamber of His Majesty Gardwig with all courtesies. She dropped in a curtsey.

"Your Majesty,"

She lifted her eyes after he ordered, "Come closer, Countess."

༄ ༅

Despite his age, Gardwig was still handsome. Lily could imagine him as a young man.

Ah! I wish I could go back twenty years, she thought. She reflexively noticed his gorgeous golden locks, heavy build, bright blue eyes, and intelligent face.

They don't call him the Lion of Wellster for nothing!

Alas, the lion was sick. The king was half-resting on the couch, with one leg stretched forward on a stool. A strange little man was running around him.

Is he a medicus? I guess so, otherwise, why would he put leeches on his leg? Yuck!

There were a few things in medicine that Lily hated with all her might. One of them was leeches. When she was a student, she would only agree to handle the creatures while wearing gloves. Merely looking at them made her sick. She hated the little creatures with all her heart, despite their indisputable healing properties.

"Your Majesty, my king ordered me to come here."

"Yes. I need you to have a look at my ulcer," Gardwig was clearly not in the mood. "What are you waiting for? Do something!"

"May I have a look at your leg?"

"I've already told you!" snapped Gardwig.

"But your medicus—"

"OUT!" shouted the king at the little man and made a face. His leg gave him much pain. The medicus hurriedly dashed toward the door, and Lily replaced him beside the king on her knees.

"Tahir-jan, could you remove these darlings?"

Without further ado, Tahir began detaching the leeches while Lily removed a rather dirty bandage from the ulcer, wincing from the stench.

Well. How can I tell what it is?

The ulcer itself was firmly smeared with something white, a red wound with blue veins in it. The leg was swollen and had an unhealthy color. At least she couldn't see any signs of varicose.

I wonder how he got it! Lily knew a lot about ulcers. *If it's trophic, then what kind? Diabetic, ischemic, varicose—or maybe it's an inadequately treated wound that turned into an ulcer?*

Lily hoped it was the latter. The rest was impossible to treat without antibiotics. She only had traditional folk medicine at her disposal. It was possible, no doubt, but only at the primary stage, not once it had spread to the whole leg. It was impossible to tell where the ulcer initially began.

"Your Majesty, what is this balm on your leg?"

"Ask the medicus!" said Gardwig peevishly. Lily stood up and bowed.

"With your permission. Tahir, prepare the tools."

"Medicus!" The king had a strong voice, and the little man flew in like a rocket.

"Your Majesty!"

Gardwig silently nodded in Lilian's direction. The medicus glanced at Lily and flinched from the murderous cold of her green eyes.

"How long have you been treating His Majesty?"

"Pff— half a year!"

Lily's voice resembled hissing.

"What is this ointment?"

"It's a family secret!" the medicus assumed a dignified air. "It's a miraculous ointment which forms a crust and makes the wound—"

Lily nearly howled in desperation. The last thing that should be done to an ulcer of this kind was to put a balm on it. The bacteria under it thrived and flourished. She didn't yet know what type of ulcer it was.

"Tahir," called Lily. He was carefully removing the leeches. He rubbed the skin with alcohol and turned around. "We need to properly wash the wound."

"Yes, it's hard to diagnose at the moment," agreed the man sadly. "Your Majesty, with your permission."

Gardwig indignantly raised his eyebrows.

"Isn't it obvious that it's an ulcer?"

"It is, Your Majesty. I apologize terribly if what I'm going to say annoys you, but any illness has its cause. Your ulcer appeared for a reason, and we are currently trying to establish it. May Your Majesty be kind enough to tolerate our examination?"

"I may," nodded Gardwig. Although he was angry and his leg hurt, there was something about these two that inspired his confidence. Every king had to be a good psychologist. He could see that Lily wasn't merely a student of Tahir. At best, they were equals. At worst, the countess was in charge. Tahir seemed to also know a lot. Despite all the Khangan customs, he followed all her orders without question. There was something in the way he looked at her, something akin to deep respect. Their curious partnership was a worthy sight. Besides, they were the first among many who weren't blindly complacent and didn't claim that they could cure any disease. They were realistic about things. The Khangan seemed to be slightly afraid of failure, but the countess remained undisturbed. She cast a quick glance at the jar with leeches and made a grimace of disgust.

"Dear medicus, how did you catch these creatures?"

"With the pig!" the man was offended. Lily sighed with relief.

"I don't like them, although they are very good for healing wounds. You've only ever used them on His Majesty, am I right?"

"Of course!"

The medicus wasn't lying. Lily sighed with relief.

A blood infection is the last thing we need!

"You can help if you want," Lily said in a simple voice. The man snorted but didn't leave. He got closer and watched. Lily asked for His Majesty's consent. She put on a sterile shirt with straps on her back, helped Tahir to put on another one, moved her hair under a headscarf and set to work. Tahir, who had recently shaved off his beard for hygiene reasons, assisted her confidently. He passed the instruments and helped to clear the wound.

Although he was given an anesthetic, Gardwig was still pale and green. He gritted his teeth in pain. Lily cleared the ulcer. She did it slowly and with confidence, just the way they taught them to treat purulent wounds in college. She would give half the kingdom for furacilin. Finally, she managed to get rid of the upper layer and sniffed it, trying to identify a distinctive smell. The smell of gangrene was impossible to confuse with anything else. *But no, it's not gangrene. What is it then?* The ulcer was thoroughly washed with calendula tincture. Afterward, the doctors put a sea salt compress on the wound and began questioning Gardwig.

Although they used the most eloquent figures of speech, they sucked his energy no worse than leeches. Half an hour later, Lily sighed in relief. Thank god, it wasn't diabetes or varicose, which would leave her no chance to cure him. The matter was far simpler. A few years earlier, Gardwig had gotten a wolf bite on his leg. It was well-deserved, in Lily's opinion. He shouldn't have poked animals with sharp objects for fun. That was different than killing animals for food. The king, however, simply did it for amusement. As a result, he got what he deserved. Wolf bites were a dangerous thing. The wolf managed to dig his teeth into the limb and tear it apart. Considering that wolves did not brush their teeth, the wound got infected.

At least the wolf wasn't mad, otherwise so much for Gardwig! The man seemed to have a brilliant immune system. It seemed that the medicuses hadn't cured the wound properly. It was likely that the wound had something left in it. The beast could have broken his tooth against the bone. The local medicuses didn't even think to check. There was no odor and eventually, the wound healed over. *Sweet,* thought the doctors. Only later, after half a year of a merry life, the first ulcer opened up in its place. Everyone panicked. Nobody thought to link it to the wolf story and identify the ulcer as post-traumatic.

At first, the ulcer was small but deep. It was healed again. After another half a year, it grew deeper and more disgusting. The wound closed up for as long as the immune system could process the ingenious remedies. Once the immune system weakened, things got worse.

No one was going to explain this to Gardwig. His misfortune was his vile character and well-spoken doctors. Nobody dared to argue with him. He led an unhealthy lifestyle. The medicuses tried to heal him with all folk remedies, right up to using the urine of a pregnant mare. The result was disastrous. Instead of opening the wound, making a drainage, and waiting for scarring as was required, they tried to soothe his pain and make the ulcer look less inflamed on the surface. And so the ulcer grew.

How is he still alive? While Lily tried to figure out the way to put it to Gardwig, Tahir spoke out.

"Your Majesty."

Why not? Gardwig is more likely to follow recommendations of the respectful Khangan, thought Lily.

Tahir explained that the ulcer was possible to treat and cure. The process was long and costly. The king shouldn't neglect it. He had to forget about hunting, walk around with a cane and follow a daily regimen. Alcohol and other harmful foods had to be excluded. Tahir put it so eloquently, with so much respect, that even the vilest of kings wouldn't have found fault in his words. Lily only shook her head. She wasn't strong in diplomacy. Gardwig contemplated everything and decided to try their treatment. It would last a year.

A year is not so long. At least these two are telling me something new. The rest of them do nothing but shake from fear and feed me promises. My ulcer is getting worse and worse. I cannot afford to die now. My children are still too young.

Lily and Tahir exchanged glances, and the Khangan began persuading Gardwig. He said that he wanted to either stay or teach his medicus how to go about the treatment. They agreed on a compromise. Once a day, Tahir would come with ointments, sterile bandages, and tinctures and watch how the medicus carried out the procedure. From time to time, the countess would also come with him. Tahir insisted on taking the medicus away for a little briefing.

Gardwig felt easier with painkillers, lotions, and competent dressing. Therefore, he agreed to send his medicus for a lesson in medicine.

༄ ༅

Lily and Tahir dragged the royal medicus out of the king's chamber almost by force. They went to the park and sat on the nearest bench. They could finally breathe freely.

"Phew! Tahir, praise Aldonai that there wasn't any green discharge. The king has a wonderful immune system!"

"I also got scared at the beginning. Lilian, how long do you think the treatment will last?"

"Around a year, or even longer."

The medicus from Wellster listened. The two doctors discussed the king's treatment in a matter-of-fact tone. They seemed to know exactly what they were talking about. The medicus, on the other hand, was often half-guessing. He genuinely believed the ulcer was caused by internal poisoning of skin juices and bad blood. He now learned that his assumption was faulty.

Do they possess some new kind of knowledge? Perhaps the Khangan knows a lot. It was he who spoke, whereas the countess merely tended the wound.

The main trouble with people was a lack of desire to learn. The reason for it could be arrogance, self-admiration, self-confidence, or mere stupidity. Without the desire to learn, there would have been no new knowledge. Yet, the medicus from Wellster was eager to learn. The man bowed to Tahir.

"Dearest—"

"Tahir Djiaman din Dashar," Tahir introduced himself.

"My pleasure. I am doctor Leonard Libertius. Would you care to explain to me what happened to His Majesty and how to treat him?" Lily and Tahir exchanged glances. The Khangan began explaining in simple language. He could do it better than Lilian, who always switched to her medical jargon out of habit. Tahir, on the other hand, explained it the way he understood it himself. The lecture lasted about an hour. The medicus from Wellster listened with his mouth and his eyes wide open.

He didn't care about his pride. His only wish was to cure the king. Those medicuses who were dismissed from their jobs could count themselves lucky. The others were hanged. Leonard didn't want to leave Wellster or die. To cure the king, he would even follow Maldonaya if he had to.

The difference between a good doctor and a bad doctor was the ability to admit to a mistake. It had been half a year since Leonard became His Majesty's medicus, and he realized that his treatment wasn't helping. On the contrary, the ulcer had become even bigger. It wasn't in his powers to heal it.

If these two think they know how to cure the king, let them teach me. They look like they don't mind sharing their knowledge. If something goes wrong, I can blame it on them. All of us are mortal, after all.

ഓ ☌ ര

Both Tahir and Lily could read these thoughts on the medicus' face yet they didn't want to sit by Gardwig all day. Their own king and his neuralgia caused them enough trouble already. On top of everything, Edward often complained about his spine and the aching in his liver.

Leave Leonard to treat his own king. If he follows our medical advice, it will be more than enough. Either way, it cannot get worse. Treating ulcers with leeches isn't the best idea. They are more effective against other illnesses. Although maybe they did help a little...

Some people hated mice or spiders. Lily had a real bee in her bonnet about leeches.

ଓ ଓ

"Your Majesty!"

"Leir Hans!" Lily was sincerely happy to see Hans.

When the royal representative wanted to see someone, he always got his way. He and Lilian crossed each other's paths somewhere in between Taral and Laveri.

"I'm glad to see you, Lilian," said Hans with a hint of hesitation.

"You know that you can always call me Lilian."

"What does your husband think about that?"

Lidarh caught up with Hans' stallion. The horses glanced at each other but remained calm and continued walking side by side. Their owners also exchanged glances and continued talking without smiling.

"I hope he will understand me correctly and won't stand between our friendship."

Hans nodded. It wasn't a good idea to mention that Jerisson Earton didn't believe in friendship between a man and a woman. In his opinion, the only thing a man and a woman could share was a bed.

"Lilian, you can always count on me, you know that."

The answer was a grateful smile.

"I don't love my husband. But I don't know what to do next."

"Is that so, My Lady?"

"I can run out the clock. But what's the use of it?"

"Sometimes time is our everything."

"Hans, I feel like I'm being mean. I took everything Jerisson Earton offered me, but I don't want to pay my dues."

"What do you mean by your dues? Repeated attempts on your life?" the man innocently suggested.

"You understand what I'm talking about. My name, my title, money—"

"No, I'm afraid I don't. Your name? Yes, it helped you to get noticed and heard. Surely, you don't need me to tell you that had you remained Lilian Broklend you would have still achieved the same heights? Your name and your title aren't worth very much. As for money, it gives you a certain freedom, but it is your own dowry. Where did you think Etor got his from?"

"Ah, I see now!"

"Slave-trading doesn't earn that much. You achieved a lot by yourself. You can thank Jerisson for your daughter. However, would Mirrie have loved you if it wasn't for your personality?"

"I doubt it."

"You don't owe him as much as you think you do. Don't blame yourself for anything."

"I do blame myself!" Lily looked solemn. Her sad eyes touched Hans' soul. "If something happens to Jerisson because of me, I will never forgive myself."

If something happens, you won't even know, thought Hans, but didn't say anything.

"Everything that happens or doesn't happen to Jess is entirely his own fault."

"I wish it was that simple!"

The man and the woman rode side by side, accompanied by the Virmans who tactfully slowed down their horses' pace and rode behind. Both of them were silent. Sometimes, words weren't needed. The silence made the bond between them stronger than a blood oath.

๛ ☙

"Uncle, my wife is so sweet, but it's impossible to get hold of her!"

"Perhaps you don't try hard enough." Edward was evidently mocking Jess. "Only today, she managed to visit Taral, my palace, the embassy of Wellster...and that is not everything."

"I understand why she drops with fatigue every evening."

Edward snorted.

"Doesn't she fall into your arms?"

"No," uttered Jerisson with grief.

"Who warms her up at night then?"

"Miranda, Lou-Lou, Nanook and two ferrets. This menagerie seems quite comfortable in my wife's bed."

Edward laughed heartily.

"If I were you, I would be jealous of the ferrets. Women love fluffy little creatures."

"I know. I am too big for her."

"Your daughter will also grow up soon. By the way, Prince Amir spoke to me about her."

"And?" Jerisson was clueless.

"He asks to marry your daughter."

"Never!" shouted Jerisson.

Edward raised his eyebrows in surprise.

"Why not?"

"He is a pagan!"

"He's already announced that he is ready to accept our faith in Aldonai for the sake of Miranda. He would even allow our missionaries to enter the Khanganat. The aldon is very happy about it."

Edward didn't mention Amir's cunning smile during his passionate speech. In reality, the Khangans cared nothing about who their ruler believed in. Amir wasn't going to build churches in the Khanganat and forcibly convert his people. He only promised to let the aldons enter the Khangan lands.

They could preach if they wanted to, only who would listen? First and foremost, I believe in the Heavenly Mare. I don't know her stableman. It's a question of philosophy, and I will leave it to the priests.

The Khangans didn't choose their crown prince by religion. They selected the ruler by wisdom, connections, and power to keep the country together. The ordinary people didn't care about what happened outside of their own country.

"I think we need to strengthen our relationship with the Khanganat."

"But why Miranda?"

"Because the prince has chosen her himself. If he chose Angelina or Joliette, I wouldn't say a word against it."

"My daughter is still too young!"

"Precisely. Therefore, we will arrange for an engagement. The wedding itself wouldn't happen earlier than seven years from now. Amir himself said so."

The king's words only increased Jess's fears.

"Is it common for them to have several wives?"

"Miranda will be his first and only wife."

"What about the concubines?"

Edward's gaze was openly malignant.

"Am I really hearing this from the man who visited every lady of the court with his banner raised and his trousers lowered?"

Jerisson cast down his eyes. Edward continued adding insult to injury.

"If polygamy was allowed in our kingdom, you would have certainly gotten yourself a dozen wives. Without a doubt. Good luck chasing ferrets!"

"Uncle!"

"Not everything is entirely your fault. Nevertheless, you are the one to sort everything out. I pity you."

Jess sighed, realizing that he had no choice.

"Uncle, may I speak to Prince Amir?"

"You may. Bear in mind that I'm interested in establishing a close relationship with the Khanganat. It would be good for Richard to marry Anna. Our tripartite union will destroy the pirates from Loris and trade will get going. Gardwig is annoyed about the salt, but if Tahir cures him, it will make him more tolerant. Besides, we wouldn't be able to produce in such large quantities. We would have to be buying it for some time anyway. It will give them enough time to sort their produce."

Jess shrugged.

"There is no escape from politics."

"That's right. You should stay in the palace for the night and check that the guards are in order. The Iverneans come tomorrow. They are already near the capital."

"Your Majesty, but I wanted to—"

"You can see your wife tomorrow. She comes to see me every day. I must say that I feel sorry for you and envy you at the same time. I wish I was twenty years younger."

"What about my aunt?"

"I loved Jessamine," confessed Edward with sincerity. "People admire women like your wife. She is clever and useful. Think about how much she can do for the capital!"

"Are you suggesting that I should settle for being a sponge?"

"Certainly not. What an idiot!" Edward rubbed his temples. "Not a sponge, but a husband who leaves the business to his wife because she does it better."

"What would people say?"

"Go and think about it!" Edward said forcefully.

Jerisson sprang to his feet, bowed, and left the king's study. His mood was worse than ever. His daughter was given in marriage, he wouldn't get to see his wife, and he'd been given a job for the night.

He would make sure his guards got their fill of cake. Jess needed to take his anger out on somebody.
I will kill everyone right now!

Chapter 5
Princess' fickle game

"Aldonai be merciful!"

The service progressed as usual. Everything was as peaceful as ever—all but the princess who was on pins and needles.

Her wait was finally over. At the very end of the service, a large man with a black beard dressed like a wealthy merchant passed in suspiciously close proximity to the princess. She recognized her husband.

Anna capriciously chased away her maids.

"I wish to speak to the priest. Wait outside!"

They had no reason to contradict her wishes. The church was a safe place. Not much could happen there. And so, the maids were deceived. It wasn't difficult for Lons to leave the prayer book on the bench, where Anna picked it up and took it inside one of the confession rooms. She left it in exactly the same spot where she found it. The forgetful merchant returned for his prayer book after the service and found a short note inside.

Tomorrow evening, prepare everything for our escape from the eastern gates of the palace.

Lons rushed to the countess. Unlike her husband, he knew where to find her.

Lily received the news with obvious displeasure.

"So, you aren't going to Earton?"

Lons shook his head emphatically.

"No, My Lady."

"Who will replace you?"

"My friend will," smiled Lons. Lily frowned looking at the teacher of natural sciences.

"Leon Alhert?"

"Yes, madam." The teacher bowed.

"Why do you want to be my secretary?"

"Because My Lady knows more about the natural sciences than I do. Children ask me questions that I cannot answer. I feel a fool. It's time for me to learn."

"And?"

Children did ask her questions, and she answered them. They looked extremely interested.

"You will drive me away soon. I don't want to leave. I like my trade, and you pay well for it. Perhaps I will be of use. Even though I am a leir and my father is an ordinary merchant, I am well-educated and have good handwriting. I want to be your loyal servant."

Lily squinted.

"What if someone offers you money in return for information about me?"

Leon ran his fingers through his golden hair and showed a mischievous smile.

"I will obviously take it and tell everything to Sir Tremain, My Lady."

Lily grinned.

"Fine. Let's try you. I will give you a thirty-day trial. If you manage to get familiar with everything, I will leave you. If not, you will go back to teaching."

"As you wish, My Lady."

"He has good handwriting," Lons stood up for him. "He is my old friend. Besides, I am not meeting my death either. I could help him to get the hang of his new role. Until then, Taris Brok could help you. August's people would be happy to give you a hand."

Lily nodded slowly.

"Fine, Lons. When do you meet? And how did you agree to run away? Horses, carriage…"

"I will buy a few horses today. I was never short of money when working for you. As for the rest, could Erik—"

"He could. Talk to him. I can ask him myself if you want."

"Please, ask him."

"Fine. I will. You still have the horses to sort out. You also need to take care of Anna. You know what you're doing. Maybe you can come back in a couple of years when everything calms down."

Lons shrugged. It was unlikely.

"May I take my leave?"

"Stay where you are!" ordered Lily. She found her purse with coins. She didn't have much. She paid bills, salaries, and other expenses. The money dispersed in all directions with great speed. She, the owner of the trademark "Mariella," which sold its products across every state, counted copper coins. She gave him everything she had.

"Take it. There can never be enough money."

She could refuse a new dress. The old one would do at court.

Lons took his leave. Lily cast a thoughtful look at Leon.

"So, Leon. First, sort the mail. Afterward, come to my study. I have something to write up."

Leon bowed and hurried to work. Lily touched one of the drawers and took out the scroll with Lons' writing. Everything was brief and clear. It had mention of the names, described the wedding with Anna, his lawful rights, how they sold him to the ship instead of killing him and so on. Pastor Vopler was a witness, although he didn't read it himself. When Lons finished writing, he dried the ink with sand, folded it and sealed it with his own stamp. Pastor Vopler did the same.

Lily did not believe in Anna's desire to run away with Lons. *But what if it is true?* If so, she wished them happiness. The main thing was to make sure that none of her people got into serious trouble. If everything went smoothly, Lons would take Anna, drive to the shore, and depart on the ship. If not, Lily would place his confession on Edward's desk.

Lily wasn't going to admit that she knew of the plot. She would pretend that she had nothing to do with it. That did not stop her from causing a row. She wouldn't let some ladybug get away with the murder of one of her people. The truth was on her side. Every virginity check would show that the princess was lying. Let her prove that she wasn't a camel.

Lily rang the bell.

"Leon, be my friend, call Erik in as soon as he shows up."

"He is already here. He is training. Should I ask him in?"

"Do!"

She felt a duty to provide her Romeo with transportation to August's shipyards. The couple would change ship there and depart to Earton or the Khanganat. Erik agreed to take Lons with another passenger and the horses at night and take them to August's shipyards. Lily sent him to Lons to arrange everything, and could finally relax a little.

There were two scenarios.

Either Lons and his wife will depart tonight and head to the four winds. Or...

Lily didn't want to think of the second option. A miracle had saved Avels once. *Would a miracle save him again?* Lily doubted it. She didn't know what to do.

Should I take precautions and let the actions take their course? Yes.

Lily took out a piece of paper and drew a couple of lines. She contemplated.

There is no need to brood over the first option, where everyone lives happily ever after. But what if Anna tells everything to the agents of Wellster? The fact that Count Lort failed once doesn't mean that he will fail again. Lons might die tonight. The first option—they capture and interrogate him. However, times are dangerous. They won't do it so openly. The second option—they kill him. It's simple. No person, no problem. The third option—Lons will be magically saved. In that case, I will need to either immediately drive him to Edward, or hide him. They will be looking for him and will find him sooner or later.

Lily was ready to deal with the consequences. She was ready for anything. The third option was the saddest. Certain people, especially religious, would have judged Lily for her cool pragmatism. She expected a person to die and did nothing about it. Although any death brought her much grief, Lily perceived it as a part of life. Lons was a grown man and could take responsibility for himself. No one asked him to trust Anna. No matter what Lily thought, Lons would still try to get his way. She was not his mother to keep him by the tail.

If Lily didn't intervene, she would have been the first one to lose her head.

Let destiny take its course. She had to show up at the palace. The diplomatic mission from Ivernea was about to arrive.

I cannot be bothered, but I have no say in the matter.

Lily's mood was spoiled, and she decided to visit Taral in order to cool her mind. She took Lidarh and set off. *Pity they gave up horses as transport back in my own world! How smart and beautiful they are! Where is Aliya Skorolenok? She's lost forever. I am Lilian Earton now. There is only one trouble. I fell out of my century but haven't gotten used to the new one. I need at least three or four more years to make it feel like home. Will they let me live that long?*

૪૭ ◻ ଓ

Lydia of Ivernea looked at Laveri. *A beautiful city. It smells of the sea.*

"How are you, sister?"

It was her elder brother. The princess was accompanied by Prince Adrian and Prince Miguel. Bernard had decided not to go.

"I am fine. Only a little tired. Where are we going now?"

"To the king. We will go to the embassy after, to rest."

Lydia was sad. They spent the night near the capital, sent the messenger, and had time to get ready in the morning. Such was the etiquette.

Nevertheless, she didn't want to do anything. She couldn't bear the pains of her unfortunate first love and shameful blackmail. Lydia was smart. She understood that she wasn't beautiful. She knew that the prince would always choose Anna over her. She realized that her dowry wasn't much.

There were a lot of reasons for her sadness. She felt terrible. Yet, even though it was hard, she had to keep a good face during a bad game.

An honorary escort took them to the king. Lydia furtively glanced around. It was beautiful. It smelled of the sea, and she could hear the scream of seagulls—a pleasant place. The procession went through the city. Lydia hid in the carriage and didn't look out of it. It had recently rained, and the streets were dirty. The Royal Palace was a beautiful place. It had white stone and tall walls and was decorated with flags.

Edward received them cordially. He sent the honorary escort, the guardsmen with naked sabers, and the trumpeters. The brothers were happy. Lydia was sad. She wasn't loved by anyone. No one cared about her. She was in a state of melancholia. Miguel helped his sister get out of the carriage, and they followed Adrian, who carried the credentials.

Lydia looked around. Small groups of men and ladies ambled around the palace. Not everyone fit into the Royal Hall, but everyone was interested in watching. People peered inside from the corridors. Lydia wasn't a fool. She noticed pity in the eyes of the women and disgusting indifference in the eyes of the men. No one liked her there. She was a blank space.

They reached the Royal Hall. A herald announced the titles. Lydia listened nonchalantly. It was the looks that really got to her. No matter how hard she tried to turn a blind eye, no matter how much she told herself that she was stronger and more intelligent, no matter how proud she was, those looks still got to the bottom of her soul. She was hurt. It was like sand and granite. One could ignore a grain of sand, but suddenly there were tens, hundreds, thousands of them, and it became a solid mass of granite. Lydia lifted her forehead, but it didn't help. She had dull hair, an unfashionable hairstyle, an old dress, coarse shoes, and cold manners. *Aldonai, help! Make it all end!*

Lydia endured the reception until the end. She returned Edward's compassionate smile and spotted the malicious grins of the courtiers when Richard kissed her hand. Their thoughts resounded through her head.

You can be thrice a princess, but he will still sleep with others. You are a tart. A smart tart! What could be worse?

Unfortunately for Lydia, a silly woman wouldn't realize the true horror of her position. She did her best to show no emotion. She managed to hide her feelings in the palace. Yet, she lost it as soon as she got to the embassy. She threw herself onto the bed, sent all her servants to Maldonaya, and cried her eyes out.

It is shameful, humiliating, disgusting! I could see them gloating when Richard chose Anna over me! Nobody will say it to my face, but their eyes still scream, "even the title of a princess didn't help this scarecrow!" They will repeat it behind my back many times. No matter how much I say that I don't like Richard, nobody will believe me, even if it's thrice the truth! Aldonai, be merciful, how sick I am.

✥

Lilian Earton was also sick, though for a different reason. She didn't meet the diplomatic mission itself, but Jerisson Earton caught her in the corridor, gallantly bowed, and kissed her hand.

"You look wonderful today, dear Countess."

Lilian was wearing a simple ash-rose dress, her hair was decorated with strands of pearls, and she had pearls about her neck and wrists. She looked splendid.

"Jerisson," she smiled to her husband, having remembered her promise to fix the relationship.

"Lilian, you have an incredible smile!" The way he said it—although not entirely sincere—was quiet and heartfelt. He looked her right in the eyes and held her hand. Right at that moment, Alexander Falion appeared around the corner. Jerisson lifted his head and looked at him with a predator's eye. He was like a street cat trying to drive away a rival. As for Falion himself, he didn't say a word. He only bowed and walked past. Lily saw his eyes. He had almost imperceptibly pulled himself together, but a trace of feeling remained. Lily mechanically smiled at her husband, chattered, let him walk her home, and even let him be present when she put Miranda to bed. There was a dark leftover pain at the bottom of her soul. *What should I do now? Write a letter, like they would do in a bad play? Express her repentance and declare her love? Run after Alex and ensure him that it was nothing; that it was not what he thought? The worst thing is that it wasn't a mistake.*

How sickening.

൚ ൏

Lons Avels was happy. He was going to get the woman he loved. Anna would finally reunite with him. She was his wife, his little girl, his lover. She didn't abandon, betray, or fall out of love with him. They were separated by the cruelty of life, but they would soon reunite. *How wonderful!* They would live together, have children, grow old, and in some fifteen years, they would remember the present with a smile.

Anna, Anneli, my love! I miss you so much!

He was immensely grateful to Lilian Earton. If it weren't for her, nothing would have been possible. But now, everything was fine. They would be happy. If they had a daughter, he would name her Lilian, in honor of their savior.

The embassy was still a mile away. He would wait there for Anna and head back. Two of Leis' people rode next to Lons. One of them was from Earton, and Lons forgot his name. They finally reached the Embassy of Wellster and the old back gates, dirty, used by the guards.

"I will go alone." Lons dismounted the horse and threw the reins to one of the men. The man shrugged.

"Go. We will wait for you here."

Lons slowly walked to the gates. It was dirty, and it reeked. There were a couple of barrels there with human excrement. He waited for Anna.

The last thing he heard was the whistle of the arrow. He even managed to feel the pain when it broke through his chest. Lons let out a cry, dropped onto his knees, staring in amazement at the plumage sticking out of his chest. The last thing he saw was Anna's face. She was waiting for him with a smile on her face. The pain quickly retreated, and Lons had suddenly found himself running down the field of chamomiles, just like he used to do in his childhood. Leis' people also turned into unwitting victims. The agents of Altres Lort had been waiting to ambush him from the very beginning. They had expected that Lons wouldn't come alone.

Lons didn't know that three arrows had whistled almost simultaneously and that six people descended from the trees. Lort's people were very well prepared. They delicately touched the veins on the victim's necks and quickly nodded to each other. The targets were all dead. The first thing they did was search the bodies and put everything they found into one pile. Second, they broke off the ends of the arrows without pulling them out of the bodies. Third, they crammed the bodies inside the barrels with human excreta (also known as honey wagons) that stood on the cart outside the gate and smelled terribly. Even though the task wasn't pleasant, one couldn't think of a better way to remove corpses.

The cart would go along the road and turn toward the shore. Usually, there was nothing for the honey dippers to do by the sea, but that time it was different. Now their task was to fill the honey wagons with rocks and dispose of them. The waves were high and smashed against the rocks. The fishermen never went to that spot, but the fish would soon.

Afterward, the killers looked through the confiscated stuff. There wasn't anything unusual. Lons had significantly more money than the other men—a whole purse. It didn't have any crest on it. Lily had recently gotten it from the local market. It would have been good to question Lons before killing him, but it was impossible to do in Ativerna. It wasn't Wellster. The embassy had local servants. Every second man was a spy. It was extremely risky.

The count's agents worked quickly and skillfully, but still didn't find anything. Back in those times, people had no ID cards or passports. Lily had once wanted to give her people personal badges but had changed her mind, and rightly so.

Erik waited for the passengers in vain. He waited all night, and at dawn went to report back to Lilian.

☙ ❧

Anna of Wellster paced around the room.

Today. Is this really happening? Aldonai help me!

She would become a widow that day if she was lucky. It sounded terrible. It was horrible to wish for another person's death. She had no other option. Lons stood between her and freedom, wealth, and becoming the queen—all because of her careless behavior. Anna wrinkled her nose at the memories of the past.

She was a small and silly girl, only beginning to realize her power and authority over men. Her breasts became full, her figure took a round shape, her voice became deeper. It had been three years since Lons joined their household. She remembered one day especially well. He talked about something stupid like geography; he stood at the blackboard when a wild ray of sunshine shone through the hole in the parchment used as a window-blind. It illuminated his face, and Lons smiled. He looked so handsome that Anna even got scared. That day she decided to get him. It was partly done to annoy her sister, who also found him good-looking.

They were so sneaky, so skilled in hiding their affair! It seemed so small and ridiculous now. She had won. Lons Avels became her legitimate prey. Despite everything, she felt fine with him. She was truly happy. She felt joy. However, he could offer her nothing but his name. To become a leira for a princess meant almost nothing. Only a simple peasant woman was worse than that.

Nevertheless, she accepted his offer. She was even happy for some while. The thought of her purest happiness didn't leave her in peace. It made the present situation worse. She couldn't throw out the lyrics from her song. She had loved him once. Only Lons was never a prince and would never become one. They had different fates. He must have realized this himself. He was the one to blame for everything. *Why did he need to come to me? Why come back from the dead?* Anna knew the answer but refused to acknowledge it. *Pathetic idiot! How dare he even think about my love! Eww. He deserved his destiny. It served him right to die.*

Yet still, at the thought of their elementary happiness in the old palace, the boiling tears marred Anna's vision. She let out a sob and threw herself on the pillow. She glanced at the moon. It was past midnight. *It's the end of him. Goodbye, Lons. Goodbye, my husband. I am truly a widow now.*

ಬಿ ೞ

Erik showed up at breakfast. Jess was already at the palace, attending to embassy affairs, therefore, Lily's sole companion was a large pink rose. Lily admired the flower and contemplated the vicissitudes of life. The Virman interrupted her.

"Erik, what happened?"

"They didn't come."

"HOW COME?"

"Nobody came, neither he, nor she, nor any of your people."

"What did you do?"

"I sent my people there. They searched everything and found a couple of drops of blood and trampled grass. They were lucky to come before the dew fell."

Lily nodded.

"Do you think it was—?"

"I am sure of it. It was a murder."

Lily threw a napkin on the table. She lost her appetite entirely.

"Hans Tremain. I need him now!"

꧁ ꧂

Hans could sense something ominous and showed up within half an hour. He stole a couple of buns from the dining room and presented himself to the countess chewing them.

"Excuse me, My Lady."

Lily waved her hand and rang the bell. The servant appeared in the doorway.

"My Lady," tried to insert the leir.

"Hurry!"

Lily was silently waiting for Hans to finish his breakfast. Only when he put aside the cutlery did the countess begin pacing the room.

"Lilian, what happened?"

Lily gathered all strength and said, "I suspect that Lons Avels was killed last night."

"What?"

Hans rose to his feet. He and Lons were friends. They had gone for a drink a couple of times and sometimes talked about life. Avels was a diligent worker, and Hans took notice of it on more than one occasion for he himself was an avid workaholic.

"Yes. They expected him today, and he didn't come."

"Lilian!"

Hans could tell that Lilian was hiding something yet he kept silent for fear of scaring her off. He was right. Lily walked across the carpet, tapped her fingers on the mantle of the fireplace and finally resolved to tell the story.

"Hans, you and I share so many secrets that one more wouldn't make much difference."

Tremain smiled sadly.

"The truth cannot leave this room. I understand. Who was Lons? A spy? A prince? Gardwig's illegitimate brother?"

"He was Anna's husband."

"WHAT?"

Hans was genuinely taken aback.

"He once taught the young princesses. Anna liked him and started making gestures of affection."

"What?"

"She began to flirt with him and tried to make him like her."

"Hmm!"

"Lons couldn't resist the temptation. Since he was an honest man, he first married Anna."

"But they didn't tell Gardwig and didn't run away either. Did they live a secret life?"

"Does that surprise you?"

"Gardwig could have easily cut off his head and sent her to the monastery."

"He could have," agreed Lily, recalling the king's recent behavior. "I bet he would've done so!"

"And then? The love ended when Anna was chosen to be Richard's bride?"

Lily nodded.

"You are smart, Hans."

"Is it time to kill me now?"

"No, it's time to reward you."

"So, what happened after all?"

"They found out about them. According to Lons, it wasn't the king. It was Count Lort. He's a dexterous piece of work."

"Very well put."

"Do you know him?"

"He is the head of Gardwig's intelligence squad. He is a beast and a piece of scum, and very smart. He is loyal to the country and his brother, the king, like a dog."

"His brother?"

"Gardwig is his milk brother."

"Wow. I see."

"Lort caught them out."

"He must have interrogated Lons and ordered his men to kill him."

"How did he survive?"

"They decided to make a profit on him and sold them into slavery."

"The guy was lucky and managed to run away."

"It seems like he's not so lucky."

"Lilian?"

"Oh, Lons! When he told me that, he asked me to help him return Anna."

"What did you get yourself into?"

For the first time in her life, Lily saw Hans turn white as a piece of chalk, jump to his feet, and grab her shoulders.

"Who else? Who else knows that you were involved?"

"Nobody. Lons kept silent. I didn't tell anyone else."

Hans let her go and almost dropped onto the chair. He sighed heavily.

"Forgive me, My Lady."

"Call me Lilian. Nobody knew about my involvement."

"Glory be to Aldonai!"

Lily nodded.

"I'm not that stupid. Such secrets reek of human blood."

"Both your blood and the blood of your loved ones," Hans responded gloomily. "What else should I know? Maybe Lidarh is an enchanted prince? By Jove, I could believe anything!"

"Lidarh is not a prince. And neither am I. I think that's it. Why?"

"Because, My Lady, you are bad at keeping secrets and bad at lying, too. Is there anything else?"

Lily hesitated. A moment later, she took out a simple scroll of parchment from her drawer.

The fireproof safe was not yet ready, but the drawer was already metal and stuffed with sand. Lily had trouble unlocking it. She didn't remember the principles of safes, and it was hard to recreate a code lock.

"This is Lons' letter. He wrote it with his own hand. It's a full confession."

Hans looked at the scroll as if it were a poisonous snake. He accepted it and turned it over in his hands.

"The seal of Pastor Vopler?"

"Yes."

"Did he read it?"

"No. Lons wrote it in front of him. He sealed it himself and gave it to the pastor to seal it for the second time."

"That means that the pastor's life can be saved. It's good. What are you going to do with it?"

Lily sighed.

"I don't know, Hans. I want you to find out what happened to Lons and the two people from Leis' guard who accompanied him. If they are alive, we need to free them. If not..."

"Do you want revenge?"

"Revenge?"

Lily's smile was bitter.

"Do I look like an idiot?" Hans was tempted to say that, in some cases, the resemblance was spot on. He refrained from making that joke. Having spotted its trace in his eyes, the countess sadly dropped her eyes.

"We have a peaceful relationship with Wellster. What would happen after we let the pig out?"

Hans was confused.

"The pig?"

"The letter that says that Anna is a tainted fruit."

"Scandal, dispute, war!"

"Do we really need that?"

"No."

They exchanged glances. They weren't going to leave the suspected murder of Lons unpunished. It was up to their conscience on how to seek revenge.

"I am going to the embassy."

"Take your people."

"I know. I won't go alone. I promise. I will try to figure out what happened. Where did they agree to meet?"

"I didn't know anything. Lons enclosed Anna's note inside. It's written in her own hand."

"Here is where!"

"Next to the gate for gold."

Hans sighed.

"My Lady, promise me to do nothing until I return."

Lily promised with a clear conscience.

ঙ০ ෫

The Embassy of Wellster, Hans had been there before—before the arrival of the royals from Wellster. It was his job. He knew the gates and already suspected why they had been chosen as the meeting place. The honey diggers came in the early morning. Even if there had been a crime, all tracks and traces would have been covered twenty times. Yet Hans wanted to double check. Still, he found nothing. The place was so trampled and packed with sewage that it was possible to murder a whole military squad there without anyone noticing.

Hans did notice several cots. *Someone must have waited here for a long time. But why?*

He suspected the killers had waited for Avels there. As for his companions, the two Virmans were a good backup, but only if they were at sea. The Virmans were good for fights and crusades. As bodyguards, they were below average. It was simply not their vocation.

Lons had most likely been killed. Hans didn't think the others less clever than himself. It was tricky to hold a prisoner for interrogation in a foreign territory where it could cause an international scandal. If Hans were in their place, he would've simply killed Lons. No person, no problem.

Let's assume Lons and the Virmans were dead. There is a letter with a full confession and enclosed proof. Should we offer it to the king? We could. How much is he interested in the marriage and the union with Wellster? Would it be better for the king to kill the agent instead?

Hans knew too much. He risked getting killed by the Crown. Sadly, the countess' joke had a shred of truth in it.

Who else could we present with the evidence? Gardwig? Very funny. The Iverneans? Could do, although such an act smells like state treason. What if we catch Anna in a trap and give the letter to Richard? That could work. The main thing is to remain unnoticed.

Hans didn't want to put the countess in danger. She was also loyal to her people. If he didn't take care of everything himself, the countess would definitely intervene.

If she gets involved, she will do more damage than a bull in a china shop! The whole party, including me, will have to flee to the Khanganat. I would like to avoid such extreme scenarios!

ಬಿ ಜ

Anna was sitting in her room when she heard a tapping on the door. The princess raised her head and saw a familiar face. The man took a respectful bow as if it wasn't him who had spoken so crudely to Anna a few days ago.

"Your Highness, everything is sorted."

"Is he...—"

"Yes. This time for real."

"T-thank you."

Anna coldly led the man to the door and burst into tears as soon as she closed the door behind him. *Is it relief? Grief? Sadness? Only Aldonai knows. Oh, how it hurts!*

ಬಿ ಜ

"Lydia, this evening we are going to the ball in the palace."

"Miguel!" Lydia looked at her brother. He was still a boy. *Aldonai knows, he is still a child!*

"What is there to be happy about?"

"Why not? You will dance, have fun…"

Lydia didn't reply. *What use is the ball to me?* Richard had already chosen someone else. Their visit was just a diplomatic gesture. It tortured her.

She wasn't beautiful. She wasn't even rich. Although Lydia was a princess, her dowry was still very little. Her soul hadn't healed yet from her betrayal. *Betrayal is an awfully painful thing. I know that the pain won't cease for another ten, maybe twenty long, lonely years!*

Her father wouldn't give her into an unequal marriage. She wondered what would happen to her. She expected malicious glances, chuckles, whispers.

I spit on them! I am Lydia of Ivernea. I don't give a damn about this trash! I am a princess!

Her chin lifted. Lydia was a fighter, only she wasn't used to fighting for her own rights.

☙ ❧

Lily was playing backgammon with Miranda when Jerisson Earton entered the house. He stumbled upon a peaceful picture: his two favorite women, wooden checkers, dice. Jess watched his wife and admired her beauty. If she had looked like that at their wedding, he would have thought himself a lucky man. He wouldn't have even thought of getting terribly drunk or sending her away. She was tall and had full breasts, a slender waist, gorgeous golden locks, white skin, a tiny sliver of a smile on her pink lips and a spectacular sense of self-worth. *How could I have been so blind?*

"Mars!"

"I will try anyway!"

"Don't give up. Who knows, you still have a tiny little chance of beating me!"

Were it not for the growling dogs, the two players wouldn't have noticed the earl's appearance.

"It's Papa! He's arrived!"

Lily slowly rose to her feet.

"My Lord."

"Madam," replied Jess, rewarding Miranda with a kiss on the nose. "Baby girl, go for a walk in the garden."

"In that case, you have to promise me not to quarrel!"

"We will try our best. Go!"

"Take the dogs with you, Mirrie," Lilian said.

The girl glanced at her, smiling, and left the room. Lily looked at her husband.

"How are you, Jerisson?"

"Better than ever! Lilian, would you accept my invitation to the ball in honor of the Iverneans this evening?"

"Uh!" Lilian genuinely didn't want to go anywhere.

"We very rarely appear in public together. Maybe it's about time to announce to the world that the Eartons are one?"

Jess made a compelling point.

"It is. Have you seen the prince yet?"

"Richard?"

"No, I am talking about Miranda's fiancé, Amir Gulim."

"Not yet," Jerisson frowned.

"I will try to introduce you to each other at the ball. I suppose he is invited?"

"I should think so."

"We will need to discuss the dowry and his future contact with Mirrie."

"You don't want to give our daughter away to a foreign country." Jess could see perfectly that Lily was worried about their little baby.

"It's true. I don't want to let her go. Yet, we have no say in the matter. Amir is not a bad man. He is smart and earnest, Mirrie knows him, and they have mutual respect for one another."

"What about love?"

"We ourselves don't love each other yet," sighed Lilian.

"But we have a chance, no?"

Lily shrugged.

"I hope so."

"I will do my best." Jerisson looked into his wife's green eyes. They were so close to each other, even a saint wouldn't have managed to resist such a temptation. He slowly leaned over, giving his wife time to change her mind and pull away, but Lilian stood still, her look fixed on his eyes. The man slowly touched her pink lips with a kiss. At first, the kiss was tender, but it gradually became fiercer and deeper. His strong male hands enclosed the woman into a tight embrace. One palm held the back of her head and drew her closer to him. *She is sublime!* The kiss could have led to something more if it wasn't for a loud "woof."

Nanook was perfectly polite, but the couple withdrew from each other as if scalded.

"Good Lord!" shouted Jess. Lily blushed and snorted.

"Jerisson, weren't you trying to invite me to the ball?"

"Yes."

"In that case, I'll go get ready."

"But wait—"

"Don't offer me your help. We would never get to the ball like that."

Lilian disappeared faster than a whirlwind, leaving Jerisson alone. He sank into a chair. His hands still retained the feel of her voluptuous body, and the kiss still burned his lips.

He felt like such a fool for not being able to appreciate his wife before.

What a woman! It's not too late to catch up. I want more, more, longer, longer! What a woman!

ಐ ☐ ಜ

Hans managed to return while Lily was getting ready. He found the countess in all her glory—white dress, flying green lace, and expensive emeralds around her neck, in her ears and on her wrists.

Her golden hair was braided in a complex braid, which was also intertwined with lace and amber.

What a beauty!

"Hans! Finally!" Their eyes met in the mirror reflection, and she noticed his meaningful glance.

"Girls, leave us alone."

Hans waited for the servants to leave the chamber, inspected the adjoining room, and sighed.

"Things are bad, My Lady."

"How bad?"

"I suppose we won't see either Avels or your people again."

"Are you sure?"

"I cannot say for certain, but the meeting place was chosen with purpose. One would never find any trace of murder in that swamping ground."

"What about the bodies?"

"The honey wagon. They were most likely put into barrels and transported along the road. Nobody would check inside of them."

Lily nodded.

"It is very bad. What are we going to do next?"

"I need to think. In any case, a slutty murderer on the throne is not the best gift for the country."

Lily sighed.

"Who knows who else might take the princess on the leash. What should we do?"

"We have to wait at least a few days."

"What next?"

"I'll think of something, Lilian."

Lily sighed. It was sad and sickening. She had already lost her loved ones. She had now lost a man who had become her friend and her teacher in this world. It hurt.

A strong hand lay on her shoulder.

"You wouldn't have stopped him."

"I know. Yet, I could have tried."

"You couldn't have. Lilian, don't think that everyone is less clever than you are." It was an insolent comment, but Hans could let himself say what he really thought. "He was going to get killed anyway. His death is a great grief, but it kept you out of serious trouble."

"They could still track me down and figure out that I was involved."

"How?"

"Pastor Vopler."

"Do you mean his seal? I can melt its surface. Nobody would be able to identify whose seal it is. Who else?"

"Lons tried not to let himself be known."

"Lons is a common name in these parts. Besides, it was hard to identify him with a beard. Have you ever told anyone about his existence?"

"No."

"Lilian, how long have you known about his chosen one?"

"Long enough. That's why he was trying to hide."

"He realized that it put his life in danger and that it could also end badly for you. I'm sure they wouldn't be able to track you down. Nobody would think that you might be involved."

Lilian nodded. If Hans said that she was safe, that was the case.

"Hans, tell me, what would happen if they find out about Anna?"

"A scandal."

"No, I mean if the princess and the prince—"

"They would most likely break off the engagement."

"What would happen to Anna?"

"They would send her to a nunnery."

Lily bit her lip. She had heard a lot of unpleasant things about the local nunneries.

"She deserves it. How would it influence our relationship with Gardwig?"

"Not in a positive way, but we could always come to a mutual agreement, especially if we don't publicize what happened."

"I remember him having other daughters."

"Yes, but the next one is around two years younger than Anna. She will reach marriageable age in about a year."

Lily nodded.

"When are you going to deliver the confession letter?"

"Either today or tomorrow."

"My husband invited me to the ball."

"I wish you to have a very good time, My Lady."

Lily made a funny grimace. Hans returned her smile in the mirror. Both of them knew that the countess would prefer a quiet evening next to the fireplace with her daughter, her dogs, and a book. Hans himself enjoyed such evenings. He remembered how, in Earton, everyone used to gather in the sitting room after dinner and set about their own business. Some preferred to read, others enjoyed talking with each other. The Virman women would usually be weaving lace. Lily was always busy writing something, getting now and then distracted by a joke or a conversation. The pastor often debated with Leif, and the children liked to sit on the floor covered with bear skins and play with puppies. Everything was so calm and comfortable. Sometimes it was noisy and fun, sometimes, quiet and peaceful. Such evenings were rare in the city, and Hans missed them.

"You have to go, My Lady."

"I have to go," echoed Lily. She stood up from her desk.

"I put my hopes in you, Hans."

ಬ ⬜ ಅ

Jess knew that his wife was a beautiful woman, but not to that extent. He saw a beautiful vision descending the staircase. Gorgeous breasts, long hair, mysterious green eyes. Lily's dress looked expensive and teased the eye, emphasizing the stunning figure of its wearer.

The man involuntarily bowed only to hide the gleam in his eyes.

"Lilian, you are lovely."

Lily replied with a bow of her head.

"May I—"

There was a tiny bracelet with emeralds in his hand. It wasn't as heavy and bulky as the titular bracelet. It was a light, elegant bezel, adorned with a rainbow made of stones and pearls. Lily held out her wrist, and Jess put the bracelet on it and touched her perfumed skin with his lips.

"Thank you for the present, my dear husband."

"They are as bright as your eyes."

"You flatter me."

"No, I flatter the emeralds."

Lily let Jess put a shawl on her shoulders and lead her to the carriage. She gave him a radiant smile. The earl was going to go by horse. Jess didn't want to scare off his prey. *Why didn't she look like that at the wedding?*

🙵 ☐ ☙

Beauties, lackeys, cadets, Schubert's waltzes and the crunch of French bread. That's how Lily used to imagine balls.

In reality, the beauties' dresses roamed with fleas, the knights scratched their genitals, dogs wandered under the guest's feet, and the music was out of tune. On any other day, Lily would have treated the ball like an amusing adventure. She walked with the noble earl and greeted the people around her. She could hear them speaking about her behind her back: whether they had reconciled or slept together, her unfeminine profession and his promiscuity. She could hear the courtiers' whispering. Lily could tell which ladies had had a romance with her husband. Some tried to touch his sleeve or batted their eyelashes, others even attempted to slip a little note into his palm or drop a handkerchief. *Silly goats!*

She was a new face at court. *They must think if Jess cheated on me before, why would he not be cheating now?* Everyone thought her the same person as at the wedding. All of them wondered why her husband locked her up in the estate and strayed. Lily was fuming, but she concealed it well. She spoke politely to the king about the state of his health and curtsied to Gardwig, who was in a good mood since his leg hurt him less. He sent Jess off to dance with the princess and invited Lilian to sit down for a private conversation.

He still had a long way to recovery. Attending balls and long voyages weren't good for his leg. Lily wielded the matter in high speeches, implying that the king should rest more. The king replied that he was happy to cut down on formal visits and dances, only to treat his ulcer. He knew that his illness could be fatal.

Lily herself realized that the local medicine had no solution against such ulcers, no matter their cause. The only thing they had figured out was that it caused "the burning of blood." It wasn't surprising, considering their poor hygiene.

Blood poisoning, gangrene, death—Lily was going to fight against all three. She had already managed to soothe Gardwig's pain. Tahir took great care of the king's ulcer, and Gardwig felt a lot better. He even expressed his favor toward Lily and invited her to the embassy and to Wellster.

"You and your husband are a beautiful couple."

Jerisson took his leave from the princess and went to speak to Edward. A minute later, Prince Amir joined them, and the three disappeared to a more private setting.

I am sure it's about Miranda. Since there is no way I could overhear the discussion I need to focus on work. The woman politely smiled at Gardwig. She wished she was twenty years older and had met him before. *Very powerful charisma! Although he changes wives like gloves, that doesn't cancel his fine looks.* After five minutes, Prince Amir Gulim approached Lily and asked Gardwig to excuse them.

"His Majesty agreed to my marriage with Miranda."

"I am happy for you."

"Your husband agreed, too."

Lily smiled. Miranda was almost a grown-up woman.

What will happen next? I want my own children, at least five, to keep my husband busy.

Lily was surprised at her own thoughts. *Devil! He's good, and he knows what a woman wants.*

ଧ ଓଃ

"Finally!"

"Richard, I want to introduce you to my wife."

"Please do. I am going to marry soon and still don't know your wife."

"What does one have to do with the other?"

"What if I want to cuckold you?" chuckled Richard, but Jess flashed his eyes.

"Be careful with what you say!"

The prince looked at his friend with curiosity.

"Are you jealous?"

"I am protective."

"Don't be protective with me. You better take care of the rest."

"Every other man looks at her."

"You are even then. Look at Ticia. She would jump out of her dress to get a drop of your attention."

Jess looked. The petite brunette was ready for anything. Yet she didn't invoke the same emotions as before. Jess used to think his type was slender, short brunettes. He now realized he preferred tall, curvy blondes.

"Forget about her. How are you, Richard?"

"I will tell Anna today that I wish to ask Gardwig for her hand."

"What about Lydia?"

"Wellster is our neighboring country, you know. A big dowry, peace, and lastly, have you seen her? Would you lie in bed with that dried oyster?"

Jess shook his head, remembering Lydia.

"I had enough of my cow."

"You were wrong about your cow."

"Are you scared that you might also be making the wrong decision?"

"Yes, I am. But I have no choice. Anna, it is."

"Let Aldonai help you. Let's go, I will introduce you to Lilian."

"Fine. Where is she?"

Jess looked for a white dress and found it next to the princesses. Angelina and Joliette were dressed in gorgeous gowns and talking to his wife. Lilian cheerfully replied to them and laughed, and the girls giggled in reply. The whole trio looked like they were having fun.

"She's with your sisters."

"Great, let's go. By the way, invite the little ones for a dance. They will be pleased."

"Okay, I will."

ಬಿ ⌷ ೧೮

"Your Highness Angelina, Your Highness Joliette,"

Jess bowed to the princesses, while a tall blonde man dressed in white and gold bowed to Lilian.

"Dear Countess, let me introduce myself. I am Richard, an old friend of your husband."

A thin diadem in his golden hair marked the man's title.

"I am glad to meet you, Your Highness."

"Me too, Countess."

Jess smiled and invited Angelina for a dance. Some duke invited Joliette, and Lily stayed one on one with the prince.

Oh yes, it's any girl's dream to stay alone with the prince. He had a perfect build, golden hair, gray eyes, and a face inspired with emotion. The women were melting, but not Lily.

I'd rather go and iron my shoelaces. She continued to observe the prince. He was a handsome boy. Jess and Richard looked like complete opposites.

"What are you thinking about, Countess?"

"You and my husband look good together, white-gold and black. The girls must be thrilled!"

Richard was taken aback by such honesty. Lily remained calm.

It was hard to say whether Lily was trying to be offensive or calculating. She needed to break the misleading impression created by Jess. Second, she wanted Richard to treat her as a friend, not as a woman. Third, she wished to show her eccentricity and make Richard get used to it. Lily realized her uniqueness. Edward and Gardwig endured her oddities because they needed treatment, whereas Richard was in perfect health. Lily needed to make the future king her close friend, so she decided to take a step back.

"Please forgive my audacity, Your Highness. It is hard to talk with people after a day of reading."

"Do you like to read?" His gray eyes sparked with curiosity.

"Among ghost candles and evening prayers…"

Richard sharpened his ear.

"Is it poetry?"

"Yes, Your Highness."

"I have never heard such poems before."

"Do you want me to recite them from memory?"

Richard was happy to listen. Lilian recited a few poems about love and about children. In her other life, Lily's housemate had admired the songs of Vladimir Vysotsky, and Lily was now reciting them as poems. Richard also recited a few couplets, and they began a discussion about rhythmic couplets. Half an hour later, Jess pulled them away and asked the prince to attend to his sisters. Richard's eyes flashed, but he followed the duty of courtesy. Jess turned to his wife.

"I can see you and the prince got along."

"He also likes reading."

"Did you like him?"

Lily looked at her husband. *Is he angry or jealous?* Lily decided to reassure him straight away.

"I have no interest in him as a man." Jess carefully inspected her face. All he could see was cold indifference, and it cheered him up.

"I brought you a present. It's some scrolls...I will bring them tomorrow."

"What scrolls?"

"You will see for yourself."

It had been a while since Jess had wheedled the scrolls out of his cousin, but he hadn't found the time to give them to Lily. *The story with the presents is a total failure!*

ఠ ❏ ß

Although Anna wasn't cruel in nature, she couldn't resist giving Lydia the evil eye. She thought her a pale, tall mole, who looked pathetic next to her. Lydia also gave an evil look to the rival princess, but with far less success. Although Lydia repeatedly told herself that her mind and soul were her main assets, she realized perfectly well that she was losing to Anna. It bothered her greatly. The other princess greatly enjoyed herself. She was dancing and laughing. Richard had already danced with Anna twice. Not once had he approached Lydia. The preferences of the prince were clear to everyone. Thus, all the courtiers swirled around Anna while Lydia stood alone in the corner. Even her brothers were distracted by other girls. Princes were rare in these parts.

Lydia would have been just fine had Anna not tried to feed her ego at the expense of her rival.

"Sweet Lydia, why are you all alone?" said Anna in a singing voice. She approached Lydia in the break between two dances and waved her hand to one of the courtiers. "Bring me some wine; I am tired." She turned back to Lydia. "So much dancing, my legs are buzzing! I'm like that girl in a fairytale, who made holes in her shoes from dancing. Why don't you dance?"

"I don't want to," Lydia bluntly answered.

"I will definitely tell off Richard for not inviting you. There are certain rules of hospitality, after all. He's a host; he must pay attention to you."

"His Majesty Edward is the host."

It seemed impolite to send Anna to Maldonaya. She wasn't openly rude. And yet, Lydia had no strength to endure it longer.

"When Richard and I host our own ball—"

"Why are you so sure that Richard is going to choose you?" Lydia made a last effort to fight back.

"He told me himself. And it is not surprising. I am young, beautiful, with a big dowry…"

Lydia could read the rest in Anna's eyes: *"You are a rat, Lydia, without a penny to your name!"*

Lydia couldn't stand it any longer.

"Excuse me, I need to fix my stocking."

She stormed out of the room and ran looking for a spare bedroom. *I don't want to do this anymore! Aldonai take me away from here!*

Anna triumphantly watched her rival leave and forgot about Lydia as soon as she saw Richard.

Maybe he will propose to me tonight! I cannot wait.

ಙ ಬ

After a pleasant and relaxing conversation with Lilian, Richard was going to devote his time to his future wife. *Why not? She is pretty, jolly, a bit silly, but the last is of secondary importance.* It was nice to meet a clever woman, but a man needed rest. Lilian also decided to take a break from conversations. She was tired from the noise and the hassle of the ball. The garter on her stocking began to drop down. She left the hall and went looking for a secluded place.

ಙ ಬ

Lily slipped down the corridor and turned the corner. She wanted to find a spare room and get some rest. *I want to sit down for a second. I'm exhausted. I need quiet.*

Finally, she found an open room. She wanted to enter but heard someone sobbing. Someone in the room was crying desperately. Lily's heart broke from hearing such miserable cries.

Don't stick your nose into every hole! Nobody asked you, Lily thought. Nevertheless, she went inside and began looking for the sufferer, who turned out to be a young woman in a simple white dress. She buried her face in the pillows and wailed so much that Lily's heart sank. It seemed like the girl had lost all joy in life, no hope for happiness.

Lily sat next to her and touched the girl's shoulder.

"Do you need any help?"

"Go away!" screamed the girl without looking. Lily stroked her soft hair.

"Do you need my help, sweetheart?"

It was Lydia. She turned around, and her eyes shone. She didn't expect to see a tall blonde who looked at her with quiet interest. Lily hadn't been present at Lydia's introduction, and she was seeing her for the first time. The diamonds on her ring were hidden by the cuffs of her dress. She looked like an ordinary young woman. She was pretty, but not in a typical way. Nobody here would consider her beautiful.

Lily assessed the girl's looks. Her hair was ash brown. Some called it a mousy color. Her eyes were gray and big, but her eyebrows needed plucking and dying. They were too wide and too transparent. Although her chin was a bit too large and her face was slightly elongated, it could be hidden by makeup and hairstyle. Her body was good. In this world, men preferred big women, but this one was almost a twenty-first-century model. She was a classic hanger for clothes, yet any woman's look depended on presentation. Lily handed the crying girl a handkerchief.

"Do you want to blow your nose, or you need help?"

Lydia shook her head, slightly overwhelmed.

"Who are you?"

"Lilian. And you?"

"L-Lydia."

"Why are you crying, Lydia?"

Meanwhile, Lily took a pretty linen handkerchief out of her purse and deftly grabbed the girl by her nose, in the same motherly way she would grab Mirrie's.

"Come on, blow your nose, breathe out!"

Having completely lost all sense of reality, Lydia blew her nose and looked at the stranger.

"Why are you so kind to me?"

"I have a daughter," Lily calmly explained. "She is slightly younger than you." Lily modestly kept silent about the fact that it was her stepdaughter. "Do you mind that I don't use titles?"

Lydia shook her head. "No."

In another time and another place, Lily would've gotten slings and arrows for her directness. Lydia was strict about her privacy. Yet, at that moment, her soul was hurting. She was in pain and screamed from desperate misery, so she was grateful to any selfless person who soothed her. Lily made her feel like someone cared.

If it weren't for her own anxiety, Lily would've never approached Lydia. But there was something similar—perhaps a shared sense of loneliness—that drew her to comfort the crying girl. She couldn't tell that Lydia was a princess.

"It's a pity there isn't any water. You need to drink and wash your face."

"I w-would like to sit here for a while."

Lydia began to stutter from the shock.

"Should I leave?" asked Lily. She didn't want to intrude.

"N-no." Lydia didn't want to stay alone. Lilian expressed her interest and participation. She comforted her when Lydia needed it most.

"I will stay then. What's your name again?"

"Lydia, and you are?"

"Lily. Call me Lily."

Lydia nodded. What she understood was that the woman had no idea that she was talking to a princess. She twisted her signet ring toward her palm to hide the crest. That woman was a countess, not a maid. There was nothing damaging for her reputation to share her worries with a countess. Thankfully, nobody heard them.

It took them fifteen minutes to get Lydia in order. Lily somehow managed to fix the girl's hair and even tried to put some powder on her face. She shook her head because there was not much she could do to get her in order.

Lily complained about the balls that she said she despised. Lydia eagerly encouraged the topic. Like Lily, she couldn't stand attending balls. The princess couldn't refrain from complaining about her fiancé who didn't seem to be interested in her anymore and spent time with her rival. He didn't even think of giving her at least a formal greeting, out of politeness.

Lily sympathized with the girl. They spent the next twenty minutes discussing the eternal female topics—fashion, make-up, and men. Lydia complained, and Lily comforted her. Lily expressed her indignation, and Lydia sympathized.

"Why does everyone care so much for appearances?"

"Because a person is greeted by their clothes."

"But even if I was beautiful, everything else inside me would remain the same. The aldons say that the soul is the most important."

"It's true, but people look at the cover first."

"It's not fair!"

"It's life. I will tell you a story."

The story was very simple.

"Once upon a time, there lived a princess. She was pretty, kind, clever, so everyone called her "miss sunshine." The time had come for the princess to marry. Different suitors came wooing to the palace. The first one was the most handsome man alive, the second was the best warrior, the third had a lot of money, and the fourth was a crippled prince. Every one of them was nice and sweet with her. The young girl was torn and didn't know how to choose between them until her nanny advised her. The next day, the princess dressed in rags, smeared her face with dirt as best as she could, turned her face away, and sat on the floor begging at the gates of the palace. Some scolded, others took pity on her. The handsome groom drove past in the carriage and gave her a haughty look. The warrior on the horse almost ran her over. The rich man was near to pulling out his whip and giving her a beating. Only the crippled prince passed her a coin and said, "Come to my household; you can work as a servant there. It's not fit for anyone to beg on the streets." This was the man that the princess chose in the end. She was happy. The other candidates were only nice and kind to a beautiful and titled lady, but the crippled prince was kind to every human."

At first, Lydia couldn't understand how the story was relevant. Lily began explaining.

"This story isn't true, but there's some truth in it. Look, only one of the four men looked into the princess' soul. There are very few people like that, the rest judge by appearance."

"I see."

"Why would you want a husband who lacks the wisdom to appreciate your soul?"

"But—"

"With such a husband, your life would be terrible. Only imagine! You marry your prince and rub it in your rival's face, only she would be one of many! It's better to give away such treasure and rejoice. Let her suffer her whole life with him if she wants to."

"But I also want to—"

"Make him realize his mistake? Make him crawl on his fours and beg for your forgiveness? You want to reject him? It's not a good thing to do. Don't destroy the man's illusions. He would make himself unhappy anyway."

When Prince Miguel came looking for his sister, he saw two happy women. Although one of them had a slightly red nose, the smile on her face was bright and wide. They talked about different hairstyles for Lydia and agreed to arrange her visit to Lily's fashionistas. Lydia was a woman after all, and she dreamed of looking good and natural, without too much pompousness.

"Lydia, are you here? We've been looking for you everywhere."

"We got carried away talking," Lydia was calm and cheerful. "Miguel, meet my friend. Lily."

Lily bowed.

"And this is my brother— his Majesty Miguel of Ivernea."

Lily felt like a complete fool, but seeing happy sparkles in Lydia's eyes, her only reaction was to take a bow in acknowledgment of her own defeat. *You tricked me well, Your Majesty!*

The girlfriends quickly agreed on a visit and parted. The countess slipped back to the Royal Hall and was immediately seized by Alexander Falion.

"I am glad to see you, Lilian. I missed you. Shall we dance?"

Lily accepted his invitation, and the marquess spun her across the ballroom.

"Are you with your husband here?"

"Yes."

"A family reunion? Reconciliation?"

Lily frowned. That information was only between her and Jess.

"Aldonai works in mysterious ways."

Falion turned gloomy. He got the hint and stopped sticking an oar in Lily's private life. They danced until the end.

Soon, Jess returned and expressed his wish to introduce Lily to Anna, only his wife politely refused. Lily couldn't contain her anger. She was ready to kill that whore for what she had done to Lons.

The rest of the evening was perfect. The couple drove home in the carriage. Jess complimented and entertained Lily on the way back. He kissed her hand when they parted. The earl didn't expect anything more, and Lilian took notice of it. She appreciated his patience. A clever man wouldn't rush when it came to seduction.

Lily went to her room, pushed the dogs out of her bed, straightened the blanket on Miranda's side, moved away the ferrets, and immediately fell asleep. The ball had left her completely exhausted.

ೲ ☐ ೬

His Majesty Richard of Ativerna went to bed even later than Lilian. He had a good reason for it. To be precise, it was a scroll left by someone on his bedside table. It was addressed to the prince, confidential and urgent. Richard shrugged and called the servant.

"Did anyone enter my bedroom?"

"Nobody, Your Highness."

"What about this?"

The questioning of the servant revealed that he was absent from his guard for some time. Perhaps it was then when the stranger had managed to leave the scroll near his bed. Richard spread his arms and ordered the servant to open the scroll as a punishment. Perhaps it was poisoned. The man obeyed the order. He waited for a couple of minutes and went out. Richard skimmed through the lines of the confession. The contents of the scroll made him knit his eyebrows. Halfway through, he had an urge to smash it against the wall but stopped himself. He read till the end, carefully placed the scroll on the table, sat on the bed, and froze for a couple of minutes.

"Bastards, scumbags, miscreants! Quarter them! Treason!"

Damned, be the day! Of course, it's a lie! But what if it's true?

Richard took a couple of sips of wine from the bottle and waited for another fifteen minutes. He read again through the confession. He had to admit to himself that even if it was a lie, it sounded very probable. A strange man, but not a stranger—Lons Avels—described his relationship with Anna of Wellster. He talked about being kidnapped, about his return to the capital, and his meeting with his wife. He also wrote that if they killed him, the confession would appear on Edward's desk. He put the rest in the hands of Aldonai.

Richard wasn't going to let this out. He didn't want to start a war, although making this woman a queen was also out of the question.

Richard wasn't a fool, and the letter sounded way too convincing for it to be a lie. In the letter, Lons described Anna's castle in all possible detail. He listed every detail he knew about her, including her personal features, such as a mole in the form of the battle shield on her lower back. He talked about the pastor who conducted the marriage ceremony and the kidnappers who took him away shortly after. The only thing that Lons Avels didn't mention in his letter was how he managed to stay alive and reach Ativerna. This he explained by the fact that his master wasn't aware of his past. Lons was grateful to him and couldn't afford to put the honest man at risk.

The story sounds probable, only what should I do with this information? The easiest thing was to wait until the morning.

Richard was too anxious to wait. He took the scroll with him, and ten minutes later, was knocking on the doors of his father's chamber.

The king's personal valet opened the door.

"Is my father asleep?"

"Not yet."

"Ask him if I can I come in."

Richard did not stand on ceremony with the old man, but that didn't mean that he was disrespectful. On the contrary, the prince rated the man who devoted his whole life to the Crown very highly and treated him like a distant relative, with a degree of warmth at a certain emotional distance. The valet disappeared into the king's chamber. He reappeared shortly, letting the prince enter the room.

The king's bedroom looked the same as before. The only new thing that struck Richard was the smell of fresh mint. The prince was astonished to see everything so clean and tidy with bunches of fragrant plants in vases.

Richard found Edward in bed. Tahir sat at the king's feet, rubbing his legs. It was hard for His Majesty to throw balls.

"What's the matter, son?"

"Here," uttered Richard and handed the scroll to the king.

Edward began reading. At first, he was reading fast, but as the letter progressed, he slowed his pace and scowled. He folded up the scroll and sat in contemplation. With a wave of his hand, he dismissed the doctor.

"Do you think it's true?"

Richard shrugged.

"I do not know what to think. It seems probable."

"Have you noticed anything unusual about Anna?"

"Even if there was something, I didn't notice it at the time. I am not going to try and interpret in retrospect."

"That's true. Are you in love with her?"

Richard shook his head.

"That's good. However, what about Lydia?"

"I pray you, anyone but her!"

Edward looked sad and solemn.

"Let's consider. We don't want Lydia in any circumstances. As for Anna, she's not a suitable candidate either. As a result, we are left with nothing."

"But—"

"If this letter is true, Anna cannot be your wife. It's not because she was previously married, no."

"It's because she is capable of betraying her husband. I understand."

"She is also a perfect target for blackmail. I am myself not without sin, but neither Imogene, not Jessamine would ever—"

"I know."

"We shouldn't get on Gardwig's bad side."

"Maybe we don't need to." Richard theatrically spread his hands. "I don't want to fall into a marriage trap yet. I could wait for a few years and maybe marry his younger daughter. Meanwhile, we could announce my engagement with Anna. If the confession were true, Gardwig would watch her with an eagle eye."

"Hmm." Edward pondered. The solution was pretty decent. Only one thing remained.

"How do we brush off Lydia? Bernard would have understood had you preferred Anna, but since there will be no marriage, it will be tricky to explain."

"I don't know how we are going to get out of it, but I know for certain that I don't want to marry this mouse. She's useful for nothing."

"She is quite smart."

"That's true, only her dowry is too small. Ivernea is further away from us than Wellster, plus we don't want to spoil our relationship with Gardwig."

"I will figure out tomorrow whether this confession is true."

"How?"

"I will meet with Gardwig and show him the letter. If it's true, too bad, if not, any midwife would be able to tell us if Anna is a virgin or not. We will find a few midwives just in case."

"If she isn't a virgin, do you think she lied to me?"

Edward gave his son a wry smile.

"It's not hard to fake virginity. Screams, chicken blood—some women tried to fool me like that a couple of times. Maybe she was planning to do the same during your first night."

"Maybe. I'll refrain from making assumptions. So, the plan for tomorrow is to talk to Gardwig, gather a commission of midwives, and wait, am I right?"

"As for now, yes. Meanwhile, think of how you can get rid of Lydia."

"Fine."

"I will order my people to check the letter tomorrow morning."

"Deal."

Richard left the scroll with his father and headed back to his chamber. No matter how hard he tried, he couldn't fall asleep. An unpleasant feeling weighed upon him.

෴

The king didn't give the job to Hans but chose another royal trustee instead, who immediately began to dig.

Chevalier Avels—the agent was first going to ask about him in Wellster. He wanted to inquire about the pastor who wedded the couple.

The only name that was given in full was the Count Altres Lort. Every secret agent of the Crown knew that the count was the head of the secret service of King Gardwig. In other words, he was the perfect person to question about Anna. However, one risked losing his life if he contacted the count directly.

It was hard to make inquiries about Avels in Ativerna. Chevalier Avels didn't mention where he lived, where he worked and wherefore he came from. Therefore, it was almost impossible to trace his steps.

As for Anna, the agent could start with her. He could ask if they met at the ball. It was possible. On the one hand, the ball was a highly secure public event where everything was regulated. On the other hand, it was very easy to lose sight of a single person. Provided one took to certain tricks, it wasn't hard to escape the public gaze. A woman could set her servants with little tasks, leave the hall to fix her stockings, and dissolve in the palace corridors, go inside the rooms or out to the park.

The agent could make his final verdict only after receiving information from Wellster and the conversation with Gardwig.

ಐ ೞ

After the events of the previous day, Lily had no idea how to behave next to Lydia. The princess resolved the tension by paying the countess a visit without unnecessary ceremonies.

"I am a guest here. Therefore, I can let myself overlook the rules of protocol," she explained. At first, the women felt uneasy remembering the events of the previous night, but soon the ice was broken. Lydia praised the meringues, Lily made a compliment about the princess' hair, Miguel, who came with his sister, expressed his admiration for the Virman watchdogs. Little by little, the tension disappeared.

Women could become friends if they have no self-interest. Neither Lilian nor Lydia was competing with the other. Lilian was married; Lydia was soon going back to Ivernea. She was intelligent and resolved to make the most out of the visit to Ativerna despite everything. Lily realized this and didn't mind taking advantage of the opportunity to advertise her trademark in Ivernea.

Lily carefully suggested helping the princess unlock her full potential and her feminine charm. Lydia turned sulky, but Lily asked her to try. Miguel also encouraged his little sister to try. They had plenty of time, and Miguel wanted to talk with the Virmans for a little longer. Lily dragged the princess to Marcia and the maids, and they set to work. Although Lydia didn't believe in the result, she refrained from complaining. The events of the previous day still made her sick at heart. She accepted that she would lose Richard, but she wanted to retain at least the remnants of her pride.

They used Basma powder on Lydia's eyebrows, which made her features more defined. Marcia selected a dress from the royal collection. Although it was pink, the color suited the princess. It enlivened her white face and gave her ash-color hair a glossy shine. The hairstyle they selected was quite fresh and simple—a slanting fringe and a few loose curls. Her new shoes had a little heel, which was unusual for Lydia. When the young woman looked at herself in the mirror, she couldn't believe her eyes.

My father would never let me show up like this! What a disgrace! And yet, I am beautiful.

Her reflection in the mirror showed a beautiful woman. She was a tall beauty with splendid posture. Her ash-colored locks were naturally loose and came down to the pink lace. The eyebrows in the mirror raised in amazement, for everyone could now appreciate their beauty. Her eyes shone from under her darkened eyelashes. Her skin didn't seem dull anymore but could be described as translucent. The faded rose color of the dress was flattering. The gown emphasized her little but high breasts and thin waist, successfully masking her narrow hips. Everyone could tell that the legs under the skirts were long and slender. Her lips were shining pink (thanks to the Khangan tints), and her chin didn't look massive anymore.

"Is this me?"

Lily's smile reflected in the mirror.

"Do you have any doubts about your beauty now?"

She had no doubts, only amazement.

"But how?"

"Very simple. I suggest you go and show your brother. Let's see what he says. I'm afraid you will need to take off the dress after and give it to the girls. It needs a little fixing." Lydia slid her fingers along the pink silk.

"How much do I owe you?"

Lily glanced at the princess, and she immediately corrected herself. She was a smart woman and quickly realized that Lilian had done this from the heart. She cared nothing for the money.

"Thank you."

Lilian softened.

"We will consider it my present, Your Highness."

"I am Lydia for you. No titles please."

"Lily, but only between each other."

Their eyes met. Lydia nodded. They couldn't show their friendship publicly. They would keep up appearances in that regard, and only privately, would they call each other by their first names. Lilian wouldn't forget the young woman, and Lydia would remember her savior. That was the start of their friendship, which promised to become stronger with time.

"Let's assume that I also got my way. I forgot about the earrings!"

Two pink pearls, the work of artisan Leitz, completed the look. Lydia admired them in the mirror.

"Wonderful! What will be your reward?"

Lily grinned.

"I want you to show up at court dressed like this and tell everyone you were dressed at Mariella Fashion House."

"Mariella?"

"Mariella was my mother's name. I want to open a fashion salon for women, where they can come and get fashion advice, just like we advised you. We can all agree that hair and clothes are trivial matters, but they make life easier."

Lydia agreed.

"Will you do it?"

"With great pleasure!"

෨ ☐ ඥ

Miguel was petting a puppy and asking about the methods of dog training when she slipped into the living room. The prince simply did not recognize his sister. She was a beautiful vision in pink and had nothing to do with Lydia.

The prince suddenly became so uncomfortable that he just sat stunned, his chat with the Virman suddenly interrupted by this strange lady. He and Erik jumped to their feet.

"Let me introduce myself, madam! Miguel, the Prince of Ivernea. You must also be one of the countess' guests?"

Lilian covered her face with both hands, shuddering from the spasms of silent laughter and not being able to keep it in. Lydia stepped forward and got a tenacious grip of her brother's ear.

"Me? A guest?"

"Lydia?"

Her brother's amazed look was payback for all the humiliation of the previous night. The admiration in the Virman's eyes was even more precious to Lydia. Erik bowed with deep respect.

"Your Highness, allow my liberty, but you look amazing." Lydia's cheeks flushed pink, and she lowered her eyes.

Lily grinned.

"You made the girl blush! Isn't she a beauty?"

Lydia enjoyed compliments for the next ten minutes. Afterward, Lily sent her to Marcia and the other maids. Lily tried to think what else might suit the girl. Cold hues didn't compliment her skin. The warm ones, on the other hand, suited her well—pink, apricot, peach, cream, and all their shades. Lily wanted to combine them with pink or green. *We'll see what else we can find.*

"My Lady."

"Hans!"

They bumped into each other in the doorway. Lily looked around. Lydia was already gone, and nobody else seemed to care about them. *Perfect timing.*

"Richard received the confession." Hans switched to half-whisper.

"So?"

"He went to his father last night and left the letter with him."

Lily preferred not to ask Hans how he knew about this.

"Do you think he will take the information seriously?"

"I hope so."

Lily lowered her eyes. She didn't want Anna on the throne. The country didn't need such a queen. *Is it an arrogant presumption?*

Remembering the twenty-first century where businessmen paid for politics, she thought herself a true saint. She was simply standing up for the truth. Nobody forced Anna to lie to her husband and deceive him into thinking she wanted to escape with him. She could've refused Richard's offer of marriage and departed with Lons instead. Lons would've accepted Anna's every decision. If it wasn't for Anna's lie, he would be alive. It was too late now. Lily would never forgive her for the death of Lily's people.

Chapter 6
The Second node

Gardwig felt a little better. His medicus washed the wound and was left amazed. The ulcer looked better after the soaking. Although it was still far from recovery, there was a good chance that everything would go well. The king hoped to live for at least five more years. Considering the former hopelessness of his situation, this was already something. He didn't want to die before his child grew up and before he lifted up the country. *Maybe by that time, the Khangans will have invented a new treatment.* He wouldn't mind adding another ten years to his life. Lily also hoped for the best. Everything was in the hands of Aldonai, including brick falling from the roofs. At least the king had good veins and no diabetes (maybe the leeches had helped, after all). With proper nutrition and care, the king could hope to live for another ten years. The most important thing was to let the ulcer scar correctly and prevent it from reopening. Gardwig heard about those truths from Tahir, who described his care in the most eloquent manner. The king was inspired by his speeches. He didn't want to pass before his time and was ready to follow any advice.

So much was he inspired by the prospect of his recovery that he didn't even get angry with the messenger, who came to him on behalf of Edward. The king wished to see his crowned brother that day for a formal meeting. Gardwig handed the invitation to his master of ceremonies.

"Tell him I agree to the meeting tonight or tomorrow."

The master of ceremonies set about his difficult task. On the one hand, the king shouldn't lose face and dignity. On the other hand, both kings were not in their best health, so a magnificent ceremony wasn't appropriate. They could even behead him for organizing one. Moreover, the man should take into account that one of the kings was a host and the other one a guest. Lastly, the two kings were good friends, which made it difficult to keep things proper and formal. Everything had to be done on the run. Being the master of ceremonies was a hard job.

ಭ ೞ

"My house is your house," said Jess with a faint smile. Lily carefully looked at his chambers. *What can I say?*

It was the sanctuary of a bachelor. Although it was cozy and nice, something was still missing. *Heat? Light? Color?*

"Do you come here often, Earl?"

"I usually stay in the palace. I feel myself at home there. As for this place, Miranda used to like coming here."

"She is a wonderful child."

Talking about her daughter was safe, and Jess gladly picked up the subject. But it wasn't all that simple.

"I am only worried about her marriage."

"Her engagement with Amir?"

"Exactly. A different faith, a different country—"

"Different customs, different culture... I understand. I am very much worried myself. Yet, I trust Mirrie. She is a strong and clever girl. If we help her now, she will be able to help herself later."

"Nevertheless, when your spouse is entitled to have concubines, and you don't even have a right to speak freely—"

"Tell me about it!" Lily couldn't refrain from giving Jess a malicious grin. "Men in our country also think that they are entitled to have mistresses."

Jess frowned but swallowed the insult. *What can he say to that? That he isn't guilty? The women cornered him and raped him? Two hundred and twice raped!*

Lily waved her hand to cast aside the unpleasant thoughts.

"It's nice here. Is this house large enough to fit all of us?"

"Let's count and think what changes to make."

Lily counted on her fingers.

"You, me, Miranda, Amalia's children, and Alicia, right?"

"Right." Jerisson frowned. "Children, yes."

Roman and Jacob had never met their uncle. It was painful for Jess to even think about the children or their dead mother. As far as Lily understood, the king hadn't told Jess the whole truth about the death of his sister. Jess didn't know much about the conspiracy, and she certainly would not be the one to tell him. So, Amalia remained a saint in Jess's memory. *All the better!* That would stop him from seeking revenge unless Edward himself pointed out the criminals.

"What shall we do with the rest of my retinue?"

"Um..."

"The Virmans, the Khangans, the artisans..."

"The artisans will soon head to Taral. As for the Virmans, how long until they go back?"

"Father and Leif signed a three-year contract," shrugged Lily. "I don't know about the rest. They could leave any time." When Lily had arrived in that world, it had been jarring to learn they only knew of one continent. The Countess of Earton wanted to take on the function of the Spanish Crown. She would set the ships to search for an unknown coast.

Lily knew that the earth poles were almost identical to the magnetic poles. She could construct a compass in no time. She needed a needle, a cup of water, and a cork that floated on the surface. She would heat a needle from one end in order to demagnetize it, put it on the cork and place them inside the cup filled with water. The heated end of the needle would point south.

A compass, a telescope, and a ship—she seemed to have everything to conquer the world. Once, after a conversation with Lily, August had begun improving the Virman ship. He also wanted more, and he had the money and resources for it. The Virmans had a job. They used to be decent pirates who competed with Loris. Since Ativerna was going to make an agreement with Wellster and the Khanganat, Loris had ceased to be a threat, and it left the Virmans short of their pirate activities.

Should we put our teeth on the shelf and go into opposition? No, thank you.

"The Khangans are soon to return to their home."

"In about a year."

"So long?"

"Amir had the most severe poisoning. A miracle saved him."

"I see. I suppose he needs to remain under constant medical watch?"

"Even so—"

"My dear wife," Jess's blue eyes flashed in a cheeky way. "Do you really not have time for your husband?"

"It depends on how hard my husband tries," replied Lilian.

Jerisson's answer was a kiss on her sassy lips. He kissed once, then twice. Her dress somehow appeared on the floor, and the underwear dropped next to it. The earl's chamber had a wonderful bed. It was made of oak, very wide and made absolutely no creaking. According to both husband and wife, the result of the night was worth it.

ಬಿ ೞ

"Edward,"

"Gardwig, thank you for agreeing to see me."

"Why wouldn't I? I guess I need to say thank you for Tahir."

"Your limp seems less."

"That's right. They're treating me."

"What do they say?"

"That I will live if I pull myself together and follow all instructions. Diet, herbs, exercises—"

"I see you've already gotten used to following those orders?"

"Nobody before could cure me. I'll give it a try."

Officially, the two rulers must communicate at a high-level meeting. Unofficially, Edward used his royal will and didn't let anyone else be present. Gardwig supported his idea. As a result, the two old men sat in an ordinary room with a fireplace, two cozy chairs, and a table.

"Something happened?"

"Why, yes. Read it yourself."

Gardwig accepted a letter from the hands of his colleague and skimmed through the text. When he got to the middle, his face turned red, then white, and he threw the scroll against the wall and shouted profanely.

Edward looked alarmed.

"Do you think it's true?"

Gardwig waved his hand, asking to be left to cool down. Edward looked at his crowned brother and against all codes of conduct poured him wine. Gardwig took a couple sips and began gradually to recover.

"Where did you get this from?"

"Someone left it on Richard's bedside table. Is the confession true?"

"I don't know," Gardwig said gloomily. "I wouldn't be surprised if Anna inherited her mother's behavior. That wench was ready to sleep with anyone. I swear I don't know anything about it."

"Is the rest about Anna true in the letter?"

"About her education? It's true. About the birthmarks, we have a family mole on the back, but I've never seen Anna's."

"What if I inspect her? I can find a midwife and a medicus. You know how it's done."

Gardwig knew. He had married widows a couple of times, but his wives were never murderers. He had known everything about his wives from the beginning.

"I understand, and I won't object. Does anyone know about it?"

"Do you think I would tell?"

Gardwig relaxed a little. Edward kept everything secret.

"Politics," was the only reply of Gardwig.

He didn't make excuses and didn't explain himself. He only repeated the known truth—that one cannot stay clean and pure on the throne.

"True. But I like the agreement with Wellster. I don't like the Iverneans, and Richard doesn't like Lydia."

"Anna is a fool! I will strangle her with my own hands!"

"If Anna is a virgin, we will announce the engagement on the same day. I promise. If not…"

Gardwig was silent. He was contemplating the situation when Edward suddenly smiled.

"If not, how old is your second daughter?"

"Thirteen."

"Richard can wait another three years, but it will mean that you will have to educate her properly."

Gardwig threw a glance at his companion.

"Are you serious?"

"Dead serious. We can wait a little, but not very long. We can even have an engagement now and sign the contract. The girl will arrive at Ativerna whenever she's ready. You can send her immediately. I will put her with my daughters with no damage to her honor. Who knows, maybe she and Richard will fall in love."

His Majesty Gardwig sighed with relief.

"Edward…"

He was short of words. The king wasn't used to expressing his gratitude in words instead of presents, and Edward saw it.

"Bear in mind, I insist on having the province of Bali for a dowry."

"I will even give you the tribute to salt. We have a problem with trade."

"Nay," squinted Edward. "We have our own salt-making technology. It will become cheaper, but we could play around with something else. Coal, for example."

"Shall we discuss?" squinted Gardwig.

"Of course, but first things first."

"My daughter Anna."

His Majesty went a little darker, though everything worked out well. His daughter was stupid, and he would see to punishing her appropriately. The interests of Wellster shouldn't suffer. His reputation would remain intact, that was the main thing.

"What do you suggest?"

"Inspection. Bring her to the palace, and my midwife will have a look. If Anna is chaste, we will immediately announce the engagement. If not—"

"If not, we need a plan."

Gardwig furrowed his brow and brooded. "If not, she will need to simply disappear."

"She's your daughter."

"So what? Do you not have prisons? We'll quietly keep her there and in a couple of years will send her to the nunnery. We could say that she ran away."

"Besides, we have your second daughter. Why not? It could work."

Edward thought about Stonebug. He wasn't going to put Anna there forever; neither did he plan to send her to a nunnery. When the time was right, he would let her out, give her money, and send her away. Another option was to give her into marriage to some low-class merchant. Either way, the options were plenty.

Edward saw that Gardwig's reason was presently marred by mad frenzy. He would later regret taking harsh measures against his own child. If Edward's girls got themselves into something similar, he knew that he'd, sooner or later, forgive their childish silliness.

The case with Amalia was different. Edward couldn't forgive what she'd done. She was a grown-up woman and deliberately provoked a rebellion. Compared to Amalia, Anna was still a child. She would grow wiser.

"When?"

"Tomorrow morning."

The kings exchanged glances. They didn't need words to understand each other. Gardwig was giving his daughter for an inspection and a punishment. All he cared about was the future of the country. Edward tried to alleviate the plight of his friend, and Gardwig appreciated it.

ಐ ಜ

"Jerisson, could you do me a favor?"

"Yes, Uncle. What is it?"

"Nothing much. Richard?"

Without getting up from his chair, Richard threw the parchment with the confession to his friend.

"This must remain between us."

Jess read through the scroll, swore, and rubbed his forehead.

"I don't understand. How can it be true?"

"Sadly, it is."

Jess sighed.

"Honestly, I have a feeling that I live in a topsy-turvy world. My wife turns out to be a beautiful woman, a mistress is a murderer, and a princess is a whore. What else?"

"Maybe you learned to see behind the masks."

"Maybe. What do you want me to do?"

"Tomorrow, I will invite Anna to the palace. You will have to meet her and lead her to me. We'll see what to do next after the medical inspection."

"Meaning what?"

"Option one: you will bring her here for an engagement announcement, and we will look for the author of the letter to punish."

"Option two?"

"Stonebug."

The word spread a heavy silence. Jess flinched.

"Your Highness..."

"She should thank me. Gardwig was going to behead her for it."

"What are you going to do with her?"

"I will let her out in a few years. She will be able to go where she pleases."

"I'll tell my people to get ready."

"No," Edward made a willful gesture. "Whatever happens, nobody should know about it. Everything must be done in secret."

"Then why don't we do it in the embassy?"

"The palace is almost empty at that time of the day. You will do it while everyone goes on a walk to the park."

"I will help him, Father."

"Whatever you wish. Don't let yourself be seen. If need be, Jess should be able to do it alone."

"I will try my best." The earl smiled. "The only woman I cannot tame is my own wife."

"Is it still difficult between you two?" Edward raised his eyebrows. Jess returned the gaze and resembled a male cat.

"It's our own business, Uncle." His reply left Edward relieved.

"If I find out that you are cheating on her, I will tear off your member with my own hands."

"I hope you are talking about my head?"

"Precisely. You don't use it anyway."

"As you please, Uncle."

"I like seeing your wife at court. However, I suspect that she doesn't particularly enjoy coming here."

"She is just like her father. If you give her a choice, she will move to the workshops. She and her doctors walk around almost holding hands."

"They're good doctors."

"The mediquses are mad!" Richard was smiling. "Maldonaya take them! The main thing is that Father is well." Edward had told Richard about his illness, and the man was sincerely grateful to the countess for curing his father. The king was already fed up with the guilds.

"Gardwig is also feeling better. If he's lucky, he will be ruling for at least ten more years, and Ativerna and Wellster will be friends."

"First things, first." Jess demonstratively waved the scroll in the air.

"Precisely. Do it without noise and in secret. Fine, take a couple of trusted people and meet the princess. After the midwife's verdict, you lead her either here or send her to Stonebug."

"Understood."

"Go home now and come back tomorrow in the early morning."

Jess happily obeyed. He already imagined Lilian's shining green eyes, her meeting him with a smile…and everything else.

His dreams came true. Although he had to shake the ferrets from his head and dogs from his feet, and even though Miranda came climbing into their bed in the early morning and painfully kicked them with her feet, Jess was happy. *Perhaps that's what they call a family.*

ಐ ☐ ೞ

Gardwig could've easily ripped off her head for what she'd done, only he didn't want to risk the reputation of Wellster. *To Maldonaya with this whore! She is like her mother. The kingdom shouldn't suffer because of them.* He risked his own honor being damaged. He failed to fulfill his parental duty. Still and all, he was worried about one more thing—Count Lort. Edward turned out to be more honorable than Gardwig thought. He didn't ask or mention Lort, leaving Gardwig to deal with his menagerie by himself. The King of Wellster appreciated Edward's tact. *What have you done, Altres! It is most likely true.* Still, Gardwig couldn't blame his brother. Although he wanted to kill him for disclosing information, there had already been cases where Gardwig had found out about Altres' activities post factum. The king had to weed it out at the very beginning. It was too late now. He had given his brother too much freedom. He couldn't get his head around how much power he should give him. If something happened to Gardwig, Altres would become the regent, with Milia and his children. He would have to get used to making radical decisions. Yet, the situation had changed. Gardwig hoped to remain on the throne.

He would tell his brother off for taking too much on himself. Gardwig could see Altres being capable of this to ensure the union with Ativerna. He could have easily removed the teacher and put fear into Anna. *How my illness tortures me! It ties my hands! I need to send a pigeon to my brother, although I expect him to know already. He surely has his agents in the embassy. I need to question all of them, starting with Baron Kilmory.*

Alas, the king didn't have time to deal with the baron when he got back to the embassy. The baron in question was away. Gardwig's leg was giving him pains, so the King of Wellster sunk into deep sleep. He woke up only in the morning, when it was already too late, for Anna had gone away to the palace.

ಌ ⃞ ಌ

Anna was not feeling very well. Something was wrong. Perhaps it was her rat instincts. They told her that she was about to be cornered. The young woman tried to keep calm, although she did check that she had her bottle of poison on her. She put it inside the pocket of her dress.

ಌ ⃞ ಌ

Upon finding out that Anna was already gone, the king became upset, but decided to leave everything up to Aldonai. If she was a virgin, she would soon become a queen. If not, she only had herself to blame. Gardwig cared nothing for family relations, except for the relationship with his brother. He loved Altres. He appreciated Milia for giving birth to sons. He loved them as an extension of himself. *Yet, how could I love children who can't even talk? It is the same as loving a dog.*

As for his feeling toward Anna, his daughter was a constant reminder of her mother's adultery. The other daughters were at least only reminders of his failures. *Out of sight and out of memory!*

Gardwig called for the Baron of Kilmory. He remembered again how lucky he was to have a friend like Edward. The union between Ativerna and Wellster was beneficial for both parties. The day before, he had almost sacrificed his daughter, and Edward accepted it but still agreed to act in the most lenient way. They would send Anna to Stonebug for a couple of years. Once everything was forgotten, they would let her go to all four corners of the earth. Nobody would give a damn about whether she was Anna of Wellster or not. The incident might have proven fatal for the kingdom and caused a war.

Gardwig never overestimated himself. His army wasn't ready for war. Lort wasn't a good military commander either. He might have been good at intrigues, but not on the battlefield. *What would happen to Wellster in the case of war? It would be torn to pieces! One third would remain of it. All of my children would probably be murdered.* Gardwig couldn't even think about such horror.

Edward acted like an honorable man. Gardwig felt like he was indebted to him. He was going to pay him back. If everything went well, the friendship between the two states would be strong.

Someone tapped on the door, and the servant reported the arrival of Baron Kilmory. Gardwig made a sign to let him in. The baron walked in and bowed low before the ruler. The king's look was condescending. With a degree of brutality in his voice, the king asked him a direct question. "Who killed Chevalier Avels?"

No matter how much the baron tried to hide the truth, his face gave him away. His lips twitched, and his eyes filled with horror. Gardwig wasn't famous for being merciful. That instant, the king realized the confession was true. Anna was indeed a married woman, and her husband had recently been killed. The baron was the one who had given the order.

"I know everything," sighed the king. "King Edward knows about it as well."

The baron's face expressed only one thought—*A catastrophe!*
Gardwig snorted.

"Lons Avels left a letter for King Edward. They told me yesterday."

The baron dropped to his knees. "I'm not guilty! Have mercy! The count ordered it!"

Gardwig let him talk for a while and waved his hand as a sign of kindness.

"Edward is not going to make a scandal. Otherwise, you would've lost your head. I won't be so generous next time."

"Never! I won't let you down! I am your loyal servant!"

The king listened calmly. His leg ceased hurting, and his soul grew quiet.

Anna will be fine. They won't even kill her. It would do her good to spend some time without men. No wonder the aldons say in sermons that abstinence ennobles.

☙ ❧

Jess waited for the princess at the front entrance. It seemed ridiculous to have the princess examined by midwives right inside the walls of the palace. *The gossip would spread, wouldn't it?*

For all its size, the palace was a very complex structure. It had a lot of corridors and secret pathways and a lot of empty rooms that were out of use. Thus, it wasn't difficult to find a private spot there.

The king was outside on his afternoon walk around the park. He would later have afternoon tea in the gardens. The whole court followed the king everywhere. All of them wanted to please the king and didn't wish to earn his disfavor if they happened to be absent when the king asked for them. Since the king didn't have a royal favorite, the afternoon promenade was a chance for the courtiers to show off their wives and daughters, as well as make useful acquaintances. The younger generation, too, found in the walk an opportunity for casual flirting. And so, it followed that the palace was completely empty during certain hours of the day.

Nobody cared about the servants and their gossip. To the rest of the court, the servant's talk was like a dog's bark.

Either way, the number of witnesses wouldn't decrease even if they invited the princess to some house in the city. There would still have been coachmen, footmen, servants, and random pedestrians. It was impossible to foresee everything.

☙ ❧

Jerisson bowed to the princess and led her to a special room. After, he would invite the midwives, and if Anna was pure, he would take her to Richard who was currently on the walk with his father. The story would end with a wedding.

If she wasn't a virgin, Jess had to stun her, tie her up, and deliver her to Stonebug. The midwives wouldn't know who they were checking. The princess had a mask and wasn't going to introduce herself. Otherwise, it was a simple common procedure.

They reached the infamous room.

"After you, Your Highness."

※ □ ※

Anna hadn't been particularity surprised to see the Earl of Earton at the gate. He was the prince's friend and a trusted person. Only when Jerisson led her along secret passageways did she suspect something scary. It was her worst nightmare. The room was empty except for the bed in the middle.

"What's happening?" protested Anna.

At first, she thought that Jerisson wanted her. The thought of it didn't scare her much. She turned around to face the earl, who obstructed her way out of the room.

"Your Highness, according to the old custom, any woman who wants to marry the prince must certify her innocence."

"What?"

Her false indignation seemed genuine. In reality, she was merely scared for her life. Any actress would have envied her acting then. Jess listened to her tantrums without a blink and shook his head.

"Your Highness, your father gave his consent. You can only leave the room after the midwives examine you."

"How dare you!"

"Or not leave it altogether. This is your father's order."

"Do you have his order? Otherwise, I refuse!"

"Your Grace," Jess's blue eyes flashed. Anna's behavior left him no doubt of the relevance of the confession. "Here."

Anna paused. She accepted the scroll from Jerisson's hands and immediately recognized Gardwig's seal. Her father had given his consent the day before during his meeting with Edward. The girl's brain ran like clockwork. Her cover was blown. She didn't care how or when. She knew she wouldn't pass the examination unless Aldonai turned her back into a virgin.

The only thing she could do now was to run away. She had an expensive dress on, which she could sell. She had expensive jewelry in her ears and on her fingers. *What a fool for dressing up! Now it is my capital. I need to get out of here. But how?*

The Earl of Earton would never let her out unless she tried to trick him. Anna's fingers touched a small bottle inside her pocket. It would take her a few minutes to take it out, but she had to do it subtly.

Anna let out a sob and dropped on the floor at the earl's feet.

"Jerisson, I beg you! Don't!"

Jess was a little confused. Anna clung to his boots and sobbed. He could hear unintelligible mumbling through the tears, "terrible," "such a shame," "my father" and so on.

It was impossible to understand her. Jess didn't notice how the woman took out the bottle with poison and placed it in her sleeve. She continued her hysterics for five more minutes until Jess managed to raise her from the floor, dust her off, sit her on the bed, and even give her a goblet of wine. Anna took a few sips and started wailing anew. Jess didn't know how to act. It was inappropriate to slap her. He stood up and started pacing around the room. He didn't notice how Anna, who was hysterical, poured half the bottle of poison inside the goblet. In a little while, the crying ceased. Anna sat on the bed with a blank expression on her face. Jess tried to offer her more wine, but the woman refused.

"Why do I have to go through this humiliation?"

"Your Highness," Jess tried to speak softly. "It's only a custom. It's a very common thing to do. Your father gave his consent."

"It is so humiliating! I am forced to expose myself to strangers!"

"Your Highness, everything is arranged in the most secret way. Nobody knows we are here. This room doesn't even have guards. The mediuses and midwives are waiting in the next room."

"They will recognize me!"

"Never! Put on this mask, and nobody will ever know!"

Anna shivered.

"I've never been with a man. But if it is necessary…"

Jess continued to convince her. He said that if it wasn't for the custom, he would've never allowed himself to drag her there in secret. He said he hoped for her understanding. Although he was convinced that Anna was lying, he couldn't know for sure.

"Put the mask on, Your Highness."

Anna nodded.

"Fine. I only want a couple more sips of wine. My throat is dry."

"Obviously, Your Highness." Jess continued to treat the princess with respect. After all, her father was the King of Wellster, even though Gardwig was close to renouncing her. Anna put the cup to her lips. She smelled the liquid and pretended to drink, not letting the wine touch her lips. Suddenly the woman winced and spat on the floor.

"Earl, how disgusting!" She grew so skittish that Jess grew quite surprised.

"What's wrong, Your Highness?"

"What is this slop? I cannot even take a sip of this wine! It's sour."

The earl shrugged.

"So disgustingly bitter," Anna stamped her foot. "I insist on you trying it yourself!"

She approached the earl.

"Give me the mask. Try the wine. You'll see for yourself. How nasty! We wouldn't offer such wine even to servants."

Jess obeyed, glad that the tantrums were finally over. Anna gave him the cup and took the mask. Watching her fiddle with the strings, Jess absent-mindedly took a couple of sips.

The wine is good, but what is this bitter aftertaste? Anna took too long attaching the mask. Jess wanted to rush her when suddenly he couldn't take a breath. The earl let out a guttural sound, flinched, and fell to the floor. Anna turned around and looked at the earl. The witch who gave her the potion hadn't guaranteed a quick death, but he would die in ten minutes.

The earl lay wheezing, scratching his throat with his nails and twisting on the carpet. An invisible flame burned him from the inside. Everything burned, hurt, his heart was panting, he couldn't breathe, his muscles convulsed and he wanted to scream from pain, but only weak moans came out of his swollen throat. Jess thought that he was yelling, but even Anna couldn't hear his moans. She looked around. She had no fears, for her fears had become reality.

Dispose of the mask. His cloak, I'll take it. It's not the best color but it will do. Money—I won't rummage around in his pockets! One thought of touching the dead or remaining in the same room with him made Anna sick. She carefully opened the door and looked out. Nobody was there.

Aldonai, help me get out!

ಖ □ ಡ

Edward ambled through the park. Looking back at the day, he wouldn't remember either the aching in his chest or his sense of evil foreboding.

Richard was waiting inside the palace. His Majesty strongly suspected that the engagement wouldn't happen. Edward was almost sure that the confession was true. It was possible to fake, but he could see no distinct causes for it. *Who would benefit from breaking off the engagement with Anna? The Iverneans? Possibly yes. Either way, Richard would never marry Lydia. He didn't need such a wife.*

Edward was a wise man, and he saw the true value of the girl. Lydia was intelligent and wasn't used to compromise, except when it came to her father. Bernard loved his daughter, spoiled her, and let her off. The woman who was cleverer than her man and stupid enough to show it wouldn't become a good wife. The only way their marriage could work was if Richard had turned into a henpecked husband. Richard needed a wife who would look up to him or at least one who got her way but still loved him. He needed a wife like Jessamine.

Edward could see Lydia seeking her former independence after the wedding. She would fail the primary task of a queen—to give birth to an heir. Richard and Lydia didn't love each other. Their married life would be reduced to a series of unresolved scandals.

The worst thing in that scenario was that the state would be the one to get the raw end of the deal.

The unhappy marriage would ruin the relationship with Ivernea. Bernard and the brothers would want to protect the interests of their beloved Lydia, causing chaos in the state. Edward didn't want Ivernea to become the second Avesterra. It was better to remain with Gardwig. Although they would have to wait a few years, they could still bring his second daughter to live in the palace. That would allow Richard to get used to his new bride.

If only Anna was a chaste woman!

Edward called forth a servant. He asked him some nonsense and received an obsequious answer. He looked at the sun. It was almost midday.

෮ ෭

That day, Anna had thought she had Maldonaya's favor. In reality, the king ordered that wing of the palace emptied. Anna wrapped herself in the green cape, threw the hood over her head, and looked for a way out. She couldn't remain in the palace. She knew that to leave the palace was dead easy, especially with a companion.

"Your Highness."

Anna raised her eyebrows. She recognized the man.

"Baron Reynolds!"

The man bowed.

"I am at your service, Your Highness."

Anna contemplated a little and charmingly smiled at the baron.

"Take me to the exit, dear Baron!"

The reason why Tarney wasn't at the walk was very simple. His servant had not woken him up in time. His plan was to carefully merge with the crowd and not let the king notice his negligence. He walked into Anna and decided to take his luck and do the future queen a service. *Who knows, maybe it can play out in my favor in the future.* Tarney realized that any queen needed her trustees at court. *Why not me?* He would happily serve the feeding hand. On their way to the exit, Tarney asked Anna what she was doing there alone and why she was dressed like that.

Inside her, Anna's heart was shaking, but she replied to the baron calmly. The cape belonged to a friend. She was there because one of the court ladies had written to her that Richard had someone else. The princess said that she realized it was a lie, and yet, she had to come. Her father didn't know she was there.

"Will you keep my secret, Baron? You wouldn't let down a lady's honor? I have no doubts in you. You are so nice. A real man!"

Tarney drank the honey of her compliments, spread his peacock tail, and supported the lady by the tip of her elbow. He tried to be as courtly as he could so he held her limb with the tips of his thumb and middle finger to show he was no village redneck.

He led the lady to the gates, helped her get into the carriage and even waved adieu. Anna did the same and dropped back onto the pillows. She had a few minutes to think everything through. If her father had given his permission for examination, it meant that she couldn't go back to the embassy. Gardwig wouldn't take pity on her for disobedience, especially after what she'd done to the Earl of Earton. Anna didn't know exactly the working witchcraft of the potion, but she strongly suspected that it would kill the earl. Jerisson was Edward's relative. She wasn't a helpless woman anymore, but a murderer. They would hunt her down. She had no one to protect her, so she had to run as far and as fast as she could.

Where exactly will I go?

She needed to make a wise decision. She was penniless and didn't even have a comb on her. Perhaps the adrenaline sharpened Anna's wit, and she reasoned quite sensibly. She needed to sell her jewelry and go to the port. She would take a ship far away, as soon as possible, to Avesterra, to Elvana, or even to the Khanganat. She didn't care where. *Anna of Wellster exists no more. I am now Anna Avels, a young widow.* A poor leira, a very poor one, without a dowry. She hoped she could remarry and start a new life. Anna gritted her teeth. *Damn you, Lons! It's all your fault!* Anna forgot that it was she who had seduced the man to show off before her sisters; she didn't remember that his death sentence, his banishment, and his death were entirely her own fault.

Despite the fact he was already dead, Lons became Anna's primary enemy. *Where can I sell the jewelry?* Anna banged on the carriage door. The coachman was now a dangerous witness.

"Hey, you!"

When the coachman bowed and inquired what Her Highness needed, she ordered him to take her to the jewelry store. The man obeyed. Half an hour later, she entered the store, slightly bending to avoid knocking the low ceiling. The jeweler turned out to be an elderly Eveer. After some hesitation, Anna put a necklace on the counter. She decided to leave the rings for later.

"How much will you give me for it?"

The Eveer looked at the woman in the cape that was evidently too large for her. He considered the price and offered a rapaciously small amount. Anna had never bargained in her life, but the need and the looming shadow of the gallows worked wonders together.

After some twenty minutes of shouting, noise, and commerce, after proclaiming Aldonai and the Eveerian gods as witnesses, the sum in Anna's pocket could be called if not decent then at least reasonable. It would last her getting to Avesterra and a couple of months of humble living, not like she had any choice.

ಐ ☐ ೞ

Jess was extremely lucky.

His screams came out as wheezing. It was impossible to get the attention of the doctors separated by two doors and a thick wall. With his last ounce of strength, the man banged against the wooden legs of the little table. *Praise the long-horn beetles, the eaters of wood!* The wooden legs collapsed and a heavy marble block shattered against the floor with a banging sound. It was loud enough to raise the dead.

The members of the medical committee next door pricked up their ears. One of them went to look outside. There was nobody in the corridor. The sounds were coming from the room next door. Lily was wrong when she said that all medicuses were silly-headed. Having noticed that the door was slightly ajar (Anna had closed it too loosely), the medicus took a step forward and glanced inside the infamous room. Upon realizing what was happening, the medicus began yelling and calling for help.

Luck was on Jerisson's side, for Tahir had been spontaneously chosen to supervise the midwives. It was a common procedure in the

Khanganat. Tahir stormed into the room to the sounds of screaming, saw Earl Earton writhing on the floor, a broken jug of wine, a goblet, and spilled wine, and figured out what had happened.

"The earl is poisoned," he snapped. "Get help!" The midwives couldn't be of much help, but luckily the two doctors knew what to do. They lifted his heavy, writhing body, moved it to the bed, turned it on its side. One of the doctors began unclenching the jaws that were cramped together by a spasm. Tahir smelled the puddle of wine on the floor, dipped his finger inside but didn't dare to lick it. Judging from the earl's state, the poison had been absorbed through the mucous membrane. Thanks to Lilian Earton, Tahir knew what to do. A lot depended on the kind of poison, on the dose, and on time.

"We need to make him throw up."

Tahir gave out calm and confident orders. The medicuses followed his advice, realizing that they would be the ones to blame if the earl died. Perhaps the king would be more lenient with the servant of the Khanganat. They blindly did as he said.

Tahir took serene and confident measures. He unclenched the earl's jaw and tickled his throat with a feather to induce vomiting. His vomit wasn't abundant.

"Water! More water! Laxatives!" He needed to clean out his stomach first and then remove the poison that had been absorbed into the intestine. Tahir didn't know about aconite or nice supplements like arsenic salts or other useful herbs. Even so, that didn't make him a bad doctor. He was fighting for his patient's life.

ಖ ೞ

Lily didn't feel the trouble coming. She was at her father's place. August gave her a tired smile.

"How are you, my little girl?"

"Phew!" Lily plunked herself down in a chair. "I went to check up on my fashion house today. Everything is almost ready, they only need to mud the roof. In about a month or two, everything should be ready. The doors of Mariella Fashion House will open in winter."

"Mariella! Your mom would be proud of you." Lily smiled at her father. August Broklend, despite all his flaws, had become a father to her. Strong, earnest and intelligent, he was always ready to help his daughter, be it with advice or money.

"Honey, your ideas, such as the compass and maps with a grid, are worth thousands. Sailors would bite off your hand to get these objects. You do it for the state, but it wouldn't be kept in secret for long. We will always have money."

The royal treasurer was pleased with Lilian Earton and her work. He could also provide her with a loan, only Lily didn't want to live in debt. She didn't feel the same strain when borrowing money from her father. She would give him back everything to the last penny. First, she had to start the project and think about the profit after.

"How are things with your husband?" Her father was the same as Lily. He would first think about his work and about his private life after.

"I hope everything will be fine." Lilian shrugged her shoulders.

"Try to fix things. I'm expecting to see grandchildren soon," August said.

Lily nearly blushed having remembered something from the past, but she coped with her emotions and flashed her green eyes.

"What about your children?"

The shipbuilder turned crimson.

"I—um..."

"I know about you and Alicia."

August was a little embarrassed, but not for long.

"Do you like her, Lily?"

"Very much. I want you to know that whatever happens between Jess and me, I am on your side. Go for it! My children will need such a grandmother as Alicia."

"Do you really think so?"

"I don't want to end my relationship with him, but I'm preparing for the worst. He is domineering. Quite smart. Time will tell if we can get along together."

August's thinking was more practical.

"If you ask for a divorce..."

"The king will immediately find me a new husband."

"What if you find him yourself?"

"And displease the king?"

"You can't find someone worse than Jess."

"If ifs and ands were pots and pans. Six of one and half a dozen of the other?"

August realized that it was hard to find a decent candidate, but he urged his daughter not to give up.

"We could leave."

"To where?"

"To the Khanganat."

"I will feel even less freedom there. No, Father. I prefer to finish what I've started here. I will enjoy what I have."

Lily put her head in her hands and rubbed her eyes.

"I can handle it."

"That's it. You handle too much. You leave yourself no time to live."

"I can live with Jerisson Earton, or to be more precise, I can survive."

August gave his daughter a meaningful look.

"You can always count on me, Lily, no matter what."

Lily hugged and kissed her father.

I love you too, Dad.

ଔ ଓ

Richard was in shock. Jess had been poisoned, allegedly by her Highness the Princess of Wellster. *How do they know? If there were two in the room and one of them escaped, and the other one was poisoned, the suspect wasn't Aldonai.* Richard remembered sitting down and reading through the confession, waiting for the result of the medical examination, when he heard screams. The prince hurried to the source of the noise and discovered Jess convulsing in pain and covered in vomit. A few midwives and three doctors tried to hold Jess down in order to pour water inside his mouth.

"What is going on?"

"Your Highness!" cried one of the midwives. Tahir didn't even lift his head. The patient's life came before everything. Even though his patient was the husband of Lilian Earton, Tahir didn't get distracted by extraneous thoughts.

Lily could be proud of her student. For Tahir, the body on the bed had neither a name nor a title. Before him was a man who was ill, who needed his help and salvation. The rest was unimportant. The most important thing at that moment was water.

"Praise the Heavenly Mare! Careful, he might choke!" Tahir was optimistic. He prayed, *Let him survive, let him live.*

"What happened?"

The midwife approached the prince and dropped in a low curtsey. She explained how they'd been waiting and how they had heard a cry.

"We ran in and found him thus. He is bad, very bad. Tahir said it was poison."

"Was there anybody else?"

"No, nobody."

Richard looked at Tahir. The only thing he wanted was to be reassured, to ask a childish question: *You will save him, won't you?* He realized that he shouldn't distract the people in their attempt to save Jess. Another thing he should do was to run after Anna. *Was it really her? It's hard to believe. On the other hand, everyone has their dark side.*

Richard hastily rushed to the guards, but luck wasn't on his side. Anna of Wellster wasn't seen at the palace. Having remembered his father's stories, Richard sent messengers to Lilian Earton, to both the city home and Taral.

Maybe she will help? Aldonai, have mercy!

೫ ⃝ ೫

Alicia Earton was on a walk with His Majesty. Everything was peaceful, until the arrival of the guard. His hair was messy, and he looked dispirited.

The king raised his eyebrows in surprise but let the guard finish. He didn't expect to hear what he heard. Edward went pale. The Duke of Falion, who stood beside him, didn't think twice before grabbing the king under the arm. Breaking the code of conduct was better than His Majesty fainting and dropping to the floor. The Old Pike took some smelling salt from his pocket.

"Your Majesty!"

After a few breaths, Edward felt significantly better. Yet, the healthy glow of his face didn't return.

"Countess Earton!"

Alicia instantly appeared before the king.

"Accompany me back to the palace."

Alicia obeyed, and the king almost ran toward the palace.

"Your Majesty, what's the matter?"

"Jess was poisoned."

"How?"

"It doesn't matter."

Alicia flinched.

My son— poisoned? How? Why? She thought about Lily and Mirrie. *I hope it doesn't affect them.*

‍ஐ ◻ ☙

    His Majesty walked fast. He dragged Alicia to his chamber, went up to one of the walls and pushed it. It was a secret passageway. Alicia obediently followed behind. She painfully banged her foot against the step and let out a short cry. Edward turned around and offered his hand.

    "Careful, Alicia."

"Thank you. It's dark."

    "We're almost there."

    "What exactly happened, Your Majesty?" she dared to ask. For a few seconds, Edward remained silent but finally spoke.

    "I received a letter. Anna of Wellster couldn't legally enter another marriage because she was already married and had a living husband. We decided to carry out a test, to see if she was chaste." Alicia nodded, forgetting that the darkness made it impossible to see.

    "I understand."

    "The examination was going to happen this morning, and this is the result of it."

    "Aldonai!"

    Although the explanation was brief, Alicia could figure out the rest by herself. Although a virginity check wasn't a common procedure, it happened if the bride was particularly suspicious. It didn't matter if the girl was from a royal family or a family of coal-miners. If the woman had been married before, she had to declare it. She also had to prove her virginity, at least with words. Aldonai advocated for the purity of the soul. Nobody wanted a promiscuous wench. Horns were an unflattering decoration.

    "And Jerisson?"

    "I asked him to meet the princess, invite her to a specially prepared room, explain the procedure to her, and invite the midwives."

    Edward pushed the wall, and it opened. It was a secret door. The room was empty, and hearing the sounds next door, the king rushed out. Nobody dared to stand in the king's way. Edward's face was a mask of horror.

    The door opened by itself.

    "Your Majesty."

    Alicia could see Jess on the bed. It seemed like they were pumping his stomach. The room smelled awful.

    "Tahir," the king said sharply. At first, Alicia didn't recognize the serene Khangan in this disheveled monster, smeared with dirt. He finally left the patient's side. "Continue. We need to clean everything out," he ordered.

He rose and turned to the king.

"Your Majesty."

The bow wasn't too low, but the time wasn't right for ceremonious greetings.

"How is he?"

"I suspect it was poison. Medicus Hale heard a noise and ran into the room. He found the earl lying on the floor and saw traces of spilled wine. I suppose the poison was added to the drink."

"What will happen to him?"

Tahir shrugged.

"Your Majesty, you can behead me, only I don't know. It seems like he didn't drink much, but I don't know the nature of this poison."

"Find someone who knows then."

"Baron Donter might know, Your Majesty."

"How would he know?"

Edward looked frightening, but Tahir only shook his head.

"His grandmother was an herbalist. I am a stranger in your blessed country. The herbs I know are uncommon here. My colleague says that the poison is called the 'lilac slayer.'"

Edward groaned.

The lilac slayer was a fearsome plant. Every part of this plant was poisonous—flowers, fruits, stems. There was a story about a noble lady who received a bouquet with a bunch of lilac slayer in it. She breathed its poisonous perfume for several days and died.

"Will you save him?"

Aldonai, be merciful, don't take away my son! I beg you. Take my life instead, but let him live.

Tahir cast down his eyes.

"I will do everything in my power, Your Majesty. I hope that his heart can last through it."

It was true, Tahir did everything he could—cleaned out his stomach, gave him a laxative and water, poured in the antidote. He didn't know how effective his antidote was against the 'lilac slayer.' It was a truly a fearsome plant. The mucous absorbed it instantly. Anna had poured almost half a bottle of poison into the cup. Jess was stupid enough to taste poisoned wine, rolling it in his mouth. Tahir couldn't do anything but pray to the Heavenly Mare.

ಠ □ ೦ಽ

Lilian Earton found out about her husband's illness on the way to Taral. The messenger intercepted her on her way. He knew the countess by sight. She was a famous person in the capital. There were not many blonde women on an Avarian stallion and with Virmans as a retinue.

Lilian didn't hesitate for a minute. She turned her horse around and patted him on the neck, asking him to run faster. Lidarh rushed to the royal palace. The situation was worse for Lily than for Edward. Considering her knowledge of medicine, she wasn't as optimistic.

Yet, if death wasn't instantaneous, it meant that the poison wasn't cyanide. There was hope. On the other hand, she feared that it would be impossible to treat her husband properly. They didn't have hemodialysis, nor plasma, nor blood serum, not even a simple dropper. *What is this poison? I wonder if they have fugu fish here. Wolfberry, belladonna and other joyful plants are known here. What about strychnine or arsenic flower? It could've been anything. It doesn't matter much. It's harder to cure than to get poisoned.*

The palace welcomed the countess with the buzzing of the courtiers. She had no time for greetings. The king sent footmen for her and, bowing on the run, they led her to the infamous room. Edward was waiting in the room next door. Lily hastily greeted him and rushed to her husband.

Husband? No. He is now one of my patients. Lilian Earton never mixed her job and her personal life. She wasn't pleased with the sight of Jess's pale skin, blue lips, cold sweat, and dilated pupils. *What on earth is this poison?*

Lily counted his pulse, checked his heart. The pulse was no more than fifty, and the heart was barely beating.

"How long has he been in this state?"

"Three hours."

"Did you figure out which poison it was?"

"It seems to be the lilac slayer."

Lily bit her lips.

"Cover him and warm him up. Do you have any sample of the poison?"

As it turned out, there had been some poison left in the bottom of the goblet. Lily brought the cup to her nose.

"My Lady." Tahir got worried.

"I won't try it," said Lily.

She tried to remember all the poisonous plants. The substance strongly smelled of metal goblet and wine. Lily dipped her finger inside the poison and held it to her face. She began to sniff carefully.

It's no lab technique, but who cares! The tip of my finger feels—numb?

Lily knitted her brows in concentration. *It seems to numb all nerve terminals. How interesting! I've heard about it. Numbing... I remember something from childhood. That's it!*

"Give me a needle."

One cute little plant produced a certain characteristic numbing of lips, tongue, face, and limbs. The woman poked her husband with a needle. The earl wasn't completely unconscious. He reacted to external stimuli such as light. The enema didn't please him either. Jerisson reacted to the pinprick in the chest. He jerked with his whole body, except for one leg and his face. His pupils were dilated, and his saliva was abundant. Lily sighed and looked at Tahir, who froze in waiting.

Tannin was a good antidote. The only trouble was that they didn't drink tea and Lily couldn't find it anywhere. They did have pomegranates though.

"Tahir, my friend, we need to give him a hot infusion of pomegranate peel, the same as we did for Amir. It wouldn't hurt to strengthen his heart. What do we have from the tinctures? Let's also have mustard plasters and oils."

Tahir perked up and ordered the servant to bring hot water. Lily sighed and left the room to see Edward and Alicia. The widowed countess was trying to comfort the king when Lily walked in. Two pairs of searching eyes turned to Lilian.

"Countess?"

"Your Majesty, he's very weak."

Edward turned pale, but Lily wasn't going to hide anything.

"I assume the herb is the lilac slayer." Lily remembered this herb from Jamie's stories. "There are also some nasty impurities. Otherwise, he would at least have been conscious."

"So?"

"If his heart is strong, he will survive. If not..."

The unsaid echoed in the killing silence.

"He has a strong heart." Edward looked hopeful.

"It's not only about the heart, Your Majesty. I don't know what else was in the poison, but the lilac slayer makes the heart beat very fast to then make it cease beating at all."

"Countess..."

Lily understood him without words. He would get her a star from the sky only to save his nephew. She didn't exactly know how to remove the poison from the body and how to help the heart without surgical intervention. She could strengthen the heart with tinctures, but they weren't as effective as say kordiamin or cardioprotectors.

"I swear to Aldonai I will do everything in my power to save him. Pray for him." Lily took her leave and left. She didn't want to witness the king's suffering.

☙ ❧

Anna looked around in terror. The sight of the port invoked disgust and fear. There was no way back. The coachman had brought her here, and now she had to find a ship that could take her away from Ativerna. Slipping in the mud, she slowly walked along the quay. She noticed a large ship and squinted to read the name. Anna knew nothing about ships, but judging from the load, she assumed it was heading far away. *The 'Silver Shark,' why not?* Anna moved closer to the ship. The sailors noticed her and whistled. Had she come here at night, she would've found herself in serious trouble.

"Are you lost, madam?"

Anna turned around and collided with a man. He was tall, handsome, with dark hair, and with a dagger in an expensive sheath on his belt.

"Erm,"

"Peter Levorm. It's my pleasure to be at your service, madam."

"I need a ship!" Anna gathered her courage.

"Excuse me?"

The princess sighed and told him the story she had invented while sitting in the carriage. She introduced herself as a widow, whose husband died two days ago. Her relatives were going to hide the poor woman in a nunnery. Therefore, she decided to take some valuables from home and escape. She would be unhappy where everything reminded her of her dead husband. She needed to leave for Avesterra or the Khanganat.

The man listened carefully and nodded.

"I feel your pain, madam."

"Anna Ulter. I am not a noblewoman."

"Anna, darling, let me invite you on my ship."

"Your ship?"

"The 'Silver Shark' departs this evening, with the tide."

Anna nodded.

"Where are you heading?"

"To the Khanganat."

"How much is the fare?"

The captain named a price that Anna could afford. She thought a little and agreed.

"Fine. I'm going."

"In that case, welcome aboard. I will show you to your cabin. Where are your things?"

Anna shook her head.

"I didn't want to risk being caught by his relatives."

Peter nodded. *Of course, the relatives. It's clear that this wench is running away from someone. And that her story is a lie from the first to the last word.*

Peter was not a saint. He told the truth about going to the Khanganat, but he didn't mention what he was taking there. He would set sail along the shores of Wellster and Elvana, and collect a cargo of female slaves. Beautiful girls were in demand in the Khanganat. He would happily add Anna to the headcount. He offered the woman his hand and led her onto the ship.

I wonder if what she said about her husband was true? If she isn't a virgin, I could use her on the way. A nice kitty!

Anna had a dark future ahead of her. Yet, not as dark as the one she would've gotten at the hands of her father, Count Lort, or Edward.

ఈ ☐ ఆ

Lily lost track of time. It had been several hours since she sat down at her husband's bedside. They cleaned out his stomach, gave him enemas, tried to strengthen his heart.

God, how I hate death. It knew no time, no reason, no mercy, and took away the closest people to unknown faraway places. Whatever the Bible said about death, Lily didn't believe that the dead departed to a better place. She wasn't going to sit back and watch them depart to that better world. She wanted to fight. She viciously fought for every patient's life. Sometimes hopelessly, but she continued the fight until the end. It wasn't fair when the young and strong died before their time. Death was always painful, sometimes too painful.

Out of nowhere, Miranda appeared, pale and crying. Her searching look asked one question, *My Papa will live, right?*

Lily sent her to Alicia and Edward. The child clung to Alicia's chest like she was her real grandmother. She was sharing her living human warmth. Lou-Lou was whining softly, clinging to the feet of her little mistress.

The earl was vomiting. His heartbeat was weak and inconsistent. Lily decided to take more serious measures. Atropine could help, but if she didn't guess correctly with the dose, it could be fatal. Atropine was found in belladonna, a deadly poisonous plant. The dosage was crucial. The earl's heartbeat was fading out, and Lily decided to take the risk. *It can't get worse than this.* She diluted a few drops in a cup of water.

Jess's heartbeat evened out slowly. One minute, two minutes, ten minutes. Lily was treating poison with poison.

The earl flinched and ceased to breathe.

"NO!"

Lily wasn't going to give up. She knew it wasn't the end. She didn't care about the smell or the vomit and shouted to Tahir, "Push on his chest!"

He was a healthy young man, he would cope with broken ribs if they came.

"Lily!"

"Come on!"

A breath, one more—push! A breath, and again, and again!

Her hands were numbing, tears came running down her cheeks, her lungs hurt.

Come back! I'm not letting you go. Two more breaths then push!

Minutes felt like years and added gray hairs to Lily's blonde. Only when Jerisson's chest started moving, when he began unevenly rattling and started breathing by himself, did Lily drop to the floor near the bed.

"He will survive. Tahir, he will survive!"

Tahir was a Khangan, and the thing he did next went against the customs of his country. He bowed deep before Lily and kissed her hands slowly, first one, then the other. He kissed the hands of the doctor, the hands that saved lives.

Lily looked at her wrists and burst into tears. *Impotence? Anger? Stress?* Tahir helped her to a chair and left her alone. He looked at Jerisson.

That man won't cross the great divide today!

He would let the others know that the danger had passed. A lot of people were waiting for the verdict: Edward (who was unwell because of his nerves), Miranda (who needed comfort), Richard (who was worried about his friend's fate), and Alicia. August Broklend was also there to support his daughter. Everyone thought an attempt had been made on the king, but that they had poisoned the earl instead. Fortunately, nobody said anything about Anna. Nobody linked her to the attempt.

All of them waited.

Edward was first to take a step forward, but as soon as he saw Tahir's eyes, he was relieved.

"He's alive."

"Lily said he will live."

Edward sighed in relief and slowly dropped to the floor. Miranda squeaked and ran next door to see her parents. She snuggled on Lily's knees and couldn't stop crying. *Papa will stay alive! Papa will live!*

Nobody took notice of the crying women. The doctors in the room were busy with Jerisson Earton. The rest surrounded the king, helping him to recover from fainting. The king was old. Thankfully, it was nothing serious.

The only person who didn't make a fuss, but instead got Tahir's silent reassurance and left the room was Richard. He was the future king, after all. He had to behave accordingly.

⊰ ⊱

Jerisson, the Earl of Earton, opened his eyes, and in the moonlight, saw his wife sleeping in a chair by the bedside, close enough to be touching his hand with her fingers. There was a mattress on the floor near the bed. On it, in the company of two big dogs, slept Miranda. It went against all code of conduct, but nobody dared to turn them out. The palace servants didn't even try; they feared punishment.

Lily opened her eyes and looked at her husband.

"Water?"

A glass was brought to Jess's lips, and the man greedily sipped. He was about to ask something when Lily covered his mouth.

"Be quiet. I will tell you everything. I don't know what Anna of Wellster gave you to drink, but she poisoned you. You should thank Tahir. If he hadn't been there, you wouldn't have been saved. I wouldn't have managed to get here on time. I hope there won't be any serious consequences."

Jess slowly lowered his eyes.

"Your body might hurt; it's the consequence of the treatment. I will tell you later. You need to sleep now."

"What about—"

"Anna? We haven't caught her yet. Sleep."

Jess thought he was lucky to have his family and sank into a deep, heavy sleep. He saw no dreams that night.

⊗ ☐ ⊗

Edward was ghastly pale and looked aged. He tried to stay strong. Richard understood him. Experiencing such shock at his age was difficult. Yet, things had to be done. The king had to look after the kingdom. It was his duty.

"What do we do with Wellster?"

Edward gave his son a searching look.

"What do you want to do?"

Edward was testing Richard. He was to become king, and it was the king's duty to decide. *Is it disgusting? Alas, the life of the king is like that.*

"It's fine," said Richard calmly. "We have two choices. The first one, to make everything public and announce a war with Wellster. The second option would be to keep everything quiet, see Lydia off, and hold Gardwig accountable. How old is the second princess?"

"She is two years younger than Anna."

"Let's invite her to come here and stay with the princesses. Sooner or later, I will still need to marry." "What about revenge?"

"I would've strangled Anna with my own hands." Richard bared his teeth, which for an instant made him look like a beast. "That filthy woman managed to escape. As for the war with Wellster, Avesterra would only benefit from our feud."

Edward looked at Richard with a degree of respect. His decisions might have seemed savage or even beastly, but not for a king.

"Well done, Son."

Richard sighed.

"Father, you better go rest. I will make an announcement to the court myself."

"How could I fall asleep?"

"Don't put strain on your heart."

Edward also realized that it was best for him to rest.

"Fine. Call Tahir."

ಐ ☐ ೞ

The next morning, Lily woke up with a terrible feeling. She had dreamt of India, which at that time was a barbaric place. She had been a criminal sentenced to be trampled to death by an elephant. The elephant had stepped on her head and kept pressing it down. *Finish me off, you brute! I haven't got any more strength to endure it!* She had howled in her sleep and woken up. Although she saw no elephant, the rest was there—a terrible headache. Her mouth tasted of street cats, and her stomach seemed to have turned into a wasp nest. Her feet were freezing cold. The rest of her body was kept warm by a blanket. Jess was sleeping on the bed. Miranda's cover had come off, but she didn't have to worry about a cold with such warm-blooded creatures as Nanook and Lou-Lou by her side. Lily carefully moved the girl to the chair. She touched her husband's cheek. It was warm and full of life.

At moments like that, Lily understood how well she had chosen her profession. *A doctor? A healer? A medicus? One could even name it 'devil.' The most important thing was the saved life.*

Jess opened his eyes.

"Lily?"

She could see it was genuinely hard for him to speak. He almost whispered. Lily smiled at her husband.

"Shall we go home?"

Jess slowly closed his eyes. *Yes, home. Praise be to Aldonai! I've been such a fool!*

Lily was not present during Jess' confidential conversation with Aldonai. She had already left to organize the servants and the carriage. She couldn't put Jerisson on a horse. There was also Mirrie and the dogs.

How would I have looked my daughter in the eye if I had let her father die? Praise be to Aldonai.

ಐ ☐ ೞ

Meanwhile, Richard consulted with his father.

"Tomorrow you will go to Gardwig and tell him everything."

"What next?"

"You will agree to the arrival of his younger daughter. He owes us."

Richard sighed.

"You bet!"

"Take a draft of the agreement from the table. Read and make a note of it."

Richard only shook his head. His father's skin was gray, he couldn't stand on his feet, but that wasn't a reason to shirk responsibility. His brain worked relentlessly. He thought about the future of the state. *Aldonai, be merciful, do all kings become like that? I'm scared to become like him.*

"I will give it a read."

"Don't be angry at Gardwig. We can't afford to be."

Richard understood his father. Kings weren't ordinary humans. They couldn't afford to get revenge, be happy, love, and hate. Although everything was fine in the end, the whole royal family had to go through a lot. Edward sighed heavily.

"You know, I sometimes think that I shouldn't have allowed myself to be loved."

"But—"

"I love my baby girls. As for the rest, children pay for their parent's sins. But if the parent doesn't die on time, he is also forced to pay."

"Don't talk like that."

"I am old, Richard. I haven't got much time left. You know I would've wanted to pay my own dues."

Richard shook his head. He didn't understand what his father meant. Edward looked at his son and thought that he would never reveal the truth to him.

One day, he had allowed himself the liberty of falling in love. He didn't let Jessie go; he didn't let her be happy or at least safe with someone else. The result was his daughter, who was consumed by grief. His son almost died because of some stupid wench. He was grateful to Lilian Earton. She was a walking miracle, and the king owed her unto death.

Everything could've been different. My one weakness cost a lot of lives. Imogene, Jyce, Jessie, Edmund, Amalia, her children—they all died because of it.

The crown was a terrible burden. Wearing it demanded the king to commit to terrifying things. Such a life was painful and frightening.

Aldonai, I beg for your understanding, not forgiveness. I forgive myself anyway.

※ ❦ ☙

In the morning, Richard departed to meet Gardwig. The King of Wellster was already waiting for him. He dismissed his medicus, looked carefully, and nodded at the chair.

"Sit down."

"Thank you."

Richard measured his opponent. The king was pale, red-eyed, and evidently tired. On top of it, Richard noticed the special way he had arranged his injured leg.

"How do you feel?"

"I will feel better once I find out what happened," snapped Gardwig.

It had caused him a lot of trouble to keep everyone silent when Anna didn't return to the embassy. The rumors had spread fast, and the king had said that she had left to the monastery for prayer. She was accompanied by Edward's guards.

Gardwig's wrath was terrifying. The servants didn't dare to speak about Anna in his presence, and rightly so.

※ ❦ ☙

"Anna arrived at the palace. The Earl of Earton met her and notified her of the details of the medical procedure," announced Richard without much emotion. "Having found out why she was brought there, she poisoned the earl and ran away."

Gardwig angrily swore. He looked at Richard.

"Is the earl alive?"

"He miraculously managed to survive. We still haven't managed to capture her."

"If I had known about it I would've killed her myself."

Richard carefully looked at the speaker. Gardwig wasn't lying. It was clear he really thought that.

"Nobody knew."

"What are you going to do next?"

The old man's voice was tired and desperate. He knew that Jerisson was like a brother to Richard. If he were in Edward's place, he wouldn't have forgiven him and would have started a war. Being in Ativerna made him feel like a hostage. *Aldonai, have mercy on Wellster!*

"What is your second daughter's name?"

Gardwig looked at Richard with mistrust. Before him was not a boy, but a man who was no less tired than he, with sad eyes, a man who nearly lost his best friend and still found the strength to not seek revenge, to not shed blood and drag the country into a well of misfortune.

Gardwig sighed with relief.

"Richard, you and your father,"

"It wasn't easy for us. I hope that we didn't make a mistake."

Gardwig could've said a lot to this, but the words were unnecessary. He simply extended his hand to Richard. It was a gesture of understanding, gratitude, and respect. A lot of things were left unsaid between the two. Gardwig had long ago gotten used to making hard decisions. For Richard, it was only the beginning.

A common idea brought them together. Any proper king was prepared to sacrifice everything for the sake of his people. They both realized that one couldn't remain on the throne for long if he only took. Both men had to fulfill their royal duty.

Their hands met, and their eyes met. No matter what, Wellster and Ativerna would forever remain neighbors and friends, as long as the kings, their children, and their grandchildren lived, they would remember this testimony.

The moment passed, Gardwig sighed and smiled.

"Your father must be proud of you."

"I hope so. Let's discuss the matter."

"Maria, my second daughter. She is a year and a half younger than Anna. I will write to the regent today and will stay here until she arrives. I will attend the engagement ceremony and give you my blessing. Besides, it would be good for me to get a bit more treatment. As far as I understand, Sir din Dashar won't go to Wellster.

Richard replied with a smile.

"I suppose he won't, Your Majesty."

"Call me Gardwig."

"I assume, dear Gardwig, that he will not leave his student."

"Do you think the countess will stay with her husband?"

"If it weren't for her…"

Gardwig nodded and remembered.

"I'd be happy to have her as my guest in Wellster, together with her teacher."

"We also need such doctors!" Richard joked.

The main things were already said and taken into account.

"Fine," Gardwig said with a smile. "I will send my mediucuses to them for training. Maybe there will be some use in it."

"Do you feel better?"

"Not much, but at least Tahir didn't lie to my face. I cannot stand the doctors who give nothing but promises, but in reality, wish to leave you as soon as possible." Richard nodded sympathetically. Gardwig looked at the table.

"I cannot offer you wine. Wine isn't good for me for medical reasons, but I can offer you cold spring water."

"With pleasure."

The men clinked cups and drank some water together. Richard was optimistic. He would look at Maria, educate her, and make her fall in love with him. She would have no choice.

As for him, warmth, care, and tenderness were a good substitute for love and passion. *Maybe I will learn to love this strange girl? Time will tell.*

Gardwig respected Edward. He wished for his son to become like Richard, only he wouldn't see him grow up. He wouldn't last to see his grandchildren. Time would tell.

"What's the official version?"

"I suggest presenting it as if Anna had suddenly felt the taste for prayers and left to the nunnery."

"Hmm."

The explanation wasn't perfect, but it gave the monarchs a chance to save face. As for the gossip, it was inevitable. Either way, nobody could prove anything. If someone tried to, Altres in Wellster would deal with them. Gardwig suspected that Edward's secret service was also up and running.

"Let it be so. I will support any version that allows you and me to save face."

The men exchanged meaningful glances.

"I wish I knew where my beastly daughter was." Gardwig sighed.

"I don't," retorted Richard. "I hope she got what she deserved."

ೞ ⃞ ೞ

The two men would've been pleased to see Anna at that moment.

After the captain tested her, the woman received the unflattering and unprofitable role of ship whore, although reserved for the captain and his officers. If she behaved well, they would sell her as a concubine into good hands. She had already received some slaps in the face. The men made her understand that the ocean fish weren't picky. They took away all her money and jewelry. The only thing she could do was pray to survive until the end of the voyage. She cried, prayed, and pined after Lons. If only she had run away with him, if only she had known.

Anna was going a long way to the Khanganat. Uncertainty loomed ahead of her. As for Aldonai, the aldons claimed he heard all requests, but answered rarely.

ಸಿ ೞ

After his visit to Gardwig, Richard headed to the Ivernean embassy, reported his arrival, and waited to be invited in. He didn't have to wait long. After about ten minutes, Adrian appeared in the living room.

"Your Highness."

"Your Highness."

The princes exchanged bows.

"Wine?"

"Thank you." Complying with the gesture of welcome, Richard sat down in a chair. He relaxed a little, and after making small talk, gradually got down to business.

"Your Highness, I beg to inform you that we have signed an agreement with Wellster."

"I suppose that means—"

"Yes. I will have to marry one of Gardwig's daughters. I offer you my most sincere apologies."

Adrian shrugged.

"We have expected such a decision. I guess we should congratulate you on a successful marriage?"

Richard smiled. Right now, he felt genuine affection for Bernard's son. After all, he could've reacted violently.

A young woman flew into the living room. She was tall and good-looking. Richard rated her highly: he noticed her thick, ash-brown hair decorated with flowers and her pink dress made of a light material. He stood and bowed. The lady responded with a curtsey and stole across the room toward her brother. She gave the prince a casual kiss on the cheek.

"Brother, I'm going out for a while."

"Where?"

"To the same place as yesterday."

"Make sure you take guards with you."

"Yes. Miguel is going with me as well."

"Your H-Highness?"

Richard faltered, for he couldn't believe his eyes.

Is that LYDIA?

Before him was a gorgeous woman with beautiful hair. She was a bit too thin, but quite fit.

Is this a joke?

Lydia laughed in a familiar, poisonous giggle.

"Your Highness, it's me. I could never imagine that the change of clothes would produce such an effect on you. Or maybe you couldn't see beyond the old dress? Anyway, it doesn't matter. Your Wellster princess is waiting for you, and I can finally enjoy freedom."

Richard only shook his head. The voice was hers as well as the nasty character.

Lydia. No, thank you. A snake can bolt, but it will never stop biting. Even if she were the most beautiful woman in the world, I would never take her for a wife.

Richard didn't say this out loud. He complimented Lydia on her looks, kissed her hand, talked to the prince a little longer to agree on the times of departure of the embassy, and left for the palace.

I wonder who could've turned this duckling into a swan! A most curious thing. No matter how much one decorates Lydia with flowers, nothing could make up for her surly disposition. I don't envy the man who will marry her.

Chapter 7.
Young fruit.

> *Brother,*
> *I hope everything is well in Wellster. I want to inform you that all our efforts weren't in vain as we finally signed the agreement with Ativerna. I demand an explanation about Anna's secret marriage. Meanwhile, send Maria to Ativerna. Dress her up and make sure she is still pure. They won't forgive us if we mess up a second time. I will stay here for now.*
> *Thanks to doctor Tahir Djiamin din Dashar, my ulcer is beginning to heal. He promises that the wound won't open up again. Provided I lead a healthy lifestyle, I could hope to live significantly longer. Send my greetings to Milia and take care of the children.*
> *Gardwig.*

Having read the letter, Altres sighed in relief. He had already received a few messages from his agents, but he still felt uneasy. Everything went against his plan. *I should've killed that whore and her husband a long time ago. The only reason I didn't was for the sake of the agreement. The most important thing is that Gardwig is not mad at me and that he doesn't remain a hostage of the situation. Thank Aldonai for prolonging my brother's life.* Altres would've paid an arm and a leg to keep his brother alive.

He resolved to see Milia. Although he thought Gardwig's wife a silly goose, she still loved her husband. She was worried about him. *She needs to be reassured, lest the milk disappear. Aldonai, have mercy.*

He didn't have to send for Maria. The girl was already in the palace. After Gardwig's departure, kind-hearted Milia brought her girls to the palace to educate them herself. Maria seemed to be a good girl. She was cheerful, flirtatious and charismatic but didn't seem to have a weakness for teachers. Altres would have to invite midwives to check her. He winked at his reflection in the glass mirror, which was unusually clear.

Let's get to work!

≈ ◊ ≈

"Lilian, this is great! Congratulations!"

Lily sighed.

"Thank you, Lydia."

As it turned out, she and Jerisson weren't careful enough, and their carelessness bore fruit. Everyone, from the king to the Virmans, wished her the best. Everyone smiled, everyone handled her like she was a crystal vase. *Ugh!*

The earl had fully recovered and returned to his duties at court. He kept repeating how much he wished to leave for Earton with his wife, but Edward wanted him at the palace. It looked like the countess had to give birth in the capital. *Not a big deal, I'm up to my ears with work.*

"I looked through your books and calculations and made some corrections. Overall, we are doing well. No larceny, we should meet the estimates and can expect profit from the very first day."

Lily sighed.

When Lydia came in for a visit, Lily was in the middle of making calculations. She obviously didn't show Lydia. She left the books on the table and went to instruct the servants about an herbal brew. Lydia opened one of the books and couldn't take her eyes off the numbers. The new method of bookkeeping interested the girl. The apologies quickly turned into explanations and had soon sparked a discussion. Talking to Lydia made it clear that she was a real Dreiserian financier. It would've been a crime not to use her quick brain. Lily was far removed from economics and finance. She took care of accounting out of necessity.

Lily trusted Lydia with the secret information. The methods of production at Mariella were real know-how. As for the profit estimations, there was nothing special about them. On the contrary, they could encourage the princess to open a Mariella Fashion House in Ivernea.

"The embassy is leaving for home soon."

"I am very sorry to hear that!"

Lily was genuinely upset. The state would have benefited from having an intelligent queen, but Richard had made a different choice. *What a pity!*

"Me, too. We didn't have enough time to get to know each other properly."

"We can write to each other and visit each other."

"Princesses cannot travel when they please. Besides, the king wouldn't let you come either."

Lydia sighed.

"In that case, we will simply send each other letters. Let them think what they want."

Lydia smiled.

"They will read them over."

"Let them read!"

The princess shook her head. Lilian was intelligent, but sometimes she acted like a small girl.

"I want you to know that I am very grateful to you."

"What for?"

"For Richard. He came in this morning to break off the engagement agreement and saw me in my new outfit. He didn't even recognize me! Can you imagine?"

Women and the subject of their gossip never change.

"No!" Lily giggled. "I hope he didn't fall from his chair."

"He nearly did! To be honest, I'm glad he didn't pick me."

Lydia didn't mention the blackmail.

"Why?"

"Although the prince is a worthy husband, and although I am a princess myself, I think we wouldn't have gotten along. He needs a quiet and home-bound life. I like numbers and freedom."

The women exchanged glances. Both of them could be quite hard to live with. It was hard to find a man who was able to look deeper, past the prickles of irritability and thorns of casual malice. Such heroes were rare. Being a hero wasn't easy.

For instance, it took Jerisson being poisoned before he appreciated his wife for her true worth. Yet, not every man could survive such an education.

As soon as Lily remembered Jerisson, he came knocking on the door. He walked in and took a bow. Looking at their love, Lydia even got a bit envious. They looked happy together. The earl couldn't take his eyes off his wife. Lily smiled.

"How are you feeling?"

She was genuinely worried about her husband's health. There was no X-ray or EKG, so there was no way to tell if the poisoning had done any serious damage to his heart, stomach or kidneys. For the first two weeks, Lily didn't leave her husband's side. Gradually, he felt better, and soon, was fully recovered. The situation with Anna made him stop trusting women. The only exception was his wife. The rest of them could go to Maldonaya. *I've had enough of it!*

Furthermore, Lily was pregnant. Jess doted on her. It was his child and a brother to Mirrie. *I cannot wait!*

❦

The month passed without any special events. Lily wasn't required to attend court and could use her status as a pregnant woman in order to get some quiet and privacy. She frequented Taral, the Mariella Fashion House, and the Royal Treasury. Mirrie followed her everywhere. The Earl of Earton would often join them, and the happy family could spend more time together.

He and Lilian weren't particularly compatible. They had conflicting personalities, education, and views on life. Yet, for the sake of their daughter, they tried to be tolerant toward each other. The fact that they never had any disagreements in bed also helped. Besides, Jerisson was grateful to his wife for saving him and remembered that a pregnant woman was a dangerous, unpredictable, and absurd being. Nevertheless, beauty was a powerful weapon. He forgave Lilian a lot of things. Gradually, he and Lily got used to each other's ways and learned how to reach a compromise.

Prince Amir's behavior was exemplary. He even managed to earn Jerisson's approval. He doted on the little girl and thought the world of her. He gave her an eagle and taught her fencing. Lily was amazed when, one day, the prince came up to her and confessed that having grown up in the Khanganat, other women only saw him as a prince. Mirrie, on the other hand, saw a person in him. It was very important. *Harem?*

"Mind me, Countess, you have very wild ideas of a harem here. Not only women live there, but a lot of cousins, second aunts, and third grandmas. The concubines barely reach ten percent. Even if I get them, they will remain the tokens of victory. It's necessary for status. As for the rest, they could go have fun with the guards, or pleasure themselves; it's their own problem."

Lily nodded and began remembering pharmacology. She needed to teach Miranda toxicology. She could've waited, but realized that Miranda urgently needed it.

❦

"Stop lying here like a sissy. I am ashamed of you, son!"
Alexander Falion turned his head and looked at his father.

"What happened?"

"It's been a month that my son has been getting wasted every night. I hoped that it would go away by itself, but you've lost your mind over that girl!"

"Don't call her that. She is Lilian."

"She is the most ordinary whore!"

"Father!"

"While you lay here sniveling—do you even know that she is pregnant?"

"I know."

"Do you want her?"

"I love her."

Falion heartily slapped his son.

"Too much is at stake. Get yourself together. I will order them to bring a hot bathtub. Have a bath and pull yourself together. I want my son back, not this sissy. Only once you look like a person, will I explain to you how to get that girl."

The Old Pike left the room. Alexander stupidly stared at the floor. *To get the girl? Really?* A sweet hope slowly spread across his body. He didn't have any reason to pay a visit to Earton. *What if Jerisson died? Why not see what my father has to say?*

෴

The diplomatic mission from Ivernea left in the morning, with friendly goodbyes. The princes thanked Edward, and Lydia thanked the Countess of Earton. All of them received an invitation to Wellster and promised to visit.

Gardwig was not going to depart. He was waiting for his daughter to sign the new agreement.

෴

It didn't affect Lily in any way. She stayed back from court because of her delicate condition. Sometimes, she did visit the king, but only in the evenings, using the back entrance, wearing a cape and a mask. Such was the code of conduct. As before, the princesses enjoyed her visits to the palace and, together with Mirrie, wrote down the fairytales Lily told them. Lily saw Richard a couple of times. He was mainly Jerisson's friend. As for Lily herself, she laughed and put up with the prince as the lesser of evils. The main thing was that he didn't get her husband insanely drunk. She could tolerate the rest.

The Eartons were in possession of a certain rare thing, something without which one couldn't build a family—namely, the feeling of family warmth. It was the feeling of warmth and belonging when one is peaceful and knows that someone is always waiting for them at home. This feeling has been beautifully described by poets and writers. Those lucky enough to experience it in real life call it different things. Some call it habit, others passion. But it took a man to truly experience it to know that he would never be satisfied with less. It was an indescribable feeling, to know that someone needed you, that they loved you for who you were, no matter what.

Lily tried to build her love island in that medieval world, where she would always feel secure. Her family was Helke and Loria with their children, the Virmans, Leif and Erik, Ingrid and the lace-makers, the artisans, Leis, and his soldiers, Taris Brok, Alicia Earton, and Pastor Vopler with his son. They were all part of the small world that revolved around Lilian Earton and Miranda Catherine Earton. Jerisson had also become a part of it, and he wanted to stay there. In good times and in bad times, that island was a safe harbor amid the seas of trouble, where nobody judged or scolded anyone, where there was no place for anger or greed. Although they weren't quite a real family yet, they were something very close. It only took Jerisson getting a taste of this warm feeling to become addicted to it. It wasn't the madness of passion, not lightning between two people, but something different. They enjoyed being around each other.

Even the strongest man needed a place where he could rest. Even the strongest woman needed the knowledge that she was not alone, that she had a strong shoulder to lean on.

It was too early to speak about the union of the two hearts. That would only become possible after a lot of hardship, difficult decisions, blood, and death.

There used to be a time when they suspected each other, when they were scared of dirty tricks, but Jerisson and Lilian had found a way to each other's hearts. Still, they had yet to go through hardship side by side. They would cope. Happiness wasn't fireworks, it was a fire in the hearth. Their fire would not go out. They would try to keep it burning.

※ ❧

Time went by. Richard's new bride arrived. They said she was pretty. Lily hadn't met her yet. Gardwig solemnly signed the contract, marked it with a ball, and left for home. His duty called him. His leg was almost painless. The ulcer was healing. Tahir equipped Gardwig's medicus with a lot of advice and healing ointments. The man received them with awe and asked for permission to correspond. He was given a post pigeon. Gardwig approved of the idea. He felt a lot better and expected to live for at least ten more years.

※ ❧

Count Lort wrote from Wellster. He professed his gratitude for curing his Majesty.

"Dear Countess, you have a friend in Wellster. If you need anything or get into any trouble..."

Lily replied with a thank you letter but said that she wasn't going to visit Wellster any time soon. She said that she felt happy where she was, especially since her husband had come to his senses. She felt secure and peaceful. *Why go to far-away lands if I can build my own happiness with my own hands, here and now?* It was difficult, but nobody promised an easy way. Happiness was worth the effort.

Lilian knew this very well. Looking into her husband's blue eyes, she saw the same understanding there. In short, if Jerisson had gotten himself a smart and decisive woman from the very beginning, there would have been no circle of mistresses or his disrespectful relationship with women.

※ ❧

Jerisson Earton was also happy. He didn't only receive the woman of his dreams, but a lot more. Although Lilian was always busy running around workshops all day and was dead on her feet in the evenings, she was a real beauty, a real gem of a woman. She was a talented inventor. The whole of Ativerna envied him for such a wife. He had to live up to expectations.

Jerisson thought very highly of himself. He very well knew that he deserved the best, and he got what he wanted. He fell head over heels for Lily.

Mistresses? When a man has such a wife, he doesn't need surrogates. Ladies! You are free to go! How silly they seem to me next to my wife, how very dumb. What did I see in them before? I do not know.

ഇ ☐ ℭ

Alexander Falion appeared two days after the departure of the Wellster diplomatic mission. He gave Lily a luxurious bouquet, supposedly for Miranda, and kissed her hand. Without much thinking, he invited her on a walk around the garden. Lily agreed. They needed to get things straight while her husband was away—once and for all.

It was solely her fault. She gave the man false hope, and she would have to pay for it. She still had no idea how it would go between her and Jerisson. *We are responsible for those whom we have tamed, and especially for those whom we have saved.* She would take pleasure in being responsible for her husband for the rest of her life.

They ambled along the path between the rose bushes, followed by a huge grey Virman shepherd dog. Alexander was the first one to break the silence.

"You seem sad, Lilian."

Lily lowered her eyes.

"I have reasons to be both happy and sad."

"Will you tell me about them?"

Why would I have brought it up otherwise? thought Lily with irritation. Her pregnancy gave her mood swings. She had to be careful with what she said out loud.

"Obviously," Lily gave him a sad smile. "Even before I tell my priest."

"Do I deserve such honor?"

Lily didn't adopt his playful tone.

"You deserve honesty. I am expecting a child with my husband, and I am happy with him."

Alexander seized hold of her hands and looked into her eyes.

"Lilian, it could've been our child."

Lily shrugged.

"I don't think so. You are married."

"That could be changed."

"Really? Would you poison your wife? Or drown her in a lake?"

The man was taken aback. Lily continued her attack.

"Alexander, do you know why smart women never cheat on their husbands?"

"W-why?"

"Because every man will ask himself if she cheated on her husband, will she not surely cheat on me? If you get rid of one wife... Do you see what I'm saying?"

Falion gritted his teeth.

"I understand everything, Lilian. But you gave me hope."

"I made a mistake."

"Should I just forget you?!"

Strong hands lay on her shoulders and turned her to face the marquess.

"Lilian! I love you!!!"

Lily didn't make a move. Nanook became tense. Everything was clear without words. Falion heard a growl. The dog was close to attacking him.

For a few moments, Falion froze. Eventually, he loosened his grip, and his face turned to stone. All his emotions disappeared as if they had been washed away with water.

"I am sorry, Lilian."

God will forgive you.

"Forget about me, Alexander. It's for the best."

"Best for you? Of course! Who would doubt that?"

Lily lost her temper.

"Alexander, what can we offer each other? Don't talk about love, better tell me what place I would have in your life. The place of your mistress? No, thank you. I will manage. Despite psychological issues, your wife is wholesome and alive, and is going to live."

"Your husband is also alive—yet."

"I don't recommend threatening my family."

Alexander was furious; Lily kept calm. Her state of mind was deceptive. She was tense as a taut string.

What the hell?

"And what will you do to me?"

"I think you need a doctor, Falion. I don't advise you to forget that you owe me anyway."

"What for?"

"For your father."

"You weren't saving him. You were saving your husband."

"I'll make a note for the future: do not ever save the Falions!" Lily was angry.

"Is this your last word?"

"And our last conversation."

Falion flashed his eyes but realized that the conversation wouldn't be productive. He turned around and left. Lily stayed alone.

She knew she shouldn't have shown her weakness because someone could strike into the most vulnerable spot.

Is it painful? No, only nasty. How did a handsome prince turn out to be like that? Should I also be wary of my husband?

Lily managed to walk into the house and reach her bedroom without losing face. She burst into tears only after locking all the doors.

Damn the hormones!! This is not love! I am so hurt!

It's only the hormones, Lily! You'll be all right.

ಊ ೮

The servants reported everything to Jerisson, and he called Falion to a duel. It was Hans Tremain who discouraged it. He had accidentally (or on purpose) entered the bedroom in the middle of a domestic dispute. Jerisson paced the room and comforted his wife. Lilian was close to tears. Mirrie was simply crying out loud. Her mother had already whispered to her to keep her father out of a duel, and the child tried her best. She gave a very talented performance.

Hans looked at the scene and asked the earl to spare him a couple of minutes. Jess pointed in the direction of the study. He didn't see Hans give Lily a wink. *Everything will be fine, my dear friend! Stay strong.* The men disappeared into the study, and Lily began to calm her daughter.

ಊ ೮

Jess sat down in a chair and nodded at the opposite seat.

"Wine?"

"No, thank you. I've heard about the marquess' visit."

"I will kill him!" shouted Jess, but Hans held up his hand.

"I beg you Earl, don't get so worked up!"

"The bastard upset my wife!"

"You want revenge, right?"

"Yes!" Jess' eyes flashed like he was a wildcat.

"I will tell you something of which not even His Majesty knows. The Falions took part in the conspiracy."

Jess was instantly alert. He became calm, and his eyes turned into slits.

"I see!"

"I beg you to not take any action for at least three more days."

"Why not?"

"I need a little more time. I will be able to catch everyone, both small fish and big fish. I beg you, Earl."

For a few moments, Jess remained silent.

"Who told you about the visit?"

Leir Hans smiled.

"I have my sources in your home."

"Who?"

"My Lord, I'm afraid I cannot tell you."

"Call me Jess. So who is it?"

"Call me Hans. Jess, I won't say who it is."

"I won't tolerate any 'songbirds' in my house!"

Hans did not even argue.

"All right. Let's finish this business with the conspiracy, and I will get rid of my agent."

"Do you give me your word on it?"

"I swear."

Jess relaxed a little.

"Fine. Tell me your plan."

ಬಿ ಜಿ

In two days' time, the report was on Edward's table. The king skimmed the report and looked at Hans.

"So that's how it is!"

"Yes, Your Majesty."

"Are you sure?"

"All too sure."

"In that case, invite the Countess of Earton to the palace."

"What about the earl?"

"Explain everything to the earl. Make him prepare for what's to come."

"What if he is against it?"

"Then I will speak to him in person."

"Yes, Your Majesty. How much time do we need for preparation?"

"At least three days."

"It will happen tomorrow then. Remember, if something goes wrong, you will be hanged."

Hans smiled wryly.

"If I fail, I shall die anyway, Your Majesty."

Edward smiled.

"Fine. Go." He rang the bell.

'Where is the prince?"

"He is with his sisters," reported the secretary.

"Send him to me immediately!"

ঔ ෫

"Read it," he pushed Hans report toward Richard. The prince read through it, and his face became stern.

"When?"

"No later than tomorrow evening."

"Those girls…"

"If something happens to them, it will be on your conscience."

"Do we have another choice?"

"I wish! It's better to do it immediately than wait for Aldonai knows what."

Richard swore.

"We have very little time then."

"Yes, and, you know, try to act as secretly as possible."

Richard understood. *How cruel is the life of kings!*

ঔ ෫

"Jess, we have no choice."

"Are you out of your mind? It's my wife and my daughter you are talking about!"

Jess forgot all decencies.

"I understand, but we have no choice."

"I am your choice!"

"Jess, it's a state emergency."

"Find another honeypot, Richard."

"There is no other, Jess. Please understand!"

"Never! My answer is no!"

It took around two hours to persuade Jess. Hans joined in the discussion, and soon His Majesty was asking Jess himself. The Earl of Earton finally agreed, but hardly to everything.

ଅ ☐ ଔ

"We need to talk, Lily. It's important."

Lily gave her husband a serious look. The urgency in his voice was unexpected.

"What happened?"

"Lily, I will understand if you refuse."

"Refuse what?"

"It's about the Falions."

Lily was genuinely surprised.

"What have they done?"

Jess sighed and began telling her. Lily listened attentively without interrupting. She waited until he finished and asked only one question.

"What do I have to do?"

"You are pregnant."

"What do I need to do so that it doesn't affect our son?"

Jess rolled his eyes and began to explain what would happen next.

ଅ ☐ ଔ

A letter to Lilian Elizabeth Mariella, Countess of Earton.
My Lady,
I ask you today to come to the palace for a private conversation. I'll be waiting for you in my office after sunset.
Edward VIII, by the grace of Aldonai,
The King of Ativerna

Lily bit her lip. *Wow, sad. How could so much be contained in just three lines?*

"Has my husband not appeared?"

The secretary shook his head. It was not easy to refuse the will of the king. *I shall go. How frightening!*

The woman's hand mechanically slipped to her stomach, protecting it from the outside world. *I would rather die myself than let anyone take you away from me! You're my child, a vital part of me. I do risk losing my life. If something goes wrong...*

"Invite the earl to see me as soon as he is back," ordered Lily.

She didn't have to wait for long.

"Lilian."

Jerisson squeezed his wife's hand, double-checked her clothes and her weapon, and hugged her tight.

"Lily."

The kiss was sincere and full of emotion. It was as if Jess was drinking water from a forest spring and couldn't tear himself from his wife's lips. Lily answered his kiss. Only a light knock on the door tore them apart. Hans Tremain stood on the threshold, and Jerisson gave him a nod.

"You are responsible for my wife with your life."

Hans wasn't going to answer back. He passed the cape to Lily and the woman wrapped herself in it and left the study. Jerisson watched her leave with great sadness. He gathered himself together and also left the room.

I will not let anyone threaten my family ever again!

༂ ༃

The palace was quiet and calm. A solitary footman waited for Lilian's arrival.

"The king ordered for everything to be got ready. The court is moving to the winter residency—Litoral."

Lily shivered. Some of the courtiers must already be there. *As for His Majesty, will I leave the room untouched?* She was scared, but she had no choice. Her fingers nervously squeezed amber beads.

At least my hands aren't shaking!

There were two people in the king's study—Edward and Richard. Edward was seated, and his son stood behind his chair. Both of them looked at the countess with a lot of suspicion.

"Your Majesty, Your Highness," Lily took a long curtsey.

The men looked without particular empathy. Lily was silent, and Edward nodded first, letting her stand up.

"I am glad to see you, Countess. I've been told terrible news. You…Lilian, was there ever anything between you and Alexander Falion?"

"Never, Your Majesty."

"Were you his mistress?"

"Never."

"Did you make any agreements with him?"

"Never."

"Have you ever led him on?"

Lily frowned.

"It's easy to wrongly interpret a woman's behavior. I don't believe that I ever gave any hope or made any promises to Alexander Falion. I think it is obvious that I cannot be accountable for his own imagination."

"This woman has a terrible memory," said a quiet voice. She recognized it and turned around abruptly. She saw eight more people enter the king's study. Lily knew three of them. It was Falion Senior, Alexander, and his friend. The rest were strangers. *To hell with you! What does all this mean?*

Lily must have accidentally said that out loud because the rest turned their eyes on her. Their look was condescending and mocking. Alexander smirked.

"Sometimes you are such a fool, Lilian."

Only when I trust ones like you! This time Lily stopped herself from saying it out loud. She didn't want to make these people angry, especially because they had swords in their hands. Judging by their shine, the swords were sharp.

"These are the leftovers of the conspiracy," calmly explained Edward. "Am I right? It seems that Hans hasn't managed to get his hands on you yet."

"And he never will." The elder Falion smiled. "He is already standing before Aldonai."

Lily squeezed the amber beads with all her force. *Hans? Is it true? God! Another one of my friends! I want you all to die—in most curious poses. I will murder you one by one!*

Lilian's fear had vanished and was replaced by fury. The Countess of Earton, who was no longer Aliya, patronizingly looked up. Her brain labored over remembering all the details of the past.

"The Yerbys did swear that you were standing behind them, only nobody took them seriously."

"For good," Falion said with a smile. "It's really true."

"You were the ones who made an agreement with the Ivelens. They would have received the Crown, and what about yourself?"

"We would receive the Crown in the future," calmly replied Falion junior. "I was going to marry Cecilia Ivelen."

"And after, you planned to murder the Ivelens," continued Richard. "It's not surprising. The Falions have some relation to the ruling dynasty."

Lily winced. *Of course, two rats can agree about the cat. Having eliminated the danger, they would start eating each other. How noble!*

"How do these gentlemen justify their behavior?"

"Be quiet, woman!" interrupted Tarney.

Lily gave him a mocking look.

"You are such a brave boy when I don't have my dog with me!" The story seemed to be famous. The baron turned red and spattered saliva while cursing, only the countess didn't even look at him.

"I thought better of you, Alexander."

A vulgar betrayal. How tasteless. To his own surprise, Falion junior felt embarrassed.

"I also thought better of you, Lilian. I even got carried away and fell in love, until you carried yourself from hand to hand."

Lily raised her eyebrows.

"What do you mean from hand to hand? The only person I have ever slept with is my husband, and that will never change. We exchanged vows at the altar."

"It didn't stop you from flirting with me."

"Flirting is not love. It's nothing more than good manners."

Lilian felt relatively confident. She trusted her husband and knew that he wouldn't leave her. Her maids had sewn the chainmail net into Lily's dress, which was enough to save her from a blow of the sword. She also had two daggers fastened to her forearms, hidden by wide sleeves. Thankfully, they hadn't searched her at the entrance.

"You betrayed me," said Alexander. "I trusted you."

Lily snorted.

"Did you decide that after we had blown your conspiracy? I cannot believe your nobleness."

She lingered on the topic according to the plan. They needed to win more time. Judging from the brisk look Edward gave her, she did everything well. *What else could I do?*

"In fact, everything is much simpler," said Edward. "After the Ivelens' death, the Falions realized their plan had failed. Finding them was only a question of time. Your pregnancy is not in question here, apart from having hurt the pride of that sissy Alexander." He nodded toward Falion junior. "Do you really think he would've married you? You are the daughter of a non-hereditary baron, almost a merchant, whereas he's a royal descendant."

"More like a descendant of a donkey," quietly murmured Lily. She couldn't deny that there had been some chemistry between her and Falion, like in *Gone with the Wind*. A man could love with his soul, his body, or his member.

"The most attractive thing he saw in you was money. As soon as Falion realized he wouldn't get that, he got furious. The conspiracy required making significant investments and eventually failed. Although they felt themselves safe."

"Marrying me would have given them the possibility of raking up big cash from both the Eartons and the Ivelens."

"You begin to realize, Countess."

Lily sighed. She was sure it wasn't only greed. *But what is an attraction when one is talking about big money?* Ladies seek "love," and gentlemen do "business."

"So what! You only had to kill my husband and my daughter. It turns out not to be that easy, right?"

"Right, although Leir Tremain and his squad have prevented three attempts of murder in one month."

Lily went pale.

"You've known it all along!"

"We needed proof." Edward sighed. "This is what Hans has been busy with."

"What are they going to do next?"

There was a sound of clinking metal.

"I assume they plan to kill us all—you, me, Richard. They might leave the girls alive to marry."

"Why did they not do it straight away? I don't assume it was because of me."

"Because of Gardwig."

"Gardwig wouldn't have agreed, and Wellster wouldn't have either. The last thing a newly-come king needs is a war with neighbors. That's for certain."

"But the Duke of Falion had nearly been killed!"

Lily felt especially silly under the mocking glances of the men. There was a feud even among the conspirators. The wolf pack tore apart its own brothers. Schaltz was only getting rid of his opponent. He would've blamed it on the battle, or the sharks, or Aldonai.

"Your guess is correct, Your Majesty." The elder Falion smiled. "We didn't expect to be that lucky. However..." The men stepped forward. Richard placed his hand on his sword. Edward slipped his hand underneath the table.

God, how have they not invented small crossbows yet? thought Lily.

She moaned. The beads fell to the floor, the countess knelt to pick them up and took the daggers out of her sleeves. She could throw them well and would kill at least two of the conspirators. *Sorry, Miranda, Roman, Jacob! Poor orphaned children! You will still have Jerisson to take care of you.*

The men looked at the weakened woman with contempt.

"Edward!" yelled Duke Falion, who very much resembled an Old Pike. "You will now write that you abdicate and consent to the marriage between your daughter and Alexander Falion."

Edward grinned.

"Is he not already married?"

"I'm a widower." Marquess Falion said with a laugh.

"It's a pity he isn't the one who is dead," a voice said quietly.

The door creaked.

"Gentlemen, I suggest you either put your swords down or quickly kill yourselves. Otherwise…"

"Hans!" Lily cried out.

Indeed, it was Leir Hans Tremain. He was quite alive and healthy, except for a torn raincoat.

"The rumors of my death are slightly exaggerated, gentlemen." Hans smiled. "You've underestimated me and my people." The king's study filled with persons in dark cloaks, under which gleamed the azure color of the Royal Guard uniform.

Reynolds' sword hit the ground. The men understood everything well. The king's study was actually quite a spacious room. Edward sat out of easy reach at a heavy table. The hands of the king were beneath the table, and it was impossible to tell his movements. *A hand grenade?* thought Lily jokingly.

Hans had arrived just in time. His people were serious.

One by one, the swords clanged against the floor. That very moment, Lily held her head up and glanced at Alexander. There was so much in his solemn look: rage, despair, pain. "Good luck to the traitors," she uttered almost inaudibly with her lips.

The traitor howled, throwing his body forward.

Nobody would have had time to help the Countess of Earton. "Medice, cura te ipsum," or as medical students used to joke, the doctor who cannot help himself is worth nothing.

There was the flash of a sharp knife. Lily aimed it at his thigh to make sure she didn't hit hidden armor. Alexander could've caught it, but his leg was injured before he knew it.

The Earl of Earton shielded Lily. *Where did he come from? Perhaps he entered the room through one of the hidden pathways.*

Edward smiled.

"Incredible! You know how to use a weapon!"

He paid no more attention to the Falions. Lily gave a sad smile.

"I did a little learning. I wanted to live."

"How would you have used that weapon?" Lily looked at the second knife in her hand and rose from the floor. She swung her arm and threw the knife with an accurate, confident gesture. The blade entered the wooden panel past the ear of Duke Falion.

"Just like that! I swear that Aldonai would've forgiven me half of my sins for killing that vermin."

Edward smiled.

"Yes, you are truly an incredible woman."

"My wife is a treasure."

Jess looked like a dragon on a pile of gold. Lily sighed and leaned on his strong shoulder. He came to save her. *I would've managed without his help, but all the same, what else do I need for happiness?* To know that someone cared about her and would even put her before the state; Jess wasn't protecting the king, he was defending her. This might have been called love. Edward spread his hands.

"Forgive me, dear Countess, for turning you into bait. You are the Countess of Earton. You are the one they've attempted to kill before anybody else. You saved Amalia in childbirth. The Marquess of Falion courted you. The duke was saved by the Virmans who fulfilled your orders. In a word, you were always in the center of events, so I had no choice but to turn you into a live lure, even though your husband fought against it like a lion."

"They would've made a move sooner or later," replied Lily. "I am not mad. Right, Jess?"

"Yes, darling."

Hans glanced at the Earton couple with a smile. He was frankly pleased with himself. He had started digging around on the Falions right after Yerby's confession. He had strong suspicions, but the evidence was scarce. The Falions were smarter than the Ivelens. The Marquess of Falion was always around the countess. Hans had to put a lot of effort into hiding unnecessary facts.

Joint trips, walks, courtship, everything was innocent, at least from Lilian Earton's perspective. Both Hans and Falion realized it. Yet, Hans couldn't bring himself to explain to Lilian how their relationship had looked from the outset. If it weren't for Hans's consistent effort, most of the courtiers would have sworn that Falion and Lilian were lovers. Lilian hadn't noticed it, but Falion realized it well. Thus, he teased the leir. *Your elbow is near, but you cannot bite it, dear.*

It took him a lot of time to carefully pull the new strings and put them together to reveal the sad truth. The Falions and the Ivelens were conspirators together. Alexander planned to marry Sessie. As for his wife, it was only a matter of time. As long as she lived, Falion's hands were tied. He was a certain romantic sufferer in the eyes of the public. As soon as she died, the man would open a hunt. The elder Falion didn't need it before the success of the conspiracy. *Later.*

At one point, Hans himself suspected the countess of adultery but quickly changed his mind. There were certain things that the countess couldn't have known due to her position, origin, and upbringing. He did everything he could. He had warned Jerisson, provided Lilian's safety, and delivered his blow. Hans tried to make Falion find out the news in the right way. He provoked him to make the first move and achieved what he wanted.

It was a big risk for the Crown, but the only way he could weed out the remains of the poisonous grass. In their turn, the royal family acted out of their wish to protect their throne and the princesses. As for the Earton family, they had no interest in the feud. They wanted to go back home to their daughter. Jess took his wife's hand, and they headed toward the exit. They didn't notice the look with which Edward watched them go. The uncle was pleased to see his nephew happy.

ʚ◦ɞ

Still, the event had an effect on Lily. She threw up in the corridor. Jess picked her up and wiped her face with a handkerchief.

"How are you, my dear?"

"The baby is okay. It is my nerves."

It wasn't the first time she had been fooled. Lily's mind was a sea of relentless contradiction.

You fell for appearances? Gold, castles, princes, and dukes, counts and marquesses, titles and nobility… Fool! I am three times a fool! Next to the palace, there is always death, dirt, poison, and blood. Did you hope to not get dirty? You got carried away by the game. Your home is Earton, not the capital. You dreamed about many things, but what did you get in the end? A lot of pain. It's okay. I am strong. I will survive. I will pretend everything is fine. How painful!

The rales in her chest were her unshed tears. There was no reason why she deserved such pain.

You wanted to live, but you forgot that you lived among real people and became a catalyst for many events. There is blood and death on your conscience. Did you hope to get away with it so easily? You forget about the laws of equilibrium.

Although Jerisson couldn't guess his wife's thoughts, he was still by her side, and it was enough. His presence soothed her. She wasn't alone, she had a family. The second time she vomited was in the carriage. Once again, she remembered Falion.

Alexander! Why did you do it to me? What went wrong? I don't understand what you feel. I know that your feelings for me were sincere. Then why?

Lilian simply didn't understand that feelings often faded when it came to money, fame, or power. That was the case with Falion.

The Countess of Earton sat in the carriage and looked into the distance. Tears rolled down her cheeks. She didn't wipe them.

Too much pain. Too sickening.

Jess hugged his wife, not knowing how to help. He knew what was wrong. It was the first time that the woman had encountered the dirty side of life and experienced betrayal and meanness. She had been within an inch of dying, and now her heart ached from the suffering. There wasn't much he could do. She needed to let it pass.

At home in Earton, the couple was met by the servants. Terrified Marta, Loria, and the other maids began running around and taking care of Lily. She gave in to their nursing. She drank something warm, lay down in bed, and thought that such an "entertaining" day would leave her lying awake until morning. She fell into a gloomy state between sleep and wakefulness. She felt a strong embrace and heard a dear voice whispering something in her ear. She was asleep before she knew it—next to Jess, under his protection.

ಠ⃝ಠ

Hans Tremain wasn't as lucky. He still had to deal with the conspirators, even though everything worked out well. His aims were achieved, and His Majesty was pleased. On the one hand, he put the life of a monarch in danger. On the other hand, there was no serious danger. He could always choose to back off, but the last criminals had to be caught. His Majesty was waiting for his report the next morning.

"Did the Falions confess their guilt?"

"Yes, Your Majesty! It was originally started by the Ivelens. After several unsuccessful attempts, Fallion had suddenly run out of money. He also had a few unsuccessful investments and decided to act. The Ivelens were too shrewd to not use their weapon."

"It didn't help him much," winced Edward. "When did the Falions get involved?"

"Almost immediately, after the first stage. Someone had to give them money. The Falions were far from poor."

"Oh, yes."

Edward grinned. *Not poor at all!* From the heirs, they only had one daughter. He could send her to a nunnery, or even give her into marriage. He would give her whatever the treasury didn't need. She couldn't do any harm. It was best not to spread rumors about royal cruelty.

"At first, the plan was very simple…"

Hans reported, the king listened, the prince joined in, and the conversation dragged on for several hours. At the end of the conversation, the man was rewarded.

"What do you want for your work? You worked hard, investigated. Without you, we would've never caught them."

There were moments in life when it was best to be proud and not ask for anything, for they would offer and give by themselves. There were also times when one had to ask. Otherwise, one wouldn't get what one needed or wanted.

Hans bent low.

"Your Majesty, I don't dare to bother you with my trivial requests."

"Speak plainly," Edward winced. He was tired and wanted to lie down. His health was poor.

"Your Majesty, allow me to marry."

"Marry whom?" inquired Edward.

"She is one of the lace-makers who works for the countess. She is from the common people, and I need your consent to marry."

Edward only waved his hand.

"I will give you both the barony. You deserve it. Is that all?"

"Yes, Your Majesty."

Hans was happy and took his leave.

☙ ❏ ☙

In the morning, Lily woke up with a bad feeling. Without opening her eyes, she remembered the conspiracy, Alexander, and the events of the previous day. Warm hands embraced the woman tighter. Jess pulled his wife closer and gave her a big kiss, making the unpleasant thoughts disappear. Lily happily gave in. *It is so good to be loved!* Lily's morning was starting well.

Hans showed up when the couple had already finished their breakfast. They were deciding where to go for a walk.

"My Lord, dear Countess, could I have a few minutes of your time?"

Jerisson looked at his wife. Lilian nodded.

"We will be happy to. What is it about?"

"Let's go to the study," Jess gave Hans a friendly nod.

He didn't speak on his behalf but on behalf of the state. Jess was always next to Lily. Hans kept his word, and Jess was quite friendly with him. The three of them made themselves comfortable in the chairs. Hans took a sip of juice (there was no alcohol in the house because the countess was pregnant), sighed, and began explaining.

"Lilian, even in Earton, the attempts on your life looked somehow unsubstantiated. Even then, I suspected several people, including you, Earl."

Lily snorted but didn't comment.

Jerisson winced but did not begin to explain. Adelaide Wells had screwed him over so much that he had barely managed to clear his name.

"When I started untangling the strings, there were times when they tried to kill me. I decided to lay low for a while. I didn't doubt your safety. I only had to wait for your visit to the capital to see. You gave me Yerby on a silver platter."

"What happened to them, by the way?"

"They all died."

Lily winced. Jess nodded approvingly.

"Good. I hope they died a painful death."

Hans shook his head.

"I wasn't the one who issued the order. I only wanted to speak to them, but the father died in his cell, and the son was poisoned. I did nothing about it but realized that I was dealing with someone of high rank. I wondered who it might be. Yerby named Falion. The elder one was away, and the younger started making frequent calls to Lilian Earton."

"Falion? I assumed he was simply looking for how to get some benefit?"

Jess shrugged.

"Am I only interesting as a source of money?" asked Lily in a sad voice.

Jess kissed her hand.

"You're amazing, my dear, but I hope that Falion didn't manage to realize that."

Hans snorted.

"He didn't. Lilian Earton is very bad at keeping secrets. I kept all my suspicions to myself. I watched and drew conclusions. Falion was quite rich, well-known, and close to the king. Why would he play games? When the conspiracy against the Ivelens became known, I noticed that Alexander Falion was generously giving out his money to his hangers-on—to Reynolds and a couple of others. Those people didn't live in grand style, didn't play, and didn't buy expensive whores. Where did the finances go then?"

"Toward the conspiracy?" assumed Jerisson.

"Mercenaries, weapons, they planned to strike soon. I didn't have any choice but to get ready."

"Did you provoke them to strike yourself?"

"No."

"Is this true?"

Lily's voice revealed mistrust. Hans noticed it but chose not to pay attention.

"Lilian, you treated Falion as a friend. Even more, I saw that you expressed interest. Did he confess his love to you?"

Jess frowned. *Falion declared love for my wife? He's lucky to be in Stonebug right now.*

Lily nodded, answering Hans' question. It wasn't exactly as he described it, but a woman always knew if a man was infatuated with her.

"There were other agents in your house apart from my own."

"Who?"

Lily understood everything straight away. Hans shrugged.

"One of Alicia's servants."

"Who?"

"It doesn't matter. He's already dead."

"You killed him?" clarified Jess.

"No," Hans was happy to change the subject. "Not me. It was Falion. When he found out that the countess was pregnant, the servant fell over. It was fatal for him.

"Did he fall on a dagger with his throat?"

"He hit his temple against the fireplace."

"I see."

"Half of the information that Falion knew came from me. It was me who passed his father the news about the countess' pregnancy and that she and her husband were insanely in love with each other."

"This must have strongly hurt his pride." Lily nodded.

"Insulted pride is a terrible thing. He sympathized with you, perhaps even loved you and thought himself a real gift for any woman. Then you suddenly rejected his feelings. You didn't even want to try."

"Try for the place of a mistress?"

"There were some women who would've fought for being a mistress."

Lily snorted.

"This is too much!"

"As for Jerisson Earton, you and Falion had a disagreement," Hans smirked.

Jess fidgeted in his chair.

"Yes, a couple of times."

"Was it over a woman?" guessed Lilian.

"The girls preferred blue eyes to gray," explained Hans. "The marquess got upset about it."

"And here, I choose you before him again." Lily nodded understandingly. "Could you share in a bit more detail?"

"One of my colleagues approached the conspirators and pretended to be one of them. He claimed that he could help to get rid of the king by keeping him in the palace. He also hinted that all of them were in danger of getting caught."

"Did they believe him?"

"We were very convincing."

"What was my part in the plan?" asked Lily.

"I caught on live bait. Otherwise, I wouldn't have lured them in so easily. One of them had hatred, the other one jealousy, the third one had his own motives. They were lured in. The only thing left was to strike and put my bait out of danger," Hans said with a smile. "Forgive me for the comparison, most noble Countess."

"I've already forgiven you."

"The earl waited in a secret passageway. You were armed; the guards were also nearby. I did all in my powers to make it safe for you. I believed in myself, and the result wasn't disappointing. The conspirators are captured; all knots are untied. The only thing left is to live happily ever after."

Lily sighed.

"Is it really true? Has the danger passed? Are there no more enemies?"

"I swear on my honor."

Jess made a joyous stretch.

"I already have a child, the second one is coming, not counting the nephews. The house will soon turn into a place of havoc!"

Lily snorted.

"Maybe I will give birth to twins. You have that gene running in your family."

Jess sighed demonstratively.

"Twins? I'm too old for it."

"I also want to marry." Hans sat back in a chair, stretched his legs, and smiled slyly.

"Marry whom?" Lily jumped out of her chair.

"Marcia."

Lily fell back in the chair.

"You're so sneaky! When did you manage?"

"Will you not give permission?" joked Hans.

"I will! Both consent and dowry."

"His Majesty has already given me a dowry. My wife and I will get a barony."

Jess whistled in appreciation. The reward was more than decent. But Lily didn't give up so easily.

"In that case, the wedding dress is on me! Marcia will be the most beautiful princess in the kingdom, I promise."

"I will be glad. What a perfect promotion for Mariella!" joked Hans.

"It will be a great promotion," snapped Lily. "I am so happy for you!"

Jess was also happy. The fewer bachelors there were, the less they would look at his wife. Richard was the only one left. *It makes me so angry how he's not yet married!*

Hans took his leave and left. The spouses were left on their own. They sat in silence. Lily was the first to speak.

"I cannot believe that there's finally peace."

"What are you talking about? What about the guilds, the merchants, Loris, not to mention Avesterra. Someone from abroad must have supported the conspiracy."

"Will they all try to kill us?"

"Hardly, but they can make our life pretty nasty."

"Will we manage to cope with it?"

"Of course," reassured Jerisson. "We are together. You, me, Hans, His Majesty, Richard, and the Virmans. Of course, we'll give them a fight."

"I pray they let us go to Earton. If not, we'll be fine here, too. We will open our fashion house and hospitals; we will live, educate our children, and enjoy life. We could think of so many more things together."

Lily looked at her husband. *Love?* She was still not sure if what she had was love. It was very different from her and Alex.

Romeo and Juliet, Edward and Jessamine, Lons and Anna—there were a lot of romantic heroes, but all their stories ended. Lily and Jerisson were different. *Was the result emptiness?* Only people who are obsessed with Mexican soap operas could say that. There were many kinds of love. There were many couples who nourished their love with friendship. Hundreds of couples first married and only afterward, took notice of looks, learned how to trust each other and how to organize house chores. Such families ended up happier than the couples who were "insanely in love." *Will I manage to create something similar with Jerisson?* Lily didn't know. *Why not try? We have already started. We've got a daughter and expect another child. The rest will follow.* Either way, life was moving in its own way. Only time would tell.

Chapter 8
A glimpse into the future.

The grand opening of the Fashion House 'Mariella' was a sheer delight. The eyes of ladies and their husbands shone with admiration, well-trained servants in liveries carried drinks in beautiful twisted glasses. A lot of luxury items were exhibited around the room. At the entrance, every visitor was given the gift of a glass rose. The owners of the salon were the centerpiece of the event—Jerisson, a tall, slim man in dark green, carefully holding his pregnant wife by the elbow and not taking his eyes off her.

Tall, fair-haired, wearing a black-and-green dress trimmed with unimaginably expensive lace, Lilian was already in the seventh month of pregnancy. Even so, she felt great. She had no toxicosis, no pigmentation or any complications. On the contrary, she was cheerful and happy. The only oddity was that she was always craving apples. *Perhaps I lack iron,* thought Lily.

So far, the pregnancy was developing normally. It wasn't even that noticeable. Many people thought her big. The closest people knew; the rest could go to Maldonaya. Lily answered the courteous bow of one countess and politely noted that jasmine scent would suit her dark hair and blue eyes. The bottles were in the left corner of the room. The samples were beautiful—fans, sprayed with perfume. Lily greeted an elderly duchess and noted in passing that their veiled hats would go charmingly with her lace mittens. "This place is delightful, Your Grace!" Jerisson kissed the woman's angular hand, making the old woman ecstatic and led his wife further through the salon.

"Baron, I hope you are here with your wife today." She was always glad to see Avermal. He reminded her about the times when Lily first came into this world and was only learning to survive. Although unknowingly, he gave her his support.

"My regards to you, My Lady. Of course, I am with my wife. She has gone to look at your glass figures."

"Is it possible to call them miracles?"

"You flatter us, Baron!"

Lily didn't consider glass flowers and animals to be works of wonder, neither had she much regard for luxurious glasses and huge mirrors. Lenses were real miracles, and they made it possible to produce microscopes and telescopes. So far, that science had remained in the hands of Aldonai. *It is better that way.*

Lily was no longer trying to speed up progress. This new world was more tolerant of novelties, and the church tried to cooperate. She would leave new knowledge in the hands of the aldons, except for medicine. Technical progress shouldn't be ahead of ethics and morality. Inventing the telescope would mean the discovery of bacteria and lead to someone coming up with biological weapons. As long as there were wars, people would try to invent weapons.

"My Lord, perhaps you will allow me to see you tomorrow and talk about business."

"Of course, Baron."

The baron addressed Jerisson, but he was looking at Lily. The earl had the last word, and the proprieties were observed. Lily's husband had greatly eased her load, having taken part of the responsibilities on himself. He was much better at negotiating than Lily, and it saved her hours. Of course, they were living in a medieval society, and he was a man and aristocrat, so everyone obeyed him. Jerisson himself became interested in experimenting with lenses.

He dreamed of inventing microscopes and telescopes. He carried out experiments with the glassblowers and little by little, was getting closer to his aim. He had to rethink a lot of things, after being poisoned by an "innocent princess" and saved by the former "pink cow." Jess had become much more responsible. He was expecting Lily to give birth and educate Miranda, hoping that the girl would grow up to be a wonderful person. It was still under question whether she would have to live in the Khanganat, besides her fate in a harem might come unexpected. Lily often told Miranda tales about the Orient based on true events. There were Roksolana and several others. Lily didn't remember their names, but those women ruled the state, albeit from behind their husbands. Their job was to raise Miranda strong and clever. She would make her own fate.

Miranda was in love with Amir. The prince had recently departed for the Khanganat and ordered his embassy to sort out the everyday morning delivery of flowers and chocolate for Mirrie. Perhaps they could be happy together. Maybe it was love. No one could say if it was a creative or a destructive feeling. Love helped Jess create, whereas it destroyed the life of Marquess Falion. He had professed his love to Lilian Earton. Hans wasn't going to conceal interrogation protocols from Jerisson. Alexander did love Lilian, as well as he could. That was the main reason why he failed. He was selfishly possessive. The feelings he had for Lilian had nothing in common with love. Perhaps he got it confused with greed, his wish to take everything for himself. Love was selfless, it only made another person more generous. Let the poets deal with possessive love. Jess knew that it had nothing to do with the real feeling.

Perhaps back in the royal study, the conspirators would've let Lilian live. She was useful for the state. It was silly to kill the chicken that could lay golden eggs. They would have killed Edward and Richard after they signed an abdication. They wanted to put on a good face. Maybe they would've abused or raped Lilian. Yet they would've let her live. When the destiny of the kingdom was at stake, it wasn't the time for personal drama, so Falion confined himself to verbal abuse. He wanted to enjoy seeing her unhappy.

ಬ ⸺ ೞ

When Lily found out about Falion's confession, she only shook her head. Hans destroyed the remains of her feelings for Alexander, having at the same time, destroyed her trust in men. Perhaps Hans had done her a favor.

She would never forgive or forget, and she would be able to trust her husband to a certain limit. *Was it different before?* There would never be a person whom Lily would open up to about her previous world. There would never be a person who would understand her completely.

She didn't consider herself better or worse than the rest. She was simply different, like a green man among white people, she was forever doomed to be an amusing alien.

The depths of her soul would remain with her. One day, she would tell her children fairytales about the other world. Her past reality would turn into a bedtime story for their children. She was expecting Jerisson's child.

ಬ ⸺ ೞ

"Countess."

"Baron."

Hans bowed. The courtiers exchanged surprised glances. There were no indifferent faces. He wasn't a leir anymore. Having received a title for destroying the conspiracy, Hans was full of new projects and ideas.

Lily told him about criminology, fingerprints, about a special coal powder, about smells and how to preserve them, and so on. Together with Miranda, he listened to the stories about Sherlock Holmes with careful attention. As a result, Hans was appointed chief of the secret royal service. They gave him the task of establishing the new secret service.

If he succeeded in this task, the king would make him a count. If he failed, he could die from excess iron in the stomach. He was required to create the second Scotland Yard. After all, this world was full of poisoning and murders. The closest analogy to Hans' service would have been the squad of Louis XIV in charge of Gabriel Nicolas de la Reynie. It would take time to create something similar from scratch. Yet, he had to start with something.

If they had properly investigated Prince Edmund's murder, Amalia would have known that it was her father who had killed him. Perhaps if she had known, she wouldn't have sought revenge. Perhaps there would have been none of that bloody merry-go-round in the kingdom.

Thus, Hans worked day and night, employed new people and set up a network of whistleblowers. He created from scratch something that was unreal to create in one year. Yet somebody had to start.

For this very reason, nobody liked Hans, but everyone respected and feared him. The man himself was indifferent to the haters. He had everything he needed to make his own happiness. He had his favorite trade, and maybe in a thousand years, they would remember him for starting something revolutionary. He had a high title and social status. He wasn't a simple royal trustee any more, without land and title; he was now a baron. If he did a good job, the king would make him a count, and maybe even a duke.

Marcia was glowing with happiness, and Hans flourished next to her. He dreamed of having a child with her. He could protect his family. He wanted a lot of sons, at least five or six. Hans firmly believed that passions, quarrels, fights and scandals, jealousy and drama were good with a mistress. The home was a safe haven, a shelter, of comfort and peace.

People want different things, but he found what he had been looking for. He didn't care about Marcia's origin. All he cared about was love, not the titles.

August Broklend was also going to marry. His chosen one was the widow of Earton. Alicia also glowed with happiness, and the courtiers changed her nickname to a "viperess in love." The courtiers hissed and effused poison, only nobody cared for it. His Majesty favored the Countess of Earton and gave her his blessing and permission to marry. Jess was happy with his mother. Although those last months hadn't exactly made them closer, they still began to understand each other better. They now communicated more warmly and freely.

As for His Majesty, Edward didn't properly recover from the conspiracy. Looking at him, Lily gave him three or four more years to live. He wouldn't last longer.

Lily's relationship with Richard was difficult. She adored his new bride. The girl was a dark-haired and charming young imp. She was mischievous and crazy, but never evil. Her smile stretched from ear to ear, her hair curled up in little ringlets, her eyes sparked, and her tongue asked around a hundred questions a minute. Her questions could be answered with a smile. Everybody liked her: Angelina, Joliette, and even Richard himself.

Jerisson didn't know who stood behind the conspiracy with the Ivelens. The king told Richard everything, so the prince and the countess took great care when talking to each other. Their secret was like a bag of rotten apples that could be overturned at any moment. Neither of them wanted to confront the other, for fear of making a mistake. One wouldn't be able to take back what had been said.

Lily's relationship with the princesses was much easier, for they became regular visitors of the salon Mariella.

ಬಿ □ ೧ಽ

"Everything here is so wonderful!" Angelina was almost an adult. How quickly the children had grown up.

"Your Highness, you look brilliant today."

"Thank you! Do you know that Father has already started the talks?"

"What talks?"

"The King of Ivernea has a lot of sons. He wants us to marry one of them."

Lily smiled.

"And what is your personal opinion about it, Your Majesty?"

"I don't know! It must be exciting there. Will you visit the palace tomorrow?"

"Of course."

"Good! I want to listen to more stories about Lord Holmes. We have written down everything, the only thing left is to proofread and send it for printing."

"I promise to come over. By the way, have you seen that we also sell books here? Do you want to have a look?"

"Where?"

"On the second floor, there is an exhibition of books in the small hall. Do you want me to show you the way?"

"I can find it myself, thank you!"

Angelina slipped away. Lilian watched her leave with sadness. The children had grown up. The girls would probably be given in marriage to Ivernea, to strengthen ties. The Avesterras weren't happy about it, but couldn't do anything about it either. After the conspiracy, they had their snout in the fluff.

Lydia frequently wrote to Lily. It's funny, her new look made her extremely popular with gentlemen of the court. Reading her letters made Lily smile heartedly, and she decided to visit Wellster. After all, Gardwig had invited her himself.

Life and everything in it was gradually falling into place. Lily learned to find a compromise with her husband, played with the children, worked, dined with the family in the evenings, and listened to the lecturing of Pastor Vopler.

Secretly, Lilian dreamed of going beyond the horizon, toward the rising sun and to the break of dawn.

The America of this world must be so different from the one I knew before!

ഓ ⬚ ഇ

"Ingrid, I congratulate you on a girl."

The Virmaness smiled at Lilian Earton.

"It's really a girl?"

"Yes. She's most beautiful. What would you call her?"

"Lilian."

"Yes?"

"No, you don't understand. I wish to call her Lilian."

"It will create confusion!"

"So what? I want her to have your name."

Over the last two years, the woman had changed a lot—not in appearance, but in character. She was still charming like a princess from a fairytale. As time went by, it became clearer how and why that shy, domesticated girl had decided to marry a stranger and run away with him. During her independent life outside of Virma, her personality had developed and become more prominent. One couldn't call Ingrid a shrew—she entwined herself around Leif like ivy— but she made the servants respect and fear her even without raising her voice.

Lilian hadn't changed much, except she had lost a little more weight. The mirror reflected a very nice-looking woman with a gorgeous form, who knew how to compliment her beauty with clothes. The double chin disappeared once and for all. The fat was replaced by muscle, and giving birth only helped. It evened out her hormones, and Lily was now happily smiling at her reflection in the mirror.

Jess admired her beauty every day. He couldn't wait to take her to bed once the post-pregnancy recovery passed. She had given birth to the boy around a year ago. They named him Jyce Alexis Earton, the Viscount of Earton. Except for green eyes, he was the spitting image of Jerisson. The child was healthy and active. He could already speak, he learned fast and developed ahead of his age. He played with Roman and Jacob, pulled the dogs by their tails, and loudly yelled when his teeth were pushing through. To say that Lily adored her son was to say nothing.

The first time she picked up that warm, desperately crying lump of life, she felt her child as an extension of herself. She was ready to sacrifice anything for his happiness. Jess's attitude was a little calmer. It wasn't his first child. He had Miranda. He didn't know how to treat small creatures. Ingrid began educating Lily's son from almost the first day. She had just weaned her firstborn, Sigurd, and offered to look after both children. As a result, for the most part, Lily's love and affection toward her son went past him, which was to his advantage. Lily would happily stay with her child day and night, but her other responsibilities couldn't wait. Her husband, her other children, her friends, all of them demanded her attention.

That year, Mariella Fashion House celebrated its second birthday, the institute of book printing was actively developing, and aldons and pastors were mastering the art of etching. Taral Castle was no longer enough to fit the whole of the production, and Lily had to move part of it elsewhere. On top of that, the castle housed the lectures for the first generation of doctors. Tahir and Jamie taught theory, and Lily gave practical lessons.

They opened the first hospital in Laveri and named it in honor of the Countess Earton. Lily would've never agreed to name the hospital in this way, but His Majesty slammed his fist on the table and issued an order.

The previous year, Richard of Ativerna had finally married the Wellster princess. It was a luxurious wedding. The charming bride wore white and diamonds. That day, the Royal Hall was full of smiles, flowers, and sheer happiness.

Lily was relieved. Now that Richard had a wife, he would stop hanging around with Jerisson so often. It would save Lily a lot of nerves. She didn't like the close friendship between the two cousins. Close friendship with kings was often dangerous. There were many times when Jerisson had been close to death. He nearly died on that ship and from Anna's poisonous drink. Moreover, Richard was more sharp-sighted than Jess, and Lily couldn't wind him around her little finger as easily as she did with her husband.

According to Lord Tremain, Jess had finally ended all his relationships with his mistresses and now devoted all his time to his family. He didn't need any other woman. They were bland compared to Lilian, like cold porridge compared to a hot roast. He wasn't interested anymore; it wasn't to his taste. If only he had known from the start that Lilian was so incredible, he would've never sent her to Earton. He would have preferred to take her to Earton himself and have been locked up with her there, away from the world.

The country was flourishing. They produced salt, amber, cured fish, made knitting and sewing merchandise, and kept peace. Emma didn't steal, Taris Brok left a smart governor in his place. The villagers considered Lily a saint. They knew no famine or hardship.

Earton Castle was polished and renewed, with new glass windows in place of the old wooden shutters.

Cozy and tranquil, how much it differed from the dirty pigsty she had once found herself in when she first saw that world.

And yet, Lily didn't want to move to Earton...yet. The days merged into weeks and months of peaceful family happiness.

I can call myself a happy person, thought Lily. *I have finally fathomed the meaning of happiness.*

Pour out your poison, and dissolve our fears!
Its fire so burns our minds, we yearn, it's true,
To plunge to the Void's depths, Heaven or Hell, who cares?
Into the Unknown's depths, to find the new.

Charles Baudelaire, Le Voyage.

Epilogue

Lily looked at the list, knitted her brows and signed the paper. *Yes, our expenses have significantly increased, but how else? It's my 50th birthday!*

She was turning fifty in a month, a milestone birthday. She could see it looming on the horizon. She would have to take the rap.

On that occasion, Jerisson decided to gather all his friends and relatives in a mansion near Laveri. After all, it was his beloved wife. He took his own birthday much more lightly.

Fifty years! So much time has passed!

The woman looked out of the window. She saw her faint reflection against the thickening light. The years had been merciful to the countess. White hair was barely visible. Her light plumpness complimented her age and made her into a charming doughnut rather than a dried apricot. She barely had any wrinkles and had managed to preserve her teeth well, except her wisdom teeth. She joked that wisdom wasn't her trait.

Lily considered herself smart, but not wise. Aldonai didn't endow her with worldly wisdom. She got used to referring to God as Aldonai.

Lily sat back in her chair, half closed her eyes and turned a golden feather in her fingers. She remembered. Almost a quarter century before, they had uncovered the conspiracy. Since then, the opposition had quieted down, and Richard reigned in peace. Realizing that the service at court had turned into a sinecure, Jess began to devote all his attention to his family. He gave Miranda in marriage, arranged the engagement of Jyce, and gave Lily three more children, two boys and a girl. They were all grown up, some were even married, and Lily was going to become a grandmother once again.

Miranda, who after all became the beloved wife of Prince Amir and moved to the Khanganat, had already given her seven grandchildren. She would've had more, but Lily was downright threatening. She demanded Mirrie have a gap of at least two years between each pregnancy. Her daughter wasn't a machine for delivering babies. Amir was slightly annoyed, but he took Lily's wishes into account. He did have a harem to keep up appearances, and even used it. He was often given concubines, with whom he rewarded his servants. It was a great honor to receive a virgin from the Khangan's harem. All of the girls were carefully chosen and very beautiful. Although Miranda was slightly jealous, she tried to contain it. She promised to visit Ativerna with Lily's youngest grandchildren, to give Amir a break from his family.

Jyce—Lily's son, her love and her sunshine—was six and a half feet of sheer charm and had been married for four years. His wife was a daughter of Count Laish and ten years his junior. Marion was a nice girl. She was a devoted wife and would go with him through fire and water. Jyce also loved her dearly and never cheated. They already had two children, and Marion was thinking about a third.

Lily's younger children weren't married yet. Her youngest daughter was making active hints. Her chosen one was none other than the son of Lord Tremain. The eldest son of Hans was always a welcome guest in their house, as well as Marcia.

It had been eight years since the death of Hans Tremain. Although he had been killed, his heir was worthy of his father. His name was Thomas, or Tom, a hereditary baron. He was a zealous successor to his father's trade. He only lacked a cap and a pipe to resemble the famous Baron Holmes. The tales of Sherlock Holmes spread across the kingdom and became well-known. The people acted them out at fairs, which meant complete recognition. Tom was more of a talented loner than an organizer and manager like his father.

He and Hans, Lily's second son, became very close friends. Tom was more talented than Hans, but every Sherlock Holmes needed his Dr. Watson. So they worked together. Lilian's third son, August Broklend, also a hereditary baron, followed in his grandfather's footsteps. They used to say among people (at least about the ships) that name determined fate. It was true about August junior, who spent nights and days at the shipyards, nearly constructing spaceships. It's funny that he also suffered from seasickness, just like his grandfather and his mother.

Both sons closely resembled Jerisson in appearance.

Nature had played a joke with genes. How quaint!

Alina was the youngest daughter. She was a boisterous little girl with little curls and was adored by everyone. A real beauty was sometimes a real pain in the neck. She was already courted by many gentlemen of the court. However, the sixteen-year-old twisted and turned them like rings on her fingers but never gave preference to any of them. Lily didn't arrange for any engagements yet. She realized perfectly well that with such a dowry as theirs, none of her children would remain unsettled. The question of how to weed out the dowry hunters was more relevant.

Someone tapped on the door and Alina's curious nose poked inside.

"Momma, are you very busy?"

"Awful."

"Awfully busy, or it's awful that I'm here?"

"Both. So what do you need from an elderly mother?"

"Mommy, I want to go horse riding. Can I take Lidarh?"

"No. Take Tashlah and enough of it. I cannot trust you with Lidarh, he's still too goofy."

"But mother!"

Lily threw a cushion at her daughter. Alina immediately stopped arguing and ran out of the room.

"For the record, I'm going with Roman Ivelen!" said the voice from behind the closed door.

"All the same, take Tashlah," retorted Lily.

Lily's Lidarh had died ten years before. Nobody was protected against death. Lily had grieved terribly. At her husband's request, Amir had sent her a gift—a young foal who was a little copy of her departed friend. Lily was moved to tears. Over the past decades, the Khangans had grown closer with the rest of the countries.

Fortunately, the twins grew up to be good people. No one ever told them the truth about their parents. The version of the accident was enough.

Lily looked through some envelopes that were lying on the table. Paper was her gift to that world. White, green, marked with various crests. There were already a couple of papermaking factories in the city. The village dwellers collected and sold them hemp, flax, and nettles, making a good profit or paying taxes with it.

She remembered how they started making paper and introduced book printing, how they labored over letters and ink, not to mention their pain with opening schools and hospitals. The lion share of her profits went there. The aldon supported her projects. Pastor Vopler was a grateful man. He saw that her ideas didn't bring evil. He had become an aldon seven years earlier, after the death of Aldon Roman. He lectured the priests about their mission as Aldonai's servants to help ordinary people. He actively supported the opening of schools and hospitals. He wished to abolish all nunneries and send the women to help in schools and hospitals for the poor. The women could gain their freedom and live as they pleased after ten years of paid social work. There were, of course, exceptions to that rule. Some women were not fit to function for social benefit. Nevertheless, the idea found support among the clergy.

The aldon and his son were also invited to the birthday celebration. Mark had grown into a real man. He often helped August junior at the shipyards. The Virmans were also among the guests. Lily didn't want to guess what they would give her. Leif and Ingrid, who not only had eight children but also fifteen grandchildren, decided not to go back to Virma. Leif changed his occupation, from captain to testing shipbuilder. Their work paid benefits, and soon they built a real caravel. The most desperate Virman daredevils (including Erik, who had not lost his agility with age) set sail to search for new lands.

That was eight years ago. Back then, something terrible had happened. America was discovered—that is, the continent Alilen, as the locals called it. Dark-skinned, black-haired, they looked very similar to the Indians and had nearly repeated their fate.

They were rich and did not believe in Aldonai.

※ ※ ※

It happened eight years prior.

"Lilian, this is a new land! Immense wealth!" Richard, who looked a little aged, was still handsome at the age of forty. He paced the room with measured steps. The countess stood by the fireplace. Her hands fiddled with the end of a fan.

Over the years, they had found the time to talk and now maintained a friendly relationship. Richard knew that Lilian would never intervene in an affair that wasn't related to her production. Lilian knew that Richard would never tell her husband about her role in uncovering the Ivelens. Thus, the matter was settled. Step by step, they tried to find a common language. Although Richard never considered Lilian his friend, he would sometimes ask advice not only from Jess but also from his wife.

Back then, the king had called a meeting. Lilian and Jess were the only ones invited.

"Your Majesty, don't do it. It is wrong! How do you not understand? Your ideas are close to genocide. We cannot exterminate the whole population of people. Although they don't believe in Aldonai, they are still human beings! The result of your decision will make the murder of a piglet equal to the murder of a human baby. There would be fire and destruction. Stop it before it's too late!"

Time had been merciful to Lilian Earton. Her white hair was almost invisible between the blonde locks, her face was smooth, and her teeth were still white. One would never tell that the woman had given birth to four children. Jerisson looked at his wife with awe and contemplated her words.

Richard was also happy with his wife. His second wife Diana was charming, and Richard strongly suspected that it was Lilian Earton who had inspired her to become so devoted and independent.

"We cannot kill them. Let's join their lands to Ativerna and begin teaching them."

"They don't need our education! We will only make their lives worse. How do you not understand?"

"Explain," offered Jerisson. Lily sighed and started explaining. She tried to choose her words carefully. The men listened and exchanged meaningful glances. Her story painted a gloomy picture in their minds. If one state got used to living at the expense of the other, the inevitable result would be their fall. One of them would meet its end from the lack and the other one from the excess. Neither Jess nor Richard wanted to start a war. After all, the lands were already discovered.

"Your Majesty, Aldon Roman wishes to see you."

"Let him come in."

Aldon Roman was a very old man. The times were hectic. Pastor Vopler accompanied the elderly aldon. Over the years, Vopler had become more earnest, his eyes were endowed with sadness and clarity, and his face was cut through by many little wrinkles. Every person who saw him sensed his radiant inner peacefulness. He didn't desire more than he already had. He was the aldon's right hand and would become the next aldon. With the support of two kings, he would surely rise up the ranks. The days when he was counting copper coins and thinking about how to feed his son were long gone. His son Mark made the priest proud. He spent all day at the shipyards, helping the old shipbuilder and learning the old secrets of his craft. August's health had significantly deteriorated since his beloved wife Alicia, the "loving viperess," had passed away. Finally, he could only move around in a wheelchair. There were things over which men had no power.

"Your Majesty."

"Speak freely, Roman. There are no false witnesses here." Richard's court resembled the "close circle" of Ivan the Terrible.

"Richard, this is a great discovery. Erik sent me a message. We have to decide what to do with those savage men. My people are ready to sail there and spread the light of Aldonai."

"No!"

Lilian Earton's scream was extremely desperate. The woman grabbed onto her throat. She had visions of the Indians driven onto reservations. Cut down forests, a wasteland soaked with the blood of its people. The imperative "no belief, no soul, no human" was the root of Nazism and fascism.

The men turned to face her. They didn't care about her emotional response. They wanted to see what she had to say. It was she who had said that there was land beyond the oceans. She had given the mariners maps and compasses.

"You have to understand," the woman's voice grew calmer. "If we begin to impose our own religion there, they will fight against it. We need to make them come to us. They will welcome us and implore us themselves. We don't want to be taken for aggressors. We want to be perceived as the bearers of light."

The aldon raised his eyebrows in surprise.

"Any child complains of bitter medicine."

"We aren't talking about a silly child here. We are talking about people. You won't be able to convince a child to do something by taking away his toy. You would show him a brighter, more interesting one, and he would happily take it from your hands. One cannot impose good by vile means."

"What do you suggest instead?"

"I read Erik's letter. He will be home soon, in Laveri. He is coming with his wife, who is a princess of that foreign land. Her name is Tial. Why don't we show her all the beauty of our country? We can send the pastors and priests with her, on her way back. We need to choose the priests carefully and send the ones who will be clever and careful, who will manage to tell about our faith in an attractive way. This will become our first step. Later, we will be able to teach them other things—glassmaking, porcelain, silk, horseback riding. We can give them as much as we want to take from them. It will be better to become their allies, to remain their friends. Gentlemen! Please hear me out," Lily started nervously pacing the room. "We can take that land by force, but this prey is too big for Ativerna, even in coalition with Wellster. If we decide to create a bigger alliance, it would inevitably lead to more dispute. We already have to deal with Avesterra and Elvana. You know I am right."

The men considered her words. All she said made sense. There were currently seven states on the continent. Ativerna, Wellster, Ivernea and the Khanganat formed a coalition. That left Elvana, Avesterra, and Darcom. The relationship between Wellster and Ivernea was somehow strained. They still hadn't forgiven them the secret marriage of Lydia, that time she had escaped with one of the courtiers.

Lydia though was immensely happy. She shared her happiness with Lilian in her letters and during their meetings. She had given birth to six children and was content with her life. The relationship between Ativerna and Ivernea was also not very smooth. Lydia's secret marriage hurt her brothers' pride. Had Richard married their sister, it wouldn't have happened.

Since the death of Edward and Gardwig, the relationship between Wellster and Ativerna had worsened. Although there were no apparent disputes, some topics were extremely hot.

"Any contract can be sealed with a marriage," innocently suggested Earl Earton. Lilian gratefully touched her husband's hand. At least someone supported her.

The aldon pondered, but Vopler said that they shouldn't be too extreme. They needed to remain gentle. Richard waved his hand in agreement. They would try the plan with the marriage. Lily gasped in relief, grabbing her husband's hand. She was grateful for having his support. Lily was sure that the subject was not closed yet, but she hoped that her words would make them settle for a softer approach, which wouldn't do harm to either Ativerna or Alilen. Considering the delicate political situation, the king was inclined to prevent any possible feud. Although it was a little too presumptuous, Lily still wondered whether she had been sent to that world to help its people choose the right way on their diverging path. One of the roads led to bloodshed and misery. Had they turned the wrong way, fortune's well would have turned into a well of misery. So easy to destroy, so hard to get back.

ఠ ౦౩

"Darling, let's go ride!"

It was Jerisson. He looked stunning for his age. He was almost sixty but had remained as charming as before, only his hair had turned gray. His blue eyes shone, and his body hadn't lost its strength or sensibility, his smile still retained its shine.

Lily stood up from the desk and gave her husband an affectionate kiss. Fifty years was not old.

"I have a lot of things to do. Guest list, bookings…"

"Leave it to the secretaries."

"I have, and now I have to double-check their work."

"You can finish later."

"Jess."

"It is beautiful outside. The sun is shining bright, and the breeze is just wonderful."

Lily sighed. Maybe it was a good idea to leave everything and go for a ride with her husband. It wouldn't hurt to disappear for a few hours.

"Leif invited us for a gathering. They're having everyone to their house tonight."

That was the last straw. Lily put down the paper.

"Okay, let's go."

Sometimes, she prioritized her work far too much. She decided to seize the moment and enjoy the sun, the wind, and the company of her dear husband. She considered herself lucky. Jess was a loving husband. She loved her trade, which would live on even after she died. She had wonderful children and incredible grandchildren. She and Jerisson were happy. As for her descendants, it didn't matter what they thought of her. She wanted happiness, and she got it. It was a peculiar kind of happiness, different from everyone else's, but it was hers. She was unique, a traveler through time and space. One day, she would finish writing her story and tell her descendants the whole truth. One day, but not today. She was done with overthinking. She and her husband were going on a voyage.

Lily kissed her husband on the cheek and went to get dressed. Thanks to the Mariella Fashion House, she could do it with no effort and without any help from the maids. She would take Lidarh.

Lily followed her husband up the hill and glanced down at the fires beneath and the sunset above. She smiled at the evening sky.

I love you, my dear world! Madly, deeply, forever!

A light breeze, like a blessing from above, ruffled her hair.

I also love you, my dear child. Be happy.

Post-epilogue.
Two hundred years later.

Ativerna, Laveri. The Grand Royal Museum. Exhibition of Wax Statues.

A young female teacher leads her serious and extremely curious students to the central museum. They obediently line up in two rows. Before entering the museum, the teacher looks at her pupils.

"Tom, take off the cap! Lily, rearrange your braid! Your bow is falling off. Does everyone remember how to behave?"

The children answer with haphazard nodding.

"Do not touch anything with your hands, do not wander around the museum, do not yell, listen to the guide. Let's go."

A girl with messy golden hair quickly fixes her braid. *Done! My hair is always getting in the way.*

The young faces shine with anticipation of the new and the unknown. Their class came first in the competition, and this little voyage to the museum is their reward. The exhibition presents the figures of the Prenaissance epoch. The guide lovingly looks at her young listeners.

"Good morning."

"Good morning," answer the higgledy-piggledy voices. The children aren't so young anymore, around seven years of age and already very independent. Each one of them is unique in their own way.

"Today we have an exhibition of the most prominent characters of the Prenaissance epoch. Does anyone know when it started?"

The guide tries to get the kids interested. She is a young student, and this is her graduation practice. Her main aim is to spark the children's curiosity. *What could be more important than the history of one's native country?* The young girl realizes the responsibility of her task and is visibly worried.

"Two hundred years ago," the children respond.

"Correct! At that time, His Majesty Edward the Eighth ruled in Ativerna. His reign marked the beginning of what we now call 'development.' Back in those days, schools did not exist. Instead, there were guilds. The master of the guild employed many apprentices, who were children like you. Those children were forced to work for them in return for shelter and food. They were often denied even those basic needs, got sick, and died of hunger."

The baby faces are getting sad.

"In order to become a member of the guild, one was required to pay a fee and pass the exam. But the masters didn't want to have too much competition, and it often happened that a child could remain an apprentice for the rest of his life. There were cases when the masters forcibly enslaved their apprentices, lent them money, and charged high interest. In a word, it was very difficult to break free from the vicious cycle. There were no hospitals either. Medicine was very, very undeveloped."

One of the boys raises his hand.

"In the lesson, we read the play called "Sick deceiver." The doctors in the play treated their patients with either laxatives, sleeping pills, or bloodletting. Is that true?"

The girl smiles and her pupils' eyes light up in response.

"Not exactly. There were also herbalists, but knowledge of medicine was scarce. They considered the herbalists to be shildas and daughters of Maldonaya. The medicus' guild didn't tolerate competition."

The children comprehensively nod. All of them study in a special school for future doctors. From the age of six, they are taught to dress wounds, care for the sick, help doctors, and perform medicine. All of them know that there is no other such honorable profession like the profession of a doctor. Every one of them wants to become a good doctor.

"Edward the Eighth was the first king to fight against this system. Of course, many of his servants did not like that. They conspired against him; they wanted to make him abdicate."

The children look at the figure of an elderly man with a serious face. The man is dressed in luxurious clothes. A simple Ativernian crown gleams on his head. The artist managed to convey the expression of this face. It is tired and calm, and the king's eyes express sadness.

"It was under his command that the new doctors' guild was organized. The most interesting fact is that a foreigner was appointed its head. It was the great scholar from the Khanganat, Tahir Djiaman din Dashar. He was forced to flee from his native country and found refuge in Ativerna, where they appreciated him for his knowledge. His Majesty affectionately received the scholar at court, which was not little in those days. Tahir Djiaman din Dashar cured the king of several diseases. He wrote works on anatomy and pathology. Din Dashar was the first person who bequeathed his body to his disciples for experiments. He believed that it was impossible to identify an illness without knowing what was inside the person. It later became a tradition in the guild of doctors to dedicate their bodies to science. Can you tell me the name of the second head of the guild?"

"Baron James Donter," answer the children.

"Correct. Come, I will show you their wax figures."

The children obediently follow the guide. The young girl continues telling them on the go.

"Tahir was a celebrity in those days. It is widely known that His Majesty Gardwig the Twelfth, the ruler of Wellster, corresponded with the wise doctor and followed all his advice and recommendations."

"He's a doctor!" says one of the children. "It is silly to not follow his advice."

"Back then, many doctors could prescribe bloodletting or aconite!" replies a second child.

The guide and the teacher exchange meaningful glances. It was the teacher who asked the young guide to organize the tour around medicine. These children don't care about palace intrigues. They are eager to know about the origins of their profession. In a few years, they would start learning politics and the art of diplomacy. They would learn about the plots and conspiracies that grew like mushrooms during the reign of Edward. They would be told about the secret agreement between Edward and Gardwig, according to which the kingdoms strengthened the friendly union by marriage at least once in two generations, strictly following genetic timeframes to avoid the passing of hereditary diseases.

The wax figure of Tahir Djiaman Din Dashar looks quite alive. He is dressed in the traditional white clothes of the Khangans, with a clean-shaven chin and a smile on his lips. He is seated at the table holding a pen and is about to write down some important thoughts.

"As you can see, back in those days, the beard was considered a sign of wisdom and was important for the Khangans. But Tahir was the first one to note that it was unhygienic and despite his custom, he shaved his beard off. He also introduced the first medical uniform. Have a look!"

A simple uniform consisted of white linen trousers and a shirt for men, and a dress for women. Lily never liked caps, so she suggested something like bandanas for men and a headscarf for women. The uniform had several pockets. Everything was comfortable and functional.

"Next we see his successor, Baron James Donter. It was Baron Donter who laid the foundations of pharmacology, compiled several herbal mixtures that are still used today, and started expeditions in search of undiscovered plants. For his time, he was an outstanding biologist and chemist."

"Did I read that he was an herbalist?"

"That's right." The guide says with a smile. "Because of intrigues, the baron's mother was forced to flee and find shelter among the common people. She found refuge in the home of a village herbalist, and her son grew up to be an herbalist."

The children nod. They continue to listen to stories about medicine, about famous students of din Dashar, about the students of Lord Donter, about the fact that even up to the present, every member of his family has been a doctor. They finally hear about the first female doctor.

"Lilian Elizabeth Mariella Earton," the guide leads the children to the wax figure of Lily. The woman is depicted sitting in a chair. She leans back on the armrest with a medical scalpel in her fingers. Her lips stretch into a smile. She looks pensive. Her long blonde braid almost reaches to the floor. Her ears and her neck are decorated with emeralds. Behind her stands her husband, a blue-eyed man with a stunning smile. The girls smile back at him.

"What a handsome dude!" says one of the high-pitched voices.

"This is a very curious character of our story," the young guide involuntarily lowers her voice, "after Countess Lilian Earton lost her child, she became the first student of Sir din Dashar. It was she who insisted that both girls and boys should be trained in medicine. She generously donated to hospitals and schools. A lot of medical schools are named after her. She was also an outstanding surgeon. I must say, she was a lucky woman in many ways."

"In what ways?" ask the high-pitched voice. The guide begins her tale.

"Lilian Earton was an outstanding woman, unusually well-educated for her time. She read a lot and wrote stories and fairytales. She discovered many old scrolls about medicine. She managed to translate them and preserve them for future generations. She gave them into the hands of those who could truly appreciate the importance of old medical discoveries. She later asked to be a student of the great din Dashar."

"What about the Mariella lace and glass production?"

"Yes, that was the main occupation of the Earton family. In those days, it was considered unworthy of a nobleman to trade or engage in production. But the Eartons were out of this line. Several generations of their family were engaged in trade. It was their family who invented microscopes and telescopes. That age gave us a lot of interesting objects, such as compasses, the meridian, a lot of geographical knowledge, and the discovery of new lands."

"They were discovered by Erik Thorson, right?"

"That's right. The brave Virman and his team made a voyage across the ocean. He discovered the land, previously unknown to the inhabitants of the continent. Its inhabitants called it Alilen, that is, the beloved home. Since they had never seen Virmans before, they took Erik for a strange king. Eventually, he did become their king by marrying their princess Tial."

"Weren't they going to start a war?"

"You are right, young man," agrees the guide. "There was a serious argument. All of us believe in Aldonai, but the inhabitants of that land worshipped pagan gods. This sparked a great dispute, which almost split the continent between two parts. Avesterra and Elvana believed that those people, who didn't believe in Aldonai were savages and treated them worse than animals. They wanted to take over their land and either convert its native inhabitants or destroy them."

"I know! They formed the union of the five," shouts another boy. His peculiar eye shape clearly indicates his relation to the Alilen.

"Exactly." He gets an approving smile. "Ativerna, Wellster, the Khanganat, Ivernea, and Virma united against this savage approach. They managed to defend the right of Alilen to independence. The descendants of Great Erik have been ruling there until this day. There hasn't been a single war at Alilen. Perhaps it would've been impossible to avoid the war if it weren't for Aldon Roman and later Aldon Vopler who firmly stood for peace, and declared the violators of Alilen's independence the servants of Maldonaya. By the way, we have a sculpture of Erik." The huge Virman stands tall, casually leaning on his axe. His blonde hair falls down to his shoulders. Next to him is a woman with bronze skin. Her thin hand rests on his huge paw. She is wearing an exotic costume made of feathers.

"The Great Erik and the Princess Tial."

The children attentively examine the figures.

"Life back then was so exciting!" sighs one of the pupils.

The teacher and the guide exchange glances.

No one would ever find out how it felt when the war had almost broken out, when it almost claimed thousands of lives and nearly flooded a peaceful continent with blood. Nobody could ever feel the passions that boiled within the blood of these peoples.

"We have a whole film about it," replies the guide.

"We will leave you to wander around the hall and look at the wax figures by yourselves. We will give you around half an hour and will soon call you to see it. Besides, the first camera obscura was also invented during Prenaissance by Lilian Earton's son, Hans Earton and his friend, Lord Thomas Tremain."

"Is there a wax figure of them?"

"Of course."

A tall young man with disheveled dark hair and brown eyes smiles thoughtfully, with a clumsy box in his hands.

"Thomas Tremain. And here is his friend, Hans Earton."

A bulky young man with dark hair and blue eyes kindly smiles at the pupils, as if bewildered by his own discovery.

"This is what the first camera obscura looked like. You can later take a picture with it." Under the watchful gaze of the teacher, the children disperse around the hall.

A fair-haired girl freezes in front of the statue of Lily.

My great- great- great- wait! How many times is she a great-grandmother to me?

Lilian Earton is giving the little girl an ironic look. Jerisson is still standing behind her, as always protecting his wife. He is also looking at the girl.

Is his look approving? I cannot tell.

The girl's name is Lilian Broklend. In honor of the greatest of her grandmothers. Because of her age, the grandchild knows very little about this great woman. She doesn't know that Lilian lived for almost seventy years, that she was accepted at court, that she treated people until her last day, that she personally sat at her hospital and took patients, and that her advice had a great influence on world politics. The small children aren't yet told that the countess' life was constantly in danger and that villains tried to kill her. They don't know yet that the countess is one of the greatest figures in the history of Ativerna and that the details of her life are still surrounded with a lot of mystery. *Where could she have gained such education? How did she become the main authority in medicine? Why was she one of the key royal trustees, for both Edward and Richard?* Nobody could answer those questions, apart from the Tremain and Broklend families. They keep silent and don't let the historians study their family archives.

Especially precious are the diaries of the first female doctor. The children of Tremain, Earton, and Broklend families aren't allowed to read them until they come of age.

This girl also wants to do something important and be remembered in history. Yet, her parents don't put pressure on her. Lily is eager to study medicine, she is interested in continuing many of the family trades, such as lace-making, knitting, and glassblowing. The only thing that her parents insist on is for their children to be inquisitive. It was Lilian Elizabeth Mariella who first encouraged her own children to learn as much as they could. A child with less than two or three trades was considered inferior in the Tremain, Broklend, and Earton families, as well as in many others. Over the years, the number of aristocrats increased. All of them were somehow related.

The granddaughter and her grandmother look each other in the eyes. One should be worthy of the memory of one's descendants, as well as one's ancestors. One should always remain a good person.

No matter where life takes you, no matter how hard and curious it gets, you need to remain a worthy person, even if it goes against your own wish.

"I promise to make you proud," whispers the girl. "I will become a worthy person." Suddenly, she gets an odd feeling that the wax figures of her ancestors have come to life. They give her an approving smile.

Do you believe in reincarnation of the body? What about the soul? Do you believe in real magic?

Bread should be warm, grass should be green, water should be cold, and the children's future should be bright. These are the things that constitute happiness.

> *Life is a ray over an abyss of pain,*
> *Its pathway goes through the wind and the rain.*
> *We never know what we will meet on the way*
> *Perhaps we will know at the dying of day.*
> *Fate laughs at our voyage, asking us "Why?"*
> *"To know that our children shall never cry."*

Chronology

1460 Edward marries the princess Imogene of Avesterra
1462 birth of Edmund
1463 Amalia Earton is born
1466 birth of Richard
1468 Jerrison (Jess) is born
1468 Imogene dies
1470 Edward marries Jessamine Earton
1471 Edward ascends the throne and becomes king
1473 Birth of Lilian Brocklend
1476 First engagement of Jerrison Earton to Eliza Errolston
1479 Engagement of Amalia Earton to Peter Ivelen
1480 Death of Eliza at the age of 12
1480 Wedding of Amalia Earton and Peter Ivelen
1481 Birth of Amalia's son Jess
1483 Wedding of Jerrisson Earton and Magdalena Yerby
1484 Birth of Amalia's daughter Sessie
1489 Birth of Miranda Catherine Earton
1489 Death of the second wife of Jess, Magdalena Yerby
1491 Death of Jessamine
1492 Death of Jyce Earton and Edmund
1495 Wedding of Jess and Lilian Earton
1496 Aliya appears in Lilian's body

LitHunters:

Hi! We're LitHunters, a digital publishing house that specializes in diamond-in-the-rough book series.

Our selection process is thorough as we choose which book series we want to devote time to and invest in completely. We select books based on their popularity online and their social media following. We publish books that are already famous with the most important people: you, the readers! As well as the book series, we also pay attention to the author's presence in social media and transfer their success on a global scale.

At LitHunters, we focus on the highest quality and most entertaining stories for our readers. That's what you can expect from all of our books! Thanks for checking out our book, and if you like it, we have a few recommendations of some of our other series.

Please remember to leave a review of this book and remember you can connect with Lina J. Potter on Facebook. Just search For Lina J. Potter. Also you can find the full series here: **https://amzn.to/2WqhY10**
We would like to show you some other great series.

Lina J. Potter's pen now takes us to the mystical lands of the Kingdom of Radenor suffering under the reign of the unjust King. His sister, the Princess of Radenor is determined to have him dethroned. Her half-demon son, Alex conceived by a demon father, becomes the ultimate weapon of her bloody revenge. A magnificent tale of blood magic, necromancy, court intrigue and family revenge.
Order the opening book *Half-Demon* on the link below.
https://www.amazon.com/dp/B07KJG9H5L

Now available for order, the uplifting Sci-fi Space Opera *Kiran: The Warrior's Daughter* (The Rights Of The Strong) by Ellen Stellar
Meet Kiran; the young, reckless, and wild cadet of the most prestigious university. Beautiful, free-spirited, jolly, clever and fun-loving. Her life is one of organizing underground races, gambling, skipping classes, issuing fake IDs and having passionate love affairs… Until one day she is abducted to her native planet as a captive, forced to marry the

strongest warrior by the law of the strong. Her restless soul won't abide, to her cruel father nor to her supposed husband. She is a cadet after all. You can order the book via this link:
https://www.amazon.com/dp/B07GGYH8PL

A new dark romance now available for order, *Two Months and Three Days* (Sinister Romance) by Tatiana Vedenska

18-Year-old Arina studies Veterinary Medicine in Moscow during the day and works in a veterinary clinic at night, struggling to make ends meet. When she wanders into the photo exhibition of Maxim, she is struck by the cruelty and violence erupting from his world. Son of an oligarch, Maxim is handsome, talented, and rich… On his turn, he is dazzled by Arina's innocence, beauty and otherworldliness. He offers her a contract for the next two months and three days.

Hence, somewhere in the grey area between art and erotica, both Arina and Maxim embark on a life changing romantic adventure. Little-by-little Arina uncovers the truth behind the secrets and the family tragedy that marks Maxim's personality.

You can order the book via:
https://www.amazon.com/dp/B07FQT51NS

Made in the USA
Lexington, KY
16 March 2019